THE ÀCADEMY

THE ACADEMY

LUBOV LEONOVA

Contents

"When you think life is over,
it's actually just about to begin."

\- Lubov Leonova
Excerpt from *The Academy*

Story 1

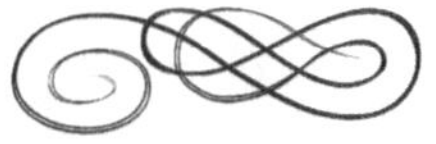

Welcome to the Club

1

A Sparkle

Jackie sat in a large chair, drumming her fingertips on the wooden handle. Waiting had never been one of her favorite things. To pass the time, she looked up at the perfectly white ceiling, scanning it for cracks. Finding none, she let out a sigh.

In the heavy silence, every small sound was amplified – the wind whispered through the tree leaves just outside the wide-open window; the paper sheets rustled in the hands of the man seated across from her.

It was Don, the head teacher of The Guardian Academy, who conducted interviews with new students. He appeared to be in his mid-thirties, with a streak of gray hair in his short beard. His long face was lined with a few wrinkles. Now, he was on the verge of making one of the most important decisions of her life. Jackie clasped her hands together, hoping for the best.

The time crystal on her wrist glowed a disturbing red – *still noon*. Damn time, as it always seemed to fly by when she was enjoying herself, yet drag on in moments like this.

Finally, Don placed the papers in front of him. "So, Miss Robinson, everything looks good."

Jackie let out a deep sigh of anticipatory relief.

"But you need to answer one question," he added.

Her heart raced. "A question?"

"Yes." Don's brown eyes fixed on her with curiosity. "Why do you want to become a guardian?"

Jackie ran her fingers through her short auburn hair, pondering the question. *Why did I sign up for this?* It was a good question that she struggled to answer. Her thoughts swirled in her head as she was coming with an honest reply. *To escape the confines of a small, suffocating town where everything felt unbearable, why else?!* Jackie gave him a sad look and remained silent, sensing that her true motivations were not what he was looking for.

"Listen, Jackie," Don began. "I can call you Jackie, right?"

"Sure."

"Being a guardian isn't an easy job. Studying here, in a group full of young and ambitious men, won't be a piece of cake. But you can handle anything if you have a strong reason to do so," he said, leaning back in his chair. "So, what's your 'Why,' Jackie?"

She lowered her eyes, her thin hands resting on her lap clad in black pants. Jackie had chosen to wear something resembling a guardian uniform, even before being accepted, as a sign of her readiness. *He must think I'm a complete dummy,* she thought to herself. *Which means I have nothing to lose by being honest.* Jackie raised her hand and unrolled her sleeve, revealing the healing black marks. "That's why," she blurted out.

Don gazed at her, waiting for a more detailed explanation.

"Because I've been through hell," Jackie continued, tears welling in her eyes. "If you allow me to study here, I promise – I'll do everything in my power to prevent such violence and assist women like myself. And I won't give a damn about any mean guys in the group." She paused, trying to compose herself. "Oh, I'm sorry. I didn't mean to sound rude –"

"It's alright," Don said, picking up a feather pen and signing at the bottom of her application. "From now on, you'll need to be firm. Sometimes, that's the only way to communicate with the mean cadets."

He finished signing and handed the papers back to her.

With a shaking hand, Jackie took the paper and read the single word written in ink: *Accepted.* Her heart fluttered in her chest, brimming with joy. From that moment on, she would be the first woman to ever study at The Guardian Academy! Lost in the moment, she didn't notice Don waving his hand, ushering in the next candidate.

"Let's see," Don said as he looked through another set of paperwork. "So, you are from Triville, correct?"

Jackie raised her eyes in surprise. "What? No."

"Yes, I am," a woman's voice chimed in from behind her.

Startled, Jackie slowly turned around, her eyes widening as she struggled to find her voice. A young woman entered the room, appearing to be around her age, if not slightly younger. She was undeniably beautiful – her golden locks cascaded down to her chest, and her sapphire blue eyes locked onto Jackie's. A thin red scar marred her left cheek, but it did little to diminish her beauty. Clad in a light-blue dress and matching leather gloves, she carried a small road bag in her hand.

Interesting, what is she doing here? And more importantly, who is she?

"Elisa Palmer," the woman introduced herself, approaching Jackie and extending her free hand. "And from what I overheard, you've been accepted. Congratulations!"

"Thank you." Jackie touched the soft leather of Elisa's glove as they shook hands. "I'm Jackie, by the way."

"It's really nice to meet you," Elisa responded with a charming smile before taking a seat in the chair beside her.

Elisa gave Don a curious look. "So, what's next?"

"Papers first," Don replied.

Jackie froze for a moment. *Will she be studying here?* Seizing the opportunity while Don was occupied with the paperwork, she turned to Elisa. "I didn't expect to see another woman here."

Elisa removed her glasses and placed them on her lap. "I arrived this morning and was accepted before you."

"So, you –" Jackie began.

"Are going to be a guardian, yes," Elisa confirmed with a cheerful expression. "I bet it will be a lot of fun."

Don handed a blank sheet of paper to Jackie. "The Academy policy. Read and sign at the bottom."

Jackie skimmed the text. "I can't use my Gift against a cadet unless I have their written permission?"

"Or verbal. But it must be witnessed then," Don clarified. "It's a standard form, Jackie. It's in place to ensure that you all respect each other's boundaries during your studies, especially with your mind-reading Gift."

"Fine," Jackie said as she signed the document. "Besides, I don't really like invading people's minds."

"Then it should be easier for you," Elisa remarked with a chuckle. "I know a mind reader, and her Gift has led her into all sorts of confusing situations!"

"What about *your* power?" Jackie inquired.

Elisa nervously crumpled the hem of her dress. "I... I'm still learning how to control it."

Don relaxed in his chair. "Don't worry. That's what all of you will learn here – to master your Gifts and use them to help others."

"I can't wait," Jackie said, placing the signed paper on the desk and returning the feather pen to the inkwell.

Don clasped his hands and surveyed the two women, who held their breath in anticipation. "As of now, you are both cadets, and due to the unique circumstances that these walls have never seen, you will be given a special mission." He opened a desk drawer and pulled out a small cotton bag filled with something soft. Then he handed the bag to Elisa. "Any guesses as to what this might be?"

She opened it and wrinkled her nose, "I'm guessing it's not tooth powder."

Jackie leaned in to get a closer look. Inside the bag was a shimmering blue powder that faintly smelled of dried herbs. One of the ingredients appeared to be aconite, a flower known for its hallucinogenic properties and often used in forbidden potions. "Drugs?!" she exclaimed in disbelief.

"Exactly," Don confirmed. "It's called Moon Dust. Not only is it highly addictive, but it also slowly causes irreversible brain damage."

Elisa closed the bag and placed it back on the desk. "Why do you keep it here?"

"It serves as a somber reminder of the lives I failed to save," Don explained, his gaze drifting out of the window with a distant look. "As you may be aware, we have a close partnership with the Guardian House of Middle Lake. For years, we've been working to dismantle a criminal gang that distributes drugs throughout the city. Their activities result in numerous deaths, particularly among the youth. Your mission will involve participating in a special operation to help apprehend them. The guardians will likely select one of you, as you are the only women currently enrolled in this program."

"I'm in," Elisa declared, her eyes shining with determination. "When will it be?"

"In the spring, after you have successfully completed two semesters."

"Spring?" Jackie gasped. "But why wait so long? You mentioned that people are dying every day –"

"Unfortunately, they are," Don interjected. "But I can't put you at risk and send you into a dangerous situation unprepared. Study diligently, pass your exams, and then we will proceed."

Jackie looked at him with concern, remaining silent.

"This is one of the toughest aspects of being a guardian," Elisa added, giving Jackie a sympathetic look. "Knowing that no matter what we do, we can't save everyone."

"Indeed," Don agreed. "That's why you must uphold the promise you made just before I accepted you here – to stand firm and do what is right at all costs. Any questions?"

"No more questions," Jackie mumbled.

"Good," Don said, clapping his hands together. "Then, I'll see you in class tomorrow!"

Elisa and Jackie walked through the wide yard and arrived at the bustling hall of the dorms. The place was packed and noisy, with students arriving accompanied by their friends and family who had come to bid them farewell. Everyone was dressed casually, but Jackie's black clothes looking just like a guardian uniform made them stand out in the crowd as they made their way through the hall.

Elisa scanned the list of names on the information board and found room number 207 assigned to two people.

"It looks like we'll be neighbors," she remarked to Jackie. "Isn't that cool?"

Jackie ignored her remark, completely lost in thought. "This Don. He's so mean."

"So what?" Elisa shrugged. "When the man can send shivers down your spine with just a glance, I find it pretty impressive."

"What if everyone here is like him? How will they treat us, all these men?" Jackie asked, her dark green eyes widening. Their color reminded Elisa of forest marshes.

"Oh, my dear..." Elisa smiled reassuringly. "Let me tell you something about being 'mean.' There's a bad 'mean' and a good 'mean.' Both involve showing superiority, but we can use it for a noble cause – to defend our true beliefs. And we must do so without causing harm to others."

"How is that possible?"

"Words. They can sting like an arrow, but they can also bring healing," Elisa explained. "I'm still learning how to wield them wisely, and one effective method I've found is good old sarcasm." She playfully poked Jackie's shoulder, forgetting about putting on her gloves for protection. A violet energy sparkled and escaped her fingertips, causing a loud crackling sound.

"Ouch!" Jackie jumped back.

"Sorry," Elisa apologized, pressing both palms to her chest. "I'm so sorry! It's my Gift, and I can't control it well!"

"It's okay," Jackie said, rubbing her shoulder. "Let's just say it was a spark between us."

"You catch on quickly!" Elisa laughed.

2

No Difference

Their classes started the following morning. Elisa walked into the classroom side by side with Jackie. Today, she wore a black cadet uniform with a golden dragon embroidery on the shoulder. Her hair was prudently brushed into a ponytail in the hope she would look more serious and not attract too much attention. The hell it worked.

When the heavy doors of the classroom slammed shut behind them, all heads turned in their direction. Ten young men stared at them, and a loud whistle mixed with laughter filled the room. Jackie gave Elisa a worried look, her eyes shimmering like two emeralds.

"Watch and learn," Elisa winked, addressing her. Then she clapped her hands, and the room fell silent. "Good morning, cadets! Maybe someone has a question for us? Ask it now because I'll answer only once."

The male cadets exchanged glances, and a young man with red hair who sat closer to them stood up. He was tall, so he looked down upon Elisa with his bright blue eyes. "What did you ladies forget here? The perfume shop is on a trade street!"

The rest of the class burst into heavy laughter. Elisa grinned. *Perfect, one more silly boy trying to mock me.* He was the first one brave enough to speak up, though. Maybe he wasn't a bad guy, but boys only understood one language – shameless honesty.

Elisa gazed patiently at his stern face. "Is this all?!"

The laughter died down, and now everyone looked at her in silence, anticipating the continuation of the drama.

His eyebrows twitched. "Stubborn, then."

"Don't play with fire." Elisa took a step toward him, but he didn't move back.

"Why not? I'm a masterful player." His eyes darkened, and his pupils turned red. He raised his hand, and the flames ignited on his fingertips. Clearly, the guy possessed a Fire Gift. But if he was going to scare her away with this ridiculous performance, it didn't work.

Elisa gave him a scornful look. "Sorry, pal, this isn't high school anymore. Can you behave like a real guardian?"

He scoffed. "A real guardian?! What do you possibly know about it?"

"All right, I'll show you how to behave," Elisa declared, scanning the room. "First, thank you for the directions to the perfume shop. We might buy something there, right, Jackie?"

Jackie met her gaze and nodded. "For sure."

"Secondly, we're here to make this world a better place," Elisa continued, shifting her focus to the red-haired cadet. "Personally, I aim to apprehend those who think they can harm innocent people. Is that clear?"

The cadet nodded, his eyes now filled with interest.

Elisa adjusted her ponytail, moving it to the back where it belonged. "Well," she said, "I've answered your questions, so if you'll excuse us, we'll take our seats."

A red-haired cadet quickly sat down and opened his book, pretending to be engrossed in reading. Elisa chuckled softly and made her way to her desk, ignoring the rest of the class. She retrieved her notebooks and supplies from her bag and arranged them neatly on her desk.

Jackie smiled. It looked like studying at the Academy was going to be a challenging journey, but at least she wasn't alone. She observed as Elisa settled into her seat and retrieved a heavy book from her backpack. In the morning sunlight, Elisa's golden hair gleamed like a beacon, brightening the otherwise dim classroom.

Jackie was seated at her desk when another cadet stood up and approached her. His hazel eyes held a sly expression. His naturally light-brown skin indicated he was from the South. Though not particularly tall, he possessed broad shoulders and a quirky haircut that reminded Jackie of the urchins she used to encounter in the bay, prompting a smile to form on her lips.

"Only your friend answered our questions; how come?" the cadet, whom Jackie mentally dubbed Urchin, inquired.

"Just take it as is," Jackie replied.

"But there are two of you," he persisted, his gaze fixed on her. "So, you must give *your* answers."

Jackie winced. "What else do you want to know?"

Urchin moved closer. "Jackie, right?"

She nodded, surprised that he remembered her name. But she wasn't going to let him take advantage. "Congrats, that was your only question allowed, and you just missed an opportunity to ask something important."

A smile spread across his lips, revealing his shining white teeth. Surprisingly, he was pretty handsome when he smiled. Unfortunately, attractive guys were often arrogant.

"Well played," he complimented. "But as your friend mentioned, we are all here for the same purpose, aren't we?"

Jackie nodded. The previous night, she and Elisa had discussed the importance of facing the first day of classes with courage. It was the first year women were allowed to study at the Guardian Academy, and that thought gave her the strength to meet his gaze without flinching.

"So I was wondering... How might *your* Gift help?"

"I'm a mind reader," Jackie explained. "I can freely access people's thoughts, desires, and fears when I touch them."

"Interesting," Urchin remarked, extending his hand. "Then, as my future colleague, would you mind showing it to me?"

Jackie hesitated. With everyone in the classroom as witnesses, she wouldn't be violating any Academy policies by demonstrating her ability. Even though she didn't trust this guy, there was no reason to worry. So, she touched his rough, warm palm.

It was a trap, of course. As Jackie shook Urchin's hand, she closed her eyes and delved into his consciousness. A memory flashed before her eyes: it was the previous evening, and he stood in front of a tall mirror in his dorm, completely naked. She could see every part of him, and the most intriguing one was fully aroused.

Breathless, Jackie withdrew her hand, tiny droplets of sweat forming on her forehead. Her face flushed with embarrassment. Her Gift had its limitations, and Urchin had caught her off guard. Typically, she could navigate through the labyrinth of people's memories unless someone was aware that she would be reading them. In such cases, they could control the images they wanted her to see.

Urchin gazed at Jackie, waiting for her reaction. Through her mind-reading ability, she had discerned his expectation for her to flee in tears, humiliated by the prank. And sadly, it worked. Every fiber of her being urged her to escape the room and never return. However, Jackie recalled Don's teachings from the previous day – she must not grant them the satisfaction of seeing her break.

Jackie wiped her forehead with her sleeve, summoning all her strength to remain composed. "I think I'm a bit distracted because it's the first day of classes. Perhaps my Gift isn't functioning properly."

Urchin chuckled. "I see."

"But it seems you have something important to share with us," Jackie retorted, mustering the sharpest look she could manage.

One of Urchin's eyebrows arched in surprise, indicating that Jackie had turned the tables on him. She glanced around the room. "Let's be honest, we all experience nerves on the first day of classes and could use a bit of... relief." She flashed him a sarcastic smile. "Don't we?"

His breathing grew heavier. "I suppose so."

"I assume we have different ways of relaxing," Jackie persisted.

Elisa glanced at her, then back at Urchin. Her eyes sparkled with the thrill of uncertainty, akin to a gambler unsure of the next outcome. The room fell silent, all eyes fixed on Jackie.

The conversation teetered on the edge of escalation, but to Jackie's relief, the entrance door swung open at that precise moment. All heads turned towards the man entering the room – Don. Like the other cadets, he donned a black uniform, but the dragon embroidery on his shirt was larger, holding a feather in one of its paws. The emblem gleamed on his left sleeve.

Urchin swiftly turned on his heels and made his way to his desk at the front of the class. Jackie exhaled with relief and settled into her seat.

Don walked to the desk and scanned the classroom. "Good morning, cadets! In case we haven't met before, I'm the head teacher of the Academy, Donahew Wilson. But you can call me Don."

Jackie opened her notebook, poised to take notes.

He continued, "First and foremost, you should understand that you are all equal in my eyes. Want to know why?"

"Because you're fair?" someone in the room ventured.

"Exactly! And because each of you is a dumb rookie," Don declared with a grin. "You believe you can dive into investigations and show off. In reality, you're merely a group of incompetent kids who think too highly of themselves and could easily screw up a case. Remember this – any mishap occurs due to your overconfidence. You won't earn the title of guardian until you grasp the importance of respecting the guardian code and one another."

Jackie bit her lip. It was clear that the path ahead wouldn't be easy.

Content with his introduction, Don made his way to the board. With a swift motion, he unfurled a poster from the top, revealing a crime scene. Jackie blinked, focusing on the image of the victim. The girl lay on the grass, her charcoal eyes wide with fear. Her pale, lifeless body was surrounded by a pool of blood.

The gruesome sight caused Jackie's eyes to blur. It was too overwhelming to see all the harsh realities of the world – cruelty, suffering, and pain. Unable to compose herself, Jackie averted her gaze back to her notes. She stared at her pencil, feeling her heart thud heavily in the pit of her stomach.

A pair of heavy boots approached and halted at her desk. Summoning her courage, Jackie lifted her gaze to meet Don's.

"What can you deduce from this murder?" Don inquired. "As a guardian, you must scrutinize closely, identifying small details that could ultimately lead you to the killer."

Jackie nodded. Attention to detail was crucial, so she must focus. She shifted her eyes back to the crime scene and furrowed her brow, deep in thought. Apparently, the victim in the image appeared to be a teenager, and the vibrant green grass surrounding her indicated the season. "This murder took place in late spring or early summer," she ventured.

"Well, yes," Don acknowledged, "but that detail won't significantly aid the investigation."

Laughter erupted from the men in the group, causing Jackie to fall silent.

The red-haired guy, the most annoying one, rose from his seat. "The victim has a stab wound in her stomach, indicating the use of a knife by the killer."

"A more astute observation," Don commented.

Jackie turned to Elisa, seeking support, but found her friend's eyes filled with tears and her lips trembling. Jackie couldn't fathom such a sudden vulnerability. It was Elisa who had stood by her side today, providing the strength Jackie needed to remain in the classroom. *What had caused this sudden shift in her mood?*

Don approached Elisa, noting her distress. "Cadet Palmer, it seems you're not feeling well. You're free to leave if you're uncomfortable. However, if you do so –"

"I'm fine," Elisa whispered.

Jackie shook her head. Elisa had been strong throughout the day, and now it was Jackie's turn to offer support. Failure to do so would leave them vulnerable to Don's harsh scrutiny. Her mind raced, recalling Elisa's mention of Triville, a town plagued by a series of brutal murders as reported in the newspapers. *Could Don truly be presenting materials related to those incidents?* Jackie shifted her focus to the picture. Elisa's reaction wasn't merely a moment of panic; she likely knew the victim personally.

Jackie raised her hand, capturing Don's attention. "It's Ghost's case," she declared.

Don approached her. "Correct. How did you come to that conclusion?"

"I've heard about it," Jackie replied, shrugging her shoulders. "As have many of us. Additionally, Elisa hails from Triville, so I connected the dots based on her reaction."

Elisa wiped away her tears and attempted to stand, but Don gestured for her to remain seated.

"Very well, Cadet Robinson," Don commended, scanning the class. "This is the kind of proactive attitude I expect."

A smile graced Jackie's lips as she basked in the attention and the sense of accomplishment. All eyes were on her, and she relished this personal victory.

Content with the exchange, Don returned to his position at the front of the class. He directed his gaze towards Elisa. "Given your connection to the victim, I advise you not to involve yourself further. Your knowledge could skew our further investigation."

"But how will I learn then?" Elisa protested.

"Don't fret. I have another task for you," Don assured her, rubbing his palms together. "As for the rest of you cadets, head out to the front yard. Your first quest awaits!"

After everyone had exited the classroom, Elisa approached Don with a question. "What exactly am I supposed to do?"

Don settled into a chair in front of her. "We will reenact the murder scene, and you will play the role of the sleeping beauty. Would you be willing to take a sleeping potion for authenticity?"

Elisa nodded. "That's not a problem. I didn't expect this quest to be so straightforward for me."

"I also need your consent to allow Jackie to use her Gift on you," Don added.

"What?!" Elisa's eyes widened in shock. "No way. I can't do that. It would be too much for her to handle after everything she's been through."

"Seriously?" Don's expression darkened. "You're losing your shit on the first day?"

Elisa sighed. "I apologize. But I just don't believe Jackie is prepared to witness what I experienced."

Don's demeanor remained unchanged. "Collaboration is essential here, no matter how challenging."

"But what if I harm her with my memories? She's in a vulnerable state!"

"There is no reason to worry. Jackie will only delve into that specific memory to identify who administered the sleeping potion."

Elisa swallowed nervously. "So, Jackie won't be exposed to all the details of the murder I witnessed?"

"I highly doubt she will delve that deeply. Cadet Palmer, you need to trust your team. It's the key to solving this case effectively."

"Alright, let's give it a shot," her voice carried a hint of hope. "But please, handle her with care."

"I assure you, Jackie is in good hands," Don promised with a smile. He then gestured for a cadet to bring the sleeping potion.

A Citadel of Knowledge

People lazily emerged from the building, chatting and laughing. Jackie stood alone beneath the shade of a willow tree, waiting for the teacher. Finally, Don entered the yard and clapped his hands. All the cadets lined up in a straight row, their arms at their sides.

"Well, rookies, welcome to the Guardian Academy of Middle Lake city!" he announced.

The cadets nodded in unison.

"Today marks your first lesson," Don continued. "It is the most crucial lesson in your guardian career. Each of you must utilize your Gifts, just as real guardians do. The victim, your fellow cadet Elisa Palmer, has been put to sleep and hidden somewhere in the building. Your objective is to locate her before time runs out. There are two rules: do not leave the building until the mission is complete, and do not harm each other with your powers. The team that finds Elisa will emerge victorious."

They were each given a small crystal of time attached to a rope. Jackie placed the rope around her neck and concealed the crystal beneath her shirt. The cadets were then divided into three groups. Jackie found herself in the same group as Urchin.

"Looks like it's you and me again," Urchin remarked with a grin.

Jackie gave him a weary look. "Listen, I don't even know your name –"

"Howard."

Jackie gave him a teasing smile. "You know what, Urchin suits you better!"

"Urchin, it is!" one of the guys from their assigned group chimed in.

"Agreed," another added.

"It appears you've just acquired a nickname," Jackie teased him.

He waved his hand dismissively. "Can we just drop this subject?"

"No way," Jackie said, raising her index finger. "I bet from now on, people will refer to you as Urchin for the duration of your guardian career." She laughed, and the rest of the group joined in.

He snorted and headed towards the building.

At 9 in the morning, the time crystal turned a soft lilac hue, signaling the start of the quest. Jackie and her group were the last to reach the lobby. Upon receiving an envelope, Urchin opened it. They silently read the letter, not to give the competing team any clues.

The message simply stated:

"Team #1.
   Knowledge is a great power,
   I can be found in the library."

Without further discussion, they hurried towards the library located on the second floor. As they neared the stairs, Jackie glanced back. Weirdly, the other team was heading in the opposite direction. She furrowed her brow, sensing something suspicious about their actions, but there was no time to dwell on it. They pressed on toward the citadel of knowledge.

Inside, Jackie surveyed the vast expanse of the library, holding her breath in awe. The room boasted a towering ceiling, lined with shelves brimming with books that spanned every wall. In the center, square pillars adorned with more bookshelves stood, each pillar housing the knowledge of generations of mages. Perhaps this library held the entirety of human history, along with its secrets, rare Gifts, and magical spells. Recognizing the immense power of knowledge, Jackie resolved to frequent the library to expand her worldview.

A sudden clap of hands drew her attention, and she turned to see Urchin, now surrounded by the other cadets, taking charge with evident enthusiasm. "Guys, let's put our heads together. Don emphasized the importance of teamwork in locating the victim!"

Two of the cadets nodded in agreement, and when their eyes met, Jackie joined in with a nod of her own.

"We all possess unique Gifts that we must utilize," Urchin stated, his gaze fixed on Jackie. "Jackie is a mind reader, which makes her useless right now."

Jackie gasped in offense but remained silent.

Urchin turned his attention to the cadet beside her. "And what about you?"

"I'm Riley. My ability is to see dreams of the future. Today, I saw that we would locate Elisa!"

"And where did we find her exactly?" Urchin inquired.

Riley frowned, thinking. "Well... I actually just remember we shared that moment of joy... And everything else was blurred. I wish I had seen more."

"Wait... So, you knew that Elisa would be the victim?" the other cadet inquired.

Riley nodded in affirmation.

Urchin raised his hand to regain focus. "Let's keep brainstorming, alright? Riley, your vision gives us a good chance of success, but we still need to act swiftly!" He then turned to the other cadet. "And you, what's your name and Gift?"

"I'm Simon. My Gift is telekinesis. I can move objects with my mind."

Urchin rubbed his forehead in mild exasperation. "Telekinesis is the most common Gift. Everyone knows what it does."

Jackie cleared her throat, drawing their attention.

They turned to her expectantly.

"What about you, Urchin?" Jackie inquired.

He raised his hand in protest. "I asked you not to call me that!"

Ignoring his reaction, they continued to gaze at him, awaiting his response.

Urchin let out a sigh. "My Gift is Invisibility."

Jackie paused, considering his ability. "And how exactly would that aid us?"

Simon, the cadet with telekinesis, stepped forward to join Urchin. "Guys, this is all just a waste of time. People rarely succeed in this game."

"But I saw us winning!" Riley insisted.

"Come on, man! You simply knew we would have a girl in our group and let your imagination run wild!" Simon retorted.

"I didn't imagine things!" Riley defended himself.

Jackie gave them an annoyed look. Men seemed to enjoy arguing without considering the time they were squandering while the supposed 'victim' awaited their assistance.

"Jackie," Urchin called out.

"Yes?"

"I'm starting to think that you might be able to help."

She raised her eyebrows in surprise. "Really!?"

"You and Elisa are friends," Urchin explained. "And girls often share belongings like clothes or hairpins. Perhaps you have something of hers?"

"Why?"

"We could perform a Searching spell," Urchin suggested.

It was actually a good idea. Jackie patted her empty pockets, but regretfully, she did not have any of Elisa's belongings. "I'm sorry, I wish I had something. We only met yesterday, and we haven't shared anything."

Undeterred, Urchin proposed another plan. "Then... we can go back to the teacher's room, and you can read Don."

Impressed by his resourcefulness, Jackie couldn't help but be surprised by his cunning ideas. "Don is an experienced guardian. He will simply put a mental block, preventing me from any attempt to read him. I think we must drop this idea and focus on searching the library."

Riley chimed in, offering his support. "I agree. We will find her. Let's thoroughly search the area."

Urchin shook his head. "It's best to split up, then. You two can search the library. Check for the clues under every shelf! But be quick – we have only forty minutes remaining." He then turned to Jackie. "And we'll return to the class together and try to read Don."

Although she wanted to protest, Urchin was already heading towards the exit. Jackie sighed and followed him.

4

⚬⚬⚬

Hens Matter

This task turned out to be a waste of time – they spent around fifteen minutes searching for the room where their morning lesson took place. Much to their disappointment, when they finally located the room, it was empty. Jackie noticed a sheet of paper stapled to the board and read it. Confused, she handed it to Urchin.

He took the paper and read it aloud. *"If you are smart enough to go beyond the given rules, you have a chance. Keep thinking!"*

"I don't understand," Jackie said.

"Me neither." He crumpled the paper and threw it on the floor.

As they walked in the corridor towards the local performance hall, they asked each other questions that they couldn't answer yet.

"Don said, 'use your Gifts' and 'work as a team.' How the hell it's supposed to help us?" Urchin complained.

"He said we went beyond the rules, so we must have done something right, didn't we?"

"But we all read the initial letter, which said, 'I'm in the library!' But all the time we were there, I didn't see anyone from the other two teams."

Jackie shook her head. "It's just torture!"

"Agreed," Urchin said as he slowed down his steps and glanced at his time crystal. "But the good thing is – we only have 20 minutes of this torture left."

A noise from the performance hall caught their attention, causing them to stop in their tracks.

Jackie tugged at his elbow. "Urchin, look! It's the other group! They're in there!"

"I see." He gave her a puzzled look. "But why are they searching for the victim *there*? On the opposite side of the building?!"

Jackie stood frozen, a new idea forming in her mind. "I think it's time to try using *your* Gift."

Urchin narrowed his eyes. "You mean we shall take a peek at what they're doing?"

"Sure!"

The Gift of Invisibility proved to be quite intriguing. Jackie had only read about this Gift in books before, but now she found herself experiencing it firsthand. Urchin took her hand, and then he slowed his breath. A cloud of mist enveloped them like a giant bubble, rendering them invisible. Jackie couldn't see her own body anymore, but she could still feel it as usual. Urchin's invisible hand gently guided her, and she followed him into the hall.

As they entered, they neared four cadets standing in the middle of the stage, engaged in a heated argument and gesturing wildly. One of them was a tall, red-haired young man who had given Elisa a hard time earlier that morning. As Jackie got from their conversation, his name was Theo. A folded envelope lay abandoned on the floor near his feet.

"Let's see what message they have," Urchin whispered in her ear. His warm breath tickled Jackie's cheek, causing her to blush. Thankfully, their invisibility masked her face, preventing her from another embarrassing episode with this guy.

They approached the cadets slowly, and Urchin took the envelope. As they were walking back, one of the guys noticed them, or rather, he noticed the piece of paper floating towards the exit. It was a side effect of the Invisibility Gift – Urchin could make himself and things around him disappear, but not the objects he touched *after* activating his Gift.

"Hey!" someone shouted.

Urchin placed the paper in Jackie's hand and uttered just one word. "Run!"

Then he let go of her hand, and Jackie suddenly reappeared in the middle of the hall. Feeling betrayed, she opened her mouth to yell at him, but before she could speak, two guys reached her and shoved her to the floor. She landed with a sharp pain shooting through her right hip.

"Give it back!" one of them demanded.

"No!" Jackie yelped, clutching the paper tightly.

Urchin appeared at the entrance door and whistled, catching the attention of the others. He waved a piece of paper in the air, taunting them.

"Looking for this?" he grinned before turning and sprinting down the corridor.

"What the hell!" The guys released Jackie and chased after him.

As they exited the hall, Jackie opened her palm to reveal the crumpled piece of paper. She unfolded it and read:

"Team #3
  Entertainment is my name

Now I'm in the performance hall."

She groaned in frustration. How was it fair to give each team completely different messages?

Rubbing her sore hip, Jackie limped out of the hall. At the far end of the corridor, she stopped by the group of cadets. Urchin was on the floor, surrounded by the guys who were shaking him and demanding to return their letter. Now, it dawned on Jackie. Despite the danger, Urchin had entrusted her with the stolen message and put himself at risk. *Ah, if I only knew what it meant!*

Theo, the red-haired cadet, loomed over Urchin, flames flickering from his palm.

"Stop it!" Jackie shouted.

Theo turned to face her, his glowing burgundy eyes sending a shiver down her spine.

"Came to save your prince?" Theo grinned.

Jackie pulled out the crystal of time, its presence reminding everyone that they had less than 10 minutes left. All the men fell silent.

"So, we received two completely different messages," she said, clarifying her point. "Our note instructed us to look in the library while yours directed you to the performance hall. The question is – what does it mean?"

Theo clapped his hands together, causing his magical flame to vanish. His eyes returned to their standard light-blue color. "I think I know exactly what it all means."

"What?" Jackie blinked in confusion.

Theo smacked his forehead. "I can't believe it! How foolish we were! We never should have split up. We need to put the letters together to understand the message!"

"Who would win then?" the guy holding Urchin asked.

Urchin moved his hand away and sat up. "I've got it, guys. Our personal victory doesn't matter."

"All that matters is to save the victim," Jackie added.

Theo nodded. "That makes sense. Gentlemen, we need to find team #2 to read all the messages as one to crack this case."

"And where should we look?" Urchin asked. "This building is too huge!"

Theo scratched his chin. "They literally split us to the opposite sides of the building, and I guess team #2 is in the middle."

"Is there anything in the middle?" Jackie asked.

"The lab," Theo replied. "I bet they're in there."

They sprinted as fast as they could, united in their purpose and leaving behind any pointless arguments. Together, they assembled all three pieces of letters and read:

"Team #1.
Knowledge is a great power,
I can be found in the library."

"Team #2
The potions might be dangerous,
Can you find me in the laboratory?
Hens might know the truth."

"Team #3
Entertainment is my name
Now I'm in the performance hall."

Theo smiled and traced his index finger from the top to the bottom, touching the first letter of each line. Aloud, Jackie read the hidden word. *"KITCHEN."*

"Three minutes, gentlemen!" Theo reminded them. Then he gave Jackie a respectful look. "And a lady."

As they made their way outside, Urchin recalled their team members were still in the library.

"We need to bring them along," he said, addressing Theo.

Theo turned to the cadet walking behind the group. "Tim! Inform our guys in the library to head to the kitchen."

Tim nodded, and in the next moment, he shifted his feet and vanished. A gust of wind brushed against Jackie's face, leaving her in awe of this rare Gift. Individuals with the ability to move swiftly like the wind could outrun even the fastest runners. However, such power came at a cost, requiring a significant amount of energy as their metabolism functioned like a furnace.

Urchin gently touched her hand. "Let's go."

"Did you see that?" Jackie asked, gazing at the spot where Tim had just stood a few moments ago.

"We won't accomplish this quest if we linger here," he replied, pointing towards the empty corridor. The group of cadets had already reached the stairs.

"Oh, how considerate of you to think of me," she teased.

Urchin chuckled and sprinted towards the stairs. Jackie hurried after him.

5

At the Labyrinth of Fear

They reached a massive kitchen door where the rest of the group was waiting. Tim, the speedy guy, was already here, which meant the rest of the team would arrive soon.

"One-minute warning!" Theo waved his time crystal in the air.

Riley's voice echoed from the stairs. "I told you we'd find her!"

Jackie smiled. They were all together, all three teams united by the same purpose. At this moment, as they were about to 'rescue' Elisa, nothing else mattered – not their previous misunderstandings, not a desire to win. It didn't matter who was taller or smarter, and it did not matter what gender they were. Now, they were all one complete team – The Guardians.

Theo pushed through the heavy door, and they walked inside.

Elisa lay on a table with her arms crossed, her eyes shut. Don stood nearby. Seeing the cadets, he smiled and began clapping. "Congratulations on cracking my message! Now, please prepare to listen for the last part of your quest."

The cadets lined up along the wall, and Jackie took a place closer to Elisa. From where she stood, she could see Elisa's eyelashes trembling. It was as if she was only pretending to be asleep.

"Today, you have the privilege of solving Ghost's case as a detective," Don continued as he stepped aside and pointed at Elisa. "You might not know, but by the time the last victim was found, she was unconscious."

"And she was rescued," Jackie interjected.

Don nodded. "Yes, but let's consider a different scenario now. The victim is still alive, but considering a massive blood loss, she's on the brink of death. Also, you know that the criminal who put her asleep is one of the people in this room. It is the one whom you started to trust."

Jackie exchanged glances with Urchin. "You mean we must apprehend someone from our group?"

Don grinned. "Exactly. So, Cadet Robinson, you are a guardian, and you know that this criminal is a serial killer. If you don't interfere, he might kill again very soon. And here is the question – what would you do to prevent the next murder?"

"Elisa is a witness," Jackie said. "So, someone can heal her –"

"You don't have a healer in your team," Don reminded her.

Urchin raised his hand. "One of us can read her thoughts while she's asleep."

Everyone looked at Jackie, so she had to step up. Remembering that she couldn't touch Elisa's hands, she stood over her head. Her golden locks appeared to be soft and warm to the touch.

Jackie raised her eyes at Don. "I don't have to read her for real, right?"

"You *must* read her," Don pressed. "No worries, she gave me her permission."

"I won't do that."

"Why not?!"

Jackie sighed. "If I read her, she might... I mean, if it was exactly like in your quest and I used my Gift on her, the weak victim would lose her last energy, and it might lead to her immediate death."

A murmur rolled across the room.

Don smiled. "You guys are smarter than I thought. Well, you're right."

She caressed Elisa's hair. "I would rather wait for someone to heal her."

"If you wait, she will die anyway, and the other victims will follow. If you read her now, she would die an hour sooner, but we will know who the killer is."

"This isn't fair! I won't let her die without trying to save her. Then, what's the purpose of this job?"

Don shifted his gaze to the male cadets. "Well, here is the greatest dilemma of being a guardian. How ethical is it – to let someone die so the others can live?"

A heavy silence hung in the room.

Jackie shook her head. "I would wait for help, anyway. Until the last moment, as long as there is hope."

Don softened his voice. "And this is what we must do – when such victims are about to die, in their last minutes, we try to bring a mind reader to get the trace of the killer from memory. Sometimes, they are lucky enough to get help from a healer. But as I said, now we play the tough card. The victim literally has a few minutes left, and you must act now."

Jackie lowered her eyes. Elisa's facial expression remained calm. No, she couldn't hear them talking. Otherwise, she would show it with her expression. She must be asleep, most likely under some potion.

"Of course, in reality, she won't die after reading," Don assured her. "Our 'criminal' gave her a persuading potion, and I hypnotized her. After you read her, she'll simply wake up."

"All right, I'll do it," Jackie said.

Don touched her shoulder. "Remember, whatever happened to the victim in the past is not your fault, but it's your responsibility now – to find the 'lawbreaker' and prevent other crimes that might follow."

Jackie closed her eyes. It was a game, just a practice, but she didn't want to be in this situation – where she had to make a choice like that.

She landed her palm on Elisa's forehead, and her Gift sank into her memories. Jackie didn't need to go too deep. It was a moment when Elisa turned in front of the mirror in her brand-new uniform and pulled her hair up, choosing her new hairstyle. *Today's morning.* Jackie delved further into her memories. First, to the morning drama in a classroom, then to the moment when she saw the dead girl in a poster that Don had shown them. *A crime scene.* That memory made her stop breathing.

The picture of the victim faded, and the poster became black. Captivated by the darkness, Jackie moved closer. The blackness started twisting, raising a cold wind to blow into her face. Staring into the depths of an abyss, she trembled. *Who was this girl?* She must have gone through terrible, unimaginable things, and if she had stayed alive, she might never heal from it.

A sour moan burst out of Jackie's chest. She couldn't go back and save that girl. She doubted if she could save someone else like her. She promised herself to make this harsh reality a bit brighter... But what if she was too weak for it? Jackie was just taking her first awkward steps on this path without knowing if she could ever make a change.

Jackie extended her hand to the black abyss, her fingertips tingling from the icy wind. A sharp pain pierced her heart, and Jackie withdrew her hand.

She could have delved into those dark memories and uncovered the truth about this girl, but it would only bring despair. It was just an imprint of Elisa's memory, frozen in time. As Don had warned her, everything that happened in the past wasn't her fault, but it was within her power to make a difference in the future. At least, to try to do so.

Jackie had to continue navigating through Elisa's mind to find the 'criminal' and complete the quest. She blinked and found herself in Elisa's most recent memory.

An empty classroom. It was the moment when the cadets had left the class, and Elisa sat in front of Don, listening to his plan. Then the guy walked in, and Jackie recognized him immediately. He was with Jackie in the library earlier, and if memory served her right, his name was Simon. He handed Elisa a bottle with the potion.

Jackie released Elisa's head and took a deep breath. She was back in reality, in a kitchen room full of cadets.

Elisa's eyelids fluttered, and her magnificent sapphire eyes looked at Jackie.

"Are you all right?" Jackie asked.

Elisa sat up and smiled. "I knew you would make it!"

Jackie scanned the room and spotted Simon in the crowd. He stood at the corner, staring at her. She pointed at him. "Simon did it! He gave the potion to Elisa."

Don stood up and clapped his hands, and soon, everyone in the room joined in.

Jackie smiled. Now, after this challenging quest was finally over, all her worries vanished in the glow of victory. This case was closed, and she put the last dot on it. In that moment, she understood what it meant to belong. To be one of these people who courageously face danger to save lives. And it was only the beginning.

Story 2

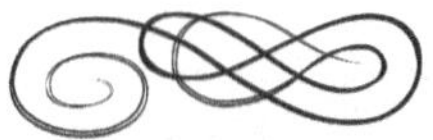

True
Flame

6

❧

The Journey

Elisa stepped into the glade, her hands laden with a bundle of dry branches. She knelt in front of the firepit and carefully placed the brushwood on the ground nearby. Recently, the evenings had grown colder and shorter, signaling the need for a strong fire. Removing her gloves, she began her preparations – arranging the thick branches vertically and interspersing the smaller ones with chips in the middle.

"Need a hand?" Jackie inquired from her spot beneath the bright-red maple tree. She sat there with her diary in hand, diligently making her weekly records. Her emerald eyes fixed on Elisa with a hint of uncertainty.

"It's fine," Elisa replied, placing her right palm over the wood. "Get ready to document the second night of our incredible journey."

Jackie sighed. "Fine. But please, be careful this time."

Now came the most crucial part – using her magic. Elisa took a deep breath and concentrated on her right hand. Purple sparkles crackled on her fingertips, growing stronger until they coalesced into a ball of electricity. With a determined exhale, she released it.

The energy struck the branches with a deafening noise, causing the wood to explode. A cloud of sawdust billowed and twisted in the air, slowly descending to coat the ground, the grass, and Elisa's head.

"Shit!" Elisa said.

Jackie approached and sat beside her. Gently, she ran her hands through Elisa's hair, removing the sawdust from her bright locks. "I'm so sorry. Maybe it will work next time."

"I hate my power..." Elisa muttered, staring at her trembling palms. "I can't touch anyone. I can't even start a fire! I'm useless."

"I understand it's challenging." Jackie offered a sympathetic smile. "Sometimes, I wish I never knew the secrets hidden in people's minds."

"But you have the choice to delve into them or not," Elisa pointed out.

Jackie retrieved a navy-blue handkerchief from her pocket and handed it to Elisa. "Now I can. But before I learned to control it, I read everyone I touched. And it was overwhelming. You know, most people are selfish, and some can be cruel. But it's all just a facade. Deep down, they're like wounded children, burdened with fears and doubts. Many adults feel trapped in their lives, suffocating under the weight of their unprocessed grief. I felt all of that when I touched them. And the worst part – I couldn't do anything to ease their pain. When I was fifteen, my Gift turned my whole world upside down."

Elisa wiped her face and clenched the handkerchief in her hand. "How did you learn to cope with it?"

"I didn't," Jackie replied, her gaze fixed on the ruined fire pit. "One day, I simply became one of them. Now I carry my own scars, a sign that I've grown into adulthood."

"Now I feel ashamed for complaining about a ruined fire."

"Don't be," Jackie reassured her, patting her shoulder. "You'll learn to tame your magic in time. Not just how to start a fire but also how to protect others. Just be patient."

"Time is merciless," Elisa observed, glancing at her wrist. The time crystal on her bracelet emitted a blue glow, indicating it was already seven in the evening. "The sun will set in less than twenty minutes, and we're far from prepared for the night. What if we freeze or get attacked by wild animals?"

"I highly doubt that will happen."

"Why are you so unnervingly calm?" Elisa eyed her suspiciously. "You've mentioned you hate long journeys because of the potential dangers."

Jackie blinked. "That's true. I'm just trying to stay positive..."

"Or perhaps you're certain we're not in danger." Elisa narrowed her eyes. "Did you tell Urchin about our trip?"

"Of course not! We agreed that I wouldn't disclose our trip to him."

Elisa twirled the handkerchief in her hand. "Hmm... If I recall correctly, Urchin used a similar cloth to make objects vanish in class. He even marked it with his initials in the corner for easy identification."

In a swift motion, Jackie snatched the handkerchief from Elisa's grasp. "You're talking nonsense."

"Am I?" Elisa maintained her gaze. "You've grown close to him, and he could exploit your trust. If Urchin gave you that handkerchief, he could easily locate us with a Searching spell."

"He's not interested in finding dragons." Jackie hesitated before adding, "Even if I were to tell him."

Elisa folded her arms across her chest. "And why should I trust you?"

"Because we're a team," Jackie asserted, rising to her feet. "Alright, let's not waste any more time. I'll go gather some brushwood, and this time, we'll stick to a standard Flame spell."

Elisa sighed. "Fine."

Jackie ventured deeper into the darkening forest in search of dry branches. Coming to a halt by a stout oak tree, she looked around, admiring the beauty of nature. The golden hues of autumn had arrived in the Lake Kingdom, painting the leaves in a fiery spectrum of yellow, orange, and red. The vibrant canopy rustled above her. Autumn days were fleeting, particularly in the forest where the trees cast shadows over the path, yet the sky remained a deep blue, reminiscent of Elisa's eyes.

Jackie smiled to herself. Despite Elisa's initially prickly demeanor, she had swiftly become her closest companion. A friend she sorely needed in this harsh world dominated by men. Not all men were cruel, though. Urchin had proven to be a nice guy, and she was gradually growing accustomed to his presence. It was a shame she couldn't have brought him along on their journey.

The sudden loud crack made Jackie flinch. She turned around, but there was no one in sight. While she could have assumed it was just a squirrel, the noise seemed too pronounced for such a small creature. *What if it's a bear lurking nearby?*

Jackie stopped breathing, fixing her gaze on the trees where the sound had originated. Her instincts urged her to flee, but she found herself rooted to the spot. Movement stirred the bushes, causing them to quiver, and the footsteps drew nearer.

Her hand instinctively went to her chest pocket, where she had concealed Urchin's enchanted handkerchief. At least with its magic, she could turn invisible and make her way back to the glade, where Elisa might be able to protect her with her powers... if she could wield them effectively. *Was it a mistake to venture here alone?*

As the leaves rustled on the ground before her, Jackie retrieved the handkerchief. She shook it to remove the remnants of sawdust from the failed attempt to start the fire.

The air in front of her shimmered, and Urchin materialized. He waved his hand and took two short breaths, followed by a loud sneeze that pierced the silence. A bird perched on a nearby tree squawked in alarm and hastily took flight.

"Damn it!" Jackie exclaimed, pressing a hand to her chest. "What are you doing here?"

Urchin wiped his nose, a smile playing on his lips. "I'm pleased to see you too."

"You promised not to follow me," she reminded him, her brow furrowed.

Urchin averted his gaze. "I didn't follow you."

She continued to glare at him in silence.

Walking over to the oak tree, Urchin reached out and touched the bark. The moss seemed to stir, slowly awakening and revealing its faint night-time luminescence. By this time of year, it had taken on a vibrant orange hue. "Look at how beautiful nature is. Yet, it's also teeming with dangers."

Jackie scoffed. "So, you were just strolling around, getting all philosophical about nature?"

He turned to her. "I missed your sense of humor."

"That was sarcasm," she clarified.

"I see." He chuckled. "I didn't intend for you to notice me."

"Well, you failed," she retorted.

"Probably," he admitted with a nod. "Listen, I just wanted to check if you're okay. And it seems you could use some help with the fire."

She frowned. "How do you know about the fire?"

"I bet that the explosion was heard by folks in the city," he remarked, glancing around. "Anyway, I just wanted to ensure you're safe, and now I can go –"

"Hold on!" Jackie grasped his sleeve firmly. "I confided in you about our little journey to High Canyons, and you promised to keep it under wraps and stay out of it. Yet here you are, clearly following me and lying about it." Leaning in closer to his face, she lowered her voice, a tactic that always seemed to affect him. "What's going on, Urch?"

His breathing quickened as he spelled his confession. "It's Theo. He became overly enthusiastic about dragons, and we decided to embark on our own journey. Please, don't be angry."

"Theo?" Her eyes widened in disbelief. "You brought him along? Despite knowing how much *they* despise each other?"

"Theo is my closest friend. He's the one who actually discovered how to locate the nearest dragon habitat."

Her cheeks flushed with frustration, and Jackie retreated to the shade of a nearby tree. She had to gather the brushwood needed for the night as darkness descended. Kneeling down, she began collecting the branches. Urchin joined her.

"I don't need your assistance," she stated firmly.

"Why not?"

"Because I can't trust you now, okay?" Jackie took a deep breath. "Please, just go."

Urchin scoffed. "Fine, maybe it's best for you to put your trust in Elisa. But you don't have to involve yourself in her conflicts with everyone. It will only bring you trouble."

"I don't want to be involved in any conflicts," her voice quivered. "You just... you don't know what she's been through. And Theo... he just wants to have fun. You're right, he's your best friend, but she's mine. I'll stand by her no matter what. Please, let's not make this more complicated than it already is."

"Alright, I won't," he relented, taking her hand in his. "It's just unfortunate that their quarrels impact us. It shouldn't be this way."

"There's nothing we can do about it." She sighed. "But I suppose I'll see you in three weeks when we return."

"Three weeks?" Urchin knitted his brow. "The dragon habitat is only two days away from here."

"No way. That's not what I saw on the map." Jackie narrowed her eyes suspiciously, but Urchin appeared to be sincere.

"Your map must be outdated then," he mused, scratching his chin in contemplation. "I think I know what's going on. The cartographer who created your map might have overlooked the fact that dragons frequently migrate. However, Theo was aware of this. After some brainstorming and research at the library, we discovered that dragon scales could enhance Searching spells. Consequently, we devised a method to locate the habitat of the nearest dragon species, and it turns out they're not too far from here. We found a quicker and simpler route."

"Simpler?" Jackie's eyes lit up with anticipation. "You know how much I detest long journeys."

"Oh, I'm well aware." He laughed. "I'll never forget the look on your face when you heard my footsteps."

"Shut up!" she playfully jabbed his chest.

"By the way, I have a spare map," he mentioned.

Glancing back at the trail leading to the glade, she hesitated. "When Elisa discovers that you're helping me, she'll have our heads."

"You mean *if* she discovers it," Urchin corrected her. "What if you two happen to run into us occasionally, and we happen to share a map?"

Jackie shook her head. "That's highly unlikely. Theo isn't one to readily share."

"What if it's a fair trade?" Urchin proposed.

"What do you have in mind?"

"Let's say, if you can offer some spare wine, we might consider exchanging it for a map," he suggested.

She gave him a quizzical look. "You didn't bring wine on your journey?"

"We did, but last night was chilly, and we finished the bottle."

"Not surprising... Alright, I'll leave our second bottle in my travel bag. Just be cautious when taking it, so we don't catch you in the act."

"You didn't catch me checking on you last night," Urchin said.

"Last night?!"

He rose to his feet. "Well, I'll see you soon then. But you won't see me!"

With that, he turned and vanished before Jackie could respond. As it appeared, Urchin had been watching her and Elisa closely during their trip. Perhaps she must be furious about this discovery, but right now, it brought a sense of relief. Gladly, she and Elisa were not totally alone in this wilderness. Jackie took a deep breath, gathered the firewood from the forest floor, and made her way back to the glade.

7

A Wine Thief

The firepit was almost ready. Jackie wrapped herself in a blanket, anticipating the warmth of hot, spicy wine. It was known that half a mug of this wine before sleep could prevent catching a cold, but for her, it was a special moment when she could get a bit tipsy and enjoy some girl talk.

Elisa finished arranging the brushwood and stood by her side. Her voice was as soft as warm liquor. "You know, I'm not a fan of long rides either."

Jackie locked eyes with her. Even though she had agreed to this long journey voluntarily, it was better to start convincing Elisa to change her mind about the guys. "You know, dragons can migrate, and we might never find them."

Elisa shrugged. "I'm sure we will. Sooner or later."

Jackie raised her eyes to the darkening skies. "It's not so easy to find their habitat. Even if we do, who will believe us?"

"I don't care about people's opinions, Jackie."

"Then why are we doing it?"

Elisa opened her mouth, but no words escaped her lips. She stared over her shoulder with wide-opened eyes. Jackie fell silent.

Something moved behind her back, and by the quiet rustle of their road bags and someone's puffing, she concluded that Urchin hadn't broken his promise about stealing their wine to compensate for it later with the map. However, he had forgotten to be quiet.

"Is it a raccoon?" Jackie whispered.

Elisa's voice was hushed. "Raccoons don't play tricks. Just look at it!"

Jackie slowly turned her head. The bottle of wine floated slowly towards the bushes.

Elisa gave her a sharp look. "I asked you not to tell Urchin about our trip."

Jackie mustered an innocent look. "We don't know if it's him."

"Really? Well, who else could it be?"

"Maybe just an occasional mage with the Gift of Invisibility. You know, this magic is very common among thieves –"

"Enough!" Elisa raised her palm. "I'll show them how to steal from us."

Without any delay, she walked in the direction where the bottle had flown. Jackie had no choice but to follow her to the forest.

"One day, you'll become a great thief!" Theo stood over the burning fire, mixing the wine in a steaming pot. The flames danced on his cheerful face.

Urchin waved his hand. "Stop saying that! I'm a future guardian, not a criminal."

Theo covered the pot with the metallic lid. "You just stole a bottle of wine for us. I assume it was fun."

"It was. But it doesn't mean that I've crossed over to the dark side of the law."

"Why not?" Theo teased him. "Isn't it boring to constantly follow the rules? Haven't you ever dreamed of being a little adventurous?"

"Nope. All the men in my line were guardians, and I'll do the same. It's my destiny," Urchin said as he started extracting the blanket from his backpack. The night might be cold. Good thing he managed to get some spicy wine from Jackie. Soon, she and Elisa would come here to demand fair compensation. Then, they might even end up continuing this trip together. *Ah, that would be so nice!*

"Destiny..." Theo stared at the flames. "Can someone decide for us what to do? Maybe we can direct our lives, and everything is in our hands. What if you can choose not to follow your father's steps and create your own future?"

The bushes shivered behind his back, and then two familiar women walked into the glade. They both held silver Paralyzing spells in their hands. This spell was the most popular among the guardians – it allowed them to neutralize criminals.

Elisa targeted him and grinned. "Your destiny will be decided right now, thief!"

"Whoa, Sparkle!" Theo grinned. "What's up?"

She breathed heavily. "Don't mess with me. I know you two stole our wine."

"And why does everyone blame me?" Theo raised his hands to the night sky. "I'm just a cook here."

Urchin stepped into the circle of light and stood near Jackie. "So, you lost your wine. But how do you know it was us?"

Jackie gave him an annoyed look. "When you stole it, you were as accurate as a drunk bear."

He blinked. "Was I?"

They stared at him in silence. The wine quietly boiled in a pot.

Urchin sighed. "Fine, you caught me. But we can suggest something in exchange –"

"No way." Theo took a step towards Elisa. "As I understand, it didn't take you too long to find us. Let's say we're impressed, so you can go back to your place and continue your journey without any further interruption."

Elisa glared at him. "Not until I get my wine back."

"Okay, Sparkle." He shrugged and pointed to the pot. "Take it back. If you can."

Elisa reached the fire in two steps, and her fingers touched the handle. The skin hissed, and the smell of burning flesh filled the air.

"Fuck!" Elisa jumped back, shaking her right hand. She dropped a Paralyzing spell on the ground, and it left a circle of frost on the earth.

Jackie dropped her spell and jumped to Elisa, catching her by her sleeve. She blew on her fresh burns, trying to relieve the pain, but it couldn't fix the damage – her magic channels were injured. Of course, it was temporary, and the channels would heal, but it was still unpleasant to lose her powers, especially in the night forest.

She turned to Theo. "Are you out of your freaking mind?! Now she won't be able to use her magic!"

Theo's face became alarmed. He approached and moved his palm over Elisa's burns. The red skin slowly took on its normal pink color. Jackie glared at it in awe. He could use his Fire Gift in a good way when he wanted to.

"See? You ladies are too impulsive," Theo said. "You could have just suggested we share the wine, and we would have had fun."

Elisa rubbed her palms. "Forget the wine. Why are you chasing us?"

"No one is chasing you." Theo rolled his eyes. "It's just a coincidence."

"It's bullshit!" Elisa glared at him in hatred. "You used the Searching spell to locate us, didn't you?"

He paused. "Maybe."

"Why?" She gasped. "Did you worry about us or just wanted to rob us to bring some colors into your miserable, pathetic life?"

Theo chuckled. "So many epithets for one sentence!"

Elisa crossed her arms on her chest. "That's all you can say?!"

Jackie shook her head. Urchin, who had stood aside all this time, now came to Jackie and pulled her elbow. They walked to the side of the glade, where the guys couldn't hear them.

Jackie lowered her voice. "Did you attract our attention on purpose?!"

He looked at her with puppy eyes. "I just tried to be proactive. You noticed me, so it was easier for you to follow me."

"And how do you think it will end?"

He glanced back. Their friends were standing at the fire, waving hands and arguing. The shadows cast by them nervously moved over the surrounding trees.

"Now we can help them," Urchin said.

"You're killing me from inside." She groaned. "What can we possibly do?"

"At first, you have to understand that they are acting like kids."

"Yeah, I kind of see that."

"A constant misunderstanding between Theo and Elisa is poisoning everything. But I have an idea. Once, I read about an interesting way of reconciliation."

"And what's that?"

"Do you trust me?"

Jackie sighed. "I really want to."

He raised his hand, and a silver Paralyzing spell shone in his palm. "Then let's shoot these birds."

"Shoot?" She widened her eyes. "I would never do that. Elisa would never forgive me."

"She will understand." His eyes gleamed. "As my father says, 'One time of being sorry is better than a life of worries.'"

She kept gazing at him. "Who's your father?"

"He used to be a guardian. A Captain, to be precise."

Jackie raised her hand, casting a new Paralyzing spell. "Well, I hope he is right."

8

The Truce

Theo slowly opened his eyes. The last thing he remembered was standing by the fire and messing with Sparkle, and then everything went blank. Now, he was lying on the ground beneath a big tree. The branches above were covered with a web made of ropes, and now these ropes shone with a bright green color. *Shit... it's a trap!* Judging by the pattern, this trap was made with his own hands. It was unbelievable that the people who attacked them found it and used it against them.

He lay quietly, listening to every sound. The air was fresh and rich with the fragrance of raw leaves. The glimpses of the burning fire played on the foliage above. There were two people at the fire, quietly discussing something. And one of the voices belonged to... Urchin. *What a betrayal!*

"Lying bastard," he whispered. "You'll pay for this."

Someone moaned to his left, and Theo turned his head. Elisa was lying nearby, her eyes shut. He moved closer to check the pulse on her neck. *Please, be alright.*

Elisa opened her eyes, her face taking on a puzzled expression.

"It seems they caught us," he clarified, trying to keep his voice as calm as possible. "Be quiet."

"Oh, shit," she muttered, pressing her palm to her forehead. "That's all I need now. Who the hell are they? Forest thieves?"

He sighed. "I'm afraid it's our friends."

"What?!" She sat up and rubbed her eyes, refusing to believe him. But Theo didn't lie – Jackie and Urchin sat on a cozy blanket, holding steaming mugs in their hands. They noticed that she was awake and watched her in silence.

Elisa stood up, but she couldn't take a step forward – an invisible trap held her under the tree. Only now did she notice that she was barefoot. Her guardian boots with special protective soles that could let her step over any trap now rested at the fire. Theo's boots were near hers. Obviously, they were trapped well.

"What the fuck, guys?" Elisa shouted. "Let me out of here!"

They exchanged glances, and Jackie gave her an apologetic look. "I'm sorry, but it can't last any longer."

Elisa narrowed her eyes. "As well as our friendship."

"Elisa, please –"

"And how could I ever trust you?" Elisa placed her palm on the invisible wall and concentrated on her power. But no single electric sparkle came out. Perhaps this trap also blocked their magic. Desperate, she kicked the invisible wall of the trap. "Take it off! Now!"

Theo gave them a weary look. "The trap is based on your spell, I guess."

"Exactly," Urchin confirmed with a nod.

Theo scoffed and shifted his eyes to Elisa. "Then it would last for five, maximum six hours. By sunrise, we'll be free."

Elisa glanced at her time crystal. It shone purple, indicating it was just 9 in the evening. She gasped. "And how will I handle you until sunrise?"

"How about you shut up?" he suggested.

She clenched her fists. "If you think I'm helpless without my power, you're wrong."

"Are you gonna bite me?" he laughed. "I don't think I'd mind it."

Elisa took a deep breath, feeling a wave of irritation roll down to her stomach.

Catching Jackie's anxious gaze, Urchin stood up and approached the trap. "Guys, please calm down. We all came here for the same purpose –"

"Not really," Elisa replied. "You followed us because of Jackie."

"We just wanted to watch the dragons," Urchin said. "After all, they're the most amazing creatures in this world."

Theo glanced at Elisa. "Actually, Sparkle is right. The dragons were never your main purpose. You wanted to impress Jackie because you're into her."

"Into her?" Elisa scoffed. "No, he just wants to get into her panties. And I guess it goes according to your plan, Urch?"

Urchin swallowed nervously. "Of course not."

Elisa looked around the glade – Jackie stood aside, a thick blush covering her cheeks. The metal mug that she held in her hand fell to the ground, causing Urchin to flinch.

"A liar," Elisa spat. Then, she turned to Theo for support. Even though she disliked this guy, she preferred his side right now. 'My enemy's enemy is my friend,' as people said.

Theo paused, probably weighing his words before attacking his best friend. "That's actually true, Urchin. You once confessed that you'd been fantasizing about Jackie once you noticed her in the dorm lobby. If my memory serves, it all started just before our first day of classes."

"And I knew that!" Elisa fended off. "Now, let us out. Or we'll make sure we tell all the dirty secrets we know about you two. Trust me, after that, you'll hate each other."

Urchin sighed and turned to Jackie. "Do you want to stop this now?"

She shook her head and moved closer. "All right, let's speak the truth, then." Jackie gave her a warm look. "I know that our acquaintance with the guys wasn't smooth, but everything has changed. I believe that Urchin has worried about me recently because he is my friend. As well as you."

Elisa sneered. "I seriously doubt that."

Jackie didn't give up. "I told Urchin about this journey because I really wanted the guys to go with us but knew they couldn't. Because you two are acting like kids!"

Theo scoffed. "You know what? You try to dominate because you are scared."

"Scared?" Jackie gave him a puzzled look. "Of what?"

"I'm stronger than you in class, and I always win."

"That's not true. It's you who are scared that Elisa might be a better detective than you. That's why you mock her constantly!"

Theo shook his head.

"What about you, Theo?" Urchin asked. "Tell us why you came here."

He paused. "You know that I have a scientific interest."

"What do you mean?" Jackie asked.

Theo gave them an annoyed look. "We borrowed a dragon scale from the lab, and I discovered that we might bring new samples from the most dangerous species that no one ever dared to bring before. It would impact my average score in science."

Elisa laughed. "I've never seen this dedication to studying. You are doing everything for good marks."

"It's not only about the marks," Theo said. "Maybe you don't know, but my fire magic is an ancient Gift. It has roots in the ages when my ancestors tamed the dragons. The legend says that those people were resistant to high temperatures, so they could travel by flying these beasts. All I want is to experience touching a real dragon. To challenge myself."

Elisa widened her eyes. "But to get the scales, you don't need to be near them. You know, the scales fall off when dragons scratch their backs on rocks. So, you can search in the rocks."

Theo shook his head. "It might take forever. But in fall, their scales renew, and I bet there's plenty of them in their caves."

Elisa paused, thinking. "Can you really get that close?"

Theo shrugged. "Well, it's dangerous, but the main aim is to stay unnoticed."

Urchin nodded. "And here's how my Gift would help."

Elisa's eyes sparkled as she looked at Urchin. "Theoretically, can you bring me into the cave, too?"

"A cave?" Jackie shifted her gaze around them. "Are you all kidding?"

Elisa turned to her. "What? I actually have a purpose, too. No one cared to ask, so I'll just say it. I came here to see how to steal their eggs."

They all stared at Elisa.

"What?!" Theo asked.

Urchin echoed. "What?!"

Elisa smiled. A burgundy blush covered her cheeks, and her eyes gleamed. As a mind reader and an empath, Jackie knew that this sight usually belonged to people who were captivated by an obsessive idea. Sometimes, it was a healthy idea, like a scientific discovery or inventing a new spell. But stealing the dragon egg... it had gotten way out of hand.

Jackie lowered her voice to speak calmly as if she was a parent speaking to a disobedient child. "Elisa, the average dragon can kill you with a single puff. Think about what they might do when you try to steal their egg. Do you really think that the silly trophy is worth this risk?"

"Exactly," Theo chimed in. "We need a better plan to steal them."

Elisa glared at him. "I took some sleeping potion with me to be able to knock the dragon off. I just didn't know how to get closer, but now I know." She looked at Urchin with hope. "Of course, if you can take an extra person under your Invisible shield."

Urchin glanced at Jackie, then shifted his eyes back to Elisa. "The more people I cover with my shield, the less time I have until my magic weakens."

Theo shook his head. "It's an awfully bad idea. Firstly, your sleeping potion won't work because these creatures are too big, and you'll need a huge amount of potion to knock them off. And secondly, Urchin's Gift has a limitation – he can make objects invisible only if he touches them *before* activating his Gift."

Jackie nodded. "Yes, it's like today's accident. If we were mad because he stole our wine, imagine the dragon who will see his eggs floating away from the cave!"

"Agreed," Urchin said. "And why do you need these eggs in the first place?"

Elisa sighed. "You know what, I didn't plan for anyone to join me, so if you are scared, you can quit and go home."

"We aren't going anywhere," Theo said. "We just need to know the stakes."

Jackie rolled her eyes. Of course – all the men adored adventures. And now they were ready to join this suicide mission.

"All right," Elisa continued, "as we speak the truth – I'll tell you the damn truth. My good friends have a wedding in two weeks, and they have a dream about creating a dragon farm. A place where people would be able to get a tamed dragon."

"Is it even possible?" Theo asked.

"Wedding? Yes. The farm? Who the heck knows? But you know what, I just believe in them. The guy learned about the dragons, and he knows that if you raise them with dignity, they can become loyal friends."

"Well, it makes sense," Theo said.

"It still might kill us," Jackie reminded them.

Elisa shot her a disappointed look. "Obviously, not all the friends are loyal..."

Jackie gasped. "You know what? You could have told me about the purpose of our adventure, though."

"I was going to," Elisa pointed at Urchin. "But this guy robbed us and interrupted me."

"Come on, Sparkle, we agreed to commit a robbery with you, and you still complain about your wine!" Theo pointed out.

"I don't." She hesitated. "Actually, we can share."

"Finally." Theo fidgeted on the ground. "By the way, Urchin, where is the wine?"

Urchin smiled. "It's right behind you – on the tray."

They both looked back and found two mugs and a warm pot of wine. There were also two sandwiches because, as Jackie learned, food always made people a bit kinder and happier. To her own surprise, Urchin's plan worked perfectly – Theo and Elisa teamed up as they became trapped.

After dinner, Urchin removed the trap, and all four of them sat at the fire in a circle, enjoying a good conversation about their upcoming mission. Theo told the legend about the chosen guardian who was destined to tame the dragon and save the world from the upcoming apocalypse. According to his story, the guardian's appearance matched his.

When he finished, Jackie smiled. "You seem to know a lot about these creatures. I just don't understand one thing."

"What's that?"

"If the dragons are so intelligent, won't they look for their missing eggs?"

"Good question," Theo remarked. "It's not a problem because, in the wild, the strongest kids get out from the nest first, and they just fly away."

Elisa gave him an intrigued look. "How many eggs can we steal then?"

"I think they won't notice if we only take a couple."

"Is that it?"

"Don't be greedy, Elisa," Jackie said. "It's too risky, plus I've never heard about people who stole the dragon's eggs, which means that they never brag or end up dying in the cave. We must be really careful."

"Fine," she agreed. "Two eggs, then."

Urchin, who had been silent until now, joined their conversation. "When I was a kid, I read one fascinating legend about the dragons."

"Aren't there too many legends around them?" Theo asked.

Jackie sighed. "I hope it's not too creepy. Because a nightmare is all I need tonight."

"No, you would love this one." Urchin gave her a soft smile. "It says that the souls of people who died from unnatural reasons can come back and continue another life as a dragon – free and wild."

"You mean people who died from accidents?" Elisa asked.

Theo shook his head. "He means the ones who were murdered."

"Then, if we don't survive tomorrow, we will become the dragons." Elisa chuckled. "How ironic is that?"

"It's not a joke." Urchin frowned. "I don't know about you guys, but I'm too young to die!" He locked his eyes with Jackie. "We'll make it, okay?"

"Of course we will." She nodded with a yawn.

As the tiredness took over, Jackie laid on a blanket. It was so good to finally see her only friends in another state other than arguing. Her eyes started closing against her will. Elisa moved to her and covered her with the plush blanket they had borrowed from the dorms.

"I hope you aren't mad at me," Jackie whispered.

"Of course not. It's too hard to be angry with you for too long."

Jackie gave her a sly look. "I'll remember that."

Elisa smiled. "Sleep. We have a long day ahead."

Her heart filled with pleasant calmness, and Jackie closed her eyes, falling into a sweet, cozy dream.

The sharp piece of a dragon scale slowly floated forward, surrounded by the blue glow of a Searching spell. Their horses trotted through the narrow forest trail. Theo was first, then Elisa, then Jackie. Urchin rode behind, his horse puffing. It was the next day of their trip, and they were supposed to reach their destination soon.

The trail widened, and Urchin rode by Jackie's side. "I'm really enjoying this journey."

Jackie smiled. "Yes, me too."

He eyed her curiously. "Do you think it's just the beginning of something?"

"What do you mean?"

He paused. "I mean, this adventure for the four of us. We might be a good team."

She glanced at the guys who rode in front of them in silence. "You know you can count on me, but I'm not sure about these two. They are too stubborn."

He snickered. "At least they have something in common."

Jackie shook her shoulders. "I just hope they won't kill each other until we make it back to the dorms."

The trail ended, and they stopped at the foot of the hill, watching the Searching spell. The blue light started blinking, and the scale floated to the top. Then it landed in a pile of fallen leaves, and the light went off. It became quiet around.

Elisa frowned. "Theo, are you sure you made the spell correctly?"

He gave her an annoyed look. "I never do it wrong."

Jackie and Urchin exchanged glances and moved up the hill. Urchin moved faster and stopped at the top, staring at something with wide-open eyes. Jackie approached him with caution. The trees here parted, opening a spectacular view of the valley. Stunned, she held her breath. Surrounded by the high rocks, the valley drowned in the evening light. The gleaming curve of the river streamed among the bright red and yellow trees. But all this beauty was just scenery for the most exciting creatures who lived here – the dragons.

Yellow, blue, and gray creatures floated under the golden clouds with their wings spread. Their scales shone in the soft sunlight. They probably were hunting because one of them, a big yellow dragon with black paws and a sharp face, roared and streamed to the mountains. His mouth opened, pouring a stream of fire between the stones. The dragon moved down, his claws catching the dead wild goat.

It took Jackie some time to put herself together.

"Holy shit!" It was Elisa's voice.

Jackie turned to face her. She was by her side, as was Theo.

Jackie smiled. "We found them."

"We really did," she whispered, awe-struck.

Theo chuckled. "You see, Sparkle, this spell never lets me down."

Hidden Treasures

The bushes grew between the rocks, and the cadets lurked behind them, waiting for the first rays of dusk. Theo sat on a flat stone, his gaze fixed on the cave entrance. Urchin began doing stretching exercises to prepare himself.

Elisa removed her gloves and rubbed her palms. The sparkles lit up and melted between her fingers. "My Gift is useless here," she remarked.

Jackie smiled sarcastically. "Then what about me? My mind-reading has nothing to do with robbery."

Elisa leaned down and picked up a strange rock. Jackie approached to get a better look and raised her palm, invoking her Light. A blue energy twisted between her fingers, forming a glowing sphere.

The small rock in Elisa's hand had a dark blue color, now gleaming in her palm as it reflected her Light.

"A dragon's scale!" Elisa exclaimed.

Theo stood up and approached. "It belongs to the Nosimos. This species of dragons is quite big but not too dangerous. Some scientists even find them cute."

"They won't be so cute when you steal from them," Jackie added with a smirk.

He chuckled. "Just like Sparkle."

"Very clever," Elisa remarked, her brow furrowed.

Theo softened his voice. "Why don't you just take it as a compliment?"

"Because you have a strange way of giving compliments," Elisa retorted.

He narrowed his eyes. "As do you."

Jackie took the scale from Elisa and twisted it in her hand. Holding the scale made her feel oddly calm. "It might make a good trophy," she suggested.

"We have plenty of those in the lab. Jackie, could you look for the red or orange ones while we wait?" Theo asked. "Please?"

"I'll see what I can find," Jackie replied, offering him a polite smile before tucking the scale into the pocket of her pants.

Urchin joined them, pointing upwards. "Guys, it's time."

They turned their heads to see the pink horizon. The dark-blue dragon emerged from the cave, stretching and yawning.

"I told you they're cute," Theo whispered. "And by the way, it's a female."

The dragon walked to the edge of the cliff, her paws with violet stripes sliding forward as her mouth opened, revealing sharp yellow teeth.

"Cute, of course," Elisa grumbled.

The dragon shook her head, then roared, the sound echoing through the valley. Speechless, all four quickly retreated back into the bushes.

Urchin's voice was barely a whisper. "She's waking up the others. It's hunting time."

Jackie's heart pounded in her chest. These creatures could easily devour them for breakfast.

"Jackie, I'll need your Light now," Elisa instructed. "Split it and give me a half."

Jackie lowered her eyes, the Light ball still shimmering in her hand. She nodded and placed her free hand in the middle of the Light ball, splitting the energy into two parts. As they had discussed earlier, Jackie had to wait outside while the guys were stealing the eggs. It was decided to use her Light as a signal.

As it was two parts of the same energy, in case of danger, Jackie was supposed to destroy her Light, causing the other half to disappear as well. This was their signal for impending danger – if the dragon was about to return to the cave earlier than expected.

Jackie split the Light ball in two and handed the second half to Elisa. She then moved her hands around it, shaping the energy into a sphere. Elisa did the same with her half.

Meanwhile, the reptile spread her wings and launched into the air, kicking up a cloud of dust that settled on the nearby rocks.

"Let's go," Urchin commanded.

Theo stood up and dashed towards the cave, with Urchin following closely behind.

"Please, be careful," Elisa said, her voice filled with concern.

Jackie sighed. "I hope it's worth it."

Elisa gave her a sad smile, then pressed her palm to her mouth and blew Jackie an air kiss. "Good luck!"

Jackie's heart trembled, a pleasant warmth filling her chest. She opened her mouth to speak, but Elisa ran after the guys before she could utter a word.

Alone among the dusty rocks, with the blue Light in her hand, Jackie watched as they disappeared into the darkness of the cave. The dragons floated on the horizon, breathing fire onto the hills. Theo had mentioned that the dragons were immune to magic. *Can we truly outsmart them?* Jackie could only hope that her friends would be clever enough to steal the eggs quickly.

Elisa held a half of Jackie's blue Light as she walked into the cave. The interior was dusty, with walls covered in cobwebs. Theo used his magic as a torch, casting flickering light that illuminated their curious faces and the space around them. At the far wall, they found a nest made of branches and hay, and they approached it to inspect the contents.

Inside the nest were four eggs, their shells adorned with magnificent scales. Two eggs gleamed in shades of blue and purple, while the other two were a fiery red.

Elisa placed the Light on the ground and gently touched one of the eggs. Her magic sparkled on the scales, so she took her hand off, afraid of causing any harm.

"You can't harm them with your power," Theo reassured her. "The dragons possess a Gift of Fire. It is ancient magic, the strongest in the universe. It protects us from all kinds of destructive spells."

Wide-eyed, Elisa asked, "You mean... I can't harm you with my Gift?"

"Nope," Theo replied, shaking his head.

Elisa paused, then reached out and touched his hand. Electricity sparked on his skin, causing no damage before disappearing.

She gasped. "All this time, I was afraid to touch people, fearing I might harm them, and you didn't even bother to mention that you are resistant?"

He shrugged. "You never asked."

Elisa shot him an annoyed look, deciding it wasn't the time for an argument. To distract herself from thoughts of his arrogance, she picked up the egg. It was the size of a melon but surprisingly heavy, akin to a ripe pumpkin.

Urchin opened his road bag and spread a blanket on the floor, allowing Elisa to carefully wrap the egg. Remembering from the encyclopedia, she knew it needed to be kept in a warm place until the dragon's birth, or it would perish from the cold.

"Handle the blanket with care," Urchin cautioned. "We need to fit two eggs in there."

Wiping sweat from her forehead, Elisa hesitated. "Maybe Jackie is right. Perhaps we shouldn't be greedy. One egg could suffice as a gift."

"We must take two," Theo insisted. "One dragon is for you, and the other is mine."

Elisa shot him a sharp look. "No way. You can't just take the other one. They're not pets!"

"Guys!" Urchin called out.

But they both ignored him as the argument continued.

"They weren't yours to begin with," Theo reminded her. "And according to the legend, I must try –"

"Forget the legend!" Elisa interrupted, waving her hand. "You're the most selfish and annoying person I know, and you won't be able to take care of the dragon. You'll only end up hurting it!"

"Coming from the most annoying person I know," he teased.

"GUYS!" Urchin's voice boomed.

Startled, they turned to him. "WHAT?!"

He pointed towards the cave entrance. "Listen!"

In the tense silence, Elisa could hear approaching footsteps. Someone heavy was running down the corridor, sounding like a dragon. She glanced towards where she had placed the Light signal, only to find it missing.

"Shit!" Elisa jumped to her feet and turned towards the entrance, hands outstretched in defense. Her heart raced as she realized that the dragons were immune to her magic, meaning they were trapped. But the worst realization hit her: the signal was gone, indicating that Jackie was in danger, if not worse.

"Hold my hand," Theo said, standing nearby. "I'll create a shield, and Urchin will get us out of here."

Elisa hesitated. "What if Jackie is in the corridor, running away from them?"

"She likely found a hiding spot outside," Theo insisted, placing his hand on her shoulder. "Come on, Sparkle, we're running out of time."

Elisa stared at the entrance, her mind racing. "I said wait!"

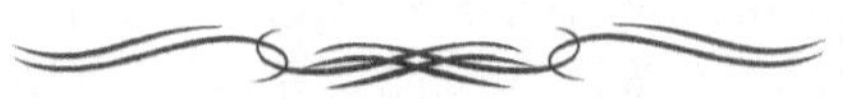

Jackie lost track of time as the sky gradually brightened, casting sharper silhouettes of the rocks around her. A glint from one particular stone caught her eye, prompting her to descend the slope to investigate. Setting her Light on the ground, she brushed away the small stones and picked up a dusty scale.

As Theo had mentioned, the red, shimmering scale likely belonged to one of the most dangerous reptiles – the Ogosis. She hadn't seen these red dragons in the vicinity when they first explored the area, suggesting their caves might be further down the valley.

The scale in her hand began to tremble and grow warmer. Suddenly, a heat spread to her hip, where she discovered a piece of a blue scale in her pocket. Confused, Jackie closed her eyes, tapping into the mind-reading Gift that connected her to reptiles through their scales. Though she couldn't see any images, her heart raced as she sensed the reptiles were alarmed.

Jackie opened her eyes to see two dragons flying in the direction of the cave. Though they were still some distance away, it wouldn't take them long to reach her. Which meant she must flee.

Quickly stashing the scales in her pockets, Jackie stepped on the Light ball, causing the blue energy to burst into shimmering sparks.

The seconds passed, but the entrance to the cave remained silent. *Had the guys noticed the signal?*

Looking down the slope towards the dense forest where the trail led, Jackie remembered the advice the others had given her the night before – to run away and hide if danger approached. But she couldn't bring herself to leave. Elisa was still inside.

Without hesitation, Jackie sprinted towards the cave entrance. The dragons drew closer, their deafening roars echoing behind her.

The cave was dark and dusty, but she pushed forward, swearing under her breath. If she stumbled now, everything would be over.

Jackie burst into the round hall, her chest heaving with exertion. Urchin was already there, catching her in his embrace. With a trembling hand, she pointed towards the dark corridor. "There!"

She didn't need to say more as the roar of the dragons reached them.

Elisa moved closer to the entrance, raising her hands as waves of electricity burst forth, destroying the ceiling over the corridor. The cave trembled as huge rocks tumbled down, blocking the passage to the hall. Dust clouds filled the space, and Elisa shielded her face with her sleeve.

As the dust settled, Elisa conjured her Light – a sphere of silver energy with golden sparkles that illuminated the hall like a glowing moon. The guys had sought refuge by the nest.

Elisa approached them, sitting on the floor to meet Jackie's gaze. "What happened?"

"Did any of you see my signal?" Jackie asked, glancing at the others.

The dragons drew closer, their claws scratching against the fallen rocks with a sound like sharp knives.

Urchin and Theo exchanged worried glances.

"We must have overlooked it somehow," Urchin said.

Theo frowned. "Sparkle was supposed to monitor the Light signal!"

Elisa turned to him, her fist hitting his shoulder. "It's your fault! I would have kept an eye on it if you hadn't been distracting me with your stupid ideas!"

A dragon roared beyond the wall, causing Elisa to flinch.

"We're doomed," Urchin said in a gloomy tone. "In a few minutes, they'll break through this wall and burn us alive."

Theo shook his head. "Not me."

"Yeah," Elisa scoffed. "But did you see their claws? After they're done with us, they'll shred you into pieces, which is a much worse way to die."

Theo gave her a sharp look. "Can you channel that enthusiasm into finding a way out of here?"

"There's no way out!" Elisa's voice trembled. "Urchin is right. We're going to die here."

"Stop it!" Jackie stood up. "We're a team, and we must figure something out."

She walked around the hall, running her hands over the smooth stone walls. In the Academy, they were taught that every situation had at least two exits, but here, there seemed to be none. It was no wonder she had never heard of anyone attempting to steal dragon eggs before; those who found themselves in such a predicament likely met a grim fate.

Taking a deep breath, she tried to push aside the fear that gripped her companions. Despair was not an option; she knew that those who lost hope were truly doomed. But she struggled to find a way to save her friends.

Urchin paced the hall, his steps quick and purposeful. "Let's think. We all have powers, right? We just need to find the right way to use them."

Elisa, now seated on a fallen stone, rested her palms on her lap. "What can we do? I could attempt to create another exit with my power, but I doubt I'd have enough energy to move us from beneath these rocks."

"Sparkle is right," Theo agreed. "Also, her power won't be effective against the dragon if we try to fight them."

Jackie sat on the warm stone floor, hugging her head in despair. Among them all, she felt that her power was the most useless. But then, an idea sparked in her mind.

She reached into her pockets and retrieved two scales, both clearly belonging to the reptiles that inhabited the cave. Somehow, these scales held a connection to the dragons. When Jackie was outside, she had sensed the dragons' emotions by holding their scales. It seemed she could tap into their minds through the scales. The solution might literally be in her hands.

Placing both scales together, Jackie closed her eyes and delved deeper into the dragons' minds. She sensed their fury, which was understandable as they were protecting their home and unborn offspring. She had to try to soothe their anger. There had to be a way to communicate with them and find a peaceful resolution.

As Jackie delved deeper into the dragons' consciousness, she scrolled through images of their hunts and flights among the clouds. She continued to explore until she reached a moment of peace and tranquility when the two reptiles sat together in the cave. The nest was prepared, with a thick layer of hay and branches awaiting the mother's eggs. Then, the moment of laying arrived, and four eggs appeared in the nest – two blue with purple stripes and two red ones. The eggs glowed from within, radiating heat and the power of fire.

Jackie opened her eyes. Obviously, the dragons' behavior was driven by a deep connection and protective instinct towards their offspring. No ordinary animal would leave their babies unguarded, but dragons were different. The scales and her ability to read them were just a small piece of the puzzle. The dragons must have shared a strong bond with each other, and when the eggs were stolen, the parents sensed the disturbance from a distance.

Jackie had to find a way to communicate this understanding to the dragons and seek a peaceful resolution to the situation.

Elisa approached Jackie, her voice filled with emotion. "Why didn't you run away when you had a chance? You could hide in the rocks."

Jackie met her gaze. "I couldn't. If something happened to you in this cave, I would never forgive myself. You clearly missed my signal, so I had to try to save you."

"I'm so sorry," Elisa's eyes welled up with tears. "If I only were more attentive…"

"It doesn't matter now," Jackie reassured her.

A solitary tear rolled down Elisa's cheek. "Jackie, dear. If we really die –"

"Not today," Jackie interrupted, wiping her own cheek with her sleeve. "We'll be fine. I promise."

"You can't give such promises."

"I can. Because I know what to do."

Theo and Urchin drew near, visibly ready to hear Jackie's plan.

Jackie stood up, her resolve firm. "These reptiles are the parents of these eggs, and when you guys stole their babies, they sensed it from far away. They became furious."

"Can we just return them?" Urchin suggested.

Elisa shook her head. "I think it's too late for that. And even if we did, our risk would have been for nothing."

"We won't need to return them," Jackie said confidently. "I'll try to connect with the minds of the dragon babies and soothe them. If they are calm, the parents won't be as agitated."

"But magic shouldn't work against the dragons," Theo pointed out.

Jackie shrugged. "Somehow, I was able to connect with them through the scales, and you were able to use a Searching spell to locate them. Maybe certain types of magic can affect them?"

Urchin smacked his forehead. "Of course, that's what the legend said – magic can't *harm* them!"

"But if we approach it with the intention of not causing harm, it might just work." Theo's eyes lit up. "It's brilliant!"

"Alright," Elisa said, turning to Jackie. "Now it's your turn to use your Gift."

"I'm not sure if I can do it well. It's a spell of emotional influence."

Elisa gave her an encouraging smile. "As a mind reader, you have a natural strength in this. You must try."

Theo retrieved a blanket from the road bag and laid it on the floor in front of Jackie. Two eggs rested on the blanket, their colors vibrant and beautiful – one shining red and the other navy-blue with purple stripes.

Jackie took a deep breath and placed her hands over the eggs. A soft blue light emanated from her fingers, enveloping the rough shells. Lacking a specific calming spell, she recalled an old lullaby her mother used to sing to her. She began to sing softly.

"The star is blinking in the sky,
It's guarded by the glowing moon."
Elisa's voice joined in. *"Because of you, I'll steal this star."*

"I'll turn the world to be with you," Theo and Urchin chimed in, completing the verse together. *"To be... with... you."*

As they sang the lullaby together, the gentle blue light continued to glow around the eggs, creating a soothing and calming atmosphere in the cave. The dragons' roars outside seemed to soften, and a sense of peace settled over the group. They waited, hoping that their efforts would reach the dragons' parents and ease their anger.

After a minute of peaceful silence, it was clear that their plan had worked. Together, they carefully wrapped the eggs that had been lulled by Jackie's magic, and Urchin placed them securely in his bag.

Urchin slung the bag over his shoulder and locked eyes with Jackie. "I think my shield can cover you as well."

"You already have two dragons to hide. I'll stay here," Jackie insisted.

"It's okay," Theo interjected. "Your mission is to get to the forest unnoticed. Don't worry, I'll protect them both."

Urchin nodded in agreement and made his way to the wall. Taking a deep breath, he focused his power, and his figure became invisible.

Elisa summoned her electricity, and a powerful wave crushed the remaining stones between the cave and the dragons. She then reached out her hand, and Theo took it. Jackie grasped his other hand firmly.

"When they enter, don't let go of me, no matter what you see," Theo instructed.

"Trust me, I won't," Jackie replied.

The blue dragon entered the hall, her scales shimmering from her throat to her belly. Her intelligent yellow eyes fixed on the group. The heat radiating from her body made Jackie break out in a sweat. The dragon let out a sigh and made her way to the nest, wrapping her tail protectively around her two babies, soothing them with her presence.

As the blue dragon settled in the nest, the red dragon followed, causing the stone walls to tremble with each heavy step. This dragon was twice the size of the blue one, its head nearly reaching the ceiling. Jackie's heart pounded in her chest as she watched in fear.

"And here comes the daddy," Elisa remarked.

The red dragon's nostrils flared, and he opened his mouth, revealing his menacing yellow fangs. A wave of flames erupted from his jaws, engulfing the group in a wall of fire. Theo held their hands tightly, his eyes glowing a dark red through the intense heat. The scorching flames felt unbearable, akin to the burning sands of a summer beach.

Despite the searing heat and danger surrounding them, Theo's shield held strong against the flames, but the intensity of the fire took its toll, and he fell to his knees. Jackie also stumbled but held onto his hand tightly. Elisa, her expression filled with concern, held onto Theo's other hand, silently urging him to hold on.

As the flames dissipated, the air grew cold, and the dragon turned away, heading back to the nest.

"Move to the exit. Slowly," Theo said in a weak voice.

Elisa crawled towards the exit, with Jackie following closely behind. Theo remained behind, ready to create another shield in case the dragon unleashed its fire once more.

In the forest, Urchin awaited their return, carrying the bag with the stolen treasures. "I told you we make a great team, huh?" he remarked proudly.

They exchanged silent looks, their uniforms dirtied and sweat-soaked, but they were all alive.

"We are," Jackie agreed. "And we all definitely need a good bath."

The group shared a moment of laughter. Jackie pressed her hand to her chest, grateful to have made it through.

10

The Father of the Dragon

That night, Jackie didn't sleep well. The images of the furious reptiles haunted her every time she closed her eyes. When she finally awoke from a short, anxious dream, she sat up, her face covered in a cold sweat. Desperate for some relief, she longed to cool off in the cold water.

The guys were sleeping near the fire, and the eggs were placed close by. Theo had mentioned that they needed to be kept warm to continue developing until the baby dragons were ready to hatch. Jackie looked around, trying to spot Elisa, who was supposed to be on watch tonight. But she was nowhere to be found. *Where had she gone?* It didn't bode well, so Jackie rose to make her way to the forest.

The pale-orange forest shimmered around her, and the creek bubbled nearby. She discovered Elisa at the shore, kneeling and gazing at the flowing water. A lonely waxing gibbous hung low in the sky above the treetops.

Jackie scooped up some water from the creek and washed her face to freshen up.

"Are you okay?" Elisa asked.

"Yes," Jackie replied, settling down beside her on the ground. "And you?"

Elisa sighed. "I was reflecting on this whole dragon journey... All I wanted was to impress my friend from the past. But instead, I put all of us in danger and nearly jeopardized our future. What kind of person does that make me?"

"You're an amazing person," Jackie reassured her with a smile. "I would follow you to the ends of the earth if you needed me to."

"Really?"

"Why not?" Jackie replied, gazing up at the night sky. "Remember the lullaby we sang in the caves? We successfully retrieved all the stolen stars, so now we can fulfill our guardian duties and fix everything that's gone awry."

"Sounds like a plan," Elisa agreed with a chuckle.

Jackie turned her attention to the river, marveling at its beauty. "We all risked our lives today. Perhaps it's because we're capable of doing extraordinary things for the people we care about."

"What do you mean?" Elisa asked, looking puzzled.

"When you initially mentioned the wedding, you said it was for your friend. Yet, you ended up stealing from the most dangerous creatures in this world. You must truly love this friend to put yourself in such peril."

Elisa adjusted a lock of her hair. "Okay, I wasn't fully honest about this friendship. I was in love before. Perhaps that's why I took on the challenge – to prove my worth. But I became consumed by it... I must never repeat that mistake."

"It's alright." Jackie offered a sympathetic smile. "We all make mistakes."

"That's true. It took me a while, but I understand now. True love is being able to let that person find happiness, even if it means being happy without you."

Jackie nodded in understanding. "Then, I hope you won't attempt to disrupt the wedding."

"Of course not." Elisa brought her hand to her chest. "I swear, I've learned my lesson."

"That's reassuring to hear," Jackie said, locking eyes with her. "You deserve someone who will love you as much as you love them."

Elisa cast her gaze downward. "You know, for me, the prospect of being loved is slim, so I've learned to live without it."

"But Theo –"

"Oh, please don't," Elisa interjected, shaking her head. "I'm not interested in him, and I never will be."

"Why not?"

Elisa turned towards the creek, the moonlight illuminating the water and casting a somber light on her face. "Because... you are my friend, and I'm asking you to respect that."

"Of course, I'm your friend," Jackie affirmed. "No questions asked. I promise."

They sat in silence for a moment. Interestingly, Elisa had never shared her past with Jackie, and Jackie had never probed. She was grateful that Elisa didn't press her with inquiries.

As if she could read her thoughts, Elisa gave her a curious look. "Have you ever been in love?"

She hesitated to respond. Opening up was daunting, almost impossible.

"Was it that bad?" Elisa inquired.

"I was once engaged," Jackie revealed. "It didn't end well for me."

"I'm so sorry, dear," Elisa expressed sympathetically. "You know what? You don't have to talk about it if you don't want to. Let's leave our past behind and start a new chapter in our lives."

"Let's give it a try," Jackie agreed with a nod.

A branch cracked behind them, causing them to turn around to face Theo. *How long had he been there?*

His face displayed concern. "Why did you two leave the camp?"

Elisa mustered a smile. "Just having a girls' talk. Why aren't you sleeping?"

Theo gestured back towards the campfire. "You've put the eggs in danger. Something's not right with them!"

They jumped on their feet and hurried back to the camp.

One of the eggs sat quietly by the fire, its red scales shimmering in the light of the flames. The other egg was trembling.

"Jackie, go check on it," Elisa instructed.

Theo's eyes begged her silently, so she had to rush to the nest.

Jackie placed her hand on the egg. She closed her eyes, feeling a sense of wonder. But there was nothing wrong with the egg.

She stood up, smiling at them. "It's just playing inside. Nothing to be afraid of."

The egg continued to shake, prompting Theo to kneel down and place his hands on it. The warmth from his palms caused the shell to crack.

Elisa's eyes widened in alarm. "You've broken it!"

Jackie smiled knowingly. She touched her index finger to her lips. "Shh... Just watch."

They fell silent. The eggshell trembled once more, and a tiny paw emerged from the crack. It was a blue paw with violet stripes running along it. Small, sharp claws broke through the shell as the creature inside struggled to free itself. Theo leaned back, his eyes wide with amazement.

Finally, a large piece of shell fell away, revealing a dragon's head. The creature gazed at Theo with its big yellow eyes and grinned. It leaped onto his chest, and Theo caught it, turning to face Jackie and Elisa. The dragon uttered something, and Theo gently stroked its scales, still at a loss for words.

Jackie and Elisa moved closer to admire the newborn reptile, but it flicked its tail, keeping them at a distance.

"No fucking way." Elisa chuckled. "He thinks you're his daddy."

"He's absolutely stunning," Theo remarked with a smile.

Jackie's heart swelled with emotion. She had never imagined witnessing the birth of a real dragon, and the experience was truly priceless.

Urchin approached, scratching his cheek. "Why are you guys so loud?" Upon spotting the dragon, his eyebrows shot up in surprise.

"I can't believe you overslept, Urchin," Jackie teased, breaking into laughter.

The following day, they reached a fork in the road. One path led back to Middle Lake city, where the Academy was located, while the other led to Triville – Elisa's hometown.

Given the situation with the newborn dragon, Theo had to accompany Elisa to the wedding as the creature refused to leave his shoulder. Despite Elisa's initial complaints about Theo disrupting their plans, she couldn't help but smile when she looked at him with the dragon perched on his shoulder. Theo decided to name the dragon Rei after an ancient mage known for controlling the wind.

Carrying Rei with pride, Theo led the way as the dragon gazed at them with round, yellow eyes.

After bidding a lengthy farewell, they set off on their respective paths. Jackie remained in the forest with Urchin. With the absence of the guys' voices and the baby dragon's fussing, the forest became eerily silent.

Urchin regarded her with a suspicious look. "Are you feeling jealous?"

Jackie flinched, feeling an unpleasant twinge in her heart at the sight of Theo and Elisa together, a worry she hadn't realized was there until now. "No, I'm not," she denied. "Why would I be jealous?"

"Who wouldn't be?" Urchin shrugged. "Now Theo has his pet dragon, and I bet they have a bright future ahead. Maybe once the farm flourishes, you could have one too."

"I don't think so. But I wish I could come back as a dragon in my next life."

He gave her a worried look. "What do you mean by that?"

Jackie gently urged their horses to move along the wide forest trail, her gaze drifting up to the cloudless blue sky. "When I pass away, I envision myself as a magnificent and liberated creature. No burdens or obligations – just soaring through the skies and hunting all day."

"Dreaming about death is creepy, especially at your age," Urchin remarked.

"Why not?" Jackie countered. "I'm a future guardian, and anything can happen."

"Don't be silly, Jackie. You have your life here and now, so live it."

"It's not that easy," she replied, her thoughts lingering.

"As my father always says, 'Life is tough, but it's filled with beautiful moments to cherish,'" Urchin shared.

"Perhaps he's right. But those moments of joy seem so few and far between."

"Yes, but we have the power to create them," Urchin encouraged her with a reassuring look. "I wonder, who will reach the next crossroad first – you or me?"

With a playful grin, he spurred his horse into a gallop along the trail. Jackie laughed and swiftly followed suit, racing after him.

11

Little Dirty Secret

The evening approached Triville, and the sun illuminated the golden leaves. The horse with a small carriage was waiting in the front yard. Carrying a big wooden chest, Theo walked on the wide porch with Rei sitting on his shoulder.

"Yes, your bro or sister is really heavy," Theo complained.

Rei nodded in understanding and circled around the carriage, choosing a place to sit. Then he landed at the horse's saddle.

"Smart choice," Theo remarked with a smile. He placed the trunk on the bench and covered it with a blanket. *Now, it should provide enough warmth for the red dragon's egg. And as for Rei...* he looked at the little blue dragon, and his heart ached. After everything they went through, it was too hard to imagine saying goodbye to this wonderful creature. But there was no other way. "I'll tell you one thing, Rei. Life isn't fair, and they won't let you live in the Academy." He patted Rei's head, and the dragon purred in response. "Very soon, we'll split, but I'll come back to visit you. Sparkle said the farm owners will take good care of you and your sibling."

Rei's yellow eyes gave him a sad look. Then the dragon jumped back on his shoulder, his short tail hugging his neck. Theo looked up, where the sky was empty and silent. "I promise I'll visit you often."

"Look who can be sentimental," Elisa's voice cheered nearby, causing Theo to flinch.

How did she get so close unnoticed? He turned to face her. Elisa had changed her usual black uniform to a snow-white coat that partly covered the hem of her long light-blue dress. Her curly hair lay on her shoulders, and it made his heart melt. He opened his mouth but forgot what he was supposed to say, so he stood silent.

"Don't worry. I won't tell anyone." Elisa playfully pressed an index finger to her lower lip. "Everyone has a dirty little secret."

He scoffed. "You have an abnormal interest in people's secrets."

"That's why I chose to become a detective," she replied, fixing a strand of hair.

As Theo learned from time with Elisa, she played with her hair each time when she was nervous.

"Is everything ready?" She asked.

He nodded. "Almost. Just one thing to clarify."

"What else?"

Theo paused. He had carried this thought for too long, and he doubted it would be a better moment to express it. Then, he must have tried. "When we get to the wedding, I guess I shall pretend to be your boyfriend."

"What?" Elisa widened her eyes in surprise. "Why would you ever need to do that?"

He walked to the horse and started checking the reins. It was better to pretend to be busy than to look into her eyes. "Well, even your aunt questioned the status of our relationship. I know something about small towns, and I guess people at the wedding will start being curious. I think it would be easier for us to pretend." He gave her a teasing smile. "Especially knowing that you used to be in love with one of the newlyweds."

Elisa opened her mouth, speechless.

"Right, Sparkle, everyone has a dirty little secret." Theo winked. He came to the saddle and pressed on it, ensuring that it was reliable. Rei, who sat on it, cocked his head in curiosity.

Elisa came closer, and Theo could hear her ragged breath. "So, you overheard me talking to Jackie last night," she concluded. "What else do you know?"

"Nothing... Listen, I don't really care about your school crush. I'm on your side. As your friend."

She gazed at him without blinking. "I don't believe you. Two days ago, you hated me."

Theo scratched Rei's neck, making the dragon close his eyes out of awe. "Things change, Sparkle. You see, now we have a commitment together."

She glanced at Rei and laughed. Using the moment, Theo took the dragon in his hands and gave it to Elisa. Relaxed, the dragon rested on her chest.

Elisa smiled, doing her best to comfort Rei in her coat. His skin was incredibly warm and not as rough as it seemed. It was great to be able to touch a living creature, knowing that her magic wouldn't hurt it. "If I ever had a dragon, I would probably never be able to let it go."

"Maybe once you will," he said, getting in a saddle. "All right, I'll ride the horse, and you'll watch him. Deal?"

"Deal."

With a heavy squeak, the barn door opened. The moonlight leaking from the small ceiling window didn't help make this space brighter. Holding Rei, Theo raised his free hand, evoking the flames. The fire illuminated the cozy space – hay was stacked at the walls, preventing the cold from entering the barn. Here, he found a torch and lit it up.

"Welcome home," he whispered, afraid to disturb Rei's nap.

The steps sounded at his back. It was Kyle Turner, the groom, who left the wedding dinner as soon as he met the dragon. Kyle was a young man who had just finished school this year, but despite his age, he seemed to be quite mature. Kyle brought the wooden chest and placed it by the haystack. His blue eyes gleamed as he opened it and took the dragon's egg – bright red and shining in the glimpses of the fire.

"This one might get hatched soon," Theo said. "Will you be ready?"

"Kidding?" Kyle turned to him, a smile playing on his lips. "It's all I could dream about."

"Said the man who just got married." He chuckled.

Kyle placed the egg in the hay, ensuring that it was covered well. "I mean, now I have everything: a family, a home, and a farm as my lifework. Once I have kids, they'll start helping me. If they want, of course."

Theo placed Rei on hay near the egg, and the dragon hugged the shells, smiling in his dream. "Aren't you afraid?"

"Of what?"

"To raise kids together with the wild dragons."

Kyle gave him a calm look. "Well, the dragons are like babies. So, I assume it's a good chance to practice before we have our own.

Of course, Rei is yours, but I'll be his uncle until you finish your studies. How cool is that?"

"I don't know." Theo patted Rei, and the dragon purred in his dream. Now, knowing that it was the point when he needed to leave him on a farm, he couldn't fight with heaviness in his heart. "How can I abandon him like this?"

"I know. It's hard to let them go. But it's the right thing to do. In nature, siblings should grow up together. This is how they learn to take care of each other." Kyle took the woolen blanket from the shelf and unrolled it. "Don't worry. You can visit him whenever you want."

"I will. Thank you, Kyle."

"No problem." Kyle smiled and covered the dragon with the blanket. "Plus, as I know, our Guardian House is constantly looking for new employees, and they would be happy to accept you for paid summer practice."

Theo widened his eyes. "Would they really take me? So easily?"

"It's a small town, so I can just connect you with the right people. You can start your career here if you want."

"I would love to. I don't even know how to thank you, man."

He waved him off. "It's nothing. My father used to work here. Actually, it's a tragic story, but I know people he worked with."

Theo glanced at the window, where the night was quiet and calm. "A tragic story?" He asked to buy some time.

"I don't like talking about it." Kyle gave him a sad look. "Let's just say that after my sister died, I figured that I didn't want to follow in my father's steps."

"I'm so sorry." Theo lowered his voice. "I lost my sister, too. She was too good for this cruel world."

Kyle sighed. "Good girls die first. One thing that calms me is that I don't have to worry about Elisa. She can protect herself."

Theo nodded. "That's true. Who knew I would end up playing the role of her boyfriend?"

"At least you are aware that you're only playing this role," Kyle said.

What was that supposed to mean? Now, he had to figure it out. Theo mustered an honest look. "Elisa is my good friend, and I support her in everything. Really, I'm glad that you managed to leave all this love drama behind. It deserves respect."

"Thanks." Kyle smiled. "Good that you're okay with that. When I got to know that a girl like her is not into boys, it shocked me."

Theo stared at him without blinking. *Not into boys.* Hearing it was like receiving a knife stab right into his chest. It was terribly wrong and unfair. But the more he thought about it, the more sense it made. Elisa never treated any of the guys with affection, and all this time, she never accepted any friend but another woman – Jackie. This raised another disturbing question: Were they just friends? Unable to find an answer, Theo placed his palm on his pulsing forehead.

"Are you okay?" Kyle's voice seemed muffled.

"Sure. I just really, really need some fresh air." He turned and rushed outside.

Outside, he took the path to Kyle's house and stopped at the front yard. The windows ahead shone, illuminated by generous candlelight, revealing the silhouettes of people dancing inside. No, his place wasn't among them, neither near Elisa. It never was.

Kyle came to him and stood nearby. His breath was heavy from fast walking. "I hardly closed the gates of the barn, and you disappeared. What happened?"

Theo gave him a painful look. "Elisa. I had no idea."

"Really?" He wiped his forehead. "I'm sorry I told you. I wasn't supposed to."

Theo responded with a heavy sigh.

"Somehow, I thought that you knew her well enough," Kyle added.

"I thought so, too."

"Well, you'll get used to it." Kyle pointed at the house. "Let's go and have a drink. People are waiting for us, especially the bride."

Theo didn't move. As Elisa had mentioned, she was in love with one of the newlyweds. Knowing that Kyle wasn't her crush, there was only one option left. While they were taking care of the dragons, Elisa was interacting with the bride.

"I can't go back," Theo said. "And how can you stay so calm? Knowing she was into your wife?"

Kyle gave him a puzzled look. "It hit you damn hard, buddy. But maybe it's for the best – to know it now until you fall for her or something."

Theo lowered his eyes and stood silent.

"Unless you already did," Kyle concluded. "Crap. What can I do to make it easier?"

"Nothing. I think I'd better go home and lie down."

"Are you sure?"

"Yes." Theo extended his hand for a handshake. "Well, it was good to meet you anyway."

"Me too." Kyle shook his hand. "Come visit us in the winter holidays. I promise I'll do my best not to give you any more shocking information."

"Is there more?" Theo gave him a sad smile. "Actually, don't answer. I don't wanna know."

"Good choice."

The yard became brighter as the entrance door to the house opened and closed. It was Elisa. She ran down the porch and stood next to them like nothing was wrong. Feeling uneasy, Theo unbuttoned his jacket.

Elisa smiled at Kyle. "Congratulations again. Sorry for the short visit, but I'm just too tired after a long road."

He smiled back. "It's okay. Thank you for making it. I hope you two will visit us in winter and stay longer."

"We'll see." She moved her gaze around them. "I'm glad you two got along."

"We did." Kyle smiled and clapped Theo's shoulder. "Well, good luck with everything!"

Theo gave him a sad look. "Thanks."

12

A Piece of Truth

They walked along the road in silence, the full moon gleaming in the dark sky and lighting up the streaming river. Elisa always loved this path to her house – Triville was silent and calm, unlike the stone streets of Middle Lake city that were crowded and lit up with fake lights.

"After months of living in the capital, I started to forget how beautiful my hometown is," she said.

"You are so forgetful these days." Theo turned to her, his eyes glowing with red. "Especially when it comes to telling the truth."

"Oh, for the Divine's sake." She rolled her eyes. "What happened again?"

"Nothing." He took a deep breath, and his inner fire soothed.

"Then don't be so grumpy." Elisa poked his shoulder. "I know it's a stressful time for you, but it's not exactly easy for me either."

"Oh, really?! Cause you seem to be in a cheerful mood."

"Because it was a good evening and I really enjoyed it. But tomorrow, we'll need to get back, and then the classes will start again." She gave him a curious look. "Actually, you were the main reason why I hated some classes. How will it be when we get back?"

"I don't know, Sparkle. You'll probably keep lying to me, and I'll keep being grumpy about it."

"Even though I didn't really like you, I never lied to you."

He stopped and looked her in the eye. "Right. You just never told the whole truth to use people in your games. Even people who you call your friends."

She frowned. "I don't understand. What the hell happened?"

His voice became steel. "Does anyone in the Academy know that you are a lesbian?"

Elisa pressed her palm to her chest. It seemed that time had stopped, along with her ability to breathe. She saw a lot of arrogance among men she happened to know, but each time, they found a new way to kill her from the inside.

"Got to know my worst secret, then." Her voice trembled, but she kept talking. "Good job, detective. You won. Now you can go back and tell everyone to make sure you destroy my future as a guardian."

"I would never do that." He gave her a remorseful look. "Maybe I shouldn't have said it like this."

"Just leave me alone!" Elisa turned away and walked toward the riverbank.

He stood alone on the road, counting his heartbeats. *What have I done?* He ran his hands through his hair, trying to come up with a plan to fix everything, but nothing came to his mind.

Elisa was sitting at the shore, facing the restless river. Her eyes were moist, the tears decorating her long lashes like dew drops.

Theo stood nearby. "Okay, I'll tell you my worst secret to make us even."

"Just go home, okay?" Elisa said, her voice unusually weak. "Because I don't care about you and your stupid secrets."

"To get to the Academy, I stole the money," he blurted out.

She turned to him, her eyes wide open. "You did what?!"

Theo sighed. "The classes are expensive, and even though I worked as a bartender the whole summer, I figured that I would never earn enough. Even with all the extra shifts."

"And you robbed the bar?"

"Not like that." He placed his hands in his pockets. "Sometimes, I served rich customers, and they ordered our most expensive whiskey. After two glasses, they became taste-numb, and I sold them cheap alcohol instead. Of course, I didn't forget to charge the full price. Then, I just put the difference in my pocket."

"And you got away with it?"

"Of course not. Our owner caught me soon, and I had to share half with him. Now, I only have enough to make it through this academic year, and only if I study well. That's why I care so much about my marks and about finding a summer job."

"Breaking the law to become a guardian." Elisa raised her eyes to the indifferent moon. "What a terrible world we live in. And it's full of shitty people."

"Well, I can only try not to be one of them," he said as he sat near her. "Listen, I'm sorry I treated you like this all this time. I just tried to be on the same page with the guys whose parents are rich enough to pay for their classes. But you were the only person who impressed me from the very first day."

Elisa gave him a compassionate look. "It's okay. I just don't want anyone to know who I really am. Especially the guys who only look for the freak to laugh at."

"Does Jackie know?"

Elisa shook her head. "Please, don't tell her."

"So, you really like her." His heart beat heavily. "Why don't you tell her, then?"

"Because I ruin everything I touch." Elisa looked at her clear palms. Now, her magic was quiet, and her fingertips didn't shine. "Only if I could find a working way to deal with my power."

"I think I can help you. My Gift is one of the strongest ones, and I know some tricks to tame it. I can share it if you want to."

She gave him a hopeful look. "Will you do that for me?"

"Of course. Why wouldn't I help my friend?"

"Thank you, Theo." She moved closer and hugged him tightly.

Her hair smelled of her favorite lilac perfume, and he closed his eyes, enjoying the scent. His hand patted her back. "You're welcome, Sparkle."

Story 3

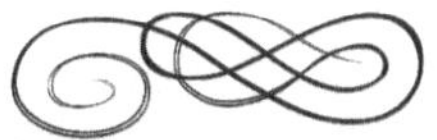

*Breaking
the Rules*

13

A Librarian

Just three days remained before New Year's Eve, yet the library was open. Jackie stepped into the citadel of knowledge and glanced around, holding her breath. After four months of studying within these walls, the place still managed to impress her. The exquisite books, clad in leather covers, stood proudly on their shelves, patiently waiting for someone to unravel their silent secrets.

The atmosphere was unusually quiet, perhaps because most students had departed to spend the winter break with their families. Jackie, however, had chosen to stay behind for her own reasons and was determined not to waste a moment of her time.

Laura, a young woman with warm brown eyes and a long plait, was diligently dusting the shelves. With a wave of her hand, the dust broom gracefully glided above the top row of books. Laura had been a part of the library staff since mid-October, and she and Jackie had quickly bonded over their shared love for books. They often engaged in lively discussions on a variety of topics, as Jackie's reading interests spanned from applied magic to modern fiction.

"Hi, Laura," Jackie called out to her.

She turned and greeted her with a smile. "Hey."

Approaching her, Jackie pointed to the top shelves where the books for the upcoming spring classes were neatly arranged under the high ceiling. "I see you've got the books for my spring classes!"

"Yep, they just arrived today."

"That's great," Jackie said, rubbing her hands in anticipation.

The art of protective spells had never been one of Jackie's strengths. She struggled a lot during the autumn term until Laura introduced her to the textbooks, which significantly improved her concentration. With Laura's help, Jackie managed to excel in her exams. Now, she was eager to continue practicing and had a unique opportunity to prepare for the next term, aiming to surpass even Theo, who seemed to possess an encyclopedic knowledge.

Laura's expression turned apologetic. "Sorry, but I'm not allowed to give you those books just yet."

"Are you certain?" Jackie asked, a glimmer of hope in her voice.

"Yes, the rules are quite strict. But I do have something else for you. I think you'll like it!"

Jackie followed her to the reception desk, where Laura retrieved a massive book from the drawer. The book had a thick gray cover adorned with golden curly letters that read *Gifts Exchanging: Techniques and Rituals*.

Jackie widened her eyes in surprise. "Seriously, 'Gifts Exchange?' Is that possible?"

"It is, but each Gift operates differently. That's why the book is so extensive. It's actually a manual for the second year of studies."

"Oh, I see." She nodded in understanding. "So, you're not allowed to give us books for the upcoming term..."

"But they didn't specify anything about future ones," Laura added with a smile.

Jackie ran her fingers over the book's smooth cover, admiring its elegant design. "You're a smart ass, aren't you?"

Laura chuckled. "I like to think so. As I always say, rules are meant for those who lack the creativity to work around them."

"It would be wonderful to delve into this," Jackie remarked, hugging the book close. "Isn't it strange? With thousands of textbooks and manuals here, I couldn't find one that might assist Elisa in controlling her power."

"Actually, that's why I gave it to you," Laura explained. "There's a spell in there that can allow you to tap into Elisa's Gift without physical contact."

"Okay," Jackie said, furrowing her brow in thought. "But how will that help?"

She shrugged. "Sometimes, you need to experience something firsthand to comprehend it truly, like tasting food or smelling a flower. It's the same with understanding others' magic. As a mind reader, you might discover a way to harness a power like hers."

"I'm not sure I can make it work –" Jackie began.

"Please, don't be so hard on yourself," Laura interrupted, raising her hand to dismiss any self-doubt. "I know how much you want to assist Elisa, and this is the best resource I could find. Just give it a try when you get the chance, okay?"

"Fine."

Jackie attempted to place the heavy book in her backpack, but it was too massive, causing the lock to remain open. *When will I even have the opportunity to practice these spells?* she pondered. With no one else around for the next two weeks, it seemed like an unlikely prospect. It was Laura's final day at work before the winter break, and Elisa was preparing to depart for her hometown of Triville with Theo, who eagerly anticipated reuniting with Rei, his dragon. Theo had been forced to leave the dragon at a farm due to the dangers and strict prohibitions against raising such creatures within the Academy.

"Jackie, you really shouldn't stay in the dorms all the holidays," Laura advised, now organizing notebooks on her reception desk. "I insist that you join my family for New Year's Eve. My home is just a couple of blocks away from here."

Jackie shook her head. "Thank you, but I'm fine."

"Are you sure?" Laura inquired, giving her a curious look. "Or perhaps you've had a change of heart and decided to visit Urchin's place instead?"

Jackie chuckled at her teasing. Their conversations often veered towards discussing guys, and Laura never missed an opportunity to playfully prod her. Following their daring mission of stealing dragon eggs, Jackie formed a close friendship with Urchin. He had even extended an invitation for her to celebrate New Year's Eve at his home, located not far from the city.

"I turned down his invitation," Jackie explained. "It wouldn't be appropriate for a female cadet to spend the night at someone's home."

She narrowed her eyes. "Why do you friendzone him so hard?"

"Friend... what?"

Laura often surprised her with her modern slang, which was commonplace in larger cities like Middle Lake. So, now she was explaining this one, carefully selecting her words. "Okay, it means that you see him only as a friend and nothing more."

"Well, in that case, you're right," Jackie admitted.

Laura shook her head. "Please, stop doing that. I can see how Urchin looks at you. But he won't wait indefinitely, especially with the new year approaching. He might find someone else. Don't miss your chance, Jackie."

"I just want to focus on more pressing matters," she replied, adjusting her backpack. "After all, I came here to study."

"Sometimes I don't understand you, Jackie. You're surrounded by men. If I were in your shoes, I wouldn't waste time."

"And who would you choose as a partner?" Jackie inquired.

Laura looked up, her chest rising and falling. "Actually, it's the one who visits me almost every day. A tall, handsome guy kissed by fire."

"Theo?" Jackie guessed.

She nodded in confirmation.

Jackie narrowed her eyes. "Is it because of him or because of Rei?"

"Let's just say I like the guy, and hearing his stories about his dragon is an added bonus." Laura's eyes sparkled. "I hope one day he'll take me to the farm."

Jackie smiled, appreciating Laura's tendency to romanticize situations and view the world through rose-colored glasses. It was one of the qualities she admired in her friend. With Laura, she could freely discuss topics that were off-limits with Elisa, who tended to shy away from conversations about men.

"Theo is indeed a handsome guy. But honestly, I think he frequents this place because he enjoys reading," Jackie remarked.

"You see, we have a lot in common."

"Moreover, he dedicates all his free time to Elisa, and I suspect there's more than just friendly interest motivating him."

"Oh, please!" Laura waved her hand dismissively. "Have you ever noticed how she treats him?"

"You think it's another case of friend-zoning?"

"Exactly," Laura affirmed confidently. "Listen, I may not be as close to Elisa as you are, but she exudes an icy demeanor. It won't be long before he gives up on her. I'm just waiting for the right moment. Then, I'll find a way to convince him to be mine."

"Well, that's a good plan. But please, don't involve me in this strange love triangle, or whatever it is."

"Alright. Just promise me you'll consider giving Urchin a chance."

"I think I'll leave things as they are."

Laura fixed her with a long, silent gaze.

"Fine, I'll think about it," Jackie relented, rolling her eyes before making her exit.

The book that Laura had given her was heavy, but not as heavy as the burden in Jackie's heart. Pausing by a window in the corridor, she gazed out at the winter yard, watching as the snowfall ceased and the first stars twinkled in the darkening sky.

Examining her wrists, which had long since healed, Jackie pondered Laura's words. Perhaps her dedication to her studies was a way to prevent herself from dwelling on the painful memories of her past that she sought to bury. Despite all the spells she had learned, there was nothing that could heal the deep-seated traumas she carried. Time had not lessened the pain; it had merely pushed it to the back of her mind, allowing her to focus on creating new distractions.

Jackie let out a heavy sigh. She had a task at hand – finding a way to help Elisa. It was better to channel her energy into this new challenge rather than dwell on the past that haunted her.

14

A Wish

"Just focus on this damn wick." Theo pointed at the thick lilac candle on the floor among the islands of white and yellow wax chips. "When you close your eyes, you must feel this connection. It's just you and the wick."

"Okay, I've got it." Elisa shook her right hand, preparing for another attempt to light up a candle. Her palms burned after two hours of unstoppable practice, but she couldn't give up. Not on the last day of their training.

"It's the last candle we have left in your room," Theo reminded her. "And as far as I know, this was Urchin's present to Jackie, *A Lavender Cloud*. Expensive thing, I must say. If you ruin it, she'll be mad at you."

"Then I have no other choice but to do it, right?" She gave him a look full of hope.

"Exactly." He nodded and walked behind her.

Today, Elisa wore a black tank top and shorts, her hair tied in a horsetail. Practical rather than attractive, considering she was sweating a lot during their exercises. Meanwhile, she couldn't help noticing his craving glances. It was another reason to finish their exercises as soon as possible – then Theo would have more time for his meetings with the other women, and she... she would finally be able to touch Jackie. Elisa tried to be realistic and didn't hope for much, but even a slight touch would be bliss. Just to be able to hold her hands in hers, or to hug her shoulders when she needed her support... *Interesting, how would it feel?*

"Relax." His warm hands touched her naked shoulders. "You are like a guitar string!"

"Because I'll never make it," Elisa moaned.

"You'll do it. For *her*," he whispered over her ear.

Elisa closed her eyes, relying on her instincts, as Theo had taught her. The wick was in the candle, and the candle was right in front of her. She imagined the waves of electricity gently touching the wick, lighting it up, and the room slowly filling with the scent of lavender. Her power leaked through her fingertips, and Elisa released it.

The sound of an explosion hit her ears, and then the wax dust reached her face. Well, at least she was right about the lilac aroma.

Theo sighed. "I won't tell her, I promise."

Elisa opened her eyes. The entire floor was covered with wax powder. "I'm hopeless."

"Maybe you just need some rest," Theo suggested. "You know, just switch into vacay mode when we leave. Chill, drink some hot cacao, and talk to your friends. Next year, we'll try again."

Elisa looked at her palms with pity. "Then that's it. Let's clean the place so Jackie won't get upset."

The door opened behind her, and Elisa stood motionless.

"Why would I get upset?" Jackie asked. Then she stared at the floor with wide-open eyes. There was one thing about her that Elisa couldn't stop admiring. At the moments when she was sad, her emerald eyes took on a dark, marsh color, like now.

"Seriously?!" Jackie said in a voice full of disappointment. "Guys! It was *my* present!"

Theo and Elisa exchanged glances in silence.

"Well, I think I'm gonna go," Theo said after a long pause.

"Go." Elisa waved to him.

"Not so fast." Jackie looked at him curiously. "So, Theo... You must be excited to see Rei."

"I am." He stopped at the threshold, unable to dismiss the topic. "Kyle wrote that both dragons grew up a bit, and now they have the size of a medium dog."

Jackie chuckled. "Kiddos grow too fast."

"Yes, when you feed them well."

Elisa laughed. "Okay, daddy, go get ready. We need to wake up early tomorrow."

"Right." Theo smiled and left the room.

Jackie walked to her bed and took the book from her backpack. She placed it on the plush cover, ensuring that Elisa saw the title. All this time after their trip, Elisa avoided practicing any spells with anyone but Theo. Maybe this time, Jackie would make her change her mind.

Alas, Elisa sat nearby without paying any attention to the book. "Don't worry, dear. I'll buy you another candle. Exactly like the one that I've destroyed."

"It's fine." Jackie locked her eyes with hers. "Is it that bad with your Gift?"

"Honestly, I don't know what to do." Elisa shook off the leftovers of the wax from her tank top. "Except for trying to focus on something else and not to think about being a pathetic loser."

"Did you ever think of..." Jackie paused, afraid to scare her away. "Doing it with me?"

Elisa climbed on the bed with her feet, her face taking on a playful expression. "Dear, I often think of doing different things with you." Her eyes shimmered. "But I can't."

"You're afraid to hurt me?"

"More than anything." Elisa lowered her eyes, her cheeks blushing.

Jackie placed the book on her lap. "What if I found a safe way of taming your Gift?"

Elisa glanced at the cover, her eyelashes moving as she read the title. "'*Gift Exchange?*' And how would it help?"

"You never know if you never try." Jackie gave her a teasing look. "Let's figure it out together."

"Why not?" Elisa shrugged and jumped from the bed. "But let's first clean this mess."

Outside, the night was cold and starry. The snow had stopped, so a full moon lit up a snowy yard and the roofs of the Academy building. They both agreed that it would be too risky if someone saw them practicing the spells too close to the dorms, so they headed to the nearest park.

They walked along the trail. Jackie liked the night nature, especially wintertime – the naked tree branches were covered with snow, and the blue shimmering of the tree barks created a unique holiday atmosphere. Like in her distant childhood when she was confident that every wish made tonight would come true. But even with her vivid imagination, Jackie never expected to become a guardian cadet. Now, it was happening for real – they walked with caution, and the fresh snow squeaked under their heavy uniform boots.

When they almost reached the lake shore, Jackie opened the book.

"I always wanted to read someone's thoughts," Elisa said, not hiding her excitement.

Jackie shook her head. "Actually, you can't read my thoughts using my own Gift. Similar Gifts don't work against each other, and I'm immune from mind reading."

Her look became perplexed. "So, no one can perform this ritual with you?"

"It's possible, but not today. We need a third person for this purpose."

"Will Urchin fit?"

She shrugged. "Probably."

Elisa narrowed her eyes. "But what about limitations? I have a friend with your Gift, and she can't read the thoughts of people she loves or once loved."

"That's true. I also can't read my close blood relatives." Jackie raised her eyes to her. "And by the way – I'm not in love with him."

"Whatever you call it," she said sarcastically. "So, what are we going to do now?"

Jackie turned the page and found the Lightning Gift. "Here. Just the two of us are needed. We both have to combine our Lights, and then, I'll read the spell."

Elisa raised her hand, and silver energy started leaking into her palm. When she finished, a silver sphere glowed in her hand. Golden sparkles shimmered inside, illuminating her excited face. Every person had their life energy, the Light, and it was unique. Jackie admired Elisa's Light – silver was a rare shade.

"Your turn," Elisa urged her.

Jackie transferred her energy into her hand, and a pure matte blue Light filled her palm. In silence, they merged their energies, and the spheres started vibrating. This sound soothed Jackie, and her heartbeat calmed.

"Beautiful," Elisa whispered in awe.

Jackie took a deep breath, focusing. Now, it was important not to mix up the spell because Elisa's Gift might literally kill her. She closed her eyes and started reading.

"Your Gift. I welcome it inside.
I let it find me through the Light."

These two simple lines had an incredible power. The heat increased between their palms, and Jackie extended her free hand, facing a palm to the nearest tree. Her fingertips itched. She let the energy of her Gift leak freely through her hand.

Jackie was expecting to see some sparkles of violet energy, but their connection was stronger than she had imagined. With a deafening thunder, powerful lightning escaped her palm, the wave of energy hitting the branches. The fire enveloped the tree. In several seconds, the smell of smoke filled the night air.

Elisa took her hand off and looked up. "Holy shit!"

The flames reflected on her face as the fire played in her wide-open eyes. Jackie closed the book, and the sparkle of electricity dropped from her index finger, leaving a slight burn on the cover. She inspected her palms – they still were warm. The book said that she might keep the Gift they exchanged for a while, so it was better not to touch anyone. Elisa's magic was dangerous, but somehow, experiencing it was the most exciting thing that had ever happened to her.

15

Going Under

Jackie was sitting on the ground, staring at the book, when Elisa's alarmed voice interrupted her. "Someone's coming!"

Jackie turned back. Someone ran to them from the side of the lakeshore. It was a woman in her early forties. Her face was red and wet from tears, and she was shivering under her shabby black coat. Jackie raised her hand to comfort her but stopped halfway. The leftover power of Elisa's Gift was still in her, and she could hurt the woman. To avoid trouble, Jackie hid her hands in her pockets.

"Are you lost?" Elisa asked.

She shook her head. Her voice was quiet. "Me ... my husband..."

Thankfully, Elisa took the situation into her hands. She gave the woman a comforting look. "It's okay. We are guardians."

Jackie nodded. In fact, they were just cadets, not guardians. But there was no one else around, so it was their duty to help. "Is anything wrong?" Jackie asked.

The woman took a deep breath and pointed at the side of the lake. "There!"

Without delay, they rushed in the direction of the lake, with the woman following closely behind. When they arrived at the lakeshore, the trees parted, revealing the water encased in ice. A full moon illuminated the smooth white surface, and a round hole blackened the ice a few feet away. The local men must have made it for fishing.

They walked over to the ice hole, where something dark lay nearby, resembling a piece of cloth. Jackie leaned down and picked it up – a dark blue scarf belonging to a man.

"My poor husband, we were skating," the woman explained, pointing at the ice hole. "And he fell in there!"

The hole was wide enough for an adult man to fall into. If the man had indeed fallen in, he was likely dead by now.

"When did it happen?" Jackie asked in a firm tone, following Don's strategy. He believed that clarity helped victims recall important details more quickly, saving precious time in cases like this.

The woman shrugged her shoulders and sobbed. "Several minutes ago. Then I saw the fire and ran there to call for help. Oh, my poor Jonathan!"

"I see," Elisa said. "And what's your name?"

"Kathy."

"Don't despair, Kathy. We can still save him," Elisa said confidently.

Jackie looked at her in hesitation, trying to understand how exactly they could save a man who hadn't been breathing for several minutes.

Elisa shifted her eyes to her. "Jackie, can you evoke a Searching spell?"

She nodded. Without further questions, she placed the scarf back on the ice and covered it with her blue Light. Then she whispered a spell. The scarf shimmered and flew up, slowly floating further to the northeast, with all three women following it. The current likely carried the man away, but not too far.

"You see," Elisa explained as they walked, seizing the moment. "The water is icy cold, which means that even if his heart stopped beating, his body is frozen. This protects the brain from decay, giving us more time to find him. And when we do, he can be brought back."

Kathy sobbed. "Oh, I can't believe he is gone!"

"He is NOT gone," Elisa insisted. "Trust me, I was in a much worse situation. Hope dies last."

As the scarf fell on the ice, the light dimmed. Jackie sighed, recognizing that the color change indicated a weakening connection with the man.

"But we better hurry up," Elisa concluded, raising her hands. "Everyone, step back!"

They stepped back, watching Elisa's magic in action – the electricity concentrated in her palms, crackling, twisting, and dropping violet sparks. Then she moved her hands, and the lightning struck the ice, melting it. Jackie couldn't believe her eyes. Despite Elisa's complaints about her Gift, she now controlled her killing power with unbelievable accuracy.

As the layer of ice melted, water splashed, and a human face floated up. Elisa put on her leather gloves, leaned over him, and started pulling the man out of the lake.

Kathy fell to her knees, touching his head. "Jonathan!"

He lay on the ice, unconscious, his eyes shut. His motionless face appeared white in the moonlight, while his beard resembled charcoal. Elisa placed both her palms on his chest and pressed, then repeated the action. The man didn't move.

"Oh, he is gone! Gone!" Kathy moaned.

"Jackie, do something!" Elisa shouted, pressing his chest. "Come on! We must make him breathe!"

Kathy stood up to give them some space. Stepping back, she covered her mouth with both palms, her eyes glittering in the moonlight.

Jackie leaned over the man and froze. *How many seconds would pass before his soul left his exhausted body? Did he deserve to die at such a young age?* Jackie didn't know the answers to these questions, but her guardian instincts kicked in.

Obeying her inner impulse, she slid her hand under the man's shirt and touched his icy-cold bare chest. A spark of Lightning Gift that she had acquired from Elisa pierced his heart. His body convulsed heavily on the ice, and he opened his eyes.

His lips moved, but he struggled to inhale air. She and Elisa turned him to the side, and he began expelling water, coughing.

"Oh, dear, you saved him!" Elisa exclaimed.

"With your magic!" Jackie smiled, still unable to believe they had almost witnessed his death.

The man stopped coughing and began shivering. Jackie removed her coat, and they placed it on him over his wet clothes.

Jackie sat on the ice near the man they had just rescued. He lay under her coat, breathing slowly. She hugged her shoulders, realizing that her woolen sweater wasn't enough to keep her warm now that the adrenaline had subsided.

Elisa was at the shore, sending a Light signal to the guardian team as part of the regular procedure. When something happened, people sent the signal, and the local guardians on duty rushed to help. Elisa created a Light ball, and it shot into the night sky. After a loud burst, silver sparkles dissolved beneath the shimmering stars.

Kathy approached and stood over Jackie, her face as calm as if she were wearing a clay mask.

"Isn't it a miracle?" Jackie smiled. "He is alive!"

"He is," Kathy replied in an indifferent tone.

Jackie stood up, remembering that victims might be in a state of shock. She had to comfort her before help arrived. "Listen, you might blame yourself for this accident, but it wasn't your fault –"

Kathy took an awkward step back and started laughing, tears rolling down her cheeks. Obviously, she was in a state of turmoil.

"The guardian team will be here soon," Jackie said. "We almost made it."

"He beat me," Kathy suddenly confessed.

Jackie frowned. "What are you trying to say?"

"He beat me," Kathy repeated. "And our daughter."

Jackie's eyes widened. "Why didn't you ask for help?"

"I did," Kathy said in a murky voice. "The guardians didn't believe me, so I took matters into my own hands. He can't be brought back."

Jackie gazed at her in silence. All for a sudden, all the pieces of the puzzle came together in a clear picture. Only a blind person wouldn't have noticed the ice hole on the white lake surface in that bright moonlight. Kathy said they were skating, but she wasn't wearing any skates. It all meant she never wanted to ask for help. She had noticed the fire they accidentally made and pretended to need help because no one would suspect a wife who seemingly did her best to help her dying husband.

"Look," Jackie said, trying to buy time. "I'll personally talk to the guardians, and they'll help you."

"No! They won't believe me! Please, just turn away. With my Telekinesis Gift, I'll pull him back!"

Kathy extended her right hand towards her husband, and Jackie leaped forward to stop her. Alas, the recent experiment with the Gift exchange played a cruel trick – unintentionally, she hit Kathy with electricity. It wasn't a strong hit, but enough to make her angry.

Kathy screamed and began shaking her hand, her face contorted with malice. This was the last thing Jackie saw before a wave of invisible energy pushed her back. She fell into the ice hole, her body sinking into the dark water.

Jackie began drowning, her body descending into the dark water. Despite the instinct to swim to the surface, she remained still. Her heart pounded heavily in her chest, and the water pressed on her, disorienting her senses. It was winter, but the water felt scalding, burning her skin like charcoal in a hot stove. Gradually, she stopped feeling anything. The surroundings grew eerily quiet, and her body went numb.

As she sank deeper, memories of her life flashed before her eyes – the joyful days of her childhood, her mother's voice... Then came the painful recollection of the day she met her husband-to-be. Despite months passing, she couldn't shake him from her mind, unable to forget the torment he had inflicted upon her. Now, as the water chilled her to the core, she welcomed the cold. A gentle current cradled her, carrying her beneath the icy surface, and Jackie drifted into the depths.

Somewhere on the surface, shadows moved through the dark layer of water. Several figures were present. Jackie speculated that the guardians had arrived. It was fortunate that they were late, as now she would finally be free. Free from the torment of her life.

A blinding electric light sparkled above, striking the layer of ice that loomed far above her. Jackie closed her eyes and let go of all her thoughts.

16

Bounded by The Oath

"It wasn't your fault," the guardian's voice sounded in her ears, but his words couldn't comfort her. Elisa stared at him. In his late thirties, he was a man with blond hair and calm blue eyes.

"What's wrong with Jackie?" Elisa repeated. He didn't provide any details, and the lack of information was worse than anything. But she wouldn't give up trying.

The guardian sighed. They were sitting in chairs in the hall of the dorms, and the fire was crackling in the fireplace, illuminating the space. But it didn't make the room warm. Jackie was on the sofa, covered with Elisa's white plush blanket from their room. The Doctor had recently checked her and allowed her to come in.

"Listen, girl –"

"Elisa," she introduced herself. "And what's your name, by the way?"

"Walter. Walter Mills."

Elisa nodded. "So, Mr. Mills, thank you for helping pull my friend from the lake. It was the most impressive use of a Telekinesis Gift that I've ever seen."

He relaxed in his chair. "No worries. It's my job."

Perfect. As Don had trained her, the most important part was establishing a connection with the person, and then she could try to learn what he wasn't telling her. "So, what the heck is going on with Jackie?"

He gave her a sad look. "The doctor said that there's still hope. Now everything depends on her."

Elisa glanced at Jackie. Her head rested on a white pillow, her face pale and lifeless. Elisa was ready to do anything to wake her up. Sadly, she couldn't even hold her hand without wearing her leather gloves.

Walter's face took on a compassionate expression. "Were you good friends?"

"She *is* my best friend." Elisa hugged herself, shivering. "I don't even know what to do if she... I can't lose her."

"Then you need to help her."

"How?"

"She just needs rest and care, so her body will recover," Walter said calmly. "She'll wake up eventually, but the actual healing from her condition might take years."

Tears welled in her eyes. "What do you mean?"

"She was too deep in the water. It only means that she didn't try to fight for her life." His hand rested on the chair arm. "Did you know that she was depressed?"

Elisa wiped her face. "I don't... actually, we both have an uneasy past. But we prefer not to talk about it. Not here."

"At this point, you *must* talk about it." Walter looked at her without blinking. "It's the easiest way she can let it go. Then, she will heal."

"But what if she doesn't want to talk about it?"

"Alright, I'll explain," he said patiently. "Emotional trauma is a part of being a guardian. And as you probably noticed, this path doesn't start in the Academy. It starts much earlier, in your real life. When you face unfairness, injustice, or tragedies caused by someone's neglect. This darkness is too hard to bear because we often think that we are alone in it. But when you have the support of someone who went through the same, it hurts less. To leave her pain behind, Jackie needs a friend. The one that she can trust."

Her fingers squeezed the chair arm. "I just don't want to make it worse. To hurt her."

"Just take it slow. You need to open up first, and then she will feel more secure. But don't push her. You need to guide her and support her when she needs it."

"Does it really work?"

"Every single time," he assured. "It's called mentoring. I know it's hard for you, too, but it's just a rehearsal. The guardian's path consists of dangers, hard choices, and losses."

Elisa gave him a sad smile. "Sounds exactly like my life."

"Then you shall be fine." Walter looked around the hall, immersed in his own nostalgia. "Here, in the Academy, I thought I was alone in my problems. In fact, most people who came here to study were pretentious pricks looking for a well-paid government job. Only two guys were the same as me – devoted to making this shithole that we call Middle Lake city a better place to live."

Intrigued, Elisa fidgeted on her chair. "What happened to these guys?"

"They became my best friends. Whatever happens, they are the pillars I can rely on, even after so many years. Actually, you know one of them. His name is Don."

"Our Don?!" She smiled for the first time that night. "Oh, that explains why you both have a similar subtle sense of humor. Perhaps you communicate a lot."

"Well, thanks." Walter chuckled. "So, the point is that it might be hard to be honest with someone. But when you open up to someone you trust, you can build an unbreakable bond."

"Fine. I'll try."

"Good." He clapped his hands. "Oh, just one more thing before I go. There's so much fuss around female guardians right now... Don will probably explain it to you later, but as we talk, I wanted to give you a heads-up."

"Female guardians?" She knitted her eyebrows. "I sense it's something about me."

"It's all about new relationship rules. Now, if two people work on the same case, they must not be in a relationship unless they are married."

She twisted her hair lock. "I don't really plan to get married."

"You never know. Anyway, it's just at the top of the list. As for the cadets, there is a one-year no-dating rule."

She blinked. "What rule?"

"That might apply to you. You can't date any cadets or guardians as long as you are in your freshman year. And when you are a sophomore, you can't date the cadets from their first year."

She paused, thinking if she could trust Walter. "What about the girls?"

"The same rule for boys and girls. It's for your own safety."

Elisa sighed. She didn't know if Walter understood her or not, but she must figure everything out just to know if she ever could be her true self. "I mean... you said that I can't date guys, but... can cadets of the same gender date each other?"

His face expressed a person who had just eaten a raw lemon. "Phew, Elisa! Where do you get these ideas?! No, same-gender relationships are strictly forbidden by law. Everyone who breaks this rule is to be kicked off by having their rank taken away. It doesn't matter if they are cadets, captains, or whatever they have achieved in their guardian career."

Her heart sank. "Why?"

He shrugged. "Rules are rules. It's not that I'm a gay-hater, no. Sometimes people... date. But they prefer to keep it a secret so as not to get in trouble. You see, it is one of the guardians' tasks to find and arrest those people. As for me, I have nothing against it if they are regular civilians, so I just leave them alone. But I believe there must be no precedents within our guardian team."

"What if two guardians fall in love?"

"There is a code, and there must not be any misunderstandings among the guardians. I assume that relationships can cause cases of harassment. You know, people tend to make everything complicated when they have a chance."

"And I make it more complicated, then," she concluded.

He shook his head. "You are here because of your spirit, Elisa. Not gender. And you need to respect the rules that have been adjusted for you. It shouldn't be that hard."

Elisa lowered her eyes. "I suppose it shouldn't..."

"Well, times change. People don't." He stood up. "Don't overwhelm yourself with this. Just focus on the current problem and try to be a good friend. Then, you'll see what to fix next."

She nodded. "I'll do my best. Thank you, Walter."

"Always." He smiled before leaving. "Whatever happens, remember that you are the guardian, Elisa. A true one."

When she was left alone in the room, Elisa stood up and approached the sofa. Her gloves were somewhere on the chair, but she didn't have any energy left to come back for them. Thus, she just sat on the floor and rested her hands on the sofa arm.

Jackie was so close and, at the same time, too distant. Deep inside, Elisa always knew that they would always be just friends. At the same time, a weak hope still warmed her heart. *Is it love?* Elisa didn't know for sure. So far, love has been an endless challenge of heartbreak for her.

The anxious thoughts twisted in her head. *Why didn't I fall in love with an ordinary girl?* Elisa sighed. Right, all the 'regular' women seemed to be too boring. Her Jackie was different – funny, compassionate, sometimes reckless. She was perfect. Before tonight, all Elisa thought of was gaining the ability to touch her. Now, she would agree never to touch her again, just to know that she was alright.

From now on, Elisa must help her heal. And to do so, she must let her foolish hope die.

Elisa took a deep sigh. "I hope you hear me, dear. Just wake up, please. We'll fix everything together. I promise."

17

New Beginning

The next time Jackie opened her eyes, she found herself lying beside the crackling fireplace. The warmth caressed her face, reminiscent of the water that had engulfed her moments before. *Am I still alive?* Jackie sat up, realizing she was on the sofa in the dorm living room, draped in a white plush blanket. Feeling overheated, she pushed the blanket aside, revealing her nightgown drenched in sweat.

Elisa entered the room carrying a teacup in her hands, a smile lighting up her face. "Glad to see you awake again."

"Hi, Lissy," Jackie replied weakly.

Elisa's expression turned surprised. "No one calls me that except my aunt."

Jackie gazed at her in silence, recalling Elisa's Lightning magic that had saved her from the depths of the lake. Gratitude swelled in her heart. "I should thank you. You rescued me."

"My dear, you saved all four of us in the caves. We are now even," Elisa said, offering Jackie a teacup. Jackie accepted it, inhaling the fragrant blend of honey, ginger, mint, and other unfamiliar herbs.

Jackie took a big sip, the taste triggering memories of the day in the caves when fear had gripped her heart. Elisa must have been terrified as well when she had plunged into the lake, seemingly seeking an end to her own life. *What did I put Elisa through?*

"I'm so sorry for everything," Jackie murmured after finishing her drink.

"Please, don't dwell on it now. Your priority is to rest and recover, okay?"

Jackie nodded in agreement.

The sound of a New Year song drifted in from the street, and Jackie turned to the window. There, fluffy snowflakes gently descended from the evening sky.

"How long was I asleep?" Jackie inquired.

"Long enough for me to wish you a Happy New Year," Elisa replied with a smile. "Today is Eve."

Returning the smile, Jackie echoed, "Happy New Year."

And so began her journey to recovery. Jackie soon learned that Elisa had not left with Theo that day. Instead, she had penned a letter to a close friend in Triville, explaining her absence, and had chosen to stay by Jackie's side.

On the morning of New Year's Day, they sat on a carpet near the fireplace, indulging in cinnamon cookies for breakfast. The snow had ceased, leaving behind a day that was pure and bright outside the window.

"I called for Urchin," Elisa announced. "He'll be arriving later today."

Jackie placed a glass of milk on the floor. "Why?"

Elisa shrugged. "He would have been worried about you, so I sent him a letter. Thankfully, he lives close to the city, so he should be here soon."

"It's probably not a good idea to interrupt his family time," Jackie said, shaking her head. "Besides, I'm feeling much better now."

"What do you remember from that night?" Elisa inquired.

"I recall hearing a man's voice. When he carried me, I briefly opened my eyes. I initially thought it was Urchin, but then everything became hazy, and I can't recall much after that."

"It was a local guardian," Elisa explained, her expression tinged with sadness. "And you referred to him as 'Howard.'"

"Is that Urchin's real name?" Jackie asked.

Elisa nodded. "I'd forgotten that he even had a real name."

Jackie chuckled softly. "Me too."

"If it weren't for that guardian, we wouldn't be sitting here right now," Elisa remarked, her expression turning serious. "I'm truly grateful that you survived."

A somber silence enveloped them as they listened to the tireless crackling of the fire. Jackie chewed on her lip, grappling with conflicting emotions about her survival. She had been managing well until the day she had nearly drowned. Despite her efforts to move past the pain, she found herself trapped by her own past, the darkness overshadowing any glimmer of hope and leaving her feeling empty.

Elisa was the only person who understood that darkness. It lingered within her own soul. Jackie had sensed it during their first day of classes, recognizing a shared struggle. She had believed she could handle it as well as Elisa, but now she felt her own weakness acutely.

"Sometimes I feel like I can't go on," Jackie confessed with a heavy sigh.

"Can't go on with what?"

"Pretending to be normal. Because I'm not," Jackie said, her voice tinged with despair. "I'm not as strong as I thought I was."

"No one is truly strong," Elisa said, her expression clouded with sorrow. "I carry my own shadows, stemming from a dysfunctional family. When I was eleven, I became an orphan after my father was imprisoned for killing my mother."

Jackie's eyes widened in shock. "I had no idea. I'm so sorry."

Elisa forged ahead, recounting her harrowing experiences without hesitation. "But it didn't end there. Last summer, I was abducted by a serial killer who targeted schoolgirls. I narrowly escaped by sheer luck. My friend wasn't as fortunate. You saw her in the photograph from our first day of classes."

Taking a deep breath, Jackie absorbed the weight of Elisa's words. "I remember... Lissy, it's horrifying! The horrors they inflicted upon us, they just continue, with no end in sight!"

"It is indeed horrific. But isn't that why we're here? To bring about change."

Placing both hands over her heart, Jackie confessed, "I don't know. This pain still lingers within me, and it's unbearable."

"It is," Elisa acknowledged, her tears glistening. "My past was shrouded in darkness, too grim to share the complete truth with anyone, not even myself. But after facing death's door, I realized I couldn't cling to that past any longer. I had to release it from my chest before it consumed me. In my darkest moments, I had a friend who supported me." She locked eyes with Jackie. "I want you to know that you can confide in me. Whatever it may be, you can share it."

"It won't change anything."

"No, it won't. But I believe that the burden will lighten with time," Elisa reassured her.

Jackie turned her gaze to the fireplace, the memory of her recent ordeal resurfacing vividly. "You know, when I was submerged in that lake, one thought consumed me – *now I understand how it would feel to escape this pain.*"

Elisa remained silent, offering Jackie a safe space to express her innermost thoughts without probing questions, allowing her to voice words she never imagined speaking aloud.

Jackie wiped a tear from her cheek and continued in a hushed tone. "When my father introduced that man to me and hinted at a potential marriage, I naively believed he could be a good husband. He appeared polite and intelligent, expressing concerns that my Gift could jeopardize our relationship.

"Foolishly, I suppressed my Gift whenever we were together. He wasn't terrible, and we had two months to acquaint ourselves before the wedding. We strolled and talked, and he even managed to make me laugh. He seemed like an ordinary man, and I never anticipated any harm. All I desired was to be loved and lead a normal life... If only I had used my Gift against him... Just once." Her shoulders trembled as emotions overwhelmed her, rendering her speechless.

Elisa, sensing the unspoken anguish in Jackie's narrative, gently interjected, "He harmed you."

Jackie nodded, taking a deep breath before continuing. "That day, my father had gone hunting, and my mother was at work – she's a teacher. We were alone in the house. It was noon, and we were sitting in the living room, engaged in our usual conversation. He brought me tea with honey... The honey masked the taste of the potion."

"A sleeping potion?"

"I'm not sure," Jackie replied, her voice muffled as she sobbed into her sleeve. "I felt numb, yet fully conscious, enduring every agonizing moment. It was excruciating..." Her voice quivered with emotion. "I was lost after that. My own father blamed me, refusing to call off the engagement." Jackie wrapped herself in a shawl, her shoulders shaking with the weight of her pain, tears streaming down her cheeks uncontrollably.

Elisa sat silently beside her, offering a comforting presence as Jackie struggled to regain her composure. "Oh, my dear. I'm glad you found the strength to break free from that marriage."

"I didn't have much of a choice. I endured days of agony, but my father insisted that seeking medical help would bring shame upon our family... So, I escaped a day before the wedding. In the capital, I sought help at a clinic and met a guardian who helped me. However, my family remains unaware of my whereabouts. To them, I am as good as dead."

"Do you have any desire to reach out to them?"

Jackie shook her head. "Not really. But it feels strange to be on my own now."

"You're not alone," Elisa reassured her. "You have me."

"Thank you, Lissy," Jackie expressed gratefully, wiping her tear-streaked face. "Your support means everything to me."

"Always," Elisa affirmed, her gaze filled with warmth.

"I hate myself for being so stupid! How could I be so blind? How didn't I see it?" Her lower lip trembled, and Jackie went silent.

"The burdens you've carried were not your fault. You just thought you were safe, that's it. Now, you must forgive yourself. You need to release yourself from this guilt because it's the only way to keep living."

Taking a deep breath, Jackie nodded. "I'll try."

"Now, I have something special for you," Elisa announced, rising to her feet and making her way to the festively adorned New Year tree in the corner. She retrieved a small box with a silver ribbon adorning it.

"What is it?" Jackie inquired as she accepted the box.

Elisa smiled. "Just open it."

She opened the box to reveal a stunning silver pendant in the shape of a heart, adorned with a tiny sparkling diamond that shimmered in the daylight. It hung delicately from an elegant thin rope.

"It's beautiful," Jackie remarked, admiring the pendant.

"It's a gift for you, Jackie."

Jackie turned the box, observing the diamond's radiant sparkle. "I can't accept this. It looks way too luxurious, and I... I don't even have a gift for you!"

"Don't worry about that. It brings me joy to give this to you," Elisa insisted. "This pendant holds ancient magic within."

Intrigued, Jackie accepted the silver heart, watching as it caught the light and sparkled between them. "What kind of magic does it possess?"

"It carries the power to bring good luck in love. It will guide you to find the right person, and this magic is unwavering," Elisa explained.

"I fear I'm too broken for such magic," Jackie confessed, her gaze falling. "I'm sorry, but romance isn't something I feel capable of."

"Perhaps it may not have an immediate effect, but it will certainly aid in your healing. Love possesses a formidable strength that can vanquish pain," Elisa asserted, her cheeks tinged with a blush. "With love, anything is possible."

Jackie pondered for a moment before asking, "And what about you?"

"I no longer need it. Please, do me the favor of wearing it."

Jackie complied, fastening the pendant around her neck. Though she harbored doubts about its magical properties, she was willing to entertain the idea if it brought comfort to Elisa. Perhaps by wearing it, she could at least pretend to be on the path to recovery, alleviating Elisa's concerns for her well-being.

18

A Spell Whisperer

Jackie woke up in her room from her afternoon nap. Despite the rest, she still felt weak. The doctor had advised her that she needed at least one more week to recover. Putting on her sweater, she stopped at the mirror. Her reflection revealed a sickly pale face, and her sad green eyes resembled deep marshes. The silver necklace on her chest gleamed as she fixed it and forced a smile. Despite her condition, Jackie was grateful to be alive, a feeling she hadn't experienced in months.

Perhaps she needed to write about this moment in her diary, which she had abandoned after the dragon journey. She retrieved a leather notebook from the depths of her nightstand and held it close to her chest before heading downstairs.

In the living room, the fireplace still burned brightly. Elisa and Urchin sat on the sofa, engaged in conversation and laughter. Jackie leaned against the wall, a smile spreading across her face at the sight of them. She was pleased to see him; his changed hairstyle gave him a more serious appearance, and the nickname Urchin no longer seemed to suit him. He was Howard now, a future successful guardian and her dear friend. Jackie didn't rush to embrace him; instead, she found comfort in simply observing them together.

Her attention shifted to Elisa, whose hair cascaded freely down her chest, illuminated by the generous sunlight that made her head shine. A warm feeling enveloped Jackie's heart, prompting her to place her palm against her chest and blink in surprise. It was a new sensation for her, and she couldn't help but wonder about the significance of the necklace that Elisa had given her earlier in the day. Its purpose was to awaken her dormant love. But why do I feel it when I look at Elisa?

Jackie shook her head, dismissing her earlier thoughts as silly. The surge of emotions she felt was likely a result of the near-death experience and the adrenaline rush that followed. It was gratitude towards Elisa for saving her life, nothing more.

"Hey, there you are!" Howard's voice interrupted her thoughts.

Jackie smiled and walked over to them. Howard enveloped her in a hug, and she returned the embrace, her arms wrapping around his broad shoulders.

"You have a new haircut," Jackie observed as they settled on the sofa.

"Yep," Howard replied with a smile.

Elisa glanced at them slyly. "Well, I'll leave you two alone," she said before exiting the room. Jackie felt her heart pounding in her chest as she watched Elisa leave.

"How do you feel?" Howard inquired, breaking the moment of silence.

Jackie turned to face him. "The doctor said I can't use magic for a week, and I need to rest more to recover."

"So, you'll be skipping classes?"

She nodded. "Just for the first couple of days."

Howard took Jackie's hands in his, a gesture that was supposed to cause her heart to tremble. But she didn't feel anything romantic. Indeed, the accident on the lake and the pendant had strangely influenced her heart's desires.

"Howard, do you know what happened to that unfortunate couple on the lake?" Jackie asked, attempting to change the subject.

He squeezed her palms gently. "You remember my real name."

Jackie bit her lip, realizing her slip-up. "Right, I said 'Howard.' But it doesn't change anything." She continued to gaze at him in silence, waiting for his response.

Releasing her hands, Howard began to speak. "Yes, the couple. The guardians arrived at the shore just before that woman used her Telekinesis Gift to push you. Now she's in prison."

"But it was an accident! I accidentally struck her with lightning," Jackie protested.

Howard gave her an agitated look. "You mean... Elisa's magic?"

"It's a long story," Jackie replied, waving her hand dismissively. "This woman, Kathy. She shouldn't be in prison because it was unintentional."

"Yeah, if you don't consider the fact that she tried to kill her own husband," Howard added solemnly.

Jackie sighed, defeated. "What about the man? Is he alive?"

"He's recovering at home. They have a six-year-old daughter, and someone needs to take care of her."

Jackie exhaled deeply. "The woman claimed he abused her and their daughter."

Howard shook his head. "Of course..."

Frustrated, Jackie stood up. "What do you mean, 'Of course'? None of this would have happened if her husband wasn't such a jerk!"

Howard also rose from his seat. "Jackie, I understand. Life isn't fair, and yes, she may be a victim. But the real question is, why would she resort to killing him? She could have sought a divorce or asked for help."

"She said she tried, but the guardians didn't believe her," Jackie retorted.

"Regardless, she attempted to kill you!"

"I told you, it was an accident!"

Howard placed his palms on his head, a gesture he often used to gather his thoughts. "Okay, don't be upset. I'm on your side."

"Are you?" Jackie questioned, searching his eyes for reassurance.

He nodded. "Yes, Jackie. This case is currently under investigation, but if you're willing, you can assist. You can visit the Guardian House and provide your testimony once you've recovered."

"I will."

"Good. Are we clear on this now?"

"Yes," she replied, looking at him with admiration. Howard truly was a good friend. "I'm grateful for your support."

He smiled before leaning in to kiss her. Jackie reciprocated the kiss, but to her own dismay, she found herself pulling away.

Howard looked at her with uncertainty.

"Howard, listen..." Jackie began, her voice trailing off.

He locked eyes with her. "I understand."

Jackie blinked, puzzled by his response. "What do you mean?"

"It's all about these new rules of dating."

Jackie furrowed her brow, trying to comprehend his words. If there were rules, why hadn't she been informed of them? Aloud, she said, "Exactly."

"It's alright; we can wait until the next academic year," Howard reassured her, gently caressing her shoulder. "For now, focus on your health."

"Sure," Jackie replied, her gaze shifting to the window where winter had blanketed the yard in white. She had ample time, as Howard had mentioned, to navigate these new rules and come to terms with her emotions.

"It takes time to recover from such an accident, both physically and mentally," Howard said.

"I'll be okay. Eventually."

Howard nodded and moved to stand by the fireplace. "When Elisa wrote to me about your condition, she mentioned that you were on the brink of death. It was a shock to me."

"I'm sorry that I scared you all," Jackie offered apologetically.

He gave her a concerned look. "Why did you go to that lake?"

Jackie shrugged. "We were experimenting with a new spell from The Book of Gift Exchange."

Howard's eyes widened. "For what purpose?"

"I wanted to understand how the Lightning Gift worked," Jackie recalled. "To potentially assist Elisa."

He paced the room, deep in thought. "It's actually not a bad idea."

"Really?"

"Once, I encountered a man struggling with a Poisoning Gift. A witch used a spell to experience it through his Light," Howard shared.

"That's what I did. We did an exchange by touching our Lights."

He nodded in understanding. "Then, another witch crafted a spell to tame this Gift."

"She was a spell whisperer?" Jackie pondered.

"Being a spell whisperer is a skill, not a Gift. She was a mind reader, much like you. Jackie, you have a unique ability to write any spell you desire. You are creative, inventive..." Howard's gaze was warm as he complimented her. "And very charming."

Jackie blushed at the praise. Though Howard wasn't the object of her affection, his kind words still brought her joy. "Thank you, but –"

"No 'buts,'" Howard interjected, raising his index finger. "Remember when we were trapped in that cave with the furious dragons? You whispered a spell that saved our lives. You may not realize it, but I believe you have the capability to create any spell you wish."

Jackie gave him a hopeful look. Maybe Howard wasn't a bookworm, but his eloquence and charm always allowed him to effortlessly connect with a wide circle of friends and acquaintances. Even the meanest men in a group preferred to be on good terms with him. And at this moment, she wanted to believe his words.

She looked down at her palms, still hesitant. "I probably need to wait for my magic to recover."

"Not really. Just focus, meditate, or whatever helps you gather your thoughts. Then, write a spell," Howard advised with a smile. "When your magic returns, you'll be prepared."

"Thank you," Jackie replied with a smile.

After Howard departed, Jackie found herself alone in the spacious living room. Despite it being dinner time, she wasn't hungry. Holding the diary in her hands, she settled onto the sofa, engrossed in the process of writing. The spell flowed effortlessly from her pen, akin to the poems she enjoyed composing in her leisure time.

Content with her work, Jackie closed the notebook. If Howard was right, then Elisa's struggle with her Gift stemmed from fear, much like how most people fear the unknown. Elisa lacked belief in her ability to control her Gift. As a friend, it was Jackie's duty to instill that belief in her.

19

A Way of Heart

The library was usually quiet. The classes had already started, but Jackie still had her medical leave, so she decided to use this time wisely. She sat on the floor, holding her Light ball. Now, its color seemed almost transparent in the bright daylight, just a clear sphere, looking like pure ocean water.

Laura sat nearby, twisting her bright green Light in her hands. "Are you sure you feel well?"

"Absolutely. My magic returned two days ago," Jackie replied. "Ok, let's focus."

Laura nodded and moved her hand, letting Jackie merge her energy with hers. The spheres of Light synchronized and became brighter.

"A soft touch," Jackie smiled. "We're getting better each time."

"I feel like I can become a witch after all this practice," Laura said with a chuckle.

"Just one more time, okay?" Jackie took a deep breath, concentrating on her inner balance. "Now try to remember the times when you couldn't control your Gift."

Obeying her, Laura closed her eyes. Jackie moved her free hand up, letting the Telekinesis Gift go through her magic channels. She aimed to make a book from the reception desk float. However, the wave of invisible energy hit the vase with fir twigs. Before New Year, Laura nicely decorated it with paper flowers and candies. The vase swung under the motion and fell on the floor.

A loud clanking of broken glass made Laura open her eyes. "This time, you're responsible for cleaning," she said in a weary tone.

"Hold on." The merged Lights became smaller between their palms, but Jackie could still use this energy. "Keep in contact. Now, remember the time when you just learned to control your power."

"Fine." Laura sighed and closed her eyes again.

Jackie focused on reading Laura. She was immersed in a memory of her past when Laura stood over a broken pot in her garden. Her face was covered with tears, and she was looking at her palms with disappointment.

"What have you done?" Jackie asked.

Laura's voice sounded from her sides as she replied from the real library room. "It was my mom's favorite pot. My dad made it for her garden when they had just bought a house. And I broke it."

"Did you fix it?"

"Just watch." Laura's image in her memory finally stopped sobbing. She placed her palms on her chest and took a deep breath. Then she raised one of her hands and moved her fingers. The flowers torn from the earth started flying around, dropping the dirt from their buds. Cleaned and fresh, they landed on the soft flower bed, and their roots sank to the earth, finding comfort in a new place.

"Jackie, look!" Laura called her from the library.

Jackie opened her eyes and held her breath in amazement. The fir twigs flew over them, along with candies and the paper flowers of red and golden colors.

"Incredible!" Laura laughed and moved her hands up, arranging the vortex of New Year accessories. First, the twigs landed on the floor, and then the candies dropped into the empty crystal vase on the shelf one by one. She left the flowers for the ending, making them cover Jackie's head like giant snowflakes. Their thin knits attached to her hairlocks.

"Your Gift is fun." Jackie couldn't stop smiling. She was wiping the water from the floor while Laura got rid of the broken glass. Her Gift could let her do it without risking cutting her fingers.

"It is sometimes," Laura replied. She closed the paper garbage bag, ensuring it was properly sealed. "And you look so pretty. Now you can go on a date."

"Which date?!" Jackie scoffed. "You know about the new rules."

Laura gave her a sly look. "You know what I think about the rules."

Jackie shook her head. Since the day she learned about the rules, it had become a hot topic for discussions among the guys in the group. Undoubtedly, they were waiting for a moment when she or Elisa would make a mistake. Then, they would complain to the teachers, putting them in serious trouble.

Laura came closer, her eyes gleaming with interest. "Relax. I know about your kiss with Urchin."

Jackie widened her eyes. "What? But how?"

"You just confessed." She smiled widely. "Then, you two finally made out."

"Maybe," Jackie replied with bemusement. "But still, how do you know it would happen? Did he tell you?"

Laura shook her head. "Of course not. He asked me for a piece of advice just before winter break."

"Oh, Laura. What did you tell him?"

"The truth. That the only way to know for sure if someone likes you in a romantic sense is a good old kiss."

Jackie walked to the chair and sat down. "I didn't even like it."

Laura sat in the opposite chair, not forgetting to bring a crystal vase with candies. She waved her hand, making a kettle with hot tea fly from her reception desk to the coffee table.

"Something must be wrong with me," Jackie complained. "He is a good guy and everything, but –"

"But it's not *him*." Laura poured the tea into a mug and gave it to Jackie.

She took a sip. *The lemongrass.* It always helped her feel better if she was sick, but not today. Even the ritual and magic tricks couldn't make her stop thinking about her weird feelings towards Elisa. And it wasn't right.

"As I say, the heart doesn't understand orders." Laura gave her a knowing look and leaned back in her chair. "So, tell me, who is it?"

Jackie had almost choked on her tea. She wiped her lips and gave Laura an anxious look. "Can I not tell?"

Laura kept looking at her with uncovered interest. "Whatever. I'll know it sooner or later."

"You can't know everything."

She laughed. "As long as people talk, there will be rumors."

Jackie lowered her eyes. "I just... I don't know what to do. Can I get rid of it somehow?"

"Nope." Laura sipped her tea with the confidence of a true expert in the field of relationships. "Love is higher than magic. You can't tame or control it. So, you must learn how to live with it."

"By the way, I read your memory." Jackie narrowed her eyes. "And this is exactly how you learned to control your Gift. You thought about your parents at that moment, and it worked."

"Maybe." Laura's face became intrigued. "As I know, there are two ways of taming a Gift like mine – control or trust. The first is a way for most men. It's because the strong Gift is a part of their nature, so they trust it when they manifest their power. So, all they need is to practice gaining control. For most women, it's the opposite – we must let go of control. Fully. We need to learn to accept this Gift with all its consequences. Then, we tame this magic."

Jackie drummed her fingers over the chair handle, thinking. "That's true. Gifts may be so different, and mine was natural for me. I only learned how to block it, not to read people accidentally, that's it."

"If it worked for me, it might be the same with the Lightning Gift," Laura suggested. "What an interesting time we live in. People never allowed women to have destructive power, but, in fact, it might work the same as telekinesis."

"I never thought of it like this."

"If my theory is correct, maybe that's why it's so difficult for Elisa." Laura waved her free hand, pondering on her new discovery. "She tries to do it the hard way."

Jackie took a candy and twisted it in her hand. The shining wrapping gleamed in the daylight. "Only if I could find a way to make it easy for her."

"Then use my experience and make her think of someone she truly loves," Laura suggested. "Like parents. It might work just fine."

Jackie shook her head. "Not in her case."

"Then someone from her past."

Jackie ate the candy, and a sweet-sour taste of salted caramel filled her mouth. She had all she needed to help Elisa. But her heart ached in her chest when she thought about awakening Elisa's romantic feelings. It wouldn't be easy, but she must do it even if it meant breaking her own heart.

20

Last Date

Jackie placed a piece of chalk on the drawer and wiped her hands. With a smile on her face, she admired her work. A white chalk circle looked impressive on the dark wooden floor. Six white candles burned at its sides, crackling. Her leather diary lay in the middle, opened to the proper page. To create a special, cozy atmosphere, Jackie ensured that the curtains were closed tightly, not letting any daylight in.

With time still before Elisa would return from her classes, Jackie approached the mirror to check her appearance. Her hair had grown a bit since summertime, now reaching her shoulders. Red and golden paper flowers adorned her head – a gift from Laura. To enhance her image, she wore a red cardigan without buttons, revealing her elegant black woolen dress and heart-shaped pendant.

Jackie gave a sad smile to her own reflection. She really wished it could be a real date, but she knew it was impossible. At least she could make it beautiful. Lost in her thoughts, she didn't notice the door opening. She watched Elisa in the mirror, approaching her from behind.

"You look terrific!" Elisa exclaimed in a cheerful voice. "What's the occasion?"

Jackie turned to face her. "It's my turn to give you a present."

"What present?"

Jackie touched her pendant. "Just a little magic."

Elisa looked around the room with suspicion. "I hope this time it's nothing forbidden."

"Don't worry. It's a new spell." Jackie walked to the wardrobe and retrieved her black scarf. "Are you in?"

Without waiting for a response, Jackie stepped into the chalk circle and took a seat. Elisa followed suit, settling on the opposite side.

"And how does it work?" Elisa asked.

"First, use this." Jackie handed her the black scarf. "You must cover your eyes."

Elisa paused, examining the black cloth. It was made of good quality wool, specifically for the guardian's winter uniform. "And what will happen after?" she asked.

"We will read a spell together."

Elisa gave her a hesitant look. "Jackie, I don't want to hurt you —"

"Do you trust me?" Jackie interrupted.

"Of course. It's just —"

"You won't hurt me," Jackie reassured her with a smile. "I know you never will."

Elisa fidgeted. "I'm afraid my Gift might."

"I promise I'll be gentle," Jackie said playfully. "We will proceed with small, cautious steps."

"Fine." Elisa sighed and covered her eyes with the scarf, enveloping herself in darkness.

"What do you see?" Jackie inquired.

"Not a damn thing."

"What do you hear?" Jackie's voice remained calm and confident. "Tell me."

Elisa slowed her breathing, focusing on the sounds around her. "Besides your voice, it's the crackling of the candles."

"Very well. Do you feel their warmth?" Jackie asked.

Elisa shrugged. "Maybe. A little."

"Now, could you notice this warmth with your eyes open?"

"Maybe. If I paid close enough attention," Elisa replied, biting her lip in impatience. "Should I try to blow out the candles now?"

"No, you shouldn't touch the candles."

"Why?"

Jackie moved closer, lowering her voice. "Because that's not how you harness your power. As you have the opportunity to experience, your vision only distracts you. When you stop focusing on what you see, you can pay attention to what you feel."

"I think I've tried this already," Elisa whispered.

"Today, it's the same but different."

Elisa sighed, feeling resigned. She had already attempted everything from the books provided by Don and all the exercises given by Theo. Even if she failed, it couldn't possibly make things worse.

"So here is the wisdom of the day," Jackie continued. "The power bestowed upon all mages is the blessing of the Divine. It is rooted in two forces – trust and control. All this time, you have been trying to exert control over your Gift. Is that true?"

Elisa nodded. "I believe so, yes. But it hasn't worked."

"If you want to tame your power, you must first trust it. Absolutely, unconditionally. Can you trust your Gift, Elisa?"

Elisa shook her head. "No."

"What do you need to know in order to trust it?"

Elisa fell silent. It was a new perspective, as no one had ever posed this question to her before. But it resonated deeply with her. "I want to ensure that I won't harm innocent people," she finally articulated.

"Has your power ever caused harm to anyone?"

"Well, I've exploded many candles and ruined all the campfires I tried to create. And recently, I accidentally burned a tree."

"Has it ever harmed a human being?" Jackie questioned.

"Yes. It struck you on the first day we met," Elisa recalled with a smile. "Do you remember? You joked that it was a spark between us."

"Of course, I remember." Jackie chuckled. "But it merely felt like a tickle. Has your Gift harmed anyone else?"

"Oh, dear," Elisa paused, reflecting. "I'm not sure. I may have accidentally touched a few people in the group."

"Has it caused any fatalities or significant injuries?"

"No."

"Okay, Now I'll ask the next question. Take your time to think carefully. Has your Gift ever saved someone's life?"

Elisa's heart raced as she recalled fragments of memories. "When we were stealing from the dragons, I used it to seal the entrance to the cave. It gave us some time to find a solution."

"Agreed," Jackie acknowledged. "What else?"

"I'm not sure. There was a recent incident with the man who nearly drowned. It was actually you, but it seems that my Lightning Gift helped restart his heart."

"And the most recent instance is…" Jackie prompted.

"You." Elisa exhaled. "I shattered nearly all the ice on that lake to locate you. While it didn't directly aid in finding you, it cleared the surface, allowing the guardians to retrieve you more swiftly."

Jackie fell silent, leaving Elisa to wonder about her thoughts.

Finally, Jackie spoke. "Would you be able to save me without your power?"

Elisa shook her head in silence.

"So," Jackie concluded, "The Gift has been with you for half a year, and it has helped you save several innocent people. Isn't that enough to deserve your trust?"

"It is. But what about me? What if I make a mistake?"

"The Divine power bestowed upon you by your wise ancestors will never allow you to harm yourself or others. You must let go of your fear. Can you do that?" Jackie asked.

"Yes. But how?"

"Your heart will guide you. You must allow your Gift to flow through your heart while reciting a sacred Spell. This is how you can fully embrace it," Jackie explained.

"Let's try," Elisa agreed.

The pages of the diary rustled as Jackie flipped through it. "Okay, then. Place one hand on your heart and the other on the top of your head."

Elisa followed the instructions, feeling her heart beating steadily in her chest.

"Now, think of someone you truly love. Can you do that for me?" Jackie requested.

"Of course," Elisa responded without hesitation. The only person she could think of at that moment was right in front of her, and it brought her joy to think of Jackie.

"Well," Jackie's voice carried a hint of sadness. "Now, just repeat after me:

Sometimes, we choose the path;
Sometimes, it chooses us.
Sometimes, we open doors;

Sometimes, all doors stay closed.
Sometimes, we run away;
Sometimes, we must come back.
The whisper of your heart
Will help you to decide."

Elisa took a deep breath, allowing the tingling sparkles to envelop her body from head to toe. As they dissipated, a sense of warmth and comfort washed over her. It felt incredibly natural. She lowered her hands in silence.

Unexpectedly, Jackie's fingertips brushed against her palm. There was no surge of electricity between them. Elisa squeezed her hand, finding it hard to believe that it was actually happening.

"See, you did it," Jackie whispered.

Elisa moved her free hand to Jackie's shoulders, then to her face. Her skin was warm and smooth, just as she had imagined.

Jackie leaned in closer, and they shared a kiss. Elisa responded, feeling the soft and tender touch of Jackie's lips, which seemed to illuminate her from within, soothing all her worries. Jackie continued to kiss her smooth neckline, and Elisa leaned back, embracing this new sensation.

Jackie's breath was ragged, causing the electric sparkles to shimmer in her blood, from her fluttering heart to her fingertips. She wished this moment could last forever, but the kiss ended as abruptly as it had begun.

As Jackie leaned back, she slowly removed her scarf.

"The spell worked," Jackie said softly, her cheeks blushing.

"It did," Elisa replied, adjusting the collar of her shirt, trying to process what had just transpired. Her mind was still struggling to comprehend the situation. "Thank you. It was the best New Year present I've ever received. But I didn't expect the bonus kisses."

"I'm sorry, Lissy," Jackie said, averting her eyes. "I don't know how it happened."

Elisa stood up, feeling conflicted. *This kiss was a mistake, but why did it feel so right?* Her heart raced in her chest. "Listen, I really care about you, but you know the consequences if anyone finds out. It could ruin our careers."

"I know," Jackie said.

The candles around them almost burned down, casting a dim light in the room. Jackie began to blow them out.

Elisa went to open the curtains, revealing the fading daylight outside. *How much time do we have before darkness descends?*

Elisa turned back to Jackie. "Let's just forget about this slip-up."

"How can I forget?" Jackie's hand brushed against a pendant. "You mentioned that this jewelry brings good luck in love, and it led me to you."

"Are you certain about that?"

Jackie nodded.

Elisa paced across the room, her thoughts racing. If the pendant truly worked as intended, it meant they were both in a precarious situation. She took a step towards Jackie. "What if you just take it off and give us both some time to cool off?"

Jackie crossed her arms over her chest. "Is ignoring my feelings your solution?"

Elisa met her gaze in silence. Jackie moved closer, her warm breath brushing against Elisa's ear, causing goosebumps to rise on her skin. "I know you enjoyed it," Jackie whispered.

Elisa's head spun. "We can't be together, Jackie. It's against the law."

"Then we won't tell anyone," Jackie suggested.

Elisa took a step back. "Someone will find out. We can't take that risk."

"Isn't love worth the risk?"

Elisa shook her head. Jackie may be intelligent, but she couldn't read her mind at that moment. There was only one way to prevent Jackie from making a grave mistake. "I'm not in love with you, Jackie. I can't endanger you for a fleeting moment of passion."

"A fleeting moment?" Jackie blinked. "So, I mean nothing to you."

Elisa's heart sank as she turned away, her voice filled with compassion. "I'm still your friend, Jackie. You know that. That's why I need to be honest with you. Urchin is a great guy, so give him a chance. Don't waste your time on someone who will never return your feelings."

Jackie clenched a silver heart in her hand, causing the thin rope to snap. The jewelry fell to the floor between them, resembling a shard of shattered glass.

"What are you doing?! That was a gift from me."

"It didn't suit me," Jackie replied as she retrieved her winter coat from the wardrobe. "Please, take it back and keep it hidden in the darkest corner of your jewelry box."

"Where are you going?"

Jackie picked up her scarf from the floor and hastily tied it around her neck. "Don't worry. This secret will stay within these walls. But I need to leave."

"When will you be back?"

"I have no idea. I just need some fresh air," Jackie responded, turning on her heels. As she made her way to the door, she glanced back. "By the way, congratulations on your tamed Gift."

As the door closed behind Jackie, Elisa sank to her knees on the floor. She picked up the broken rope from the fallen pendant, attempting to align the torn ends, but they refused to fit together.

Tears welled up in her eyes as the weight of the situation pressed down on her, making it difficult to breathe. The harsh reality of love's complexities was overwhelming, and Elisa struggled to come to terms with it.

Suddenly, the door opened, and Theo entered the room. "What's wrong?" he inquired.

Elisa wiped her face, trying to compose herself. "Nothing," she replied with a heavy heart. "Nothing good. As usual."

Story 4

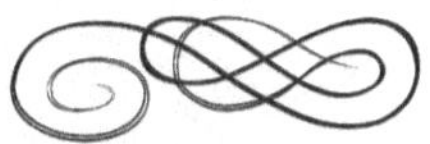

Insidious Truth

21

The Eyes of Justice

The main hall of the courthouse was almost empty. Jackie sat on the bench near the small fountain with her diary on her lap. The crystals of time on it shone with a yellow hue, making the moving water look like bubbling lemonade. Open windows let the spring air in, filling the space with the aroma of blossoming trees.

Jackie bit a pencil as she re-read the notes she had prepared for the hearing. This past winter, she had almost drowned. Kathy, a woman abused by her husband, had pushed her into the lake that night. Today, Jackie was the only one who had volunteered to become her attorney at law. This decision came to her after learning that the guardians usually punished such females by taking away their magic in cases like this, rendering them Incapables. After that, Incapable women were forced to live the rest of their lives in special isolated communities. Jackie couldn't let this happen. Not this time.

She turned several pages, searching for the spell of self-confidence that she had recently written for herself. Instead, the diary opened to the spell she had written for Elisa.

"Sometimes we choose the path..." she read, her heart racing. Since the day they kissed, Jackie couldn't find a better solution than focusing on her studies and spending all her free time preparing for the court hearing.

Placing her free hand on her chest, she hoped to discover that the love she carried there had finally disappeared. Alas, it was still there, and it had only grown stronger over the past several months. She missed Elisa badly. Even knowing that Elisa would never love her back, Jackie craved her. Every evening, all she wanted was to hold her tight and keep kissing her again and again, without caring where it would lead them. Instead, she stayed late in the library, reading law books. Jackie usually returned to their room close to midnight because not talking to her helped a lot.

The shadow of a man's hat fell on the diary page, and Jackie raised her eyes. It was Don.

"What are you doing here?" Jackie asked.

He sat on the bench and took his hat off. His hair was neatly brushed as if he were prepared for an important social event. "Just came to check on my loyal student."

Jackie closed her diary and sighed. "I don't think I'm that loyal."

His brown eyes smiled. "You studied night and day. I'm intrigued to see how this case will end."

"Really, how much can a rookie like me change?" She stared at the fountain, now with a light-green shade to the water. They only had several minutes left before the hearing started.

"Lack of confidence is normal for a beginner." His voice lacked its usual sarcastic tone. "Jackie, I don't often tell my students this, but you have a real talent for putting words together. If you keep practicing, you can become a good lawyer."

"Really?"

Don's face was serious. "Why not?"

"Well, I'm not a good liar."

"You won't need to lie. In fact, there is no such thing as absolute truth. All you need to do is to show the judge *your* version of the truth."

"But which version is right to show?"

He gave her a sly look. "It depends on what you want for this woman. Why did you take part in it in the first place?"

"I just wanted to prevent cases like this from happening. When Kathy experienced domestic violence, she couldn't even find where to complain!" Jackie paused, remembering all the events that led her to become a guardian cadet. "She was vulnerable and unprotected. She was... like me."

"Exactly." Don stood up. "I'm sure your vibe will help persuade the judge and people in the courtroom. Now, let's go."

When the hearing was almost over, Jackie stood up for the final word as the attorney in law. The hearing room was smaller than she had imagined – no statues of justice or rows of benches. There were around thirty regular chairs for attendees and a lattice for the suspect in the corner. It seemed that such cases were common in Middle Lake, and the smaller rooms were used for hearings. Additionally, everything moved quickly, lasting less than half an hour, leaving Jackie with little time to present her arguments.

Jackie walked towards the chair where the Judge sat. He was a middle-aged man wearing a purple mantle. His pale eyes had a tired look.

"Your Honor," Jackie began her speech. She pointed at Kathy, the suspect sitting behind the lattice, awaiting her verdict. "This woman, Kathy, has clearly made several mistakes. However, upon closer examination, it becomes evident that everything she did was to protect herself and her daughter from constant assault.

"When I met Kathy, she had argued with her husband and left home to avoid waking her sleeping daughter. Her husband followed her to the lake, where they began to fight. Please note that Kathy wasn't the one who initiated this fight – it was an act of self-defense. Regrettably, this altercation resulted in him falling into an ice hole. However, we were able to rescue him, so technically, no crime occurred."

Jackie paused, glancing at the judge. His dull blue eyes showed no expression, but she continued. "According to our laws, women are not permitted to engage in violence, but this case clearly was not an intentional act of murder. It was an attempt to prevent harm to herself. Today, we witnessed a failure in the system that was meant to protect this woman and her child. As I mentioned earlier, there is documented evidence that Kathy had made multiple complaints to the local Guardian House, yet she was never provided with assistance or shelter. The guardian's negligence drove her to despair and forced her to fight for her own life.

"Undoubtedly, Kathy made mistakes, but there were also errors on the part of the law. If we acknowledge this, we can work towards improving the system to ensure that women like her receive the support and assistance they need. This would not only prevent similar cases in the future but also maintain the existing order of things."

Jackie locked eyes with Don. He nodded, showing satisfaction with her brief speech. Apart from him, no one from the Academy was present. Her friends had stayed in the dorms at her request, as she knew their presence would only make her more nervous. Now, she was grateful that Don had broken his word. His presence provided incredible support.

"Thank you, Miss Robinson," the judge said. "You may take your seat."

She nodded and returned to her place beside Don.

He smiled, his voice so quiet that only she could hear him. "That was a good performance. Let's see what this grumpy face will say."

The judge decided to impose the full punishment and promptly delivered the verdict. As Don led Jackie out onto the street, those words continued to echo in her ears. Even the bright sunlight failed to dispel the gloom of the day.

"It's not fair!" Jackie almost screamed. "We need to go back and explain it's a huge mistake!"

"Calm down!" Don shook her shoulders, silencing her. "Listen, I understand how painful this is, but Jackie, now you understand how this process works."

"So what?"

He released her shoulders, allowing her to steady her own trembling body. She was shaking, unsure if it was from the cold or anger. Perhaps it was the latter. Her sole focus for months had been to win this case, to achieve a small victory in the sea of disappointments. Now, that dream lay in ashes, along with her hopes for a better future for people like herself.

To hold back her tears, Jackie looked up. They stood beneath a large apple tree, and white petals slowly drifted down upon their heads.

"Today, we witnessed a failure in the justice system, and this is a crucial lesson for you. What did you learn, Jackie?" Don asked.

"That failure sucks," she replied with a nervous chuckle.

"That's correct," Don agreed. "But here's another truth - when faced with such failures, most people choose to give up. Some do so quietly; some seek solace in others. Others openly confront it, often with unfavorable outcomes."

"Then what should I do?" She furrowed her brow. "Just accept defeat without a fight? Like a coward?"

He shook his head. "No. There's a third type of people. We observe, learn, and then we find the right way to effect change. We reshape outdated, ineffective rules that have become harmful to people rather than protective. And we do so without hesitation."

Jackie looked back at the court building. "But Kathy... she is a victim here, and no one cares."

"You do, and that means a lot," Don reassured her, glancing around to ensure no one was listening. "I have a feeling that cases like this have a hidden layer. I've been observing this judge for some time, and it's not the first instance of him disregarding pleas like yours."

Jackie stared at him, the realization sinking in. It was unsettling to imagine how many more victims of injustice might have had their fates sealed by the same judge.

Don gave her a concerned look. "Alright, I think that's enough for today. How about you head back to the dorms and work on memorizing your oath?"

Jackie blinked. Amidst the intensity of the hearing and the emotional turmoil within her, she had completely forgotten about the upcoming ceremony. She was on the verge of completing her first year of studies and would soon become a sophomore cadet. This milestone would involve taking an oath and beginning to assist real guardians. However, the thought of facing Elisa during the official proceedings was daunting.

Don smiled. "Alright, take your time."

"I will."

22

A Farewell Party

The dorms were bustling with activity – servants coming and going, carrying trays of food and drinks. The party was set up in the backyard, adorned with tables, chairs, and vases filled with fresh flowers for the first time in years. Elisa perched on a chair at the entrance, securing a large flower garland above the doorway. The scent of daffodils brought back bitter memories of the previous spring. If someone had told her then that she would become a cadet, Elisa would have never believed it.

After fastening all the ribbons in place, Elisa hopped down from the chair and smoothed out the hem of her light-blue dress, making sure she looked presentable.

Theo approached with two glasses of champagne, offering one to her. "Would you relax already and have a walk with me?"

She chuckled. "Sure."

They strolled through the yard, basking in the warmth of the spring evening.

"I told you the flowers would add a nice touch," Elisa remarked with a smile. "Hopefully, the evening won't turn into a drinking spree."

Theo took a sip of his drink. "Well, there's still a chance it could. There will be thirty-four intoxicated men here, after all."

"Are you planning on getting drunk?" Elisa teased. "With three women in attendance, you might need to stay focused."

He twirled his glass, watching the bubbles rise. "And you've decided I should hit on Laura?"

"Why not?"

"We actually talked and agreed to remain friends," he explained.

"Oh, really?! I can't believe she let you go so easily. She seemed really into you."

He shrugged. "I think that spark just fizzled out."

"What happened to your hunter instinct?" Elisa playfully poked his shoulder.

"Nothing," he teased back. "And what about yours?"

"Touché." Elisa sighed, taking a big gulp of her drink.

Ever since she kissed Jackie and then pushed her away, Elisa couldn't stop thinking about her, even in her dreams. Surprisingly, her lie seemed to have a positive impact as Jackie focused on her studies and significantly improved her grades in law and history. The least Elisa could do for her was throw a surprise party, a small gesture to lift her spirits after a challenging year.

His hand landed on her shoulder. "Sorry, Sparkle. Sometimes, I forget that you still have feelings for her."

"It's just so strange that being in love is considered illegal in my situation," Elisa whispered. All these months, since she had confided in Theo about the kiss and her subsequent heartbreak, he had been a constant source of support.

"You've done nothing wrong," he reassured her. "And with the upcoming summer practice, you'll likely move on from her by fall."

"I hope so."

"Speaking of practice... Are you certain that going to Santos is a good idea?"

"The farther away from her, the better," Elisa declared, finishing her drink and placing her empty glass on the table.

The waitresses she had hired had yet to arrive, leaving no one to serve the drinks. Luckily, Urchin was at the entrance, engaged in conversation with Riley, a guy who claimed to see the future in his dreams. Elisa was drawn to the bottle of fine whiskey that Urchin held, so she waved him over.

"I thought you didn't particularly care for Urchin."

"Today, I appreciate anyone who helps me forget my worries." Elisa winked at Theo. "Let's go."

Tonight, Urchin was the center of attention as everyone eagerly anticipated trying 'the real guardian drink' he had brought. As Elisa waited for her turn to get a serving of whiskey, she approached Riley. "How come you foresaw Jackie failing the hearing and didn't warn her?"

Riley shrugged. "If there's one thing I've learned this year, it's that too much knowledge can only lead to frustration. If someone is destined to fail, they will, regardless of any warnings."

"But what if she could have prevented it?" Elisa pondered.

"Not everything is within our control," Riley replied, giving her a somber look that weighed heavy on Elisa's heart. His words made her feel like they were mere pawns in a cruel game with uncertain rules, rendering everything seemingly meaningless.

Urchin chimed in, "Riley is right. Life is a series of lessons. Some may be harsh, but they are necessary for growth."

"And what did you learn from your failures?" Elisa asked with a hint of teasing in her voice.

"That hard times are inevitable. But when they come, everyone needs a friend," Urchin responded as he filled Elisa's glass and handed it to her.

Elisa took a whiff of the brown liquid, its scent reminiscent of oak tree bark warmed by the summer sun. She exhaled and took a sip, feeling the warmth cascade down her throat and relax her body. Urchin was indeed a good friend, capable of bringing happiness to Jackie when she was ready. Yet, letting go of Jackie was proving to be a difficult task.

"So, what do you think of the drink?" Urchin inquired.

Elisa smiled. "I like it. Where did you get it, Urch?"

"From my dad's pantry. But if you ever meet him, don't mention it."

Theo laughed. "I've always said you could make a good thief."

"I'm not a thief!" Urchin protested. "And I never will be."

"This is the second time I've caught you stealing," Elisa remarked, handing her glass to Riley, who was next in line. "And I'm willing to bet you took this bottle because of Jackie. Again."

"Wrong guess, detective," Urchin said, clapping a pocket of his black shirt. Clearly, it was a small square box inside. "I got her something better."

"A special farewell present?" Elisa blinked, feeling a mix of dizziness, unsure if it was from the drink or jealousy.

"Yes. In the morning, I visited a jewelry store and bought a special gift."

Elisa frowned. "Who gives expensive jewelry to a friend?"

"You do," Theo reminded her. "You gave Jackie a pendant as a New Year gift –"

She turned to him; her eyes bore into his. "Thank you for mentioning it, but still..."

"Relax. It's just a small present," Urchin interjected, glancing around as the silence of onlookers settled upon them.

Elisa bit her tongue, mindful of the rules. As the guardian, Walter, had warned her, there was a one-year no-dating rule in place, which would expire the following day. "Okay," she said, adjusting her hair, styled in a long plait adorned with small forget-me-nots. "As they say, a little attention never hurts anyone. After all, that's why I suggested throwing this party."

"Exactly." Urchin nodded. "Well, Jackie might arrive any minute. I'll go check the entrance."

The cadets around them nodded in agreement and made their way back to their tables. As Urchin departed, Elisa gazed up at the deep blue sky, the sun casting golden hues on the rooftops, serving as a reminder of the impending conclusion of the day. It was the final day of her freshman cadet year. Despite the challenges she had faced, she had nearly made it through.

Carrying her backpack in one hand, Jackie strolled towards the dorms. Despite the day taking a turn for the worse, the warmth and coziness of the spring evening made it perfect for a leisurely walk. The evening sun hung low in the sky, its rays gently caressing her tired face.

Following the trail, she found herself in the deserted front yard of the dorms. Jackie stopped by an empty wooden bench, immersing herself in the quietude and pondering where everyone had vanished.

"Here you are!" Howard's voice startled her.

Turning to face him, Jackie greeted him with a simple "Hey."

Clad in his black uniform, Howard held a small velvet box. "I knew you could use a pick-me-up."

"Has Riley seen it? Seen how I messed up?" Jackie asked.

Howard nodded.

Feeling disheartened, Jackie sighed. "I feel like such a fool."

"You aren't a fool." Howard walked over to the bench, patting the wooden seat, and gestured for Jackie to join him. "When you truly believe in something, you always hope for the best. And I think that's beautiful – to keep hope alive despite everything."

She gave him a weary look. "What do you believe in?"

"In you," he replied with a smile.

Jackie blushed. Howard had been nothing but supportive and kind all this time. Since their kiss in winter, he had never pressured her about their relationship status and had always been there for her when she needed him. She couldn't help but wonder when he would grow tired of waiting.

"The deadline for the summer training application is tomorrow," he mentioned.

"I know. Don already reminded me," she said, placing her backpack on her lap. "I just haven't decided where to apply yet."

Howard sighed. "Jackie, listen. I think I'm tired of waiting –"

"Oh."

He locked eyes with her. "I mean, I was waiting for your application so we could go together, but I think that was foolish. So, I've decided to apply to the local Guardian House."

"In Middle Lake? That's a good choice, and it's close to your home," she remarked.

He nodded. "I believe gaining experience with a strong guardian team in the capital is the right move. It will also benefit my future career."

"That's a wise decision."

"Yes. Plus," Howard lowered his voice. "Today, I overheard something about the local guardian team."

"What's that?"

"They will be selecting two students tomorrow for a special undercover mission. It's an opportunity for me to test myself in a real criminal case and build my reputation."

"How do you know if you'll be chosen?"

"I can only hope."

"Who knows..." Jackie shrugged, though she knew the truth. Howard was referring to the operation involving catching drug dealers. When she first entered the academy, Don had shown her and Elisa real drugs, a bag of Moon Dust, and mentioned that one of them would be involved in that investigation.

Howard gave her an intriguing look. "I do know one thing for sure – it's the beginning of a new chapter in your life."

Jackie held her breath, wondering what he meant.

Howard smiled and gave her a small red box. "This is a gift for you."

Opening the box, Jackie discovered a thin silver chain with a snow-white crystal hanging from it. "A memory crystal?!" she exclaimed, her eyes widening in surprise.

She had dreamed about memory crystals ever since learning about them in the *Stones and Minerals* book. These rare crystals could serve as temporary vessels for various spells, with this particular one having the ability to record sounds.

Howard took the chain and opened the tiny lock. Jackie turned away, lifting her hair to allow him to fasten it around her neck. As the lock clicked into place, she turned back to him, touching her new pendant.

"It fits you perfectly," Howard remarked.

"This present must be too expensive."

He smiled. "Perhaps. But you deserve it."

She laughed and embraced him, feeling grateful for his thoughtfulness. What a wonderful guy he was. It seemed foolish to continue harboring feelings for someone else. She knew she should let go of Elisa and choose Howard, but it would entail yet another deception.

Leaning back, she gazed into his warm eyes, finding solace in his comforting presence. "I don't know what to say. I hadn't even planned on celebrating."

Howard stood up and took her hand. "Don't worry. We've arranged something special for you."

"Who exactly?" Jackie inquired.

He gave her a mischievous look. "Let's find out together."

As they entered the spacious backyard of the dorm, they were greeted by all the guys from their group who were waiting for them. The group surrounded them, offering applause and cheers.

"Screw the first trial!" they shouted in unison.

Among them was Elisa, looking stunning in her light-blue dress adorned with tiny blue flowers in her golden plait. *Forget-me-nots.* She smiled, admiring Jackie's new pendant. "You look perfect."

"Thank you."

Elisa planted a kiss on her cheek, sending shivers down her spine. Thankfully, Howard was nearby, offering her a glass of champagne.

"Bottoms up!" someone called out.

Jackie downed the glass, feeling the bubbles tickle her nose. She wiped her mouth, laughing. While she wasn't particularly fond of drinking, it did help calm her racing heart at that moment.

Amidst the personal drama she was facing, Jackie found solace in the fun and camaraderie of student life. She had never been one to seek the spotlight, but on this day, she embraced the attention and enjoyed every moment of it. Laughter filled the air as they danced and played the game *All the Stars*, where they placed cards with the names of famous individuals on their foreheads and tried to guess who they were. The festivities continued with more dancing and champagne, creating a lively and carefree atmosphere that allowed Jackie to forget her worries momentarily and simply revel in the joy of the present moment.

After indulging a bit too much in the drinks, especially whenever she caught sight of Elisa, Jackie found herself in a haze of intoxication. She proudly showed off her new crystal to the guys, who recorded silly messages and songs with it. However, as the night progressed, her memories became fragmented and disjointed, akin to shards of drunk recollections. This experience served as a stark reminder of why mind readers should never overindulge in alcohol. Given the nature of her Gift, the effects of alcohol caused a chaotic mix-up in her mind, making it challenging for her to piece together her own memories.

Later that night, Howard carried her to her room, with Elisa assisting him in settling her into bed. Elisa helped her undress and tucked her in with a soft blanket before Howard departed. As Jackie drifted off to sleep, she found herself consumed by a deep and anxious dream, the events of the evening swirling in her subconscious mind.

23

❧

Mind Games

When the sky turned gray in the early hours, Jackie opened her eyes. Elisa sat on her bed in her nightgown, gazing out the window. Jackie wrapped herself in a blanket and sat up, feeling her head spin.

"Why aren't you sleeping?" Jackie asked, her voice hoarse.

Elisa turned to her. "I was thinking."

"All night?" Jackie questioned.

Elisa nodded.

Jackie leaned against the wall, her heart burning in her chest as she continued to stare at the woman she loved.

Elisa turned her face back to the window, the sounds of the first carriages filling the street. Some farmers were likely hurrying to set up their goods on a trade street. Jackie noticed a teacup on her nightstand, filled with her favorite mint tea. Elisa must have prepared it for her, and Jackie was quite thirsty. She drank it down to the bottom.

Elisa watched her with sadness in her beautiful dark-blue eyes.

"What were you thinking about?" Jackie inquired, placing the empty cup on the nightstand.

Elisa sighed. "Of you."

Her heart sank. Elisa seemed to be toying with her like a cat with a silly mouse. "Tell me."

"I don't want to talk about it."

Jackie squeezed her blanket tightly in her hands, her knuckles turning almost white. It was enough. She stood up. "Then let's play a game."

Elisa gave her a confused look. "What do you mean?"

Jackie sat on her bed in front of her. "We won't talk, we'll show instead."

"Didn't we have enough charades last night?"

Instead of answering, Jackie continued to tease her. "Are you afraid of something?"

Elisa sneered. "No!"

"Then let's do it." Jackie raised her hand.

She moved closer and clapped her palm. "Fine!"

Jackie looked into Elisa's eyes, smiling. It was incredibly easy to engage her. Now, she needed to be careful not to scare her away.

"Who goes first?" Elisa asked.

"You. Ask any question, and I'll answer without words," Jackie challenged.

"Ok." Elisa paused, then asked, "How drunk are you right now?"

Jackie raised her hand and put her thumb to her index finger, then slowly moved them apart until there was an inch between them.

"Really?" Elisa narrowed her eyes.

Jackie smiled and made it two inches. They burst out laughing.

"Okay, my turn," Jackie said once their laughter subsided.

Elisa's eyes sparkled. "Go ahead."

"How badly do you want me?" Jackie asked, looking at her without blinking. *Elisa Palmer*, she thought, *brave with men and damn scared with women.* Who knew what was going on in her mysterious head?

They were supposed to leave for summer training the next day, and Jackie wouldn't see Elisa for three months. But in that moment, they were here and now, sitting in front of each other. Jackie felt like she was on the edge, anticipating Elisa pushing her away. She was prepared to hear the ugly truth and face rejection, as she couldn't bear the weight of her desire any longer.

Instead, Elisa hugged her shoulders and kissed her. Her lips were soft and tender, and Jackie melted into her embrace. When Elisa pulled back, Jackie opened her mouth, ready to reveal everything she had kept hidden.

Elisa placed her index finger on Jackie's lips. "Hush-hush," she whispered. "No words."

Jackie smiled in agreement. Sometimes, words can ruin the best moments.

Then they kissed again, their embrace tight as a blanket fell to the floor. Jackie helped Elisa remove her nightgown, and it landed softly on the wooden floor, leaving Elisa in her naked beauty. The first rays of sunlight touched her messy hair, her shoulders, and her full breasts.

Jackie took Elisa's hands in hers and gently pushed her back onto the pillows. She kissed Elisa's body slowly, starting from her neck and trailing down to her belly. She breathed in the tender aroma of Elisa's silky skin, feeling her tremble under her soft touches, eager for more. Jackie let her passion guide her to sacred places where no one had been before.

She was determined to explore Elisa fully, and she didn't stop until Elisa squeezed her shoulders tightly, unable to contain a lascivious moan.

Then, they began the game again from the beginning.

Elisa moved the heavy curtains aside, allowing daylight to flood the room. Jackie rolled onto her back and moaned, unwilling to accept the reality that she had to leave the bed. Every muscle in her body ached.

Sitting in the corner, Elisa smiled. "Wake up and shine."

"Can I have five more minutes?" Jackie asked weakly.

"It's already breakfast time."

Jackie sat up, her head feeling as heavy as iron. She squinted and glanced around, realizing she wasn't in her own bed. Weirdly, she was in Elisa's bed, completely naked under the sheet.

"What the heck happened last night?" Jackie inquired. The effects of drinking hit her hard, and it was embarrassing to admit it. She knew her memories would return eventually, but at that moment, she was completely blacked out.

Elisa knitted her eyebrows. "What do you remember?"

"Not a damn thing," Jackie said, rubbing her forehead.

"Well, maybe it's for the best." Elisa stared out of the open window. "You know what, nothing serious. You just fell into my bed, and I left you here."

"I'm so sorry."

"Don't be sorry," Elisa replied with a sly grin. "It was actually fun."

Then Elisa stood up and walked to the door. Pausing at the threshold, she glanced back. "The ceremony is in half an hour. Please, pull yourself together and come down to the kitchen."

Jackie's stomach rumbled loudly.

"I'll get you some oatmeal. Food for champions," Elisa said with a wink before walking away.

Jackie dressed quickly, trying to maintain her balance. Her clothes from the previous night were strewn on the floor, along with Elisa's nightgown. *What a mess!* She touched her neck, where Howard's gift, the memory crystal, was safely secured.

Looking in the mirror, Jackie saw a tired reflection staring back at her. Since autumn, her hair had grown to shoulder length, and she appreciated her new look. While brushing her hair, she noticed a blue mark on her neck, causing her heart to skip a beat.

She rubbed the mark on her neck, hoping it would disappear like a spot of dirt, but it stubbornly remained. *Because it's not dirt,* she realized. *It's a kiss mark!*

In shock, she slid down to the floor. Her lips muttered swear words she had picked up during a year of studying in a male-dominated environment. Actually, she had learned most of them from Elisa. Damn, she had been too drunk last night, which meant... Well, at best, she had kissed someone, but at worst... It was pathetic. Jackie gazed at her pale reflection. Elisa knew something. In the morning, Elisa looked at her slyly and said it was fun. *What did she mean by that?*

More than anything, Jackie wanted to hide in her room until everyone left for their training. However, she had learned an important lesson that year – if she wanted to become a guardian, she must put her emotions aside and face reality. It meant Jackie had to go to the dining room and confront the situation head-on.

The crystal on her neck glowed, and Jackie sighed. If she had used it the previous night, it might help her make sense of what had happened. With shaking fingertips, she touched the crystal.

"Listening," she commanded.

The room got filled with sounds of rustling sheets and kisses. Cold sweat trickled down her back as she listened intently, afraid of recognizing the voices she might hear. But she needed to know what had transpired.

Then, she heard her own moan and Elisa's voice whispering, "I love you so much."

The sounds faded away, leaving Jackie stunned. She didn't know how long she sat on the floor, her head in her hands. The spinning in her head ceased as all the memories and fragments came flooding back, and she remembered everything. However, now that she knew the truth, she wished she had remained in the dark because she had no idea how to handle her newfound knowledge.

24

A Chosen One

Downstairs, everyone sat at the big table, enjoying their morning tea and coffee. Jackie adjusted her black silk scarf, which draped elegantly around her neck. Then she made her way over to where Elisa had placed a plate of oatmeal for her. She took a seat.

"You look like crap, Jack," one of the guys remarked.

Ignoring the comment, she scooped up a spoonful of cold porridge and popped it into her mouth. Glancing up, she locked eyes with Simon, the most irritating member of their group.

"Oh, shut it," Jackie retorted.

The guys around the table chuckled.

"Come on, we all had a blast last night," Elisa chimed in.

Jackie shot her a look of disappointment. "Yes, I remember."

Elisa narrowed her eyes, and Jackie met her gaze without blinking. "I remember everything," she reiterated.

"Everything?" Elisa asked.

Jackie nodded.

Howard tugged at her elbow, diverting her attention. "The ceremony starts in five minutes."

Jackie knitted her brow. "Which ceremony are you guys talking about?"

"Someone seems to have a serious memory issue," Howard said with a chuckle.

Jackie burst into laughter. It was awkward, but at that moment, she was unable to contain herself. Tears welled up in her eyes.

Elisa handed her a handkerchief. "We must attend the ceremony and take our guardian oaths. Afterward, we can go upstairs and talk."

"Why do we need to talk?" Jackie wiped her face. "You already said it was just for fun." Elisa attempted to pat her shoulder, but Jackie pushed her hand away. "Enough with the lies."

Elisa remained silent, her cheeks flushing as she breathed heavily.

One of the guys laughed. "Looks like the girls are having a disagreement!"

"That's quite the spectacle," another chimed in.

Jackie dropped her spoon and stood up. "There is no disagreement! The ceremony starts in five minutes, and I will be there."

Howard also rose from his seat. "Let's go then."

They stood in a line in the front yard – thirty-six student guardians, with only two women among them. These cadets had just completed their freshman year at the Academy, where they were being trained to potentially become detectives, lawyers, or engineers skilled in creating potions and spells.

The 'special undercover mission' was scheduled to commence immediately following the ceremony. Jackie gazed up at the cloudy sky, silently hoping that Elisa would be chosen. It would buy her some time to gather her thoughts before their impending conversation.

Glancing to her left, Jackie spotted Elisa standing on the opposite side of the yard. When their eyes met, Elisa quickly averted her gaze. Jackie gritted her teeth in frustration. She was seething with anger towards Elisa for keeping her in the dark about the events of last night, and she doubted whether Elisa had any intention of coming clean.

Fingering the pendant hanging around her neck, which contained a memory crystal, Jackie couldn't shake the memory of Elisa's parting words: "*I love you.*" Was it just a lie? Was everything merely a game to Elisa?

The sound of a horn cut through the air, prompting the cadets to turn their attention towards the wide porch. The head teacher, Don, emerged from the building, flanked by two guardians. One of the guardians struck a chord of recognition in Jackie – with his round face and tousled hair, he appeared to be in his mid-30s, just like Don. It suddenly clicked in her mind – he was the one who had rescued her from the lake after the winter accident. Catching her eye, he offered a warm smile, to which Jackie responded in kind.

Don positioned himself at the center of the porch and raised his hand, signaling for silence. The gentle rustle of the wind through the trees was the only sound that filled the air. "Dear cadets," Don began, his voice carrying across the yard, "I congratulate each of you on successfully completing your first year and passing your final exams. Many of you have already applied to join one of the three Guardian Houses for practical training."

His gaze lingered on Jackie. "For those who have not yet submitted their applications, I must remind you that the deadline is midnight tonight!"

Jackie nodded. Right, she needed to make her decision today; any delay would render it too late. Elisa had chosen Santos, where her friend resided, and Jackie could opt to follow her there.

"Now, let's make it official," Don declared, raising his hands as the golden dragon atop the rooftop began to glow, casting a radiant light akin to a miniature sun.

Mesmerized, Jackie gazed at the soft light emanating from the dragon, feeling a sense of warmth envelop her heart. She felt a deep connection to this sacred brilliance and considered it an honor to stand among these individuals – the guardians.

Following the lead of her fellow students, she placed her left hand over her chest and recited the oath along with Don.

"Today, I take the oath to fight,
To carry hope through darkest nights,
Protecting every human being
From the injustice that I see.

Despite the hardships and the pain,
I'll choose the right and honest way.
Today, I swear with all my heart –
I am a guardian of Light."

Jackie smiled, savoring the moment of inner peace before opening her eyes. The glow from the dragon statue on the roof had faded, but the yard seemed to be bathed in a brighter light as the clouds parted, allowing the sun's gentle rays to filter through.

"Beautiful," Howard whispered beside her.

Jackie turned to him, surprised to find Howard in close proximity throughout the ceremony. "Yes, I feel so... refreshed."

"That's because Don used special ritual magic," Howard explained, gesturing towards the porch. "Look, here comes the final part."

A guardian handed Don a letter, which he opened with a chuckle before addressing the assembled cadets. "Today, you have the opportunity to participate in a special mission alongside the guardians of Middle Lake city. They have selected participants based on their Gifts. When I call out your Gift, step forward and choose a partner whom you believe is the most suitable to work with."

"Invisibility is quite rare," Howard remarked, rubbing his hands together eagerly. "If they select me, I'll have you on my team."

"Thank you," Jackie replied.

Don waved the letter in the air and announced the selected participant. "A mind reader."

Jackie blinked in surprise as all eyes turned towards her, but she remained rooted to the spot.

Howard nudged her shoulder gently. "Go!"

Taking a deep breath, she made her way to the porch and stood beside Don.

"Congratulations," he said.

The guardian, who had been her savior, approached and extended his hand in greeting. His blue eyes twinkled as he introduced himself, "Walter Mills."

"I'm Jackie Robinson," she responded, a sense of gratitude washing over her. "I remember you. You saved me in the winter. Thank you for that."

"Always a pleasure," Walter said before turning his attention to the expectant crowd.

As she stood there, Jackie decided that whatever had transpired before that moment was inconsequential now. She needed to focus on the task at hand and select her partner for the upcoming case. Elisa shot her a curious glance, but Jackie couldn't choose her. Their earlier rift could lead to further misunderstandings, and it wouldn't be deemed professional. Additionally, selecting another woman among a predominantly male group of guardians could be seen as provocative.

She glanced over at Howard, who was eager to be her partner. Jackie shook her head, feeling a pang of guilt for neglecting him. While he was caring and supportive, she knew that his emotional attachment could potentially complicate the case. Instead, her eyes sought out Theo in the crowd. With his exceptional intelligence, he seemed like the ideal partner for this mission.

"Theodore Thomás," she announced firmly.

Theo's face lit up with a smile as he made his way to the porch, where he exchanged a handshake with guardian Walter Mills. Jackie avoided meeting the eyes of the onlookers, anticipating their disapproval of her choice. However, she had to maintain a clear boundary between her work and personal life. This decision allowed her to focus solely on her guardian career, free from any distractions.

25

Miss and Mister Chillicothe

The Guardian House appeared to be gorgeous, and not only from the outside. In the wide corridor, their steps echoed over black marble floors. Theo walked along the walls, marveling at the paintings in golden frames – scenes from guardians' lives. The men in black uniforms stood on different backgrounds, using their magic. One of the guardians had a Lightning Gift, like Elisa. Some of them moved the subjects with the power of the mind – Telekinesis, the most popular Gift among all mages. Then he found a guy who held a ring of fire in his arms.

"Look, it's me," he said to Jackie in a whisper.

"Impressive," she replied, looking around. "I don't see my Gift here. It's probably hard to capture it in a picture."

"Actually, mind-reading Gifts are very rare among men."

She widened her eyes. "How come?"

"Just biology. It's mostly found among women because of your nature – women are more empathic."

She smiled. "Now I remember – once Laura explained to me how it works. She said that men are more likely to have strong destructive Gifts – to fight and protect."

"Exactly," Theo replied, turning to the pictures. *Why must every-one mention Laura?*

Jackie touched his elbow. "Sorry."

"For what?"

"You always pull a face when someone says her name."

He frowned. No, Jackie couldn't read his thoughts without his permission. He simply needed to take control of himself. "Let's just focus on this mission, OK?" he suggested.

"Sounds good to me."

"I've heard that the guardian chief is strict," Theo said, changing the subject.

"He isn't that bad," Jackie replied, her cheeks suddenly blush-ing. "You'll see."

Does she know the chief? Theo wondered. He kept the question to himself. After all, he had plenty of time to figure it out.

The corridor ended, and the guardians who followed them opened the massive door. They walked into a round hall where a dozen guardians sat around a long table. At the end of the table, a gray-haired man with intelligent blue eyes was waiting for them.

"Welcome," he said.

It was Trevor Harland, the chief of the Guardian House and one of the most powerful men in the capital. *It's better not to let him down,* Theo remarked silently. Pressing his hand to his chest, he bowed as a gesture of polite greeting.

They took their seats and prepared to listen. The guardians around looked at them with curiosity, mainly focusing on Jackie. One of them was Walter Mills, the man who greeted them on the stage. He was now sitting next to the chief, and Theo assumed that he had an important role in this mission.

"So," Trevor addressed the guardians, "Here are the fresh cadets for our secret operation. Jaqueline Robinson, a mind reader, and Theodore Thomás, who has the Gift of Fire."

One of the guardians glanced at her. "With all due respect, chief, is she the only mind reader around?"

Jackie gave her opponent a sharp look. "It's not my fault that Mind Reading Gifts are rare among men. Women are more empathic; didn't you know that?"

He sneered and shook his head.

Satisfied, she glanced at Theo, who gave her an encouraging smile.

"That's correct," Chief Trevor said to the guardian. "And it's actually beneficial for our team to have a woman. No one would suspect she's working for us."

Theo sighed but said nothing. Most people underestimated women as future guardians, and a year ago, he was just the same. Things had changed for him, but not for those guys sitting beside them. Honestly, both Theo and Jackie were considered inexperienced rookies. They could do nothing but try to prove themselves through their work. Setting aside the harsh comments, Chief Trevor was right – Jackie being a woman gave her an advantage in working undercover. Perhaps that's why they chose her in the first place.

Chief Trevor waved his hand, and Walter stood up to come to the board. He began to explain their roles in this undercover operation.

The roles were relatively straightforward – Theo and Jackie were to pretend to be wealthy young siblings, the Chillicothe, for one evening. The capital, Middle Lake, was a popular tourist destination, and a local criminal gang took advantage of this by selling drugs in the nightclubs.

The guardians had been organizing operations to arrest this gang for several years, but they had never succeeded. Even when they managed to apprehend a seller, it was impossible to reach the gang leaders because the lower-level members did not possess the necessary information. Additionally, the sellers had their memories blocked after being caught – they were given a forgetful potion, rendering magic ineffective in extracting information.

Jackie's task was to approach the seller and read the information while it was accessible. They emphasized that even a small detail could be valuable – locations, faces of individuals, exchanged phrases. Her job was to memorize it all. Theo's role was to provide cover and protection in case of any danger.

Jackie touched the memory crystal on her chest and glanced at Chief Trevor. "Should I record the criminals to have proof?"

He shook his head. "I see you can use the crystals, which is good. But wearing a memory crystal on your neck is a dumb idea – it will give away your intentions of recording them."

The guardians around chuckled at the remark.

Jackie lowered her eyes. "I understand."

"Don't worry," Chief Trevor said in an encouraging tone. "We'll provide you with something smaller that you can use."

She nodded in acknowledgment.

Chief Trevor then turned to Theo. "Do you have any other questions?"

Theo scratched his chin, deep in thought. "If we're supposed to pretend to be wealthy, spoiled kids, we'll need appropriate outfits. How will we manage that?"

"That's a good question," Chief Trevor responded. "You'll be provided with everything you need in the locker rooms, and one of our team members will explain each of your roles in detail."

Two hours later, they stood in the expansive yard of the Guardian House, awaiting the arrival of their carriage. Jackie was dressed in heels and a long black dress with silver trimming. An elegant black choker adorned with rhinestones conveniently covered her kiss mark. Her hair was intricately braided, and a small hat completed her ensemble. A real emerald ring sparkled on her finger, catching the evening light and casting magnificent sparkles.

"Jackie, you should stop staring at the ring like that," Theo remarked.

She lowered her hand. Theo was dressed in an expensive suit, his red hair neatly brushed back. If she had encountered him on the street, she would never have guessed he was just an ordinary cadet.

"Maybe I just enjoy wearing my ring?" she retorted.

"You look as if you've never seen jewelry before."

Theo was right – her family wasn't poor, but she had never seen such a large gem up close. "See, that's why I chose you. You're smart."

He chuckled. "I bet that's not the only reason."

"What then?"

He shrugged. "I thought you would choose Urchin or Sparkle, but it's hard to choose between two best friends. Someone is bound to get hurt no matter what choice you make."

She sighed and adjusted her choker. "You have no idea."

The carriage, drawn by two raven horses, emerged from the far corner of the street. The horses' manes glistened in the rays of the setting sun.

Theo whistled. "The guardians always operate at the highest level."

"I've never seen such luxury," Jackie remarked.

"Me neither," Theo agreed.

An interest sparked in her green eyes. "I thought you came from a wealthy family, like most guys at the Academy."

He shook his head. "Not at all. I've spent my life reading and studying hard to become who I am. I always wanted to experience life from the perspective of a wealthy individual – no burdens, no responsibilities, just the enjoyment of life."

"Well, today, you have that chance."

As the carriage arrived in the yard, the horseman opened the door.

"Well, Miss Chillicothe, let's show them what we're made of," Theo said, offering her his elbow, which Jackie took.

26

On the Dark Side

The nightclub was located at the far end of the city, with loud music spilling out onto the busy night street. Their carriage came to a stop in front of the grand entrance. Following instructions, Jackie patiently waited as Theo emerged from the carriage, circled around, and offered her a helping hand.

With his assistance, she gracefully stepped out onto the pavement, the sound of her heels clicking with each step they took. The guard stationed at the entrance cast a scrutinizing gaze over them, his eyes lingering on her ring.

"Where are you from?" he inquired.

Jackie responded with a charming smile. "Esplendor."

The guard's eyes lit up with curiosity. "The capital of the Rocky Kingdom... Quite a distance to travel, isn't it?"

"I've just completed my studies, and my dear brother gifted me with a journey across the continent to gain new experiences," Jackie explained.

Theo took her hand and gallantly kissed it. "Any whim, my dear sis."

The guard nodded in acknowledgment and gestured for them to enter. The doors swung open behind him, and they walked hand in hand into the nightclub.

The spacious hall boasted a lofty ceiling adorned with garlands of yellow and violet night flowers wrapped around the pillars, casting a soft glow over the elegantly dressed figures within. Laughter filled the air as ladies in luxurious dresses mingled with gentlemen puffing on cigars, creating a haze of blue smoke that hung like a mist. The soothing melodies of guitars and violins added to the enchanting atmosphere.

Theo whispered in Jackie's ear, "Let's find a quiet corner."

She followed him to a secluded spot at the far end of the hall, where two plush chairs and an elegant side table awaited them. The ambiance was more subdued here, allowing them to converse without the din of the crowd.

A young girl in a form-fitting violet dress approached them with a menu, and they ordered a bottle of white wine, cheese, and shrimp. Jackie hesitated to drink, still reeling from the events of the previous night, but Theo insisted they simply keep full glasses on the table and take occasional sips to avoid arousing suspicion.

Jackie placed her full glass in front of her and scanned the room. "How long do you think this might take?"

Theo shrugged nonchalantly. "We'll have to wait and see."

She let out a sigh, her thoughts drifting to Elisa. While she no longer harbored any anger towards her, the inexplicable nature of her behavior left Jackie puzzled.

"So, what transpired between you and Sparkle?" Theo's question caught her off guard.

Jackie fixed him with a questioning gaze. "What do you know?"

He took a sip from his glass before responding. "I believe I know enough. You see, we've become good friends, so we're completely honest with each other. As I learned, lies only serve to complicate matters."

"Indeed," Jackie agreed, reflecting on the web of deceit that often required elaborate cover-ups. Whether it was the events of the previous night or her failed mission, her patience had worn thin, prompting her to seek Theo's advice. "Can I ask you something personal?"

"Of course," Theo replied, his bright blue eyes reflecting curiosity. "Your secrets are safe with me. I will never betray your trust or Sparkle's."

Jackie nodded, finding it challenging to broach her question delicately. She decided to start from the beginning. "It all began when I helped Elisa harness her Gift."

"Ah, yes, you crafted a spell," Theo recalled.

"Exactly."

"And then you shared a kiss," Theo added.

Jackie's heart skipped a beat. *He knows Elisa too well. If they are such close friends, what other secrets do they share?* Voicing her thoughts aloud, she asked, "So, you've been keeping her secret all this time."

"Indeed," Theo affirmed. "I suspect it may be the cause of the morning quarrel between you two."

"I'm at a loss for what to do next," Jackie confessed, twirling her glass between her fingers. The cool surface offered a brief respite, but it only served as a poison for her weary mind and soul.

"A heart-to-heart conversation might be beneficial," he suggested.

"That's the issue," Jackie lamented, lifting her tired gaze to meet his. "Elisa avoids discussing this matter altogether."

"You did have an argument, so I assume communication is still possible. You just have to keep trying."

"Perhaps it's not a question suited for a man... But what should I do? After she told me to forget about the night we shared?"

Theo took a prolonged sip from his glass, his gaze fixed on a distant point.

"Theo?" Jackie called out, hoping to snap him out of his reverie.

He turned towards her. "Well, firstly, not all the men are the same. And secondly..." he trailed off, struggling to find the right words. "Sorry, what was the question again?"

Disheartened by his response, Jackie shook her head. "Never mind. I see how much this topic confuses you."

"Sorry," Theo said, rubbing his forehead. "I promise to keep your secret. But Jackie, you must have an open conversation with her. I know it's daunting, but it's essentially a yes or no question – whether she wants a relationship or not."

"Fine, I'll talk to her tonight," Jackie replied softly. "Thank you."

As the music faded into the background, a round of enthusiastic applause filled the room. The atmosphere brightened as a young woman entered the hall, her melodious voice filling the space with a romantic ballad. Her poignant lyrics struck a chord within Jackie, causing her heart to ache.

She brushed away the tears that threatened to spill, the shimmering diamond ring on her finger catching the candlelight. The gem exuded a cold, sharp aura, much like Elisa's heart, harboring its own secrets within. Nestled at its base was a tiny memory crystal. With a simple touch, she could activate the crystal at any moment. Concealed within the ring, the crystal remained invisible to others.

Their wait was not prolonged as the singer began to weave her way through the tables. Theo seized the moment and approached her, whispering something in her ear. The woman blushed but continued her performance without missing a beat, casting furtive glances in their direction as she moved away.

Drawing closer to Theo to hear him clearly, Jackie asked, "What did you say to her?"

"Just trying to push our mission," Theo replied with a smile. "I have a feeling she might be aware of the Moon Dust supplier."

Jackie let out a deep sigh. Moon Dust was the drug that Don had introduced her and Elisa to on the day they first met. If only she had known that getting involved with Elisa would lead to such heartache! Nevertheless, she was determined to navigate this clandestine operation and apprehend the criminals involved.

A minute later, the waitress approached their table, casting a disapproving glance at Theo. "I was informed that you were rude to our singer."

Theo flashed his charming smile. "I offer my sincerest apologies. You see, my sister and I... We're in search of something unique. A pleasure that will leave us with unforgettable memories of this city. However, it appears I may have misjudged your establishment, so we won't trouble you any further."

The waitress studied them for a moment, deep in thought. Eventually, she gestured for them to follow her.

As they ventured into the narrow, dreary corridor, the stark contrast to the opulent hall was evident. The walls were covered with peeling layers of old, dark gray paint, casting a somber atmosphere. A solitary torch flickered at the far end, prompting them to rely on their Lights to illuminate the path ahead. This dimly lit setting was the ideal backdrop to utilize her Gift.

Jackie tapped Theo's shoulder twice, their prearranged signal, and he acknowledged her with a nod. Jackie quickened her pace, positioning herself near the waitress. With a deliberate "stumble," she feigned a fall, dropping her light-blue Light ball. The energy dispersed into shimmering fragments, resembling shards of ice that dissolved into the darkness.

Concerned, the waitress bent down beside her. "Are you okay?"

"Seriously?" Jackie feigned distress, rubbing her leg and adopting a petulant tone. "How could this possibly be okay?"

Theo approached them, holding a yellow Light in his hand. "This place gives me the creeps. Are you certain we should continue, sis?"

"I'm not sure," Jackie groaned, playing her part in the charade.

"I apologize," the waitress offered sincerely, her eyes wide with anxiety. She extended her hand to assist Jackie in standing up, and she accepted the gesture.

A touch. As soon as Jackie placed her palm on hers, her mind-reading Gift connected with the waitress's consciousness, allowing her to glimpse a flurry of vivid images. She swiftly sifted through the carousel of events that had unfolded in this place, revealing a multitude of secrets.

"Are you sure you're okay?" the waitress inquired once more.

Jackie opened her eyes, casting a disdainful glance at the waitress before rising to her feet. As they continued their journey, she held onto Theo's elbow for support.

Upon entering a small room, they were greeted by the flickering candlelight casting shadows across the walls. A man with a gray beard and piercing black eyes sat behind a desk, his eyebrows shooting up in surprise at their arrival.

The waitress approached the man and whispered something in his ear. He smiled and clasped his hands together, his voice resonating with a low, sharp tone akin to steel. "Finding our capital too dull for your tastes, are we?"

They exchanged glances, and Theo spoke up first. "Let's just say we've grown accustomed to a different lifestyle out West."

The man scrutinized him closely. "You seem too fresh. No one would believe you're into drugs. Perhaps the girl, though. She looks like she's nursing a massive hangover."

Theo was taken aback, rendered momentarily speechless by the man's astute observation.

Jackie chewed on her lip, contemplating their next move. Apparently, this man possessed a keen eye, and his intuition was sharp and unwavering. It was both impressive and perilous. Unlike the waitress, he was not easily deceived, and she needed to tread carefully with her choice of words. Thanks to her Gift, she was now privy to the various illicit activities taking place.

"That's correct," Jackie affirmed. "Our interests lie beyond drugs."

His expression became intrigued.

"We're here seeking a different form of entertainment," she continued, taking a step closer and placing her hands on the desk. This strategic move aimed to assuage his suspicions, as her bosom now aligned with his covetous gaze. "We've come to watch the fights."

The man leaned back in his chair, a chuckle escaping his lips. "And who might have informed you of that?"

Jackie responded with a cryptic smile. "I'd rather not disclose my sources. You understand, for safety purposes."

"Then you should be aware that it comes at a price," the man cautioned.

She scoffed and turned to Theo. "What do you think, bro?"

Theo smiled at her. "I'd say money is no issue."

Defeat

Once again, they found themselves in a carriage, but this time their eyes were covered with eyepatches. Unable to see the road, Theo could only guess that they hadn't traveled far from the city – the road felt smooth, and the journey was relatively short. Upon arrival, a silent man escorted them to a building.

As they entered, Theo's eyepatch was removed, and he was immediately greeted by a blinding light. It took him a moment to adjust to the brightness emanating from the numerous candles scattered throughout the room – on tables, shelves, and a chandelier hanging above a boxing ring. The hall was bustling with activity as people surrounded the ring, eagerly anticipating the upcoming show.

Theo hadn't had the opportunity to inquire about the fights Jackie had insisted on watching, but now it became clear without the need for explanation. This covert operation clearly had a hidden agenda, as they now found themselves in a secluded and heavily guarded location. Theo noted the presence of two guards stationed at both the front and back doors, as well as two more positioned at the bar. Their watchful gazes resembled that of hounds, sending shivers down his spine.

A man clad in a red shirt ascended the ring and bellowed, "Are you ready to witness blood?!"

The crowd erupted in cheers.

Jackie gripped Theo's elbow. While the spectators may have been prepared, she certainly was not. Theo acknowledged her uneasy condition with a supportive nod before guiding them closer to the ring.

They stood near an elderly couple dressed in opulent attire. The woman wore a diamond necklace adorning her tanned neck, her black hair streaked with gray meticulously styled. Her posture exuded confidence, hinting at her familiarity with such establishments. Sensing an opportunity, Theo initiated a conversation.

"Isn't it a lovely evening?" Theo inquired, aiming to engage her in dialogue.

"Indeed," she replied with a smile. "Today, they have fresh Incapables."

Theo struggled to maintain a neutral expression upon hearing the term 'Incapables' – people lacking magical abilities. They were a rare sight, often residing in secluded communities. However, some ventured into the city seeking employment as servants or housemaids. According to Elisa's accounts, many were descendants of women who had their magic stripped away.

"Incapables? How is that possible?" Jackie inquired.

The woman turned to Jackie. "You see, this year, there has been a surge in demand for Incapables in the city. Some of them actively participate in fights, and if they emerge victorious, they are granted full freedom."

Theo subtly reached for Jackie's hand, activating her ring with a concealed memory crystal. She gave a slight nod of approval. It was time to gather evidence and make their exit from this place.

"So, they make Incapables fight," Theo said, ensuring his voice remained steady. "That's intriguing. But who would truly grant freedom to an Incapable? The guardians are bound by the King's orders, and if they spot an Incapable without a permit on the streets..."

"Exactly. Eventually, they get arrested and killed as 'violators.'" The woman chuckled, her laughter akin to the creak of a heavy door. "Yet, these Incapables are too stupid to comprehend that."

Jackie took a deep breath before expressing her dismay. "That's awful."

"What's awful?" the woman inquired, her expression turning stern.

Jackie fell silent.

Theo offered the woman an apologetic smile. "We hail from the West, and it's disheartening that no one had thought of this idea before."

She scoffed and redirected her attention to the ring. "We've been dealing with Incapables like that for years. So, watch and learn."

Theo glanced at the woman's companion, a well-dressed gray-haired man who was now puffing on a cigar, releasing thick blue clouds. His gray mustache twitched as he observed the events in the ring.

"His face does seem familiar," Jackie whispered in Theo's ear. "I just can't recall where I've seen him before."

"Let's refrain from staring at people," Theo suggested, and Jackie didn't protest.

The light above the boxing ring intensified, eliciting whistles from the crowd. Two slender women entered the arena, waving to the spectators. Clad only in shimmering bikini strips that barely covered their intimate areas, they tantalized the already frenzied audience. One of the women sported copper bracelets on both hands, prompting Theo to furrow his brow. The guardians typically utilized special cuffs crafted from the same metal to inhibit magic channels and prevent criminals from wielding their powers. *Is it a coincidence?* His instincts vehemently disagreed.

As Theo scrutinized their faces, he recoiled. Though their lips curved into smiles, their eyes exuded a chilling emptiness.

The man on the ring chuckled. "Can you believe that one of them will soon be dead?"

The crowd erupted in excitement.

"It's time to leave," Theo declared.

Jackie remained rooted in place. "It's her."

"Her?" Theo inquired, his voice filled with confusion.

"Kathy. The woman I defended in court," Jackie said, her eyes widening like two vast abysses. "Shit, we have to stop the fight!"

Theo's mind reeled. If Jackie was correct, it meant they had stumbled into a dire situation, and they needed to leave immediately. The cacophony of voices, laughter, and whistles provided the perfect cover for their escape. Grabbing her hand, Theo nearly shouted, "We need to go. Now!"

A nearby couple turned their attention towards them, and the man's gaze bore into Theo, sending a shiver down his spine.

A waiter materialized from behind. "Is everything alright?"

"Apologies, my sister isn't feeling well," Theo quickly fabricated. "Where is the ladies' room?"

The waiter gestured towards a corner, and Theo guided Jackie in that direction, their hands tightly intertwined.

Leaving Jackie against the wall in the corridor, Theo approached a small window near the ceiling. Time was of the essence, as people frequented the washrooms regularly. Theo covered his eyes and extended his hand. Flames erupted from his fingers, shattering the window with a resounding crash as glass shards scattered across the floor.

Fortunately, the commotion in the main hall masked the noise of the shattered window. Amidst the clamor of the crowd, a woman's desperate cry pierced through, causing Theo's heart to sink. One person was dying on that ring, and another was on the brink of death, unaware. Despair washed over him. There was nothing he could do at that moment.

Meanwhile, Jackie remained frozen against the wall, her breaths shallow and rapid. *Is it a panic attack?* Theo gently shook her shoulder. "Listen to me, Jackie. I know you're scared, but I found a way to get us out of here."

"How?" she asked weakly.

"I broke the window glass. So, I'll lift you, and then you'll assist me in climbing out of the window."

"Just like that," she remarked nervously. "We swore to protect *every human being*, and now we're backing down."

Theo tightened his grip on her shoulders. "I'm sorry, but they both violated the law and were sentenced to become Incapables."

"So, their lives don't matter," she whispered, a tear tracing down her cheek. She wiped it, her ring emitting a radiant inner light – the energy of the sounds captured by the crystal served as the evidence they had gathered.

"All lives matter," Theo said. "That's why we collected proof against them. We'll show your ring to Chief Trevor, so he'll shut down this place. But Jackie, we must get out of here first. It is the only way to make sure that woman's death won't be in vain."

"Alright," she finally relented. "Let's go."

Jackie removed her shoes, and Theo hoisted her up, supporting her waist as she climbed out into the verdant yard. The sun was setting, painting the sky in fiery hues on the horizon.

"What do you see?" Theo inquired.

"The city isn't too far," she replied, reaching out her hand to him. At that moment, chaos ensued.

The waiter burst into the corridor and started shouting, calling for security. Theo conjured a fireball to intimidate the approaching waiter, but it was too late – the sound of footsteps drawing near echoed in the corridor.

"Run!" Theo's urgent command pierced through the chaos. Jackie hesitated, but Theo reassured her, "My Gift will protect me, but you are in grave danger."

With a nod, she turned and sprinted away. Theo faced the entrance, flames dancing in both hands. *How long would it take for Jackie to reach the road and send a Light signal?* Uncertainty gnawed at him. Now alone, he braced himself for the confrontation with the guards in the main hall.

Stepping into the hall, Theo extended his arms, creating a massive ring of fire around him. The guards positioned themselves on either side, hands poised for attack. Drawing fire from the blazing ring, he directed a fiery blast towards the ceiling, showcasing his power. The guards hesitated, stepping back in uncertainty.

Amidst the chaos, screams erupted from the onlookers, mirroring the fear and panic of the women they had watched in the ring. Despite the commotion, he had no intention of harming the innocent bystanders.

"All of you," Theo bellowed at the top of his lungs, "Get the hell out of here before I reduce you to ashes!"

The crowd rushed towards the exit door, stumbling and shoving. Theo then turned his attention to the bar, where two other guards were supposed to be stationed, but they were nowhere to be seen. *What if they have Invisibility Gifts?* Theo thought with panic. Then he shook his head, reassuring himself. Even if they had the ability to turn invisible, they wouldn't be able to use active magic while under their shield.

Using the strength of his own power, Theo gestured with his hands, sending fireballs toward the tablecloths and wooden panels on the walls. The flames quickly spread, engulfing the surroundings and prompting the remaining people to evacuate even faster.

The smoke filled the room, weighing down Theo's breath and making it difficult to see. Crouching where the air was slightly clearer, he surveyed the now empty hall. The only figure remaining was a woman who had survived the brutal fight. She was lying on the ring with her arms outstretched. The glint of bracelets on her wrists caught the light of the flames, confirming her identity as Kathy, the one Jackie had failed to protect in court. Though barely clinging to life, she still drew breath, indicating that she could potentially be rescued.

Feeling the numbness creeping through his limbs, Theo recalled the warning about the physical toll his Gift would exact. With each passing moment, he grew weaker. Removing his magic shield in the ring, he reached out and touched Kathy's hand. A faint pulse throbbed in her wrist, and her fingertips remained unscathed, signifying that her power was intact but blocked by the cuffs.

Despite the stinging smoke irritating his eyes, Theo leaned in closer, gasping for the last remnants of clean air. A shield. He needed to cover them both with it to save her.

The woman's tormented gaze met Theo's as she implored, "Please, go."

"No," he whispered, his parched lips barely moving.

She withdrew her hand from his grasp. "Leave me alone."

Theo's fists clenched, his dwindling energy and patience coalescing. *Why are women so stubborn?* She was resigned to her fate, prepared to die here. Now, he had to recall the lines from the book he had studied on how to communicate with victims. "Kathy, please listen. I came to save you."

"Why?"

He coughed heavily before responding, "You can be a witness in court. Those people who sent you here... They won't escape justice."

Amidst tears, she smiled wryly. "You're amusing. Even if you interfere, it won't change a thing."

"It will. I promise. You will reclaim your life."

"What life?" she retorted bitterly. "Playing a role to amuse you? Being obedient and feeling shame when it becomes unbearable? No, thank you. I'm exhausted from it all."

"You just need help," Theo insisted, his head spinning as he placed his hands on Kathy's shoulders. With no time to spare, he created a shield around them, providing a momentary reprieve from the suffocating smoke.

Kathy drew in a deep breath, then narrowed her eyes and forcefully knocked her forehead against his. Theo lost his balance and tumbled backward, landing on the ring floor littered with shards of glass and dried blood. His shield disintegrated instantly. Through blurred vision, he watched as Kathy sprinted towards the wall of fire. A flaming mass crashed down from the ceiling, striking her. Overwhelmed, he closed his eyes.

The next thing Theo recalled was the sensation of someone's hands gripping him under his shoulders, dragging his body across the floor. The fire continued to rage within the building, but the intensity had lessened within the hall. A thick haze of smoke lingered near the ceiling, casting a shadow over the remnants of the once elegant furniture. Breathing was a challenge, and moving his muscles felt like his skin was ablaze.

"Why are you so damn heavy?" Jackie's grumbling voice reached his ears, eliciting a faint smile from Theo. They hadn't captured her, which was a relief.

"How much do you weigh, seriously?" Jackie continued to complain as she steadfastly pulled him towards the safety of the corridor. The coolness of the stone walls promised some respite from the heat.

In the corridor, Jackie took his hand, likely to check his pulse, before darting off to the restroom. The fresh air in the corridor helped Theo regain his ability to breathe more easily.

As a wave of cold water cascaded over his body, drenching him from head to toe, Theo drew in a deep breath and sat up. Jackie stood nearby, holding an empty metal bucket in her hands. "Welcome back!" she greeted him.

Wiping his throbbing forehead, Theo took in his torn and charred attire, his skin marred with deep scratches. Despite his injuries, he was grateful to be alive. Speaking in a hushed tone, he asked, "What happened?"

Jackie settled down beside him. "I sent a signal, and our team of guardians will be here any minute. I thought you needed to cool down before facing them."

Theo released a sigh of relief. "Great job!"

Late at night, Theo and Jackie found themselves seated in the chief's office at the end of a long table. Two guardians, including Walter Mills, sat nearby, their expressions reflecting concern as Chief Trevor berated them.

"Do you realize the gravity of your mistakes?" Chief Trevor's voice thundered, causing Jackie to wish she could shrink and hide beneath the chair.

"We do," Theo responded calmly.

Jackie glanced at him, noting that Theo had changed into a black shirt and carried the scent of healing herbs prescribed by the doctor to aid in his recovery. Today, she had learned that his destructive Gift could have serious repercussions – prolonged use of his fire magic had left him dehydrated. Despite the risks, he had resorted to using his power to evacuate the building and protect himself. Regrettably, he had been unable to save the potential witness, Kathy, despite his efforts.

Jackie had changed back into her uniform, but the lingering scent of burnt barbecue clung to her, a reminder of the chaos they had faced. She knew it would take weeks to rid her hair of the acrid smell. With a heavy sigh, she realized that the unpleasant odor might be the least of her worries if Chief Trevor decided to expel her from the Academy for her disobedience.

Chief Trevor, arms crossed over his chest, demanded, "Please, explain."

Theo exhaled wearily. "Initially, I had no intention of setting the place on fire – my aim was to intimidate the criminals and drive them off. Once we were discovered, I should have followed Jackie and provided cover in case of danger."

"Do you believe you would have had enough time to escape through the window?" Chief Trevor inquired.

"I wasn't certain. That's why I stayed behind and instructed Jackie to flee," Theo said.

"That decision wasn't necessarily a mistake. Continue," Chief Trevor prompted.

Theo sighed once more. "Well, we should not have ventured to that club in the first place. We could have departed after Jackie gleaned the information from the waitress."

Jackie cast a sorrowful glance at Theo. He was correct in pointing out that it was her decision to delve deeper that had led to their failure in the case.

Chief Trevor redirected his attention to her. "Cadet Robinson, why did you two go to the fighting club?"

She gasped, her voice trembling with emotion. "Because I saw it! I learned so many things that they were concealing! The drugs are just the tip of the iceberg."

Feeling Theo's reassuring touch on her palm, Jackie fell silent.

Chief Trevor regarded them intently, his gaze unwavering. He picked up the emerald ring, still shimmering with the recorded evidence, and twirled it between his fingers. "You do have compelling evidence. However, the issue lies in the fact that we were already aware of these clubs, and yes, the drugs are merely a fraction of the problem. I would never have assigned you rookies to investigate the fighting club." Giving Jackie a piercing look, he continued, "Do you understand why you are still alive?"

Shaking her head, Jackie awaited his explanation.

"Because the criminals were in a hurry to flee and cover their tracks. Otherwise, they would have eliminated both of you!" Chief Trevor hurled the ring against the wall. It landed with a resounding clunk before rolling under the table. "This evidence is worthless! And after you scared them away, they'll dispose of the witnesses and go into hiding, plain and simple!"

Jackie's gaze fell to the floor, the chief's words piercing her like glass shards. As painful as they were, they resonated with truth.

She could have concocted any excuse to depart the nightclub after reading the waitress. Instead, she had delved deeper, leading Theo into a dangerous situation at the fighting club where his life had been endangered.

"I'm truly sorry," she murmured.

Chief Trevor approached, slamming his fist on the table. "You failed in this case the moment you deviated from your assigned task. Your duty was to gather information from the personnel and depart. Why did you choose to go further?"

Jackie found herself unable to provide a response, her gaze fixed on the chief in silent contemplation.

Trevor Harland was the last person Jackie wanted to disappoint. He had played a pivotal role in her admission to the Academy, and she promised to keep their agreement secret. When she had first arrived in Middle Lake, distraught and pleading for help at the hospital doors, he had been the only guardian to approach her, summoning a doctor to her aid. Tears welled up in Jackie's eyes as she recalled how he had saved her life, only for her to let him down now.

Theo stood up, addressing the chief. "It's not her fault, sir."

Jackie wiped her eyes but remained frozen, observing the unfolding scene.

Chief Trevor's brow furrowed, a vein pulsing on his forehead. "What do you mean?"

"When Jackie informed me about the illegal clubs, I insisted on visiting one. I believed it was an opportunity to prove my worth. Now I realize how selfish and reckless that decision was, and I don't know how to earn your forgiveness."

Chief Trevor let out a heavy sigh. "Cadet Thomás, you may leave now. And do not return here again."

28

A Letter

They walked along the quiet, sleeping buildings on the way back to the Academy. The night was warm and still, with the green tree barks glowing and illuminating the empty street. It was nearly midnight, and a crystal of memory shone on her chest, holding the memory of Elisa's whispered words from the night before: *I love you.* Jackie still couldn't quite grasp the sincerity behind those words – was it just another game, or did Elisa truly mean it?

"Not too bad for our first mission, huh?" Theo interjected, breaking her reverie.

She shot him a suspicious look. "Why did you lie to the chief?"

Theo shrugged nonchalantly. "We both made the wrong decision. I knew what was happening when you engaged with the man in the basement, and I could have stopped you at any time. But I didn't."

"But still... you didn't have to protect me in front of the chief," she insisted.

"I wanted to," he replied, lifting his gaze to the night sky. "It's all right; I hope it serves as a valuable lesson for both of us. Besides, I don't really care about Trevor Harland because tomorrow I'm heading to Triville."

She narrowed her eyes. "Why are you being so kind? I thought you would do anything for your career. But putting your reputation at risk —"

"Because you're a woman," Theo replied.

"So what?"

He rubbed his wrist, deep in thought. "I mean, it's acceptable for me to make a mistake, but you can't afford to. If you do, people will always attribute it to your gender and use it to judge others after you. Especially the older, more traditional guardians. They fear change and will always try to label you as too weak for this job."

Jackie's heart raced. Prejudice was her biggest fear when she first arrived at the Academy. It was precisely what had happened on her first day of studies, mainly due to Theo's inappropriate prank. "Since when do you care so much?"

"I think a part of me always did," Theo admitted, taking a deep breath and savoring the crisp night air. "After all, that's what friends do. We stand by each other. I'm willing to bet you returned to the burning building today for the same reason."

"And I would do it again without hesitation," Jackie affirmed, gazing at the dark walls of the Academy, illuminated by the faint moonlight. It was astonishing how much could change in just a year. This place had somehow transformed into her home, and all the people she trusted resided under the same roof – Howard, Elisa, and Don. It was comforting to know that Theo was among them, not just a classmate or a useful partner in investigations, but a true friend. "We won't see each other for the entire summer, so I hope you'll stay safe."

"You too. Wherever you choose to go."

A gust of cool wind brushed against her face, causing Jackie to hug her shoulders. "If only I knew which Guardian House to choose. And what to do about Elisa."

"You know, sometimes you women overthink. It's impossible to please everyone. Just trust your instincts, like you did today," Theo advised.

"I'll try," she replied with a smile, giving his shoulder a friendly pat. "Well, thank you for everything, brother."

He chuckled. "Always, sis."

After bidding farewell to Theo, Jackie turned and ascended the stairs, thinking of her inevitable conversation with Elisa. The thought of facing rejection sent shivers down her spine. The fear of the unknown was strong. Was it possible that Elisa was moved by her own fears when she had dismissed her? After all, being in a relationship with another woman was forbidden by law. However, Elisa also never cared what others thought, so this explanation didn't make any sense. What was it, then?

Jackie paused, placing her palm over her chest as her heart pounded loudly. How had she not realized it before? All this time, Elisa had cared for her and stood by her side. There were boundaries Elisa would easily cross, as she had done the previous night, but she would never jeopardize the people she loved. The truth was that Elisa was scared for Jackie, not for herself, which had become the reason for pushing her away.

Shit... If Jackie had explained that she wasn't afraid of losing her career, they might have had a chance.

Jackie sprinted down the corridor as fast as her legs could carry her, fearful of wasting another minute. She envisioned Elisa's face and imagined how she would kiss her, enchanted by her gentle allure. She would clasp Elisa's hands in hers, pouring out her thoughts, and Elisa would bare her soul. It had to happen like that. If it was love, there was no other way.

She pushed through the door and entered the empty room. The moonlight illuminated their neatly made beds and the writing desk, where a white envelope sat. Jackie approached the desk slowly, her hands trembling as she picked up the envelope.

The inscription read, "*Jackie.*"

She opened it and settled on the floor.

"My dear Jackie,

If you are reading this letter, it means that I'm already on my way to Santos, where I will be spending the summer training with Lana, my good old friend from Triville. I hope your mission was successful and that you have shown your true worth!

I hope it never comes to this, but if Riley was right and you failed your mission, please do not lose hope. I know that you can be curious and clumsy at times, but you are a great guardian. Give yourself the time to learn and grow.

Now, I must address the most difficult part and bid you farewell –"

Jackie set the letter aside, finding it difficult to catch her breath. She made her way to the window and flung it open, allowing the fresh air to cool her face. The solitary half-moon gazed down at her from above, and tears welled up in her eyes. It was too soon to cry; she needed to finish reading first.

Returning to Elisa's bed, she picked up the letter once more.

" – *You see, letting go of someone you love is the most challenging thing to do, but I am doing it because I love you, Jackie. The time we spent together has been a source of healing for me, and I am grateful for everything we have shared. However, things have gone too far, and we must put an end to it now.*

I cannot allow you to make a grave mistake that could jeopardize your career and your life. And not just yours.

It's time to face the truth, my dear – the world can be cruel. People will always try to undermine our abilities. It's no longer just about us; we must set a positive example for the future female cadets who will arrive to study here next year. The thought of what they might endure if our secret is exposed fills me with despair.

The idea of losing you is equally unbearable, but it's the only way to make things right. I understand that everything may seem unclear now. All I desire is to flee this city and start anew where no one knows us, but that would only demonstrate our irresponsibility. We cannot allow that to happen.

So, let's do this out of love. If you truly care for me, Jackie, please do not pursue me. Instead, focus on excelling in your profession in every possible way. I want nothing more than for you to find peace with someone who genuinely loves you. You deserve it. Even if things don't work out with Urchin, I am confident that you will find someone who brings you happiness.

I'm leaving you for the best, Jackie. I just believe that I'll feel better there, without seeing your face every day for three months. And when I come back, we will forget about this fit of passion.

Sincerely yours,
Elisa Palmer.

P.S. I hope you made up your mind about Guardian House because the due date is today!"

The letter slipped from Jackie's trembling fingers, landing softly on the cold floor. A gentle breeze brushed against the page, evoking memories of mourners bidding their final farewells with a kiss on the forehead before a burial ceremony. Frozen in place, Jackie remained seated, her gaze fixed on the open window, until the sun began to rise on the horizon. The words of Elisa's letter echoed in her mind – *cruelty, love, irresponsibility, self-worth...*

Wiping away her tears, Jackie rose from her seat. She moved to the desk, picked up a piece of paper and a pen, and at long last, made a decision she had been avoiding for far too long – she began to write an application to the Guardian House.

Sitting at his desk, Don perused the application in front of him, the morning light illuminating his surprised face. Jackie sat across from him in a chair, patiently awaiting his response.

He set the paper down. "Are you certain about this?"

"I know I missed the due date, but yesterday was quite hectic," Jackie explained.

Don steepled his fingers. "The deadline is not an issue. However, I must admit, I'm puzzled as to why you have chosen this path despite the mistakes you've made."

"You once told us that our mistakes do not define us; it is how we handle them that matters. I believe I can rectify my errors."

Don looked at her with surprise. "Very well, then. Get your things in order because you will be heading to the Middle Lake Guardian House."

She rose from her seat. "I will do just that!"

Story 5

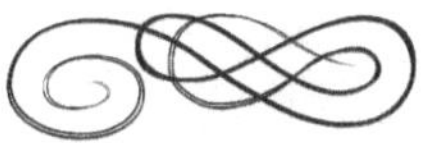

A Guardian House

29

A Diamond Mystery

The tall windows of the observation tower offered a spectacular view of the night capital. Jackie leaned against the windowsill, inhaling the fragrant summer air. Middle Lake never slept. Even when the lights in the windows dimmed, the bustling trade street came alive. Various nightclubs and pubs glowed with the vibrant light of night plants, beckoning those seeking an escape from boredom. They flocked to these lights like moths, unaware of the potential dangers that lurked in the darkness. That's why the guardians were always on watch.

The silver line of sunrise crept over the horizon, signaling that her shift was about to end. But it wasn't time to relax. Despite the quiet night, anything could happen. And when it did, she would be ready to spring into action.

"Jackie, please take a seat," a voice called out from behind her.

Turning around, she saw Walter Mills, the guardian who had saved her from drowning in the lake and had brought her to the Guardian House that spring for her first undercover mission.

As Jackie later discovered, Walter was a detective who conducted investigations in the city. He was the only one willing to take her under his wing for mentoring, showing kindness towards her, sometimes even excessively so.

Presently, he entered the room carrying two steaming cups of coffee. Placing them on a small table, he took a seat and fixed his curious gaze on Jackie with his piercing blue eyes. "Your first night duty is almost over."

Jackie looked out the window with a tinge of disappointment. "I thought it would be more exciting."

He chuckled. "That's why I enjoy working with cadets. Night duty is still an adventure for you."

Taking a seat beside him, Jackie took her coffee cup. "Is it wrong to wish for a crime to occur?"

"Not at all. I was just like you when I first started here, consumed by investigations. But I was too clumsy and eager. That's why seasoned guardians are hesitant to assign this task to newcomers."

"But you entrusted it to me," Jackie pointed out.

"Yes, because I have faith in you, Jackie. I hope you remember that."

She forced a smile. This was their ongoing game, as she liked to call it. From her initial days, Walter had been her mentor, patiently guiding her. He answered all her seemingly trivial questions and occasionally took her to crime scenes. To streamline their collaboration, they had signed an agreement on her first day, prohibiting Jackie from officially delving into his thoughts. Yet, she didn't need to read his mind to see that he was curious about what lay beneath her uniform.

Jackie unbuttoned her collar, allowing the cool morning air to caress her neck. Walter's assessment was accurate – her primary goal was to enhance her skills as a guardian, and she was content to let him believe his strategy was effective. The longer their game lasted, the more opportunities she would have to hone her abilities.

"As our duty nears its end," Walter said, "we could grab breakfast at a nearby restaurant. I know a great spot."

Running her fingertips along the rim of her coffee cup, Jackie delicately wiped away a droplet of condensation. "We still have time. Anything could happen at any moment."

Walter maintained his intense gaze, his blue eyes shining. "I start doubting anything significant will occur."

Jackie flinched. He clearly meant her willingness to cross the line and become more than just a colleague. Which she couldn't allow. "You know the saying, 'the longer the wait, the sweeter the victory.'"

He narrowed his eyes. "True. But some expectations lead to disappointment."

"Perhaps," she agreed. "All I hoped for tonight was an intriguing case, yet here I am, sitting idle."

"You will have your chance, Jackie."

"So now you're telling me to be patient?" Jackie retorted.

Walter scoffed. "Relax, no one will suspect a thing about our little rendezvous. You can trust me."

Jackie nervously nibbled on her lip. Every game had a tipping point where the stakes escalated, requiring a bold move to keep playing.

"Fine, one secret date," she relented.

His eyes lit up. "Tonight."

"After we solve the case."

"Deal."

A sudden loud bang shattered the silence, causing them to turn towards the window. Glittering orange particles from a Light signal dispersed in the morning air, originating from the western side of the trade street. Without hesitation, Jackie sprang to her feet and dashed towards the exit door, with Walter close behind.

The crime scene was a jewelry store in the city center – a luxurious establishment adorned with a grand chandelier and plush chairs for patrons. The display cases glowed with the radiance of luminescent plants, casting an enchanting aura over the jewelry, which sparkled in hues of green, purple, and yellow. In the center, a shattered showcase littered the black marble floor with glass shards. The lifeless body of a young thief lay close by.

The thief, clad in a gray hoodie, had brown eyes fixed on the ceiling. A black burn was etched on his chest. Nearby, the shopkeeper sat in a chair, his pudgy hand clutching a cup of coffee, which he sipped while shaking his head intermittently.

Walter bent over the body, examining the energy traces with Revealing Spell. His expression darkened before he straightened up, meeting Jackie's gaze.

"I have a theory about what transpired," he began. "But would *you* like to take a guess?"

Jackie smiled, ready for her detective task. "Of course."

The shopkeeper visibly relaxed as Jackie conjured a ball of Light in her hand. Ignoring his strange reaction, she focused on the crime scene, starting with the area surrounding the thief's body. Whispering a Revealing spell, she traced her hand along the floor. To her astonishment, only one energy trace was present, leading directly to the shopkeeper. As she approached him, he set his coffee cup down on the table, the scent of cognac wafting towards her.

Clapping her hands, Jackie dispelled her Light. "Excuse me, Mr. Hendricks, you mentioned there were two thieves?"

He nodded. "Yes. The other one managed to flee, but I took care of this one."

"Why did you kill him?" Jackie inquired.

Shrugging nonchalantly, Mr. Hendricks replied, "He could have killed me."

Jackie furrowed her brow, sensing that something was amiss – the deceased thief had no visible weapon on him, and there were no magical traces in the vicinity.

"So?" Walter prodded impatiently.

After a moment of contemplation, Jackie responded, "I have two theories – the second thief could be a skilled magician who erased the traces, or he could have been an Incapable. But that seems unlikely."

"Why do you think it's impossible?" Walter asked.

Glancing at Mr. Hendricks, the shopkeeper, Jackie explained, "If the thief was Incapable, it would imply that he posed no real threat. Without any weapons on him, there was no justification for killing him."

Approaching Mr. Hendricks, Walter placed a hand on his shoulder. "Is Jackie correct?"

Mr. Hendricks swallowed nervously. "Yes, but I was terrified. Picture two men in my store, attempting to steal a diamond neck-lace! How was I to know they were merely Incapables? They were brazen, I must admit. Can't you see? I was merely defending my-self!"

Jackie pressed her index finger against her lips, deep in thought. Walter had a hunch about the case, waiting for her to arrive at the correct conclusion. She had learned from him that the most straightforward explanation was often the incorrect one.

Walking along the display cases, Jackie reconstructed the sequence of events in her mind. While she could easily delve into Mr. Hendricks' thoughts, she refrained from doing so. Walter had emphasized that there would be instances where she couldn't rely on her Gift, such as when there were no perpetrators or witnesses to read or due to emotional barriers. Some criminals could even manipulate her Gift to fabricate false memories.

Piecing together the information she had, Jackie deduced the following: Mr. Hendricks had opened the store early that day, disabling the alarm. Subsequently, two Incapables had forcibly entered the premises, threatening him. In a bid to defend himself, Mr. Hendricks had conjured a Fire spell. The situation escalated as the intruders shattered the showcase, prompting Mr. Hendricks to shoot one of them in self-defense. The other thief had successfully fled with the stolen jewelry before Mr. Hendricks could cast another spell, a logical and plausible scenario. It was a convenient explanation, one that would likely not be scrutinized further due to the general disdain towards Incapables.

However, a discrepancy caught Jackie's attention – the dead thief's expression of surprise. It struck her as odd, as one wouldn't typically gaze at their assailant in such a manner unless they recognized them.

Approaching Mr. Hendricks once more, Jackie fixed him with a penetrating stare. "You knew this young man, didn't you?"

Mr. Hendricks shook his head. "How could I? He was an Incapable."

"He was," Jackie acknowledged, "And that's why you assumed no one would delve deeper into this case."

Walter nodded in agreement, a faint smile playing on his lips.

"Why did you kill him?" Jackie pondered aloud.

"There must be a motive," Walter hinted, prompting Jackie to consider the possible reasons behind the thief's demise.

"Indeed. The diamond necklace holds significant value. This establishment appears upscale but not particularly bustling. Is it possible that you are in debt, Mr. Hendricks?"

Turning to Mr. Hendricks, Walter inquired, "Are you in debt?"

Mr. Hendricks hesitated before responding, "Debt... Well, this shop is managing fine. It's just an early hour, and my clientele typically frequents the store in the evening."

"Why then did you open so early today?" Jackie probed further.

Mr. Hendricks remained silent, prompting Walter to interject, "Would you object to us conducting a thorough search?"

His eyes filled with indignation. "What do you mean?! I'm an elderly man, and this criminal met his end here! Carry out your duties, Detective Mills, and resolve this matter before I contact your superior!"

Walter smirked. "You shouldn't be so agitated, especially at your age."

Mr. Hendricks gritted his teeth, his frustration palpable. Jackie surveyed the room, her gaze falling on the door leading to the basement. *Perhaps this is how the second thief escaped – through the back door.* Alas, she couldn't check it – unlike mages, Incapables left no energy traces, rendering them untraceable by conventional Searching spells.

Contemplating the situation, Jackie considered the possibility that Mr. Hendricks had orchestrated the theft by hiring Incapables. It would be a clever scheme, as Incapables' lack of magical traces made them elusive and difficult to apprehend. By staging the robbery, Mr. Hendricks could potentially write off the stolen diamonds, declare bankruptcy, and absolve himself of debts. He could then sell the diamonds on the black market and retire to a life of luxury in the South. Given Mr. Hendricks' penchant for opulence, this scenario seemed almost perfect.

However, a lingering question remained – could a man like Mr. Hendricks truly trust an Incapable? After all, having killed one of them, would the second thief simply return with the stolen goods? It seemed improbable, unless...

"There was no second thief!" Jackie exclaimed.

Both Walter and Mr. Hendricks turned to her, their reactions starkly contrasting. While Walter's eyes gleamed with intrigue, Mr. Hendricks wore an expression of profound sorrow, confirming Jackie's deduction.

"How dare you accuse me of lies?" Mr. Hendricks retorted.

Walter intervened, placing a hand on Mr. Hendricks's shoulder, prompting him to fall silent. "Please, continue," Walter urged Jackie.

"I suspect that the necklace is still in this room," Jackie asserted confidently. "By employing the Revealing spell, I can trace your movements today and likely locate the missing jewelry."

"Do as you wish. I won't budge from this spot!" Mr. Hendricks declared defiantly.

Jackie blinked, recalling that she had previously cast the Revealing spell after Walter, which had led her to the chair. If the necklace wasn't elsewhere, it must be concealed on Mr. Hendricks or within the chair, awaiting its opportune moment.

"Search him," Jackie instructed Walter.

Mr. Hendricks gripped the armrests tightly, his knuckles turning white. "No way!"

"If you resist the investigation, the consequences will be severe," Jackie cautioned Mr. Hendricks. "Believe me, we will uncover the gems eventually. However, if you disclose the location of the necklace now, you may have a chance to mitigate your punishment."

Mr. Hendricks shot her a venomous glare before reluctantly standing up. Upon inspecting the chair, they found nothing except for a white cushion. Walter seized the cushion and gave it a shake, the distinct clinking sound indicating that the missing necklace was concealed within.

As he tore the pillow apart, a delicate platinum chain adorned with glistening diamonds tumbled onto the marble floor. Walter smiled at her. "Well done, Cadet Robinson! You may proceed with the arrest."

A broad smile graced Jackie's face, causing Mr. Hendricks to pale. Retrieving the power handcuffs from her pocket, which blocked magical abilities and prevented criminals from harming their captors, Jackie proceeded to restrain Mr. Hendricks.

"By the authority of the King of Lake Kingdom, you are under arrest!" she declared.

30

A Promise

They walked down the corridor of the Guardian House together with Walter. Jackie's heart fluttered in her chest. Their night duty was over, and they had to report to Chief Trevor. She was certain Trevor would be proud of her. After all, he had brought her to the Academy, and Jackie was on her way to becoming a guardian. This man had placed his trust in her, and she was determined to repay him with her excellent work, just as she had done now.

"This was my first arrest!" Jackie couldn't stop smiling. "It was so... so cool!"

"Yes, you did great," Walter said, giving her a cheerful look.

They came to a stop at the door of the chief's office.

"Can this day never end? Can I keep arresting people?"

Walter laughed. "Slow down. You need to have a rest before another investigation."

"I can't imagine being able to sleep after this," she said. "How do you handle it?"

"Easy. I've gotten used to it."

He gave her a warm look, and Jackie couldn't resist hugging him. Seizing the moment, Walter pressed her against the wall and kissed her.

Perhaps she was too overwhelmed with emotions to push him away, so she responded but kept it brief. "Walter, I –"

"Have a secret date with me tonight," he said, his hands still wrapped around her waist. "Remember our deal?"

She blinked, recalling their earlier conversation that morning. Jackie had agreed to go on a date with him only in case they had an investigation. But she thought it wouldn't happen because the night had been so calm... Now, she had a dilemma to navigate.

"Maybe tomorrow? I'm feeling a bit tired," she suggested.

"I can't wait until tomorrow."

"Why?"

"It will be August 1st – my birthday."

Jackie's mind raced, struggling to come up with a suitable excuse. She had been unaware of his birthday until now, and he had caught her off guard. In that moment, she couldn't imagine a more awkward situation, but things were about to get even worse.

The door to the chief's office flew open, and Trevor stood before them. Jackie's heart sank. Walter quickly removed his hands from her, and Jackie lowered her gaze. Despite her recent arrest, all her accomplishments seemed to pale in comparison now. A deep shame pierced her heart.

"Get in," Trevor said flatly.

They entered the room and took their seats. Walter presented the report, and Jackie simply nodded occasionally to affirm his words. As the meeting concluded, Trevor requested Jackie to remain behind for a private conversation.

When the door closed behind Walter, Trevor clasped his hands together and fixed her with a sharp gaze. If Jackie could have turned invisible at that moment, she would have chosen to disappear. She silently wished for Howard to magically appear and rescue her from the situation. However, there was no escape, so she had to face it.

"I see you had a busy night," Trevor remarked sarcastically.

Her cheeks flushed with embarrassment. *What does he mean by that?* Jackie nervously licked her lips, struggling to find the right words. "Trev... Chief. I appreciate the opportunity you've given me, and I promise to give my best –"

"I see," he interrupted.

She stood there at a loss for words. It seemed as though this man could see right through her, delving into the deepest corners of her soul.

Trevor stood up and walked over to the window, the morning sun casting a warm light on his weathered face. "Jackie, you must understand how much I care about your future. When I first met you last year, you were broken, but I saw potential in you."

"Did you?"

He nodded. "Absolutely. You possess the spirit of a fighter, and I have placed my trust in you. However, we are all bound by the same rules. Are you aware that engaging in a romantic relationship with a colleague who supervises you is a serious violation?"

"I'm truly sorry, but it was Walter's suggestion –"

"Don't even attempt to justify it," he interjected, raising his hand to silence her. "I can discern when someone is being untruthful. It is both my Gift and my curse. Jackie, I've been observing you since you joined our team. I see through your intentions."

"It's just a harmless game, nothing serious," she offered apologetically.

He sneered. "Are you a skilled player?"

"What do you mean?"

"Jackie, I comprehend that you are seeking to gain more experience here, but still... tell me honestly – how ethical is your conduct with Detective Mills?"

She took a deep breath before responding. "You want the truth?! Alright. These rules appear to be designed to protect me. But my life has never been fair – some people exploit their privilege because they can, while people like me are expected to adhere strictly to the rules. I suppose I grew weary of this disparity. I wanted to seize an opportunity to improve and become a better guardian. But it was a mistake to involve Walter. He is a good person who only sought to look out for me. I acknowledge that we overstepped boundaries this morning, and it must cease immediately. Please, allow me to fix everything."

He nodded. "I understand your perspective. I can only imagine the challenges of being a single woman in a Guardian House."

"Do you?"

"Of course," he affirmed, moving closer and offering her a compassionate gaze. "You see, this is what distinguishes a good guardian – knowing when it is acceptable to bend certain rules in order to do what is right. I took a risk by assigning you here, breaking a few rules in the process and jeopardizing my career. However, what you did was not appropriate, and it's good that you can acknowledge it."

Jackie nodded. Indeed, she had created this issue and needed to resolve it on her own. Uncertain of how to proceed, she was prepared to find a solution. "Thank you, sir. I promise, moving forward, I won't disappoint you."

"Honestly, I had my doubts about my decision to bring you into the guardians, especially after your past mistakes. However, I see potential in you as a future colleague. I want you to learn from your errors."

Jackie placed her hand over her heart. It was such a relief to have this man in her corner. She was determined to demonstrate her loyalty.

"Listen, Jackie, I'll always be there to support you if you require assistance or additional training. But I can't assist you if you lose the respect of our fellow guardians. Therefore, please inform me if Mills oversteps the boundaries again."

She hesitated. "How could I possibly ask you for anything after all you have done? It would be too much."

"It's not solely about you. I require a perceptive individual in my team, and that's why I chose you. In the near future, I will assign you and Mills to a case we are currently working on, and I expect both of you to maintain professionalism throughout."

"Yes, Chief," Jackie affirmed with a nod.

31

A Dealer

Elisa walked down the narrow, paved street. The rain had stopped, and now a heavy mist hung in the warm evening air. At the end of the street, she stopped. A skinny figure of a man stood by the shabby old building, waiting for his first buyers. Today, she was one of them.

Putting the hood of her red cloak on, Elisa approached the man. "Hi."

"Have you gotten lost, girl?" His pale blue eyes gazed at her from under his hat.

Elisa made her voice sound cheerful, hoping he would buy her story. "I was looking for you. I have a birthday party this weekend, and I need a package of your best product."

None of his muscles moved. "Who sent you?"

"Who cares?" Elisa rolled her eyes, playing the role of a spoiled girl. "Do you need money or not?! I can find someone else in an eye-blink."

He chuckled, revealing a golden tooth. "Okay, slow down. I'll help you. Tonight, I have something special for your occasion."

"Great." She revealed her red purse covered with rhinestones. Carelessly, she opened it, demonstrating a bunch of silver coins. "So, how much powder do I need for a dozen students?"

His eyes gleamed as he saw the money. "Depends on the quality. If you're planning something fancy, then I can suggest a new product. Moon Dust."

"Oh, I think I tried that a couple of months ago." Elisa waved her free hand nonchalantly, playing her role. "Right, at Jackie's party. It was a lot of fun!"

"I see." He looked around the empty street and adjusted his hat. "Fine, follow me. It's around the corner."

She closed her purse and put it in her pocket, making sure it made a loud clunk. In silence, she followed the dealer to the other building. Judging by the faded street sign, it used to be a restaurant. Now, the paint on the facade was cracked, and its wide windows were boarded up with wooden planks.

The man led her to the side door and walked into the spacious dining hall. Elisa followed his steps in darkness, resisting the urge to reveal her Light. It was too risky – she had been in Santos for only two months, but all the criminals already knew about the female guardian with the scar on her cheek and a rare silver Light. Even though she covered her scar with a solid layer of powder, she couldn't do anything about the rest. If he had recognized her, this undercover operation would have been over.

Finally, they reached the curtain that separated the main room from the kitchen. The reflection of candlelight and male voices indicated that it was the room where they prepared the drugs. They stepped inside.

Her guess was correct – the kitchen tables were covered with multiple jars filled with dried herb powders and suspicious dark liquids. Two young men sorted the mixtures into small cotton bags using scales. *Incapables*, Elisa guessed. It was a usual practice to hire Incapables for such a dirty job - they never left magic traces and always kept silent.

"Welcome to the candy shop," the man announced with a wink.

Elisa smiled and fixed her hair lock.

He waved his hand, and the Incapable men left the room without asking any questions. They stood alone, and Elisa's heart raced in a premonition of danger. She had done everything as planned – found a drug dealer and figured out where he prepared his goods. Even though the guardians already knew this information, she had managed to get close enough. Now, she must gather information about his supplier without giving herself away.

She looked around. "What a creepy place."

He ignored her comment. "So, how much money do you have?"

Elisa scoffed. "Enough. Show me what you can suggest first."

He approached one of the shelves and took the cotton bag. He placed it on a kitchen table. Elisa opened it with her fingertips – the powder had a blue color, and it smelled of dried aconite.

"We just got it last night. Fresh and strong," he said.

"Looks good." She mustered a smile. "If I like it, I can come back."

"I'm sure you will." His eyes gave her a sly look. "Actually, you probably put yourself at risk when you come to this part of the city."

She chuckled. "What a smart sales trick."

"Why not?" He paused, then walked to the shelf with elegant, colorful glass bottles. A dark blue bottle gleamed in his palm. "I have a bonus Gift if you buy two bags tonight."

"What's that? A perfume?"

"Do I look like a perfumer?!" He laughed. "It's a light mixture – one teaspoon of Moon Dust with our special calming potion. Two drops of it would cheer you up, whatever you feel."

He opened a glass lid and lured her.

Elisa paused. *What if it's a test?* Anyway, it was too early to ask suspicious questions, and there was no way back. Trying to look confident, she came closer and opened her mouth. The man smiled and dripped two drops of a warm potion on her tongue.

Elisa swallowed it, feeling a sudden rush of warmth in her blood. It worked fast. To help her body cool down, she unbuttoned the top of her cloak. She needed to finish this mission and get out of there. "Fine, give me two. Or better, three bags."

He nodded and placed two more bags in front of her. Trying to fight the numbness in her limbs, Elisa took her purse and gave him six silver coins.

"So, when will be the best time to get fresh goods?" Elisa asked, hiding a glass bottle in her decolletage.

"The next arrival is scheduled in two weeks," he said, counting the money. "But I prefer you to keep your mouth shut about it."

"Of course," she said. "Alright. I'd better go."

Satisfied, he placed the money in his pocket. "Be careful on your way back."

Elisa turned to the door and walked to the exit, feeling his gaze on her back. Collecting her thoughts together, she assumed that everything went smoothly. Now she knew the exact date of the next supply, so the guardians might follow the man and catch this gang soon. It felt so good. Like a dozen butterflies filled her belly with lightness and joy. At that moment, everything seemed possible. Some part of her consciousness realized that it was just an effect of the drug she had taken, but very soon, the effect would fade.

Elisa stumbled over a broken piece of furniture in the dark dining room and fell on the floor. She didn't feel any pain, but she touched her knee to make sure it was fine.

She glanced back. The gaps between the wooden planks on the windows let the dull evening light in, allowing her to see the rectangle of an exit door – a path to safety.

According to the plan, her partner, Lana, was waiting for her at the corner of the building. The curtain to the kitchen was further from her than the exit. Elisa raised her hand and formed a small Light ball to help see the way better.

She took two steps when the man's voice shouted behind her. "Stop, or I'll shoot!"

She turned and froze. The dealer stood in the kitchen, holding a fireball in his hand.

"So, it's you." He narrowed his eyes in recognition. "A guardian girl. How could I believe you?"

Elisa sighed. Once she was caught, it was over. This man wouldn't wait for an explanation. One quick hand movement, and he would kill her. Fire magic was the most dangerous one, but the Lightning Gift could protect her, as Theo had taught her.

Dropping her Light ball, she moved both her hands forward and created a shield made of violet electric sparkles. His Fireball smashed over the shield and melted.

Now, it was her turn. Elisa pushed her magic shield forward, trying to hit the dealer. Much to her disappointment, the electric sparkles melted on his skin, causing no damage.

"Oh, fuck," Elisa muttered. Obviously, he was resistant to her magic.

Slowly, he put his hand up, preparing to strike again. She held her breath, counting the seconds until it happened. Her heart beat in her chest, shifting her thoughts far away from this moment to

Jackie. *If I die, how would she take it?* No, she couldn't let him kill her like this. Obeying her instinct, Elisa turned away and ran.

When his fireball hit her, she felt a warmth between her shoulders. Then, she saw nothing but the blinding white glare.

32

Small Victories

Later that evening, Jackie sat in the pub with a glass of cold lemon water in her hand. Her diary lay untouched on the table. She wasn't in the mood for writing, so she kept gazing into the beautiful evening sky. She enjoyed watching as it blossomed with golden and red colors, then faded into shades of darkness. It was a beautiful sight, reminiscent of death.

Jackie shivered. She hadn't thought about death in this way since falling in love with Elisa. *Will I ever get over her?*

When Jackie read Elisa's letter, she couldn't believe she would be able to let her go and focus on her training. Initially, it was difficult – waking up and doing her work, pushing her foolish desires into the darkest corners of her mind. Her despair made her angry, and she didn't realize how she had started playing with Walter. But she wasn't angry anymore.

Trevor had given her good advice – it was time to take control and stop making such silly mistakes. And as for Elisa... Well, it had become a bit easier, too. Two months without seeing Elisa's face had eventually soothed her bleeding heart.

Jackie took a sip from her glass, savoring its taste. Maybe Elisa was right, and the love they had cherished so much was just temporary insanity. Perhaps they both knew nothing about love and life. At least Jackie knew something about death, and now, as the last beam of hope for being together with Elisa faded in her chest, her depressive thoughts returned. She had to do something about it before the darkness enveloped her.

Someone's hand touched her shoulder, and Jackie raised her eyes. Howard stood over her, smiling.

She managed a weary smile. "Hey."

"Congrats on the case closure."

"Thank you."

Howard looked around. "Where is Detective Walt?"

"I bet he'll come soon." Jackie sighed. She was waiting for Walter only to have an honest talk, and now, Howard showed up and made everything more complicated. *Maybe he will leave soon?*

Crushing her hope, he sat nearby and placed his beer on the table. "You look so upset. What happened?" Howard gazed at her, awaiting a response. If only Jackie could answer his question. Walter had clearly decided to take advantage of her, and there was nothing she could do about it without tarnishing her reputation.

"Why don't you tell me how you are?" Jackie asked instead of answering.

He shrugged. "Just like any other cadet. I fill out boring reports and spend most days in the archive. Not much fun."

"I could ask Walter to let you accompany him on the next night's duty."

"He won't take two cadets with him."

"Then we'll switch places. I could spend the day in the archive."

"Would he agree?"

"Why wouldn't he?"

Howard narrowed his eyes. "Why would you do that for me?"

Jackie touched her glass, the condensation that covered the rim pleasantly cooling her fingertips. "You would do the same for me, wouldn't you?"

Howard took a sip of his beer and signaled to the waitress.

The waitress approached their table with a full jug and filled Howard's mug. He placed his hand on hers. "Darling, just leave this whole thing with us."

The waitress gave them a curious look. "Of course."

Jackie turned away, gazing out the window. Since becoming a cadet and donning her uniform, women stared at her as if she were an exotic animal in a zoo. Perhaps they were unsure how to treat her. Jackie didn't fit the mold of a typical woman in modern society, yet she wasn't a man either. Maybe she should start wearing dresses like other women did. She did have a couple of dresses in her closet, but she rarely wore them.

"So, Jackie," Howard said.

"Yep?"

"Maybe you finally tell me why you chose to join the same Guardian House as me?"

She blinked. She knew Howard was going there, but it was the last thing on her mind when she submitted her application. "I had my first undercover mission here, and I simply wanted to continue working with the same team."

"But that day, you screwed up."

"You have no idea how." She poured a beer into her glass and took two big gulps. The memory of that spring night with Elisa would always live in her heart. But she could never tell Howard about it. Elisa was right about one thing – people would never stop judging them.

"When you chose Middle Lake Guardian House," Howard said, "I guess you wanted to prove something."

"Maybe." She nodded, still lost in thoughts of Elisa. "You know how it goes. At first, I was certain I knew what I was doing, but eventually, I realized I had made a mistake."

"Fixing your own mistakes is the best way to learn."

"I can't fix it. I tried, but it's just impossible." Her hands crumpled a napkin. "I can't change who I am."

Howard moved closer to her, his ragged breaths reaching her ear. "Don't say that. Also, whatever you worry about, I'll always support you; you know that."

"I wish I could tell you everything, but you might hate me if I did."

He shook his head. "Firstly, I'll never hate you. And secondly, I'm not blind; I see what's going on."

She looked at him in silence, wondering what he was talking about.

Howard took her hand in his. "I see how that bastard Walt looks at you, and I know that you hate it."

Her heart raced. "How do you know? I'm supposed to be the mind reader here."

"Maybe. But I don't just waste my time in the archive. I came across an interesting book called *Kinesics: Body Language*. Did you know that human emotions are often revealed in our subtle gestures? In our facial expressions, in our eyes?"

"Of course I do."

He smiled. "Do you remember the little Gift exchange experiment you did with Elisa?"

She nodded. Ever since she had shared the details of that Gift exchange with Howard, he had never been the same.

"More than anything, I wanted to exchange my Gift with yours," Howard said. "Just to try how it feels – to read someone. And recently, I found this book –"

"So, what about Walter?" She interrupted him. Howard enjoyed lengthy discussions and was easily sidetracked from the main topic.

"Yeah, right. I see what he wants and that you're taking advantage of it."

She chuckled. "You're quite the detective, aren't you?"

Howard's expression turned serious. "Jackie, this game won't last long. Someone will end up getting hurt."

"We only have a month left, and then I'll return to the Academy and forget about him."

"You don't have that much time, Jackie."

She narrowed her eyes. "What do you mean exactly?"

Howard glanced around. The pub wasn't very busy, but people were starting to return from their daily activities to relax under the pub's shady roof. "Listen, if anyone asks, I never told you this."

She nodded. "You know you can count on me."

"I overheard something today – Walter was furious when he returned from the chief's office, and they had a heated discussion with the other guy."

Jackie took another gulp of beer, feeling her head start to spin. She recalled the events of the morning and knew what had triggered Walter's anger. It was difficult to forget the look he had given her when he left her alone with Trevor.

"What did you hear?" Jackie inquired.

Howard leaned in closer and lowered his voice. "He made a bet on you, Jackie. From what I gathered during their argument, Walter lost a card game in the spring and owed money to the guy. However, the guy is wealthy and doesn't really need the money, so when they saw you at the Guardian House, he proposed an alternative way for Walter to settle his debt."

"What way?"

"It's difficult to tell you this, Jackie, and it's unpleasant, but you must know. They want to prove your incompetence as a guardian. Walter's deadline is the evening of August 1st, and for the proof, he must bring your..." Howard hesitated for a moment, searching for the right word. "Lingerie."

"He needs my panties, then." She paused, processing the information. "Well, that explains a lot. But wouldn't it be easier for him to break into my room and steal it?"

Howard wiped the beads of sweat from his forehead. "No. Walter must ask you to give it willingly. Another person can read the energy from the item and determine if it was taken without consent."

Her eyes widened. "That's an interesting spell."

Howard gave her a disappointed look. "Is that the only thing bothering you about this situation?!"

"Of course not." She placed her hand on his. "Thank you for warning me. I need to remember that men are not too trustworthy."

"Except for me."

"You forgot about our first encounter." She playfully poked his shoulder.

"Right, that stupid prank. But I've apologized for that several times."

"You have," she agreed with a chuckle. "Oh, Howard, don't worry about my problem with Walter. I'll handle everything."

"Will you?" He looked at her with anxiety evident in his wide, hazel eyes.

"I'll just give him the item he wants."

"I'm afraid he might use it against you. What if it ends up with the chief? I don't want that."

Jackie shook her head. "He wouldn't dare to go that far."

"Then what will you do?"

Jackie shrugged. "I don't know yet, but I'll figure it out with this information."

He leaned back in his chair. "Let me know if you need my help."

She nodded and set her empty glass aside – she had had enough for today. Though Elisa may be gone, she still had Howard by her side, someone she could rely on.

They chatted until the sky darkened. Howard was quite tipsy by the time he finished the jug, and Jackie began to worry about how she would get him home. As cadets in training, they each had their own rooms in the building rented by the Guardian House.

Unaware of the bar doors opening, Jackie was surprised to see Walter walk in with six other guardians. She had expected him to show up, but bringing witnesses along was unexpected. They spotted Jackie and Howard and made their way over to their table.

Walter grabbed Howard's shoulders and shook him. Howard gave him a bleary look. "Whatever you're going to do... don't you dare!"

Walter grinned. "This is what I find amusing about rookies. They really can't hold their liquor!"

The guardians chuckled as they settled in, and one of them called the waitress to place an order.

Jackie stood up and rummaged through her purse for some coins. Her salary was meager, and these trips to the pub were a luxury. Howard's order had left her short on funds, and with him in no condition to ask for help, she placed five bronze coins on the table.

Walter picked up the money and handed it back to her. "I'll take care of it."

"Thank you," she tried to politely decline. "But you don't have to pay for my friend."

"I insist," he said. "You don't have to pay for him either."

The other guardians fell silent, all eyes on them.

"Alright." Jackie took the coins and returned them to her purse. "He'll repay you once he's sober."

"Fine."

Walter assisted her in lifting Howard and supported him. If only she had known that Howard was such a lightweight drinker, she would never have let him finish the entire jug. But it was too late, and now they stood before six guardians who eyed her with curiosity.

Walter, seizing the opportunity, now portrayed himself as a helpful colleague. "I'll help with this bag of bones and be right back!" With that, he headed towards the exit, carrying Howard, who seemed unfazed.

Jackie had no choice but to follow him.

Their three-story brick building was just two blocks away from the pub and one block away from the Guardian House. Jackie retrieved the key from Howard's pocket and unlocked his door. Walter carried her friend's limp body to the bed.

She fetched a glass of water with lemon from the kitchen and placed it on the nightstand. As Jackie knew, lemon had antioxidant properties and could aid in faster recovery. Her student life had taught her many things, including drinking etiquette, a realm she had not been familiar with before. Being a loyal friend, she removed Howard's shoes and covered him with a soft blanket.

Throughout this time, Walter patiently waited for her, seated on a chair. His composed demeanor indicated that he wasn't planning to leave anytime soon, hinting that a conversation between them was inevitable.

Once she finished tucking Howard in, Jackie left the keys on the night table and headed to the corridor with Walter trailing behind her.

"Listen, Jackie," he began as soon as she closed the door.

She gave him a weary look. *Of course, he chose this moment to address his own agenda.* She wondered what card he would play.

"I'm listening," Jackie replied.

He placed his hands in his pockets and leaned against the wall. "I wanted to apologize. I never intended to put you in such an awkward situation."

"You mean when the chief caught us?"

He nodded. "I understand it must have been embarrassing, and he can be quite stern. I promise it won't happen again."

She crossed her arms over her chest. "Well, I'm just a rookie, as you pointed out. My future in this career hinges on what he includes in his report. I don't want him to think that you treat me well because I promised you sex in return."

Walter's eyes widened. Like many other guardians, he hadn't expected her to speak so candidly, giving her an advantage.

Her Mind-reading Gift allowed her to sense that people often enjoyed building expectations, and she typically refrained from shattering them unless absolutely necessary. This was one of those moments.

"Walter, I need you to understand – you're a good person, but this is my first experience as a guardian, and I can't do something I'll regret later. Even if I desire it."

He drew nearer, his arms encircling her. "You won't regret it."

She didn't push his hands away. "So, I can trust you. Can I?"

"Absolutely."

"Perhaps there's something you'd like to confess to help me trust you?" she proposed. Honesty could make things simpler.

He shook his head. "I don't have any secrets from you."

A liar. Jackie freed herself from his grasp. "Alright, then. Wait here."

Her room was close to Howard's, so she quickly unlocked her door and got in. Inside, Jackie leaned against the wall, her heart racing. Walter seemed inclined to tell the truth, but she could use this to her advantage. She needed to act swiftly now.

The upper shelf of her dresser opened silently. Jackie ran her hand over the neatly arranged row of lingerie and selected her favorite – a pair of red lace panties she had purchased at the start of her training program. She had intended to wear them when she would see Elisa again. But now, it was time to part with them. She placed the panties in her pocket and closed the drawer.

Walter was waiting for her in the corridor, fidgeting nervously. He froze as she approached him.

"Give me your hand," Jackie requested.

"Why?"

Her tone turned firm. "Do you trust me?"

He nodded and extended his hand, palm up.

She placed a piece of red fabric in his hand. Walter brought it closer to his eyes, his eyes widening in surprise. Then he exhaled loudly and lowered his hand but didn't release the item he held.

"You read my mind, didn't you?" he inquired. "You knew all along, and I was a fool to bring you to all those crime scenes."

"I didn't read your mind, Walter! And I never would, not since the day I signed those papers."

He placed the panties in his left pocket. "Then how did you know I needed this... trophy?"

It was a valid question, and she didn't want to frame Howard. "You're right. I did read your mind. But only today, when you kissed me." It was a lie, as she had been taken aback earlier when he had kissed her against the wall. However, he didn't need to know that. "Walter, I only did it because you broke the rules first. You crossed a boundary."

He gazed at her intently. "So, you never truly desired it. You just used me."

"I had to be cautious. So, I read your mind just in case, and after everything I saw... let's just say my interest waned."

"Fair enough. Then why did you give me your possession?"

"Because, despite everything, I want to be honest with you. How about making another agreement?"

"An agreement?"

"Yes, you can keep that item in your pocket and use it as needed. I gave it to you willingly, so it can serve as evidence."

He checked his pocket and kept his hand there. "And what do you want in return?"

She gave him a knowing look. "I simply desire the opportunity to practice and a positive evaluation when my training concludes."

"I believe we can arrange that," he agreed.

She moved closer and traced an imaginary line on his pocket. "And I trust that this little red lace secret will remain between us and whoever you choose to share it with. No gossip, no awkward situations. Do we have an understanding?"

He rubbed his chin, contemplating. "Only if you agree to the same."

She extended her hand. "Deal."

"Deal." He shook her hand.

Jackie smiled, relieved that she had managed to navigate the awkward situation without Trevor's assistance. It was a small victory, but she felt proud of herself.

"Be prepared to start at 7 a.m. tomorrow. We have work to do," Walter said.

"See you then."

He nodded and made his way down the corridor. Jackie watched him until he turned towards the stairs, finally allowing herself to breathe a sigh of relief.

33

A Fireproof One

In the reception room of a Guardian House, Elisa sat on a sofa, wrapping herself in a soft blanket. She had stopped shivering, but her shoulders and back still ached from the recent accident. Her Lightning Gift had protected her skin from burns, but the impact had been strong enough to knock her down. There was another kind of damage, too. Her hand ran over her short hair, still getting used to the new sensation.

Since she was a little girl, Elisa had always worn long plaits and tails, which had been a source of pride for her. Now, her golden locks were gone. Oh, well... It was a small price to pay for her own neglect. Today, she had made a silly mistake by revealing her Light. Usually, she would rely on her intuition before putting herself at such risk, but her inner voice had been calm and quiet at the time. And it had all happened because of the drug she had taken.

Elisa placed her hand on her chest, touching the small glass bottle hidden in her decolletage. When the guardians had caught glimpses of the fighting, they had burst into the dining room and pulled her out. They later searched her damaged cloak and confiscated the Moon Dust, but they never found the bottle.

Her thoughts circled back to the moment in the drug dealer's kitchen. Elisa wished she had never tried his product, but at that moment, it seemed like the only right choice. Otherwise, the dealer might have become suspicious. Ironically, taking the drug had led her to ruin the entire mission.

Elisa hadn't given the bottle to the guardians, and she wasn't going to. It seemed logical to keep it as a reminder of her failures, much like Don kept a sample of Moon Dust in his office.

The door opened, and a woman with kind brown eyes entered. She was dressed in a guardian uniform and had flaxen plaits. In her hands, she held two steaming mugs.

"Hot chocolate for you," she said with a smile. "And a coffee for myself."

"Thanks, Lana," Elisa smiled and took the mug in her hands, feeling its pleasant warmth against her palms. "Though I didn't deserve it."

"Don't say that," Lana replied, sitting nearby. "Undercover work is always unpredictable. You stayed alive, and we caught a dealer red-handed. He's currently under interrogation."

"Will he speak?"

Lana shrugged. "With the evidence we have, he'll likely be imprisoned for at least a decade. If he wants to ease his punishment, he has no other choice but to cooperate. I bet we'll find the suppliers soon."

Elisa nodded thoughtfully. "I saw Moon Dust samples in Middle Lake. Do you think these criminals relocated?"

Lana took a sip of her coffee, savoring the taste before sharing her expertise. "People like that don't usually relocate. They're like vermin, multiplying and staying put to avoid trouble. But they always come back to reap their profits."

Elisa gazed out of the dark window. The night was gloomy, but there was no rain. If Jackie were with her tonight, she would probably worry about how many more young people were in these streets, recklessly searching for this 'fancy' drug. After months of being her closest friend, Elisa couldn't help but admire Jackie's compassion towards everyone. *Interesting, how is Jackie doing now?*

More than anything, Elisa wanted to write her a letter just to ensure she was alright. But she knew she had to maintain her distance. Perhaps then, her inappropriate desires would fade away.

"Still thinking of her?" Lana asked, placing her empty mug on the coffee table.

"Never mind," Elisa replied in a dull voice. "I've had much worse problems than a broken heart."

"It's been two months since you arrived here, and I can't stand by any longer. You both clearly care deeply for each other. Doesn't that deserve a chance?"

"It's a hopeless case," Elisa muttered, finishing her drink in two gulps. The hot chocolate warmed her stomach, but it couldn't ease her tension in the slightest.

Lana offered an encouraging smile. "The truth is, the world is constantly changing. Just two years ago, no one would have allowed a woman to become a guardian, but look at us now. Who would have thought we'd be sitting here like this?"

"But it's different," Elisa countered. "You managed to solve a complex case and apprehend a serial killer who had been terrorizing people for years. Plus, your father is the chief in Triville."

"True," Lana agreed. "That's why they allowed me to become a guardian after I passed the exams. But I also became a guardian because I genuinely wanted to help others. I couldn't stand by when I witnessed injustice. And I still see it. In your situation, it's unjust that you have to distance yourself from your loved one to fulfill your duties."

"Well, life isn't fair." Elisa sighed, wrapping herself in a blanket. "And I can't risk putting Jackie in trouble by neglecting the guardian code."

"You're right," Lana responded quietly. "As a cadet, you don't have much choice."

Elisa winced. "That's... too honest."

"But don't you dare give up on your dreams. The rules may change when the time demands it. So, excel in your work and become a valuable, irreplaceable detective. Then, with enough support and respect from your colleagues, you can challenge and change these outdated rules."

"Yeah, like anyone would ever listen to me."

"As long as the change is reasonable. Same-gender relationships won't harm anyone, so trust me, people will eventually yield to it."

"When you speak like this, I start to believe you," Elisa admitted. Her heart beat louder in her chest, aligning with this new, remarkable dream. For now, it was just an idea, like a pencil sketch etched in her mind. But what if it could become a reality one day?

"To be honest, I believe this change is inevitable," Lana stated, her hand gently resting on the back of the sofa. "And you can be a part of it. The question is – how much do you desire it?"

"Desperately," Elisa replied without hesitation.

"Then, you will have my full support when the time comes."

34

The Truth from the Underground

The next morning, Jackie stood outside the chief's office, fully prepared for the day ahead. Walter was already inside, receiving instructions. She pressed her ear against the door but couldn't hear anything – the room was likely protected from eavesdropping with a Muting spell. Disappointed, Jackie walked over to the window. Just then, the door swung open, and Walter emerged, holding a folded piece of paper in his hand.

"What's that?" Jackie inquired.

"A search warrant," he replied. "Do you remember that case you worked on with your flame friend?"

She nodded. Since the day she and Theo had scared off the criminals, no one had been able to find any trace of the fighting clubs or drug dealers. It was as if they had vanished from Middle Lake city, leaving everyone to assume they were lying low. Perhaps the dealers were waiting for the right moment to resurface and resume their illegal activities.

Walter pocketed the paper. "We're heading to the new club that just opened at the far end of the city. There was an incident there last night, and it's likely that the owner has information on the criminals we're after."

"I hope I won't mess up this time," Jackie quipped.

Walter shrugged. "Why would you? It's just a routine check, not an undercover operation."

"Fair enough."

They strolled down the corridor. As they reached the exit, Jackie stole a glance back. Trevor stood at the threshold, arms crossed over his chest, his piercing blue eyes sending shivers down her spine. Yesterday, she had promised him to resolve the issue with Walter, and she had kept her word. Moving forward, she knew she had to tread carefully.

The new club appeared bright and spacious, perhaps due to the absence of visitors besides the two of them. Tall, narrow windows allowed sunlight to filter in, while night plants twined up the pillars, their buds tightly closed in slumber. At the far end of the hall, a small stage with a couple of chairs hinted at live performances.

"Look," Walter whispered, nodding towards the kitchen door.

A red-bearded man in a black suit approached them.

"That's the owner," Walter murmured. "Try to read him when the time is right."

"Understood."

The man drew nearer, offering a smile. Jackie sensed he was concealing something. Unbeknownst to him, Jackie possessed the ability to read minds, giving her a unique advantage.

"Detective Mills," Walter introduced himself. "And this is my colleague, Cadet Robinson."

"I've always been terrible with names," the man remarked casually. "Let's keep it simple. Just call me Joe."

"Alright, Joe," Walter acknowledged. "We're here for a quick inspection."

"Why? Your colleagues were here yesterday to handle a minor incident."

Walter retrieved the folded paper from his pocket and handed it to Joe. "Here's the warrant. We suspect this incident may be linked to one of our previous cases."

Joe shrugged. "Feel free to check whatever you need to."

"Excellent." Walter grinned. "Cadet Robinson, where should we start?"

Jackie scanned the room. "Where did the fight take place?"

Joe gave her a weary look. "Haven't your colleagues briefed you? The guy went berserk and assaulted my new waiter at the fifth table." He gestured towards a corner adorned with plush sofas and coffee tables.

Approaching him, Jackie pointed to the side tables. "Over there?"

Joe groaned in frustration at Jackie's 'dumbness.' He guided her hand to the correct spot. "There, in the middle. Look for a plate with the number 5 on it."

His touch triggered her mind-reading ability. Jackie closed her eyes, delving into Joe's memories from the previous night. She saw the battered waiter with a bruise under his eye, pleading his case to a club patron in an attempt to defend himself. It became apparent to Jackie that the altercation had stemmed from a drug-related misunderstanding. Following a faint trail, she delved deeper into Joe's recollections.

In Joe's memory, she witnessed the scene of the dark street where the waiter, Joe, and a grey-haired man with pale blue eyes stood together. The man was instantly recognizable to Jackie – he had been present at the fighting club during her undercover mission with Theo. In Joe's recollection, the mysterious man handed him a bag of coins, which Joe accepted.

Gasping for breath, Jackie opened her eyes. "How did you hire this waiter?"

Joe shrugged nonchalantly and fabricated a story. "As usual. We posted an advertisement in the newspaper, and he responded for an interview. It's a standard procedure."

Squinting suspiciously, Jackie pressed on. "And what became of the waiter after last night?"

Joe rolled his eyes before responding dismissively. "What do you think? He demanded compensation and left early. I doubt he'll return."

Acknowledging his response, Jackie made her way to the fifth table where the altercation had taken place. As Walter had briefed her, the club visitor involved was a young man who had recently lost his fiancée to a drug overdose. When the waiter asked him to leave, the visitor's emotions spiraled out of control, leading to the fight.

The authorities had taken the club visitor to the Guardian House for questioning, but little information was gleaned. All they knew was that the waiter had earlier sold the drugs to the man and his fiancée in that very nightclub. So, the guardian's focus was on identifying the waiter before he vanished from the city or had his memories tampered with.

Jackie conjured a ball of Light in her hands and murmured a Revealing spell. Gently touching the floor with her Light, she uncovered a tangle of intertwined energy traces, indicating a bustling activity the previous day. However, as Joe had claimed, no one had approached the table after the incident around 11 p.m.

Typically, energy traces dissipated after 12 hours, but they could still track down the waiter if they located his distinct trail. Given that he was the last to serve the table, his trace should stand out or be separate from the others. Jackie knelt under the table, only to find the area surprisingly pristine. There was not a single remnant of human energy.

"Damn it," she muttered in frustration.

Walter crouched beside her. "Did you uncover anything?"

"The traces. They've been wiped clean," Jackie replied grimly.

"That's not good."

He assisted her in emerging from under the table, and Jackie shook her knees to rid them of the dust.

Jackie shot Walter a puzzled glance. "Erasing traces from a crime scene is illegal and requires a complex spell. Who would do such a thing?"

"Damn criminals, who else? They likely snuck in after the incident and cleaned up."

"Why didn't the guardians notice the missing trace?" Jackie questioned.

Walter clenched his fist and slammed it onto the table, the noise reverberating through the room. "Because they're as thick as a plank!"

She flinched at his outburst. "Can you please calm –"

He shot her a stern look, silencing her. "And the bureaucratic red tape! If we hadn't waited until morning for the warrant, we might have caught the culprit."

Acknowledging his frustration, Jackie nodded. It was a harsh reality; at times, the rules hindered the guardians' efforts, giving criminals an unfair advantage.

They found respite on a bench under the shade of a maple tree, where the wind gently stirred the leaves above them, creating a soft rustling sound. Lost in their own thoughts, neither Jackie nor Walter spoke. Jackie couldn't discern Walter's thoughts, but her own mind drifted back to her mission with Theo, to the moment they were standing near the boxing ring. Back then, Theo conversed with a wealthy woman while the enigmatic man, whom Jackie dubbed the mystery man, loitered nearby with his piercing pale blue eyes. Throughout the encounter, the mystery man remained silent, observing their every move.

Recalling the man from Joe's memories, Jackie pieced together his significance in the criminal underworld. *Who was he, exactly? Perhaps a negotiator or a key player in the criminal hierarchy?*

As Jackie pondered this thought, she delved into her memories in search of any prior encounters with him. Initially, she had a vague sense of familiarity when she first met him at the fighting club in the spring, but his presence didn't strike her as significant at the time. Now, understanding his importance, she felt compelled to unravel the mystery.

Closing her eyes, Jackie focused on recalling his face within her own memories. And then, it clicked.

The memory resurfaced from the day she was discharged from the hospital. Eager to obtain her referral for the Academy from Trevor, she had arrived at the Guardian House building. Jackie had chosen an early morning hour to avoid drawing attention. Standing beneath a tree in the front yard, she had a chance encounter with the man in a hat as he exited the building. His face was etched in her memory as he hurried past her, oblivious to her presence, and disappeared down the street.

Jackie opened her eyes, her mind racing with the newfound connection between the mysterious man and the Guardian House. She rubbed her temples, trying to clear her thoughts and focus on the implications of this revelation. It seemed likely that the man had purposefully avoided detection during his interaction with a guardian, suggesting a potential connection between them.

"Walter?" she called out, seeking his attention.

He responded with a tired expression. "What is it?"

"I think the guardian from your team is involved in removing the traces."

"What are you talking about?" Walter questioned, clearly puzzled.

She grasped his elbow. "Listen, I've seen this man in three different places – paying Joe, at the fighting club, and coming out of the Guardian House."

Walter's expression shifted as he grasped the gravity of her words. "Which man are you referring to?"

"The one who holds the key to this case. We need to find him. We just have to identify who was at the Guardian House during that time."

"Do you recall the exact date and time?" Walter inquired.

Jackie nodded. "Yes, it was shortly after sunrise, around six in the morning, on September 2nd of last year."

He furrowed his brow. "Accusing a guardian is a grave matter. You can't do so without evidence."

"But Walter –" Jackie began.

He stood up abruptly. "What are you insinuating? Are you pointing fingers at me now?"

Her eyes widened in surprise. "What?"

Walter took a deep breath. "Listen here, rookie. I distinctly remember September 2nd. It was the day before classes commenced at the Academy. All the guardians who had been on summer training were absent, leaving just Dereck and me on night duty. However, Dereck left early due to feeling unwell. At five, a chief guardian arrived to take over."

Jackie stared at him, unblinking. She couldn't have made a mistake. She had practiced her meditative techniques numerous times and was confident in her memory. Yet, she also knew Walter. In truth, she had never had the opportunity to read him. The real question was – how well did she truly know him?

"Are you certain you didn't see a man in a hat that day?" Jackie asked.

"Absolutely. I was stationed in the observation tower until eight o'clock, and I only observed the guardians arriving."

"Perhaps you turned away briefly to grab a coffee or something?" Jackie suggested.

"I would have noticed a stranger near our building."

Jackie sighed, realizing that if Walter hadn't noticed her that day, he might have overlooked the presence of the mystery man as well.

"What if I speak with the chief?" Jackie proposed. "He was there at that time, so he might have seen something."

Walter's eyes flashed with a hint of irritation. "Aren't you already in frequent communication with him?"

"What do you mean?!"

"I thought we had an understanding last night. Yet, just before you mustered the courage to voice your grievances about me to the chief. This morning, I received a reprimand."

Jackie went speechless. As far as she could recall, she hadn't lodged any complaints about Walter to Trevor. It seemed that Trevor had taken it upon himself to intervene, which likely explained Walter's current agitation.

Walter's voice rose almost to a shout. "What are you attempting to achieve? Sabotage my career?"

She gasped. "Why won't you believe me?"

He turned away, taking a deep breath to compose himself. "You know what? We both need to calm down. Today is my birthday, and I don't want to spoil my mood. Let's revisit this discussion in the evening and work through it together."

"Of course," she responded softly. "I'm certain there's a logical explanation."

"I believe there is."

35

❧

What We Are Fighting For

Jackie turned in front of the mirror, admiring her reflection in the tight green dress that perfectly matched her sparkling eyes. *Why don't I wear dresses more often?* She had been so focused on work, but now she felt more like a woman, and she liked it.

As Jackie pulled her hair up, she debated whether to leave it down or secure it with hairpins. Ultimately, she decided to pin half of her hair up and let the other half cascade freely over her shoulders.

Outside, the warm summer night filled the air with the fragrance of blossoming flowers. The guardians must have already arrived at the pub, with almost everyone present except for several guys on night duty. Jackie felt ready to face Walter and put an end to their misunderstandings.

Even though she still didn't know why that mystery man was coming out of the Guardian House, she was confident that Walter would find a way to investigate it. Despite everything, he was a good detective. Jackie was still slightly shocked by his reaction earlier that day, but she hoped her pretty dress would soften him tonight. She took one last look in the mirror, grabbed her purse, and walked outside.

In the pub, Jackie had to navigate through the crowd using her elbows to reach the far table where the guys were seated. They were dressed in their usual black guardian uniforms. There were twenty-three men, including five guardians on practice, who had gathered here this summer. Howard sat in the corner, engaged in conversation with the red-haired cadet from Santos.

Meanwhile, Walter was placing an order at the bar, so Jackie made her way over to the guardians' table. All eyes turned towards her as she approached.

"Jackie!" Howard exclaimed in admiration. "You look fantastic."

"Thank you," she replied with a humble smile.

Jackie placed her purse on the table, eagerly anticipating Walter's arrival to begin celebrating his birthday. He had assured her that he would calm down and they would work things out. Little did she know what he had in store for her.

As the room fell silent, Jackie noticed Walter approaching her from behind. She turned to face him, only to see him carrying a tray with a glass of red wine. To her surprise, her red panties were provocatively displayed on the tray for everyone to see.

"Look what I brought you," Walter said, a wide grin spreading across his face.

Jackie's breath got caught in her throat. It was hard to believe that this was actually happening. "What's that?" she managed to ask.

Walter handed her a glass of wine, and she accepted it, fighting the urge to slap him. She knew that was what he wanted – to provoke her outburst, so she clenched her teeth and remained where she stood.

Pointing at the panties on the tray, Walter spoke, "I brought it back to you."

"I thought we had a deal," Jackie replied, lowering her voice, though the hushed atmosphere made it easy for everyone to hear their conversation.

"Exactly," Walter said, placing the tray on the table. "And if I recall correctly, you claimed you only read me once."

"Yes."

"Wrong answer," Walter retorted.

After a moment of hesitation, Jackie conceded, "Okay, I've never read you. Are you happy now?"

Walter gave her a scornful look. "It's even worse."

"Why are you doing this to me?" Jackie asked, her voice tinged with desperation.

Walter scowled. "Because you're a deceitful bitch. Just admit it – you've read me multiple times to advance your career. You're willing to do whatever it takes to get what you want, but in reality, you're nothing but a whore."

Jackie went numb. She considered asking Howard to explain that it was he who had warned her, but she knew it wouldn't make any difference.

Walter reached out and touched her chin, forcing her to meet his furious gaze. "You tried to manipulate me to further your own agenda. Is that how you operate, playing games with people?"

"No!" Jackie protested, taking a step back.

Walter chuckled. "You knew you were in over your head and struck a deal with me last night. Just admit it!"

Jackie shook her head. "I swear, I never read you."

"Fine," Walter said, his eyes narrowing. "If that's true, then someone must have informed you about the deal. Just tell me who it was, and I'll forgive you."

Tears welled up in Jackie's eyes, and in a moment of desperation, she remembered the glass of wine in her hand. Without hesitation, she raised it and splashed its contents into Walter's face, causing laughter to erupt from the onlookers. Jackie turned on her heel and ran towards the exit, berating herself for her actions.

Stupid me, she thought. *Stupid, stupid, and stupid once more.* After everything she had learned about Walter, Jackie could sense that he had set a trap for her. Now, with no escape route in sight, she found herself panting in the middle of the bar, her heart racing as she looked back. Something strange was unfolding before her eyes. She wiped away her tears and blinked in disbelief.

Howard suddenly stood up and vanished into thin air. In the next instant, Walter bent over and collapsed to the floor. Howard reappeared, this time standing over him. Momentarily, the other guardians became embroiled in a chaotic brawl. When these skilled men were involved in a fight, it was always something extraordinary. Jackie had never witnessed it firsthand, but now Howard was at the center of the action, and she couldn't tear her gaze away from him.

Walter moved his arm, causing several plates and forks to fly from the table towards Howard, who narrowly dodged them. Another guardian then rose, conjuring a ball of mist in his palm – a paralyzing spell. As he aimed it towards Howard, the latter vanished into thin air, causing the spell to veer off course and strike a man at the adjacent table who was enjoying his steak.

The man stood frozen, his mouth half-open. Nearby, a woman dropped her spoon and began screaming in terror.

As all the guardians rose and closed in on Walter, Howard found himself surrounded, his eyes darting around desperately in search of an escape. But it was too late – he was cornered. One of the guardians seized his shoulders, and Walter began striking his face. Jackie felt a surge of helplessness, wishing she could intervene, but what could she do with her mind-reading Gift? Then it struck her – she knew the right spell.

Summoning a fireball in her hands, Jackie hurled it towards the chandelier above the guardians. The lights flickered and went out, causing confusion and hesitation among the fighting men. Seizing the opportunity, she dashed towards Howard, who grabbed her hand. In an instant, they both became invisible, disappearing from sight.

In the late hours of the night, Jackie and Howard found themselves seated on the corridor floor between their respective doors. Jackie handed Howard a herbal compress, which he applied to his swollen eyelid.

"You know," Jackie remarked with a smile, "it's the second night in a row that I've been taking care of your health. Starting to feel a bit strange."

"It never gets easier." Howard chuckled, though the pain caused him to wince and fall silent.

"Shh," Jackie hushed him, conjuring a ball of Light in her hands and gently touching his face. Her energy worked to alleviate his discomfort. "You shouldn't have to suffer because of me."

Howard gave her a somber look. "I would do it all over again if someone treated you like that."

Jackie adjusted his compress. "Walter was right – I knew what he wanted and took advantage. I messed up."

Howard reached out and touched her hand. "Don't let him place the blame on you. He had a deal with the other guy from the start. He got what he deserved."

"Regardless, I fear I'll soon lose my career," Jackie lamented.

"You won't," Howard reassured her. "I'll speak to him tomorrow and explain that I warned you."

Jackie cast her gaze downward. "I'm so sorry. I wanted to resolve it on my own, but I put you in trouble instead."

"No. You could have easily revealed that I was the one who informed you about Walter's plan. But you didn't."

"Yet, you ended up getting hurt," she added. Amidst the chaos, she had completely forgotten about the mysterious grey-haired man who had sparked the misunderstanding between her and Walter. Jackie struggled to comprehend the situation – if Walter truly was a snitch, wouldn't he have tried to frame her instead of humiliating her? Or perhaps this was his way of trying to eliminate her from the equation? There was a missing piece to this puzzle that eluded her, leaving her utterly perplexed.

Howard gently squeezed her hand. While his knuckles had stopped bleeding, his hands still trembled. "Walter. Why didn't you tell him the truth?"

"I was too shocked, I suppose," Jackie admitted with a shrug. "You know what? I don't want to dwell on him anymore."

He nodded. "Understood."

"But you started fighting. What happened to you?" Jackie inquired, her curiosity piqued.

Howard set his compress aside and gazed at the wall ahead, his face still showing signs of swelling. "Do you really want to know?"

She sighed, recognizing his care and patience towards her. She wished she could reciprocate his feelings. "Howard –"

"Because I love you, Jackie," he interjected before she could finish. "I love you so deeply that the mere thought of someone else mistreating you is unbearable to me."

Her heart burned in her chest. Here they were, two individuals from different worlds yearning for something they couldn't have. They were both in love with someone who couldn't be theirs. Was love just an illusion, a fleeting potion that was never enough? Life seemed unjust, but Jackie knew she had a choice to make. She could choose the person who truly cared for her despite knowing everything about her. Perhaps Howard would never abandon her, explaining himself in a letter.

Jackie touched his bruised face with her fingertips, and he gazed at her with wide eyes, his body trembling. Leaning in, she pressed her lips to his.

In that moment, her Gift connected with his consciousness, and she experienced the sensation of being truly loved. There were no fears, no doubts, just the radiant glow of a bright light beckoning her to leap into its embrace. Without hesitation, she took the leap, surrendering to the overwhelming feeling of love that enveloped her.

His hands tenderly encircled her, drawing Jackie closer to him. She craved the sense of security and warmth that enveloped her in his embrace. Her hands instinctively began unbuttoning his shirt, feeling the heat of his skin beneath her touch.

"Won't you regret this tomorrow?" he asked, his gaze clouded with uncertainty.

"Let's pretend that tomorrow will never come," she whispered, a sense of urgency driving her actions.

He kissed her once more, and she surrendered to the intoxicating embrace. With a gentle sweep, he lifted her up and carried her to his bedroom. In that moment, all worries and doubts faded away as she allowed herself to bask in the light of his love, finding solace and contentment in his arms.

Story 6

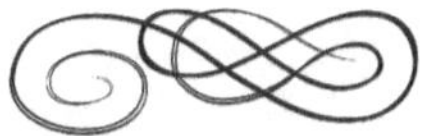

Back to School

36

❦

Embracing The Past

"You can't be serious!" Theo shook his head in disbelief.

Laura gave him a charming smile. "Life is full of surprises."

They stood in the hall of the dorms. It was the third day of September, and the evening sun generously illuminated the space. Laura wore a bright yellow dress, and her cheerful mood made her brown eyes shine as she spoke. This year, she took on more responsibilities in the Academy, and now she helped arrange the rooms for cadets. But her new role wasn't the subject of their discussion.

"Believe it or not, I saw them today," she said. "Urchin and Jackie arrived together this morning."

"It doesn't prove that they are a couple now."

She gave him a playful look. "Well, they'll share the room this year. In the morning, I gave them a key."

Theo rubbed his forehead. It had been three months since they left for summer practice, but everything was turned upside down. Starting from his own heartbreaking experience and finishing with his best friend Urchin dating Elisa's ex-lover.

275

Laura slightly poked his shoulder. "Seriously, you look too preoccupied. What's happened?"

"Too much information, I guess."

"Okay, got it." She chuckled. "Let's find you a room, too."

Clicking her heels, Laura went to the administrator's office. Theo followed her.

In the office, she opened a glass cabinet door and quickly found a key. She gave it to Theo. "I'll put you together with Riley this year. He is a good guy, so you should get along."

"I appreciate that." He paused. "Wait... but what about his neighbor?"

"Simon got fired during his practice," Laura revealed. "Which is not surprising. He often behaved like a jerk."

"True." Theo had never expected himself to be glad about someone's failure, but seeing Simon gone was a relief.

"By the way, how is Rei?"

Theo shrugged. "Growing fast. We think I might try to fly with him in two months."

"I need to hear more." Laura pointed at the small sofa in a corner. "Let's have a seat and relax a bit. And I'll make you some tea."

Theo couldn't find any reason to object, so he obeyed. It was actually pleasant to stretch his legs after hours of riding.

In two minutes, they were on the sofa, discussing their past. They shared many good memories of last year, including the farewell party they organized together. It was good that they decided to stay friends. Now, there was no pressure between them.

"We must organize something soon for the cadets." Laura waved her hand in enthusiasm. "How about a picnic at the lake? We can share the memories of summer and have some outdoor fun."

"It sounds good." Theo placed his teacup on his lap. "But not all the memories would be fun. Mine might go into the *Book of Failures*."

"Oh, no." Her brown eyes became concerned. "Whatever happened there, you can tell me. You know I can keep secrets."

"It's just... The woman I've met."

"So, it's a love matter." Laura got intrigued right away. "I'm all ears."

"I met her in Triville. She seemed to be so nice and interesting." Theo took a deep sigh before continuing. "We started seeing each other, and everything went well. I shared a lot about my work, and she always found words of support. But one day, I discovered she was involved in local criminal activities."

"She was a snitch?"

Theo shook his head. "It was complicated. All I can say is that we both learned a valuable life lesson. It's over now, so there is no reason to dwell on it."

Laura inspected his face for a minute before replying. "Whatever happened, you were in love with her. Even though it hurts, all the pain will ease with time. Eventually, it will be something worth remembering."

"I wish it could have been different," he said in a dull tone. "What is the reason for such misfortune with women? First Elisa, then this... Seriously, what's wrong with me?"

Laura took a sip of tea, thinking. "You are right. It's you."

He gave her a perplexed look. "What a wonderful support."

"Hold on." She raised her index finger, explaining. "I mean your nature, Theo. As you once told me, your bloodline belongs to the ancient generation of dragon hunters."

"Right."

"And it explains a lot. On some level, you will always be attracted to the most unreachable target. It's in your blood."

"And how to remove this curse?" He wondered. "Is it a special spell?"

She chuckled. "No spell will help here. If it's true love, you can overcome all the obstacles."

He leaned on the sofa back, his voice filled with despair. "I see. I'll die alone."

She smiled and clapped his shoulder. "One day, you will choose the right woman."

"Really?"

"Of course. Just trust my word."

The door opened with a loud creak, and they both turned to face the visitor. It was hard to recognize Elisa. She wore black leather pants and a tight red top; her golden hair was cut short.

She walked in. "Hi, guys! I hope I'm not interrupting."

Laura rose. "It's alright. Good to see you back."

"We missed you." Theo stood up and hugged her.

While Laura was looking for a key, they exchanged short greetings. Theo was afraid to mention the news about Jackie, but she didn't ask.

"Here you go." Laura gave her a key to her room. "This year, you will have your own private room."

"Awesome!" Elisa gave her a tired smile. "I would chat with you two, but I'm too exhausted from the road. I think I'll go straight to bed."

"Good idea." Theo agreed.

He watched her silhouette disappear at the staircase when she left the room. Maybe everything had changed after summer, but at least they had one more evening before they faced this new reality.

In the night, Elisa opened her eyes. The air in the room was stale, so she climbed out of her bed to open the windows. Rustling trees below her bedroom and the sweet smells of flowers reminded her of the summer that was about to die. She looked into the starry night sky, imagining her meeting with Jackie. Maybe writing her a goodbye letter was a mistake. Elisa closed her eyes, letting the warm wind touch her face. Then, she heard sounds coming from the right window.

Someone was giggling in the neighboring room. There were two voices, and one of them belonged to a man. The other could only belong to the woman she missed so much. *Jackie.* Her heart sank.

Without much thought, she took the empty glass from her nightstand and jumped on her bed. She pressed the rim of the glass to the wall and leaned her ear to its bottom. The sounds in the room reminded her of horse riding, with all the puffing and rhythmic squeaking of the saddle.

She jumped from her bed and stood in the middle, motionless. These two definitely had a wild encounter that could only be described as sex.

A glass slid from her trembling hand and fell on the floor, bursting into shards. In shock, Elisa stared at the shining pieces of glass. Her soul was torn into pieces, too, making it impossible to breathe. At first, her brain tried to suggest that it was just a nightmare and that she would wake up. She looked at her feet, covered with small scratches. Her skin pinched. No, it wasn't a bad dream. It was a merciless reality.

Slowly, she walked to her road bag and opened it. Elisa was looking for the first aid box so she could take care of the scratches.

Instead, her hand extracted a small dark-blue glass bottle from the inner pocket. The dark liquid inside lured her, offering a promise of momentary relief.

Elisa opened the lid and inhaled the strong aroma of herbs. A forbidden potion made of Moon Dust. All this time, she kept it here, promising herself to pour this potion out somewhere in the forest. She never did. Maybe one part of her secretly wanted to try it again while common sense objected. And now, when the person she loved the most was just behind the wall, in someone else's arms, her common sense was muffled... A tear slid down her cheek.

She dripped two drops on the back of her palm. Then she licked it. Elisa stood up and placed the bottle in her drawer, feeling a pleasant numbness in her fingers. The pain was numbed, too. Then she went back to her bed and closed her eyes.

37

An Arrow

In the morning, Jackie woke up in her wide bed, the sun tickling her eyelashes. The smells of coffee and fresh pastry made her smile. She opened her eyes. Breakfast was waiting for her on the nightstand along with a fresh-cut red rose that rested in a glass of water. Howard sat in the chair in front of her, wearing nothing but his blinding smile and black cotton boxers.

"Good morning," he greeted her.

Jackie yawned and stretched in her bed, her muscles pleasantly tired after everything they had done the night before.

"Did you sleep well?" Howard asked.

She rested her cheek on her hand. "If you had let me sleep."

He chuckled. "I just did what you asked me to do. Now, wake up. Classes will start soon."

Right, the classes would start that day, which meant Elisa must have come back last night. Today, Jackie would see her, and she wasn't sure what to say.

"I know what you're worrying about," Howard said.

Jackie flinched. "Do you?"

"Of course. I can read body language, remember?"

Jackie rolled onto her belly, preparing to hear his version. *Would he ever truly understand me?*

"Walter," he said.

Jackie rolled her eyes. "Howard, please. I thought we closed this subject!"

"Not yet," Howard insisted, narrowing his eyes. "I know you don't want to discuss it, but Jackie, this morning I found this." He picked up the massive book from the coffee table and showed her the cover with the title *The Book of Gifts*.

Jackie laughed. "Don't tell me you woke up so early to read it."

"Just the chapter on the Mind Reading Gift," Howard clarified.

"Oh."

"There is a way to access your memories through a third person. We can perform a ritual involving three people to uncover who the mystery man is. We just need to find someone you trust."

"Like whom?"

"I'm thinking of Elisa."

She took a sip of her coffee, contemplating a suitable excuse. "Howard, my Gift has its limitations, especially when it comes to people I have feelings for."

"Right, I won't be able to read you, but I can still facilitate the connection with a third person," Howard suggested.

Jackie bit her lip, the weight of the love triangle looming over her. She knew the ritual wouldn't work with Elisa involved, but she couldn't let Howard catch on. She needed to come up with another excuse quickly. *How long can I keep this secret from him?*

Howard cleared his throat. "I can always ask Theo."

Jackie shook her head. "The last thing I need is another man delving into my thoughts."

"Of course," Howard replied, looking out the window where the sun shone brightly. His hair was tousled, making a stark contrast to the young man she had met a year ago. Something had changed in him, or perhaps it was just her perception.

"Don't be upset," she said softly. "I appreciate your efforts. Just give me more time, okay?"

"Can you believe we'll see everyone today?" Howard asked, changing the subject. "What do you think they'll make of us as a couple?"

"Can we just stay hidden in this room?" Jackie suggested.

Howard got up and sat on her bed, his finger lightly tracing her neck. "You're so beautiful, Jackie. I wish this morning would never end."

She moved closer to kiss him, but Howard leaned back. "Let's go now. We need to talk to everyone."

"We still have some time," Jackie said, removing the blanket and giving him a playful look.

He stood up and walked to the closet, avoiding eye contact with her. "I know what you're trying to do."

"What?"

"You're trying to distract me from thoughts about the ritual. But I won't give up."

She didn't reply. Howard found her uniform on a shelf and laid it out on the bed. With no other choice, Jackie began to dress.

Within half an hour, they were already in the classroom with the rest of the group. The young men Jackie had studied with the previous year appeared slightly different. They seemed more mature and self-assured. Four guys were absent, having not passed the practice, but Theo was present, regaling everyone with tales of his summer training in Triville. The group gathered around him, captivated by stories of Rei and the dragon farm, their eyes wide with wonder. According to Theo, a young couple had begun raising dragons there the previous year, and the venture had proven successful.

To Jackie's relief, Elisa had not yet arrived in the classroom. Howard proudly announced their relationship, prompting congratulations from the others. Howard shook hands with the men, while Jackie greeted them with smiles and brief hugs. Suddenly, the entrance doors swung open, and all heads turned in unison. It was Elisa.

The room seemed to grow quieter. The only sound Jackie could hear was the pounding of her own heart in her ears.

Elisa had undergone a noticeable transformation – her once famous horse-tail hair was now cut short, and her golden locks cascaded freely around her face. Her sapphire eyes scanned the room until they settled on Jackie.

Jackie's heart seemed to stop beating, and she instinctively reached for Howard's hand to steady herself.

"I've heard you two are together now," Elisa said, offering them a soft smile. "Congratulations."

She approached and embraced Jackie, planting a gentle kiss on her cheek. The scent of her perfume made Jackie's head spin. All her hopes of moving on from Elisa and finding someone new were shattered in that moment. How foolish she had been to think she could replace Elisa – the one person she truly wanted to be with, the one who had seemingly forgotten her so easily.

"How did you find out about us?" Howard inquired. "We only just announced it."

"My room is near yours," Elisa replied with a sly look. "That's how I heard."

If words were arrows, Jackie's heart would have been pierced at that moment. The realization that Elisa had heard them having sex hit her like a ton of bricks. All Jackie wanted to do was retreat to her room, lock the door, and cry for the rest of the day. But instead, she took a deep breath, fighting back tears, and turned to Howard, whose smile remained unwavering.

"We'll use the Muting spell next time," Howard suggested.

"Good idea," Elisa replied with a chuckle.

Shooting her a playful smile, Elisa took her seat and began arranging her notebooks on her desk as if nothing had happened. *Why is she so unnervingly calm?*

Jackie made her way to her desk, her mind swirling with turmoil. She wasn't sure how she would make it through the rest of the day. However, her focus shifted when the door opened, and Don, the teacher, entered the classroom. As he began the lesson, Jackie's thoughts turned to the art of being a guardian.

Don scanned the classroom. "Congratulations! You all passed the exams and successfully completed your summer training with real cases. Look around – last year, there were twelve people in this class. Now, there are only eight."

Jackie glanced to her left, where Elisa sat. The gentle sunlight illuminated her, casting a golden halo around her head. Today, Elisa took a step closer to her dream of becoming a guardian. While Jackie knew she couldn't be with her, she understood that sometimes, the pursuit of others' happiness came at a steep cost. What truly mattered was Elisa's well-being. And as she observed Elisa, she appeared content. Perhaps Elisa had never loved her as deeply as Jackie had thought.

Don gestured with his hand, utilizing his Telekinesis Gift to move the chalk up to the blackboard surface and draw an oval shape.

"Who can tell me what this represents?" Don inquired, pointing to the drawing on the board.

A hush fell over the room as the cadets pondered the question. Don's expression turned sardonic. "This is you, cadets! And this is your greatest achievement for today. Last year, you were mere slugs, caterpillars, clueless rookies!" He paused, scanning the room. "And today... Today, you are the chrysalises. It's still a bit unsettling, I must admit, but not as ugly."

Turning to Jackie, Don posed a question. "Cadet Robinson, what do you need to complete your evolution and become a butterfly?"

"More practice?" she ventured.

Don nodded. "Yes, but not only that. To grow wings and earn the title of guardian, you must first grasp the concept of team building. Last year, your group successfully completed my quest, and now, four of you have been selected to design a quest for the new rookie team. I will name four students with the highest marks, and together, you will collaborate to create a new group quest."

Theo raised his hand. "Excuse me, which group of rookies are we referring to?"

"Good question," Don acknowledged. "It will be a class of engineers consisting of twelve cadets. You are tasked with conducting the quest in a similar manner to the one I assigned your group last year."

Elisa chimed in, "Can't we just replicate the same quest?"

"Certainly not," Don replied. "In my years of teaching, I've learned that it's impossible to give the exact same quest to every group. You can incorporate certain elements, but you must first meet the cadets you are working with and tailor the quest accordingly." Don paused before adding, "Of course, if you want to become real guardians."

38

The Rookies

Elisa walked through the corridor with Theo, her new partner for the day. While Jackie and Urchin were in the library working on a quest, they went to meet the brand-new team of rookies, as Don had called them.

Theo talked about his summer practice, and Elisa couldn't help but laugh. "I can't believe you're so unlucky," she said as he finished his story.

"I know," his face expressed sorrow. "It seems like I'm always attracted to the wrong women."

She sighed deeply. "Me too."

He stopped and touched her shoulder. "Are you alright? I know it must be hard to see Jackie –"

"I'm fine," she replied, removing his hand. When she said it aloud, it almost seemed true, at least as long as the morning dose of potion worked. "We were on the brink of making a huge mistake. I'm glad she moved on, and I must do the same."

His blue eyes locked with hers. "I know you too well. You always pretend that nothing happened, but deep down, you're broken."

"I know you, too," she replied in a calm voice. "You always exaggerate things and create unnecessary drama."

"I'm just worried about you." He glanced at the closed classroom door. "Today, I noticed how Jackie looks at you."

"She seems to be quite happy."

"It's just a mask. When we were on our mission in the nightclub, we talked. She told me everything."

"Everything?" Her voice dropped to a whisper, "what did she say?"

"Ask her yourself."

Elisa shook her head. Like a drowning man clutching at straws, she held her ground. "Jackie is my friend, and it must stay that way. I know it's not easy, but I'll handle it."

"I hope you know what you're doing," he said. "And don't worry. I'll make sure your secret remains untold."

Elisa mustered a smile. "Thanks. I'm so lucky to have you by my side." Theo was smart, maybe too smart. Now, it was becoming increasingly difficult to pretend when she was so close to the woman she loved. On the other hand, she couldn't jeopardize Jackie's relationship with Urchin.

"Let's go now," Theo rushed her as he opened the classroom door.

They entered the classroom, a magical engineering class where cadets typically mixed herbs to create potions. Colored glass bottles lined the shelves, and the teacher, the elderly Mrs. Hillstone, sat at her desk. She was an intriguing woman – her hair was gray, and her wrinkles deepened when she smiled. Yet, her bright green eyes sparkled with a fire of curiosity.

Elisa hoped to be like her when she grew old – draped in a bright shawl, hands fragrant with herbs. She was certain Mrs. Hillstone could identify every herb in existence and concoct a potion for any occasion with her eyes closed.

Mrs. Hillstone rose from her seat and surveyed the class. "These are the senior cadets, Elisa and Theodore. They will be leading a quest for you."

Elisa scanned the room. Twelve young people sat at their desks, all clad in black cadet uniforms adorned with a golden dragon on the right shoulder. A mix of excitement and fear of failure reflected in their eyes. Ten of them were men, while two were young women. It brought back memories of their first day of classes, filling Elisa's heart with warmth.

Theo approached the board. "Who can tell me what it means to be a guardian?"

"To apprehend criminals," a man with a low voice and smart hazel eyes spoke up.

"What's your name?" Elisa inquired.

He stood up. "Edward Reynolds."

"And how would your Gift help you in catching them?" she asked.

"Well, I can perceive magic connections on a deep level."

Theo moved closer. "So, you can brew potions without a recipe?"

"Yes, but that's not all," Edward said with pride. "I can decipher how spells function just by observing them."

Elisa and Theo exchanged glances.

"That's impressive. But what if you need to neutralize the criminal?" Theo questioned.

"I'll use a Paralyzing spell," Edward declared as he extended his palm, causing a silver ball to materialize like a cloud of mist.

"Good skill. Now, shoot it at the wall," Theo instructed.

Edward aimed and released the spell, the ball striking the wall and leaving a circle of frost in its wake.

Theo raised his hand, flames dancing between his fingers. "Perfect. Now, you can't access your power as your magic channels are numb. This means you're vulnerable if I were to attack."

Edward's expression fell, and he returned to his seat.

Theo surveyed the room. "Remember the first rule of the guardians – always have a partner who can provide cover. Today, you'll be working in teams, so keep that in mind."

After meeting the new cadets, they proceeded to the library, where the guys awaited them. In the vast library room, the books loomed overhead, and Elisa breathed in the scent of old papers. Jackie must have truly missed this place.

At the reception desk, Laura was organizing files. She glanced up at them, her gaze lingering on Theo. Revealing her charming smile, she asked, "How have you been?"

"Good," Theo replied. "And you? Did you find the novel I mentioned?"

"Yes. I started reading it last night," Laura said, her eyes fixed on Theo.

Elisa sighed. She was certain Laura would find a way to win over the stubborn guy. Looking around, Elisa asked, "Where are the guys?"

"I'll show you," Laura offered, leading them deeper into the library.

Jackie and Urchin sat at a desk, engaged in quiet conversation. Blank sheets of paper lay untouched before them, and they fell silent as Elisa and Theo approached.

Theo sat in a chair, placing his palms on the table. "So, our task is complete. How about you two?"

Jackie lifted her gaze, avoiding eye contact with Elisa. "We've devised the second part of the quest for the victim."

Urchin retrieved a red glass bottle from his pocket and set it on the table. "They'll need to find an antidote for this sleeping potion."

"And what about the quest itself?" Elisa inquired, taking a seat. "Did you find Don's notes about the first day's challenges?"

Laura shrugged. "Sorry, we don't have any records of past quests."

Jackie's eyes widened. "How are we supposed to proceed then?"

"We only have two hours left to figure it out," Theo remarked, twirling a pencil in his hand.

Laura joined him at the table. "I'll assist you. But first, we need to learn more about their Gifts."

"I visited Don's office and made some notes," Jackie said, placing a handwritten list of the cadets with brief descriptions of their Gifts on the desk.

Elisa examined the list. "Nice handwriting."

Jackie gave Elisa a sorrowful look. "Yes, you have a good one too."

She set the list down. "I'm glad you found my letter and followed my advice."

A heavy silence descended upon the room, akin to a looming storm cloud.

"What are you talking about?" Urchin inquired.

Laura cleared her throat, breaking the tension. "I'm sorry to interrupt, but we still need to create the quest."

"How do we go about that?" Elisa asked.

"Conversation usually helps," Laura replied, clasping her hands together. "Let's start by discussing your summer training." She turned to Theo with warmth. "You mentioned having an interesting experience in Triville yesterday. Perhaps you could share it, and we can brainstorm ideas together."

Theo regarded her with concern. "It may not directly relate to the quest, but you're correct. I encountered a Gift Reader, someone who can perceive the depth of your Gift and aid in its development. That's how I honed mine."

Elisa scoffed. "Captain Charles Braun."

Theo's gaze sharpened. "He rooted for you, actually."

"How thoughtful. Did he happen to mention how I ended up an orphan?" Elisa inquired.

Theo hesitated before responding. "No, but he did share a lot about Ghost's case."

"That case," Elisa muttered, shuffling the empty sheets of paper on the table. "They wouldn't have made progress without Lana. This summer, she confided in me about sneaking into the secret archive to steal that classified case folder. She had to enlist a witch's aid to extract her father's Light."

"The magic lock?!" Laura exclaimed, rising from her seat. "This could be the basis for the quest!"

All four of them regarded her with intrigue.

Elisa clapped her hands. "That's a great idea! Are there doors in the Academy with these locks?"

After a moment of contemplation, Laura spoke up. "No, but you can use the regular doors, and I have a book with the appropriate spell for the locks. I'll fetch it."

Elisa grabbed a pencil and began sketching lines on the paper. After ten minutes of intense brainstorming, they had a draft of the quest prepared.

According to their plan, the cadets would be divided into two teams. Each team would possess a key to the other team's door, requiring them to collaborate to unlock all the doors and locate the captured victim.

Laura returned with the book containing detailed instructions, two metal plates, and two glass spheres. Elisa placed one of the spheres on a plate and infused it with her silver Light, whispering a Locking spell. Theo followed suit, filling his sphere with yellow light akin to a miniature sun.

After completing the preparations, Laura gathered the plates and surveyed the group. "We'll need to position the locks in the center of the door, making it impossible to open without your Light. They'll have to apply the Light from the sphere to the plate."

Theo smiled. "Great job, everyone. There's just one issue. That guy who can decipher spell workings; he might solve it easily." He turned to Jackie. "What's his name?"

Jackie consulted the list and found his name. "Edward Reynolds. But you know what, we could bring him along as the victim."

Theo nodded in agreement. "That could work."

Urchin addressed him. "So, you and Elisa will handle the locks, and we'll focus on the victim."

Elisa approached Theo, taking his hand. "Let's go and leave these lovebirds alone."

"Good luck with your part of the quest," Jackie said, watching them go.

"Thanks. You too," Elisa replied with a smile as they departed.

<h1 style="text-align:center">39</h1>

Sweet and Sour

Edward sat on the kitchen floor, twisting the red bottle containing a sleeping potion in his hands. Jackie and Howard sat nearby in silence.

Edward gave them a doubtful look. "Are you guys sure it's safe to drink?"

Howard nodded. "Just take a little sip. You'll fall asleep for a maximum of half an hour. Unless your friends give you an antidote, which would wake you up."

He shook the bottle, and the liquid inside gleamed. "Sleeping potion. This one has a sweet taste. The antidote must taste terrible."

Jackie took the bottle from his hands and placed it on the kitchen table. "Good thing we chose you as the victim."

"I knew that." Edward grinned. "You isolated me because I would crack the quest too quickly."

"Bingo," Jackie said.

Edward stood up, his eyes sparkling. "That's not all I see."

"Really? And what do you see?"

"Human relationships. A love triangle."

Jackie opened her eyes wide, unable to speak. *Gee, I must have forgotten how terrible freshman year students could be.*

Intrigued, Howard came closer. "What the heck are you talking about?"

She handed the bottle to Edward. "It's time to drink the potion."

"Hold on." Howard raised his hand in impatience. "Let the guy speak."

Edward stood in front of them, grinning. It was fun for him, but he had chosen the wrong person to confront.

Jackie took a deep breath to calm her voice. "Edward, you must be careful when accusing your colleagues. Don't speak nonsense if you're not sure."

"Yes, what do you know?" Howard pushed.

"I just see some crossed connections, geometrical shapes... it has three sides."

Jackie gave him a sharp look. "Can you recall the names?"

Edward shrugged. "You guys have a problem here. That's all I know."

"Then you know nothing, rookie. Don't mess with us."

"Yes, our problem is none of your business." Howard crossed his arms over his chest. "Drink the damn liquid. Now."

Obeying, Edward took a sip. He then lay on the kitchen table, his eyes blurred. Jackie approached and gently closed his eyelids, watching him fall asleep.

Howard paced the room before stopping at the exit and pressing his ear to the door. It was quiet in the corridor.

"They have time," Jackie said. "Remember our quest last year? When we opened this kitchen door, we had only a minute left."

"Yes." He gave her a suspicious look. "Good times."

"Is everything all right?"

He glanced at Edward, who was peacefully sleeping. "Jackie, the things he said about a love triangle. Is that true?"

She gave him the most innocent look she could muster. "I have no idea what you are talking about."

He lowered his voice. "I'm talking about Theo. Something's going on between you two."

Trying to ease the tension, Jackie poked his shoulder. "Are you jealous?"

His face stiffened. "You chose him for the investigation right after taking the guardian oaths. Not me."

"Howard, stop it. I chose him precisely because there were no feelings involved. I tried to be professional, and we must do the same now."

He narrowed his eyes. "Then tell me – what am I to you? Just a replacement?"

Her heart pounded in her chest. After everything he had done for her, she couldn't hurt him.

Howard turned to the door. "Something's not right, Jackie. From your sudden appearance in a Guardian House for summer training to this very day, I knew it. You never loved me."

"I'm sorry." She touched his shoulder. "You are right. I did have feelings in the past, but it was wrong. I chose the local Guardian House for training only because I wanted to overcome my past. And you helped me, really."

He turned to her. "Have you overcome it now?"

She shrugged.

"I see." He gave her a disappointed look. "Then let me know when you're over him."

He went to check on Edward, leaving Jackie at the door. Apparently, Howard thought she was interested in Theo, which was ridiculous. But it explained why he was so pushy with the Gift exchange ritual. Maybe now, when they had this argument, Howard would stop digging into this case. It meant that Jackie was on the safe side, and her acquaintance with Chief Trevor would remain a secret. One problem was solved. However, the situation with Elisa might jeopardize their relationship, and Jackie had no idea how to fix it.

The sound of quick steps interrupted her thoughts. Several people were running to the doors, ready to open them at any moment.

She approached Howard. "Ready?"

"I'm always ready."

The doors flew wide open, and the cadets entered the room, their faces filled with excitement.

"Congratulations, guys!" Jackie said. "You managed to work together as a team and find the victim."

Howard took a step forward and pointed at Edward. "But the real quest starts now. Your colleague was poisoned, and you must find a way to wake him up."

One of the women, a red-haired cadet named Maria, stepped forward and picked up a red bottle from the floor. She opened the lid and smelled the bottle. "It's just a sleeping potion."

Howard nodded. "There are at least a dozen recipes for sleeping potions, which means there are a dozen different antidotes. He might never wake up if you give him the wrong one."

Maria approached Edward and looked at his peaceful face. "How do I know which one I should use?"

"Think," Jackie said.

She hesitated. "Can't we just wait for him to wake up?"

"Right." Jackie turned to Howard. "Sometimes, things must run their course."

He scowled. "But sometimes criminals try to buy time to finish their game. They are too greedy, but they can't have everything at once."

Jackie shook her head. "We are the guardians, not criminals."

"But we can make the same mistake."

"Yes, but I try to fix it, don't you see?"

One of the guys raised his hand, and Jackie sighed with relief. This conversation might go too far. Howard could be too pushy sometimes, and now he was unbearable.

Jackie switched her attention to the cadet. "Please, speak."

"The potions differ by taste."

"Go on," Howard encouraged.

The cadet approached the table and took a bottle from Maria's hands. He smelled it. "Hm... This one has a sweet taste. It must contain lavender and honey."

"This is the most popular one. People use it as a remedy for insomnia," Maria said.

"Or for poisoning others," Howard added.

"If this one is sweet, then the antidote must be sour," the guy said.

Maria smiled. "I guess it's lemon and absinthe."

Jackie smiled. "Good job!"

The cadets exchanged excited glances and walked to the kitchen cabinets. Among dozens of bottles on a shelf, they found a green one with a lemon picture on it. They applied the antidote to a cloth, and Maria carefully wiped Edward's lips. His eyes fluttered, and then he sat up, looking around.

Jackie started applauding, and the group joined her. Today, they tasted the sweet victory. Little did they know about the bitter disappointments that awaited them. But it was just the beginning – their beginning, and she didn't want to ruin this moment.

She looked at Howard, who was shaking hands with the cadets. Despite being too preoccupied with her past, he was right about one thing – she had made many mistakes with Elisa, and she needed to open up to her before it was too late.

40

Three Drops

That evening, Jackie didn't go to their empty room. Howard was hanging out in a pub with his friends that he hadn't seen all summer. She decided to follow his example and talk to Elisa. Hesitating, she stopped at her door and closed her eyes, listening.

Elisa was quietly moving inside, murmuring a song. Jackie could imagine how she took her perfectly ironed shirts and dresses before hanging all her clothes in the proper order in her closet. Then, Elisa would place her perfumes on the dresser. She smelled so tasty today. Jackie still had a smear of her morning kiss on her cheek.

Until the fear of failure took over, Jackie made herself knock on the door three times.

"Opened!" Elisa's voice said.

Jackie pushed the door and stepped into the bright room. The purple curtains on the windows made it cozy. Elisa even brought some matching pillows and placed them on her bed. On her dresser, the vase with lilies stood among her perfumes. The silver necklace in the shape of a heart was on top of an opened jewelry box.

"Jackie!" Elisa smiled in greeting. "Come on in."

She stopped arranging her clothes and walked to her. They hugged. Unable to speak, Jackie kept looking at her. For a moment, she forgot why she had come here.

"How do you like my new room?" Elisa asked.

Jackie walked to the window and touched the soft cloth of the curtain. "I think you have a talent. You can mask all the imperfections."

"You're right. This room was a real disaster."

Jackie turned to her. "I'm not talking about the room. I talk about *us*."

Elisa gave her a sad look. "Oh, please. Let's leave it behind."

"There is one problem."

"Which one?"

"I love you too much."

Elisa looked into her eyes, and they kissed. Her lips were soft and sweet, and her hands wrapped around her back. Jackie missed the electric magic of her love and how it made her heart flutter. When Elisa was in her embrace, nothing else mattered. They were alone in the whole world, and no force would make Jackie let her go. Only Elisa herself.

Elisa took a step back. "That was a goodbye kiss."

Jackie touched her swollen lips. They still held the taste of her kiss. "What?!"

"Jackie, I've thought a lot about it. About us." She gave her a sharp look. "We simply can't be together."

"Why?" She was still panting; her mind blurred from mixed sensations.

"It's impossible."

"When there is love, everything is possible," Jackie said with hope in her voice. "Can you look me in the eye and say that you don't love me?"

Elisa shook her head, her golden locks covering her blushing cheeks. "We already talked about it. We can try to hide, but if anyone in the Academy figures out about us, our careers are over."

"Isn't it worth the risk?"

"How do you imagine it?" Elisa sneered. "Oh, I know. I would patiently wait for you while you are fucking with your fake boyfriend next door."

Jackie stood speechless. She had never seen Elisa behave like this; she had become another person – rude and arrogant.

Ignoring her presence, Elisa walked to the opened suitcase and took a couple of T-shirts. Carefully, she placed them on the shelf.

Jackie's voice trembled, letting her down, but she forced herself to speak. "Lissy, I just... I tried to let you go, but I couldn't."

"I've heard how hard you tried," she said, her voice cold like a shard of ice.

"I'll break up with Howard."

Elisa finished arranging the clothes and closed the suitcase; she sat on the top and looked at her with pity. "Please, don't. It'll just break his heart."

Jackie approached the dresser. Elisa's jewelry box was there, and it was open. The diamond on the necklace sparkled, teasing her.

"That's what you are trying to do? Close your own heart in a box? Hide it from everyone?"

"Why not?"

"You can hide the truth from others, but not from yourself."

She shrugged her shoulders. "True. But you know what, I cried it out, and when I still couldn't forget you, I acted like a grown-up person – I found a way to fix it."

Jackie took the suspicious blue bottle filled with dark liquid. She opened the lid, and a strong herbal smell hit her nose. "What's that?"

"A potion that numbs my foolish feelings," Elisa said indifferently. "Now put it back, please."

"You can't just kill love."

Elisa gave her a weary look. "Love is way overrated, my dear. It makes you miserable and puts you in trouble. I'm not a dummy schoolgirl anymore. If I have to choose between my career and a reckless affair, I'm choosing a career."

"What would you choose without this shit?" Jackie weighed the bottle in her hand.

She took it and placed it back on the top of the drawer. "That's why I need it."

Jackie gasped, then walked to the bed and sat down. It wasn't right, and Elisa seemed not to realize the danger she put herself into. "So, this is how you would handle it. Just a drop of suspicious liquid before bedtime."

"Actually, three," she clarified, "One in the morning and two in the evening."

Jackie took a deep breath to refrain from shouting at her. "It's insane, Elisa. I bet this potion is addictive and dangerous. Trust me, I'm a mind reader, and I know how these potions work. You can't suppress your feelings for a long time. It's like an elastic band

– the more you stretch it, the harder it hits you. It would be a disaster."

"I think I'll be alright."

Jackie made herself look at her like a detective. Elisa's eyes glittered a bit, and her cheeks were covered with intense blush. Damn, that's why she was so calm and cheerful today. "How long have you been taking it?"

"Since last night. And it helped. You know, after all the noise you made."

Jackie squeezed a pillow in her hands, so her knuckles became white. "Perfect, that's all because of me."

"The world is not spinning around you. I just need a bit of dope until I get back in shape. I think I'll be over you pretty soon."

"And what would happen when you meet the next woman you fall in love with?"

Elisa rolled her eyes. "It's only temporary. You know that. When I graduate and prove myself as a guardian, I won't care."

"Really?" Her words were faster than her thoughts. "Maybe you'll start dating a fake boyfriend, too? Oh, you know what? I have a cover-up for you."

She sat nearby. "I'm listening."

Jackie took a deep breath before she could continue. "Riley has always been interested in you, and he even asked me if you might give him a chance. You know, dating, kisses, and all that stuff."

"Riley?! Who foresees the future in his dreams?"

"Exactly."

She gave her a curious look. "When did you speak about me?"

"At a party. Just before we left for summer training."

Of course, Elisa didn't know about their conversation with Riley, and Jackie was just challenging her. The only question was how far Elisa would go.

"That's a brilliant idea!" Elisa arose and started moving around the room, swinging her arms. "How didn't I think of it before? We are surrounded by boys, and they always look at me like... I would go to Riley immediately. Where is he?"

Jackie opened her eyes widely. "In a pub with the guys, I guess."

"Great!" Elisa walked to the closet and took one of her dresses. This one was white with a blue flower pattern, and it had charming open shoulders. "How is this one?"

Jackie gave her a worried look. "Seriously?! Are you going to lie to the guy?"

Elisa approached the mirror and fixed her hair. "It won't be the first time for me. In the end, we will agree that things don't work and stay friends."

"I can't believe you're doing this to us."

"Then start getting used to it." She turned to face Jackie. "We all must have a role that we play in public. So, let's just move on and live our lives like nothing has happened between us."

Jackie rose. "Listen, I know you just want to push me away, but I'll be nearby. Right now, you don't feel anything but joy, and maybe you are high. But when this potion evaporates, you will feel worse. You just delay the inevitable. And once you need help, I'll be here for you."

"Please don't." Her eyes gleamed. "I'll be just fine."

"Of course."

Elisa threw the dress on the bed. "Now, are you gonna watch me changing my clothes?"

Jackie shook her head and walked out of the room.

In a corridor, Jackie slid down to the floor and embraced her shoulders. This potion, whatever it consisted of, was the worst way to handle the situation, and the thought of the reasons why Elisa started taking it made her heart bleed.

It was only the first day Elisa had tried it, so Jackie needed to be careful not to trigger her stress. Out of sight, out of mind. Jackie must avoid her as much as possible because it would be for the best. She needed to stop being selfish and give Elisa the space she needed.

Anyway, Jackie couldn't do anything about it at that moment. Elisa was too high, and pressuring her could make things worse. Maybe it wouldn't be so bad. It was just three drops. That's what Elisa said.

Story 7

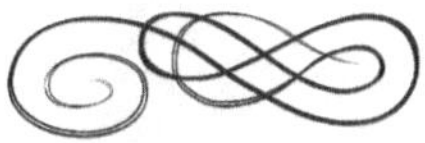

The Masquerade

41

❦

A Fallen Leaf

A scream shattered the stillness of the night, jolting Theo out of his slumber. He sprang out of bed, his hand instinctively rising in a defensive gesture. Flames erupted from his palms, casting a flickering light across his modest bedroom. His groggy mind registered that both the entrance door and window were securely locked. Beside him, Riley stirred restlessly in his bed, murmuring in distress. *Is it another nightmare?*

Theo gestured with his hand, causing the candle on the nightstand to ignite. He approached Riley and gently shook his shoulder. Despite sharing a room in the dorms for nearly two months, Theo still found it challenging to understand Riley's Gift. Often, his ability to foresee future events in his dreams was centered around his relatives or close friends. Sometimes, he saw the crimes plaguing Middle Lake city. These visions always left Riley shaken, much like he appeared now.

Gasping for breath, Riley shifted to his side and blinked his eyes open.

Yawning, Theo inquired, "What did you see this time?"

309

"She died," Riley whispered, his gaze blurred. "She was lying there, on the floor, as pale as the moon itself."

"Sounds creepy." Theo blinked, his mind gradually clearing. "You've certainly mastered the art of description. But for the Divine's sake, who is she?"

Riley swallowed hard before answering. "Elisa."

The name struck him like a blow from a sword. Theo jumped across the room and reached for his uniform hanging on the back of a chair. "Get dressed. Now!"

Riley sat up, his expression pained. "It's not something that can be prevented, Theo. I'm truly sorry."

"That's precisely why you have your Gift! To prevent this! Or at least to try," Theo urged, hastily pulling on his pants. With no time to spare, he left his shirt unbuttoned. "If you keep sitting here like a fool, I swear, I'll set this room ablaze!"

His words carried a weighty impact. Riley stood up and began dressing in his uniform, while Theo had already dashed out of the room.

Opening her room proved to be a minor obstacle – like most cadets, Elisa had secured the door with a chain lock. Theo swiftly bypassed it by using his fire magic to melt the metal. With determination, he burst into the room. The sight that greeted him caused him to come to an abrupt halt. Just as Riley had foreseen, Elisa lay motionless on the floor, her eyes shut tight, her delicate hands splayed on the rug. She was clad only in a white nightgown that now mirrored the pallor of her lifeless visage. Theo approached cautiously, his heart pounding with trepidation at the prospect of confirming Riley's prediction. Steeling himself, he extended a trembling hand and felt for a pulse at her neck.

"I'm so sorry," Riley's voice quavered as he stood beside Theo, his jaw clenched in anguish.

Theo met Riley's gaze. "Her pulse is faint, but she's still breathing."

"Really?" Riley exhaled, his hands clutching his head in disbelief.

"Yes. But she urgently requires medical attention."

Riley nodded. "I'll contact someone on duty immediately."

"The sooner, the better," Theo said. "I'll stay here to watch her."

As Riley departed, Theo conjured a ball of Light in his hands and gently placed it on Elisa's chest. Lacking a specific spell for aiding the injured, he left the glowing orb to work its magic, hoping for a positive outcome. The radiant yellow sphere emitted a comforting warmth, prompting Elisa to take slightly deeper breaths.

Rising to his feet, Theo surveyed the cluttered room, pondering what could have triggered her sudden collapse. It was uncharacteristic of Elisa to leave her belongings in such a disarray. There was clearly something amiss with her, a fact that had eluded his notice. The chain of events had commenced in September when Elisa engaged in a brief, two-week faux romance with Riley. Following their split, she withdrew from her circle of friends, citing academic commitments as her excuse for the newfound solitude. Meanwhile, Theo had been preoccupied with cultivating a close bond with Laura. If only he had been more observant!

Approaching the drawer, Theo sifted through the assortment of dusty perfume bottles, half-opened boxes, and crumpled shopping bags. Amidst the chaos, one box stood out – its lid meticulously closed with precision and care. Intrigued, Theo lifted the lid. His breath caught in his throat as he beheld the shimmering blue powder within. *Moon Dust?!* Memories of the guardians demonstrating the appearance of this illicit substance before his mission with

Jackie in the spring flooded his mind. *How did Elisa come into possession of it?*

The sound of hurried footsteps approaching broke his reverie, prompting Theo to swiftly close the lid and discreetly slip the box into his pocket. Regardless of the circumstances, Elisa's secret must remain safeguarded. Exposing her involvement with Moon Dust would undoubtedly spell the end of her career before it even had a chance to take flight.

The sunlight streamed in with blinding intensity as Elisa slowly opened her eyes. Laura was arranging vibrant autumn leaves in a crystal vase on the windowsill. Seizing the opportunity when Laura's attention shifted, Elisa sat up, wincing as a wave of pain coursed through her body.

"Good morning," Laura greeted her, approaching to adjust the blanket around Elisa.

It was only then that Elisa realized she was not in her dorm room. She rubbed her temples, attempting to piece together the fragmented memories of the previous night, which seemed shrouded in a haze.

Sensing Elisa's confusion, Laura fetched an extra pillow from a nearby chair and positioned it behind her for added comfort.

"You really gave us a scare," Laura remarked softly. "Do you recall what happened?"

Elisa met Laura's concerned gaze with a solemn expression. She recollected stashing the box of Moon Dust away and concocting a mixture. Perhaps she had inadvertently added too much powder to her drink, which knocked her off. However, the truth of her actions remained unspoken, prompting Elisa to simply shake her head in response.

"You had an overdose," Laura said.

Elisa's heart skipped a beat. If her room had been searched, she was in deep trouble. Feigning surprise, she knitted her eyebrow. "I have no idea what you're talking about."

Seating herself in a nearby chair, Laura folded her hands in her lap. "I understand that this is already a difficult situation for you, so I won't press you to reveal the truth."

"Alright. It's nothing to discuss, anyway." Elisa began to shift her blanket aside in an attempt to rise. "I need to leave."

"Sit!" Laura commanded, raising her hand.

To Elisa's astonishment, she found herself rooted to the spot, unable to move. It became apparent that Laura was using her Telekinesis Gift to restrain her.

"Let me go!" Elisa protested, her frustration mounting.

"There's no need to rush," Laura stated calmly. "The doctor advised that you remain here for at least ten days to recover. You must be in good health to resume your studies."

With her feet firmly planted and her fists clenched in frustration, Elisa could only exhale an irritated sigh. "Fine, suppose you caught me. What now?"

"I want to help." Laura's gaze softened with compassion. "Truly. I am on your side, Elisa, and I always have been. If you worry someone else might learn about your secret, don't. It's safe with me."

"Good to know that." Elisa sank back against the pillows. "Who else is aware of this?"

"Riley foresaw your demise, prompting him and Theo to intervene in time," Laura explained. "Fortunately, I was on duty. It allowed us to transport you to the hospital without involving the faculty."

"Thank goodness for that. Are you certain no staff members caught wind of the situation?"

"Positive. I informed Don in the morning that you were experiencing complications from burns sustained during the summer, though I doubt he fully bought the explanation. He may harbor suspicions and conduct tests upon your return to the Academy. You know, to make sure no drugs were involved."

"And he's quite adept at it," Elisa said. "I'll need to be more cautious with my concoctions moving forward."

Laura scoffed in disbelief. "Here you are, nearly facing death, and only care about concealing your illicit activities."

"As if you have nothing to conceal," Elisa retorted, crossing her arms defensively.

Laura gazed at Elisa with a mixture of regret and vulnerability. "I, too, was in a similar situation."

"I find that hard to believe."

Tracing her index finger along the chair handle, Laura delved into her past, lost in her recollections. "It was when my father fell gravely ill. He was in the last stage of a stomach tumor and spent his final days confined to his bed. He was heavily medicated to alleviate his suffering. Oftentimes, he would drift in and out of delirium. I took on the responsibility of caring for him, sitting by his side and listening to his tales of his time at Mercy House."

"Mercy House?!" Elisa's heart raced with a surge of emotion. "What was he doing there?"

"He confessed to me that he was a Gift Taker," Laura revealed, tears welling in her eyes. "Can you believe it? He was the man responsible for stripping innocent teenage girls of their magic, rendering them Incapables. In his final moments, wracked with agony, he cried out that he deserved his suffering as retribution for his heinous actions."

"The last Mercy House was finally shut down last winter," Elisa remarked, offering Laura a faint smile. "It's all in the past now, and possessing a destructive Gift is no longer considered a crime."

Laura's expression remained somber. "But at that time, two years ago, I was haunted by his revelations. Like him, I did nothing to change the situation. I was privy to so many damning details that I even composed a letter to the local newspaper. But the fear stopped me. I didn't want to be exposed as the daughter of the person who had committed those crimes. I believed that those in positions of authority were complicit in the wrongdoing and that they would silence me if I spoke out. It was so overwhelming! So, I started taking the drugs my father had left behind."

Elisa listened in silence. There was no doubt about the sincerity of Laura's confession. Laura's voice quivered with emotion, and tears streamed down her cheeks as she continued to share her story.

"It went on for several months," Laura recounted, her voice heavy with emotion. "Initially, the drugs provided relief. They allowed me to numb my fears and experience fleeting moments of happiness. However, as time passed, my dependency grew, and I found myself seeking out dealers to sustain my habit. My mother began to notice the changes in me, but I was indifferent to her concerns. I merely existed from one dose to the next, clinging to the hope that my miserable existence would eventually come to an end. It wasn't until I overdosed and was admitted to this very hospital last summer that I was forced to see another path. The one that wouldn't kill me."

Elisa's heart ached for the pain Laura had endured. "Did you simply stop taking them after that?"

Laura shook her head, a somber expression on her face. "I may never have found the courage to change. But I had a pivotal moment during my hospitalization. A nurse brought me a newspaper to pass the time, and as I read through it, I stumbled upon an article detailing the Triville case. It was a massive scandal that exposed the dark truths of Mercy House to the public, albeit in the form of rumors. The revelations sparked significant changes – women were now permitted to pursue roles as guardians. Witnessing the world begin to transform, I made a decision to be a part of this change. I knew what needed to be done. I sat down and penned another letter, this time including all the damning details my father had shared with me, and I sent it off."

Elisa's eyes widened in realization. "So, it was you. You made this change possible."

"I was a part of that change." Laura smiled with pride. "It turned out that there were numerous families whose daughters had suffered at the hands of these facilities. Like me, they had remained silent until they realized they were not alone in their struggles. I was among many who came forward to provide evidence against these institutions. For the first time in my life, I felt like I was doing something truly meaningful. This sense of purpose replaced all the artificial highs I had ever experienced. I finally felt authentic and connected. And I craved more."

Elisa nodded in understanding. "And that led you to join the Academy as our librarian."

"Exactly," Laura affirmed. "I wanted to be in proximity to the pioneering women who were dedicated to the guardian role and cared for others. It brings me immense joy to assist and guide you on your journey, Elisa."

She smiled warmly. "You excel at it. But why didn't you pursue becoming a guardian yourself?"

Laura shrugged. "Dealing with those kinds of crimes isn't my calling. My true aspiration is to become a teacher. Not the stern type who demands perfection, but someone who can inspire students and instill in them the belief that they can contribute to solutions, no matter what challenges they face."

"That's a beautiful dream. Promise me you'll pursue it."

"I will," Laura affirmed. "I hope you now understand why I couldn't let you slip away so easily."

Elisa's gaze fell, her mind swirling with thoughts. Laura's narrative had captivated her, momentarily diverting her from her own troubles. The pain of Jackie's absence still weighed heavily on her heart, especially when she witnessed her with Urchin. Letting go seemed like an insurmountable task. Perhaps her love for Jackie had become an addiction, a craving she couldn't resist. It was this longing that drove her to seek solace in Moon Dust, attempting to replicate the euphoria she felt in Jackie's embrace. Just like in Laura's case, it slowly consumed her from within.

"We all have our shadows," Laura offered gently. "But it's important to remember that the light is always within us. We have the power to choose it at any moment."

"I think I should relocate to another city," Elisa said.

Laura's eyes widened in surprise. "What? Where?"

"To Santos. I can transfer to their Academy, and I believe it would be for the best. Being away from Jackie worked for me before, and I don't think I can heal as long as my... temptations are right in front of me."

Laura's expression softened. "You love her that much?"

Elisa nodded. "Please, don't tell anyone."

"Of course," Laura assured her, rising from her seat. "You have a lot to consider. But before you make any final decisions, focus on your recovery first."

42

Sapphire Skies

Fall season flourished in a Middle Lake, coloring the foliage in all shades of flame. Holding Howard by his elbow, Jackie walked along the old streets. The sky was sapphire blue, with the touch of gentle silver clouds. Orange and red maple trees along the street glowed like fires at the entrances to the shops. This contrast – these flaming leaves in front of the gentle sapphire sky brought her thoughts back to Theo and Elisa. It had been a year since all four accomplished their first mission together and stole the dragon eggs. Back then, they were a team, but everything fell apart.

Jackie shifted her eyes to Howard. He walked nearby, talking about something. She tried to remember when they walked like this with Elisa. Maybe last year, before her kiss ruined their friendship. But until everything got too complicated, they had so much fun together. Now, they hardly said 'Hi' to each other. *Interesting, will I ever stop thinking about her?*

"Jackie, are you listening?" Howard slightly shook her shoulder.

"Of course," she said, guessing what he might have just asked.

Howard narrowed his eyes. "Really? Then what's your answer – yes or no?"

She helplessly looked around, but Howard wouldn't give her a clue. "Well... Yes?"

"I can't believe you are meeting my family this New Year!" His eyes filled with excitement.

Jackie stood numb. Her mind worked on a solution to get out of this awkward situation. One thing was dating him, convincing herself that it would help overcome her inconvenient feelings towards Elisa. And the other was pretending to be a loving girlfriend in front of his mom and dad, who, by the way, used to be a guardian.

Howard burst into laughter. "You must see your face now!"

"Ha-ha." She mustered a smile. "I was joking, too, so please erase this smile from your face."

"Come on. I caught you. Plus, my family is very curious about you. We've been together for almost three months, so it's time to bring this relationship to the next level."

Jackie poked his shoulder. "Isn't this conversation the last thing all men enjoy?"

"These men just don't know how wonderful you are." Howard looked at her with his puppy eyes, and her heart sank.

All this time, she managed to hide her terrible truth from him. The tragedy that happened last summer just before she got to the Academy. It was the worst part she had never told him about. She had never opened up to anyone but Elisa. But she couldn't hold it any longer.

"Howard, you must know something," Jackie said. "About me. And it might make you wish to stop everything between us."

His hand softly touched her cheek. "And how is it possible?"

"Last year I had... An episode." She lowered her eyes. "And now I have severe problems with all these kids thing."

"You can't have them?" His voice was laced with sadness.

She nodded. "The doctor said that the chance is incredibly small, and... I just want you to know that this was one of the reasons why I became a guardian. I'm not made for family and stuff like that."

He took her hands in his. "It's not a big deal. When you are ready to start a family, we can adopt and raise a child."

"Would you be able to do it?" She widened her eyes. "For me?"

Instead of answering, Howard leaned in and kissed her. She hugged him, and he started twirling her in the air. They both laughed. The gust of wind tore copper leaves from the branches, and they danced around them. It was such a relief to remove this stone from her soul. This moment with Howard was imprinted in her memory so well because it was the last happy moment they shared.

"Let's go. We need to get the costumes for the autumn ball," Jackie reminded him when he put her back on the ground.

"And the masks," he added.

She took his hand, and they walked into the glass doors.

It was a big costume shop; the rows of dresses and costumes hung on the racks, ready for the buyers. The Autumn ball was one of the most admirable traditions of Lake Kingdom. All government facilities held gorgeous celebrations at this time of the year, and the Academy was no exception. People wore fancy clothes of all shades of flame and masks that covered their eyes. As Jackie learned as a mind reader, people loved hiding their faces. She could understand why – Who would miss the chance to pretend to be somebody else for one evening?

Using the moment when Howard tried on hats at the far end of the store, Jackie approached the rack with masks and couldn't resist taking one. It was an elegant mask for the upper part of the face, made of black velvet and with golden rose decor at the side. She applied it to her face; it was soft and pleasantly warm.

Interesting, would it be possible to be who she really was, just for one evening? What if society let her and Elisa love each other freely, without this suffocating necessity to hide? Jackie turned back and froze. Theo stood right against her.

He looked like a ghost – pale and with black circles under his tired blue eyes. They hadn't spoken for a while because he spent a lot of time with Laura. Now, it was so weird seeing him in a public place without her company.

"Jackie," he called. "Is it you?"

"Damn right." She removed her mask. "What are you doing here?"

He looked around. Howard was still busy speaking with the sales associate.

"I need to talk to you." Theo lowered his voice. "It's about Elisa."

Her heart skipped a beat. "What happened?"

Theo took her elbow and pulled her to the exit door in silence. Jackie followed him to the street.

"What's the conspiracy?" Jackie asked when they stopped in the shade of a maple tree.

Theo ignored her question. "When did you talk to Elisa last time?"

"I saw her a couple of days ago. Why?"

"I mean when you *talked* to her. As a friend."

She paced to the bench and back, her hands gripping her hair. "Oh, shit. I knew it wouldn't end well."

Theo gave her a puzzled look. "So, you knew about the Moon Dust."

"Moon... what?!" Her heart leaped. Jackie had to take a deep breath to be able to speak. "I checked on Elisa on the first day of classes, and she took a suspicious potion that day. I thought it was a strong sedative. She didn't look too bad at that time, and she needed just a bit of it. Damn, Theo, what happened?"

He rubbed his forehead, thinking. "I know she is our good friend, and it's hard to believe she can do such things, but our ignorance turned out awful. I remember it in shards now, but the more I think of it, the more I see this pattern – some days, she was totally fine, even cheerful. But then, she became super excited about the small things. Last week, she had insomnia, and she studied all night."

"Just studied? That's it?"

Theo shook his head. "It's like a rollercoaster. After that high, she went to the bottom for days. Before, it was just tiredness and sadness. I had no clue that she might be taking something; I thought it was because she studied too hard. But last night, Riley had a disturbing dream, and we rushed for help. I found her on the floor, unconscious."

Jackie stopped breathing. Last night, Howard made a Muting spell to ensure no sound would escape their room. This spell worked in both directions – she slept in his embrace like in a cocoon, not hearing anything suspicious. How selfish! If not for her games with Howard, she might hear something from Elisa's room and help her.

"That's all my fault," Jackie said.

"Don't blame yourself. It's always hard to notice and even harder to believe it's possible."

"What happened to her after? Where is she?"

"In a hospital. Now she is stable, but the doctor said she is addicted to drugs, and she needs rehab."

Jackie had to sit down on the bench. A dozen questions twisted in her head like a swarm of bees. Mostly the questions that Theo couldn't answer. *Can I visit her? And if yes, wouldn't it make her condition worse?*

"Who else knows?" Jackie asked.

Theo lowered his voice. "Kidding? No one must know. Otherwise, her career is over."

"Crap."

"Agreed."

What a sad irony, Jackie thought. *Elisa started taking drugs not to let her feelings ruin her career, and they eventually almost destroyed it.*

"Can we rely on Riley?" She asked.

"Let's say we made an agreement. If he says a word, I'll burn him alive." Theo's face expressed seriousness, which erased all her doubts about any information leak.

"What can I do for her?"

Theo glanced back at the shop doors that opened and closed, reflecting the daylight. Howard still didn't start looking for her, and they had some time. Jackie lowered her eyes – the black mask rested on her lap, which meant that she stole it absentmindedly when she rushed outside.

Theo turned to her. "There is nothing you can do besides friend support and other stuff."

"Of course."

"But you can sort it out *after* her rehab. Right now, Elisa needs another kind of help." Theo gave her a sad look. "There is one thing I'll ask you to do, and you must understand how important it is."

"I'll do anything."

"This is not exactly for Elisa, but for all the people in her situation. I think you know what I'm talking about."

Jackie sighed. Apparently, the drug dealers came back to business, which meant that the gang they tried to arrest in spring became broader. And Walter was still responsible for this investigation.

"Theo, no," she said. "I had a really bad misunderstanding with Walter, and we agreed to leave it behind. And as I said, I'm not sure about that old memory with the mystery man who we briefly saw in a fighting club."

"Jackie, I understand what you told me before. There is something intimate in your memory, and you don't want me to read it by accident."

She nodded. It was exactly what she told Howard when he tried to convince Theo to take part in a Gift exchange ritual. At the beginning of the semester, Howard was jealous and wanted to ensure that she didn't have any feelings for Theo. Jackie wanted to keep her secrets untouched, so she found a way to push his ideas aside. It worked, and since then, Howard calmed down.

"Theo, that's not my secret only. It's confidential information that might compromise some people."

"I won't go that far."

"It's not only that. I know a lot about Elisa's personal life."

"The life she might lose," he reminded her.

Her hands became frozen, and Jackie rubbed her palms. One thought of what could have happened scared her to death.

"I'm sorry you have to hear it," Theo continued. "But I want to be clear – I don't just express my concerns about Elisa. I really gave it a thought. I've checked – since our failure and that trace of a mystery man that you found in a new club with Walter, the guardians couldn't find the criminals. No new arrests were made! This drug empire keeps growing, and people like Elisa keep suffering. Just imagine, Jackie. She might have died last night."

They sat in silence for a while.

"Listen," Theo said, "We both know what exactly she hides, but I don't care about her secrets as long as she is safe. I read *The Book of Gifts Exchange* all this morning. I don't need to see everything in your head, Jackie. We can make a ritual, and I'll jump exactly to that moment when you saw that man. We'll go there together, and you'll lead me and watch me. We just need someone we trust to maintain the spell. Damn it. I can sign a contract with my blood if you want me to!"

His breath became ragged, and she put her hand on his shoulder to calm him down. "No need for your blood, Theo. We'll do it, a ritual. If you say it's safe, I trust you."

Howard's voice rang above them. "What the heck is going on here?"

They turned to him. Jackie never saw him coming out of the glass doors. He must have used his Invisible Gift to approach them unnoticed.

"How long have you been here?" Theo asked.

Howard crossed his arms. "Not enough to know what ritual you are talking about, but enough to participate."

She looked at Theo. "Can he?"

"Well, if you guys trust each other, I don't see any problem."

Jackie smiled at Howard. "We're going to my memory of a mystery man. Do you think you can get access to the library tonight?"

"A drug dealer case?" Howard gave them an intrigued look. "Finally! Of course, I'll get a key. Actually, I already have a copy in my room."

"Sneaky bastard." Theo chuckled.

"Yeah, and not just me." Howard looked at her. "Jackie, the shopkeeper thought you stole a mask, so I had to deal with it."

"Did you buy it?"

He nodded. "Yes. And I must say it's quite an expensive present for the ball. But you deserve the best."

She stood up and hugged him. "Thank you. For everything."

43

The Prisoners of Consciousness

The sun was almost setting as they arranged the candles in the correct order. A chalk triangle was drawn on the dark library floor. Jackie brought the ingredients for a potion – absinthe, chamomile, and some rare plants that would lead all three into her consciousness's labyrinth.

Once everything was prepared, Theo snapped his fingers, and the candles all ignited simultaneously. They positioned themselves at the corners of the triangle, each taking a sip of the potion from the cup before joining hands. *The Book of Gift Exchange* lay in the center of the floor. This was how Howard maintained the ritual – repeating the same spell while Jackie and Theo delved into her memories.

Howard coughed, his serious expression indicating the importance of his role. "As we agreed, Theo, I will guide you through the labyrinth of Jackie's memories."

Theo nodded, while Jackie impatiently exhaled a sigh, wishing Howard would speak faster before the potion took effect.

But he apparently relished this long-anticipated moment. In a steady voice, Howard continued, "As you both know, I love Jackie deeply, so I have a limitation in my Gift when it comes to reading her mind." He gave her a warm glance before shifting his gaze to Theo. "This means that I won't be able to see any visual memories; I will be blind and can only hear your voices. Please, speak aloud so I can follow along."

"Alright," Theo replied. "Can we begin now?"

Howard nodded. "One more thing. Your shared memories may evoke strong emotions. Be cautious and avoid delving too deeply into your feelings. Excessive emotional involvement will bring you back to reality, and we won't be able to repeat this ritual until the emotions have settled."

"Understood," Theo and Jackie chorused.

Howard smiled. "Then, let's begin."

Jackie closed her eyes and focused on the sounds around her – the gentle crackle of the burning candles, the soft breeze from the open window that whispered through the endless rows of book-shelves.

Howard recited the spell, his voice taking on a silky quality that lulled her, drawing her deeper into her own memories.

"Through the night, through the fog
Let me break the sacred lock.
Let me open at once
All the doors to your past."

Theo's hand radiated warmth as he held hers. In Jackie's memory, they walked together through the fog until they reached their class-room. As the fog dissipated, Theo stood beside her, his expression one of surprise.

"Look," he exclaimed, pointing at the room.

Jackie turned to face Theo, realizing it was just a projection of her memory. It was the first day of classes when they entered the room with Elisa. In her memory, Jackie had short hair and fearful eyes. Elisa stood nearby, her hair in a horsetail, her gaze confident as she conversed with Theo. *Elisa...* She had been so different when they first met – strong and determined. Now, in reality, she was utterly broken. If only Jackie knew how to help her regain her former self.

If I only knew how to bring her back to normal. If there even is a 'normal' for us, Jackie thought as the room slightly shook.

"Where are you?" Howard's voice echoed from above. He was in the library where they were conducting the ritual, so his voice was their only bridge to reality.

Theo looked up and replied, "We've arrived. I believe this is our first shared memory."

"Is it the correct day?" Howard inquired.

Jackie surveyed the scene. Theo's projected images bantered, and all the men in the room burst into laughter. "No, it's the following day," she clarified. "It's the first day of classes."

Theo pointed to his projection. "Did I really advise you to go to the perfume shop instead of studying here?"

Jackie shrugged. "Yes, you did. I suppose you were testing us."

"That was a different version of me. Initially, I thought you were seeking a romantic escapade, but Elisa's words changed my perspective," Theo explained.

Howard's voice interjected once more. "Jackie, are you referring to the day we first met?"

"Yes," Jackie confirmed with a nod, even though Howard couldn't see her. "The day we all met. I'm heading to my desk now."

Howard's voice trembled. "Get out of there immediately."

"Why?"

"Don't you remember how we first met? How did you read me?" Howard asked.

She snickered. "I'll never forget that."

"Alright," Howard said, his anxiety palpable. "You are on the verge of using your Gift! You could get trapped in a loop and lose yourself."

Jackie's eyes widened as Howard, from her memory, approached her projection and extended his hand. Feeling Theo's reassuring grip, she closed her eyes and whispered, "The previous day. Sunrise."

Upon opening her eyes, Jackie found Theo standing before her, but the scene had shifted. They were now on the street near the Guardian House. The soft rays of the rising sun illuminated the deserted road, and her projection stood on the pavement, holding a map.

Looking up at Howard, she confirmed, "We've reached the correct moment."

"Good," Howard responded, relieved. "Just keep narrating so I can follow along."

"Now we see Jackie gazing at the map," Theo added.

"It's because I wasn't accustomed to such a large city. I took a wrong turn and ended up wandering along the street. Luckily, I left early, so I wasn't running late," Jackie explained.

"Late for what?" they inquired simultaneously.

She hesitated before replying, "To see the Guardian House. Just to catch a glimpse of the place where I hoped to work."

Theo nodded. "Then let's follow your lead."

Her projection unfurled the map and proceeded in the correct direction. Strangely, the city streets that had once seemed vast and eerie now felt familiar and comforting, almost like home. This juxtaposition of conflicting emotions was a new experience for Jackie. "Theo, can you sense what I'm feeling?"

"A little... Were you frightened when you arrived here?"

"Yes, it felt so desolate," Jackie confessed.

"I understand."

Howard's voice interjected, "I don't feel anything, so please continue talking to me. Where are you now?"

As they strolled through the backyard of the Guardian House, her projection stood beneath a tree, gazing in awe at the magnificent building with wide-eyed wonder.

"We're in the right place," Theo remarked.

"Take a good look at the man because I never really noticed him before," Jackie instructed Theo.

"Got it."

The back door swung open, and a man emerged, sporting a gray hat that partially obscured his face.

"We see him," Theo exclaimed. "Howard, it's *him*. The guy from the fighting club!"

"Fantastic!" Howard said. "Can you investigate the surroundings of the Guardian House? Perhaps there were witnesses or something that could shed light on his interactions?"

Jackie hesitated. "No! We've seen enough."

"Not really," Theo said, his gaze intense. "What did you do next, Jackie?"

Her heart raced, and the space around them began to tremble as if in an earthquake.

Howard's voice grew louder. "The connection is stable. It's your emotions. Stay calm, Jackie."

Theo gazed at her projection as the mysterious man departed the yard, prompting the image to approach the door and knock three times before it swung open.

The ground trembled once more, this time more intensely.

"Let's go, Theo!" Jackie screamed.

Already in motion, Theo sprinted towards the door. As he turned back to her, his complexion had paled. The door closed behind him, but Jackie could sense what he had witnessed.

"What happened?" Howard inquired.

Jackie remained silent. What could she possibly say? It was the morning when Trevor Harland, the chief of the Middle Lake Guardian House, had used his official position to help Jackie settle in this city. She had arrived at sunrise to avoid crossing paths with the other guardians earlier than scheduled. Trevor had welcomed her inside and provided her with a signed referral to the Academy. It was their secret. Jackie guarded this secret because the truth could ruin the chief's reputation, and now, Theo intervened with that memory and ruined everything.

Overwhelmed, Jackie sank to the ground as the world continued to shake around her as if someone were vigorously shaking a crystal ball.

Theo rushed to Jackie, shaking her shoulders in his distress, causing her to feel disoriented. Their voices blended into the cacophony of noise surrounding her, making it impossible for her to discern their words. Suddenly, the world seemed to crumble around them, and Jackie tumbled backward.

As she blinked and opened her eyes, Jackie found herself back in the library, the familiar surroundings confirming that it was reality. Howard had fashioned a paper fan from a notebook and was now waving it gently in front of her face.

"Welcome back," Howard greeted her with a smile.

Theo sat close by, his gaze fixed on her in silence.

44

The Power of Truth

They decided to occupy the spacious living room of the dorms. At this time of the day, all the cadets usually split into two groups – those who studied in their rooms or those who went to the pub. Thus, no one would interfere with their space. Jackie sat on a sofa in silence, her feet covered with a blanket. Howard set up a fireplace and settled into a chair.

Theo emerged from the kitchen with a glass of red wine. "Would you guys like anything to drink?"

Jackie shook her head. Her glass of lemon water sat on the coffee table, and she took a sip to soothe the dizziness she still felt after the recent ritual.

Howard waved his hand. "I'm good. Let's discuss what you guys saw."

Theo sat on the sofa next to Jackie and gave her a suspicious look. "Yes, let's clarify some details."

She moved to the very corner, hoping to avoid this conversation. Unfortunately, it was too late to hide the truth, so she took a defensive position. "Theo, you promised not to delve into the memories you were not supposed to see."

He placed his glass on the table, causing it to spill a bit. "You never mentioned visiting a chief that day! How do you know him, Jackie?"

"Why does it matter?" She glanced at Howard, seeking his support. "It's not relevant to our investigation."

Howard rubbed his chin, pondering. "Actually, the fact that you met a chief that day could provide us with a new perspective."

"That makes sense," Theo agreed.

"Can you explain how it might be beneficial?" She inquired. "Before I go back on my promise not to disclose this information to anyone?!"

"Of course," Theo said. "Let's start from the end and go through the facts. When you were working with Walter, you read the new club owner to find a trace of the drug dealers. In his recent memories, you saw the mystery man whom you recognized from the fighting club where we had a secret mission in the spring. You then discovered another memory about this man – he was in a Guardian House on the day you visited the chief. Am I correct?"

Jackie nodded.

Theo continued, "You found this 'coincidence' suspicious and informed Walter about it. He mentioned that he was alone in the observation tower at that time and would have noticed if a strange man had appeared in the backyard because he was on duty."

Howard shifted in his chair. "I've already discussed this with Walter, and he assured me he was focused the entire time he was in that tower."

"Perhaps he told the truth," Theo said. "But here is the question – is the entire backyard visible from the observation tower?"

Jackie pondered for a moment. "Mostly yes. However, the foliage is thick in the alley during the summer. It's possible to walk unnoticed under the trees."

"And that's likely what happened, explaining why Walter missed your visit," Theo said, rubbing his hands in satisfaction. "So, we observed the man exiting through the backdoor. Then, in less than a minute, we witnessed the chief opening the door to you, Jackie. Now, please, put two and two together."

She took a deep breath, struggling to accept the unsettling facts presented to her.

Howard gave her a strange look. "When I spoke to Walter, he mentioned that you had complained about him to the chief. But you denied ever doing so. If both of you are telling the truth, then who is lying?"

Disappointed in their theory, Jackie stood up and paced around the room, feeling their eyes following her every move.

"No, it can't be Chief Trevor," she muttered. "It just can't be." She turned to Howard. "You need to know something else about me. Before I came here, this man saved my life. He was the one who recommended me to the Academy. He risked his career by giving his referral to the woman he recently met!"

Theo's eyes widened in surprise. "That's even worse, Jackie. It's a classic manipulation!" He slapped his forehead. "And it all makes sense now. After our failed mission, the criminals disappeared."

"You mean the chief deliberately chose Jackie?" Howard inquired.

"Exactly!" Theo's eyes gleamed. "If you recall our mission, they required a mind reader, and Jackie's connection with the chief made her the perfect candidate. She was willing to bend the rules and jeopardize the case out of loyalty to him."

Jackie raised her hands in protest. "Stop it! You're not understanding. Trust me, I have my reasons to believe in this man."

Howard gazed at her intently. "Then please, explain."

Her temples throbbed with tension. Well, if the truth had to be revealed to save Chief Trevor, she was prepared to lift the veil. She needed them to believe her. Perhaps she would never have had the courage to disclose it to Howard, but eventually, she knew she had to share the whole story. So, she took a deep breath and decided to confess, even if it meant risking their relationship. "That summer when I first arrived in the city... I was engaged."

"You what?" Howard exclaimed, rising from his seat.

Theo raised his index finger. "Please, sit down. Let her speak."

Howard complied, sinking back into his chair, his hands gripping the armrests tightly.

"I apologize for not sharing this with you earlier," she began. "But it's a part of my past that I prefer to forget." She settled on the floor, the warmth of the fireplace dispelling the chill from her hands. "The engagement was arranged against my will. My father orchestrated it because the man was wealthy but lacking in intelligence. I initially thought he wasn't so bad until I saw his true nature."

Staring into the flickering flames, she gathered her courage to continue. "After our parents' meeting, our fathers went hunting the next day, leaving me alone with my ex-fiancé in my home. It was something we often did – talking and laughing together. I trusted him, and I never used my Gift on him."

"Because you loved him?" Howard inquired.

She shrugged. "I'm not sure. Initially, we agreed that trust was essential between us."

"I understand," Theo said, his gaze intense. "Please, go on."

She swallowed hard. "He brought me a cup of tea, and we chatted as usual. Then I suddenly felt numb, unable to move. He later claimed I was intoxicated, but I knew I wasn't. He had drugged me."

Howard moved closer and sat beside her. "Is this the incident you mentioned to me this morning?"

She nodded, tears streaming down her cheeks. "He changed in an instant. I was helpless, but I could feel everything when he started raping me. He... he was cruel, and I endured immense pain." With a trembling voice, she buried her face in her hands, her shoulders shaking with sobs.

A heavy silence enveloped the room.

Theo sat beside her and placed a comforting hand on her shoulder. "Jackie, that's truly awful. I can imagine the pain you must be feeling."

She met his gaze. "I doubt that."

"I've never shared this with anyone, but I have a dark past as well."

"You mentioned being poor. That doesn't compare to what I went through."

"That's not the worst of it. I had a sister once, and I lost her," Theo shared, tears welling up in his eyes. "She was a beautiful young woman. I was about ten years old at the time, and I remember how the men on the street would talk about her. One evening, one of them followed her home and raped her."

"Was he arrested and imprisoned?" Jackie asked.

Theo shook his head. "When she returned home in tears and confessed everything to my parents, my father berated her. He had already 'arranged' her marriage to a respectable man, and she had 'shamed' him."

"Holy crap," Howard remarked.

Theo continued, his voice heavy with emotion. "She ran away, and I did nothing to protect or save her. I was just a child, too scared to intervene, but I understood what was happening. A week later, her lifeless body was discovered in a river. The authorities claimed it was suicide."

Jackie wrapped her arms around herself, feeling a deep sense of empathy. "I was on the verge of doing the same. The morning after that horrific incident, I felt unwell, but my father forbade me from seeking help or disclosing the truth to anyone. He was solely focused on arranging my marriage to alleviate his massive debts.

"A week later, the pain became unbearable. I managed to escape and make my way to the city in search of medical help. I remember being feverish when I finally arrived, only to be turned away by the medical staff. They even called the authorities to remove me from the hospital building. I was on the bench near the closed entrance doors, weeping, when I encountered him. It was Trevor, a chief. He insisted that the doctor admit me for treatment. Without his intervention, I might not have survived."

"Then you understand why it's crucial to put an end to this chaos," Theo remarked. "Jackie, the hardships we've faced have shaped our lives. Now, we have the power to decide how we want to confront them. We can bury our past and keep it hidden from others, or we can confront it head-on and put an end to it."

"That's why you chose to become a guardian?" Jackie asked.

"In part, yes. Here's the rest of my story. Following my sister's funeral, my parents separated. My mother and I moved to Middle Lake in the hopes of starting anew, but on the day of our arrival, we were robbed. We found ourselves homeless and starving. It was the owner of a local bookshop who extended a helping hand. He offered my mother a job cleaning the store and provided us with a place to stay. I immersed myself in books and aspired to be like him – someone who contributes to making the world a better place."

She offered him a melancholic smile. "Trevor shared a similar sentiment with me – that I have the ability to enact change. The day I received my diagnosis, my sole desire was to plunge into the nearest river. However, Trevor visited me every evening, and we had very heartfelt conversations. He instilled hope within me and provided me with a sense of purpose. He rescued me."

Theo regarded her solemnly. "I understand that it's difficult to accept, but he may have taken advantage of your vulnerability."

She gazed at him, a sense of numbness washing over her.

In a composed tone, Theo continued, "He saw you as a shattered girl with the ability to read minds and manipulated you to serve his own agenda. He ensured your loyalty to him."

Jackie's fists clenched, her voice rising in defense. "Do not speak of him in such a manner!"

"Could you give us a moment, please?" Howard interjected, gesturing for Theo to leave.

Theo settled on a sofa, taking a sip of his wine. Howard positioned himself beside her, his presence calming her racing heart.

"Please, don't make me question everything," Jackie implored. "Hope is the only thing I had left."

"Jackie, you were alone when you first met the chief. However, now you have us standing by your side, and together, we form a team," Howard said, his expression warm. "Do you recall what Don taught us? The primary rule of being a guardian?"

"To trust in your team," she responded. "But –"

"There's always a 'but,'" he interjected. "Listen, I'm not asking you to harbor doubts about anyone; I'm urging you to act as a guardian and investigate this theory. I firmly believe that Trevor Harland is a good man, and I say this based on my knowledge of him. If he is innocent, we can confirm it and move on. Additionally, you may uncover something in his memories that he is unaware of. Perhaps another guardian conversed with the mysterious man that day, and he simply overlooked it. Who knows?"

With no valid argument to counter his reasoning, Jackie locked eyes with him and nodded. "Alright. Let's check on him."

Theo set down his empty glass, fiddling with it in his hands. "So, it's settled. Now, let's brainstorm on the 'simple' task of how to approach a guardian chief without risking our careers."

"Perhaps we could intercept him on the street?" Howard suggested.

"A masquerade," Jackie proposed.

Theo and Howard both turned to her, intrigued by the idea.

"That's brilliant," Theo agreed. "If we can get to the Guardian House's ball, Jackie could have the opportunity to dance with him. It would appear natural and not raise any suspicions."

"Howard, can you bring us to the ball using your Gift?" Jackie inquired.

He chuckled. "No need for Gifts. I'll have a word with Walter and secure the invitations."

"Walter?!" Jackie's eyes widened in disbelief. "How can we trust him after everything he's done?"

Howard gave her a knowing look. "Didn't you mention that we're all human and prone to making mistakes?"

She gritted her teeth, still struggling to comprehend how Howard had formed a friendship with someone he had previously fought with.

"Then, like any other person, he deserves a second chance, right?" Howard posed.

"Fine," Jackie relented. "But if he lets us down again, remember that I warned you."

"I'll keep that in mind," Howard assured her, leaning in to plant a gentle kiss on her forehead.

Theo smiled. "Well then, ladies and gentlemen, let's prepare for the ball."

45

❧

Ripping The Masks Off

T he spacious hall of a Guardian House was filled with people. Enjoying the gentle sounds of violins, they laughed, danced, and drank sparkling wine. Elisa stood by a pillar in her long red dress, which sparkled in the light from night flowers. She adjusted her mask, a black velvet adorned with a solitary red rose that perfectly complemented her outfit. Perhaps this would be the last time she would spend in the company of her friends, so the least she could do was play her part in this secret mission.

Theo emerged from the crowd, dressed in an orange tuxedo and a black mask that concealed his eyes. He smiled and greeted her. "Here you are."

"Where else would I be?" Elisa replied, glancing around the hall. The ball was in full swing, but there was no sign of Jackie and Urchin.

"They will be here soon," Theo assured her, checking the time crystal on his wrist. "Are you certain you need to leave in the morning? Without saying goodbye to Jackie?"

"It has to be this way," Elisa stated firmly. After she had made the difficult decision to leave the Academy, Theo was the second person she had confided in. His reaction had only added to the complexity of the situation. "It will be tough for both of us, and all I want is for her to be happy. Please, promise me you'll take care of Jackie when I'm gone."

"Of course I will," Theo replied, letting out a heavy sigh. "I just wish you would stay a little longer."

"You always want what you can't have," Elisa teased him.

He crossed his arms. "Seems like someone has been spending too much time with Laura."

"Don't be so dramatic." Elisa smiled at him, patting his shoulder. "I actually think she's a wonderful person. It's a shame she's put you in the friend zone. You two could make a great couple."

"The friend zone?" Theo hesitated. "Does that mean there's no going back?"

Elisa nodded. "Isn't that what you wanted?"

He gave her a worried look. "I did, but we had such a good time together, and I started to think –"

"Please, don't overthink it, Theo. She had enough of shattered hopes and will never be yours," Elisa interrupted, gesturing towards the beautiful young woman in the hall. "Look, there are plenty of other options."

Theo remained silent, causing Elisa to smile in satisfaction. She had kept her promise to Laura and ignited his competitive spirit. Now, it was up to him to decide whether to pursue a relationship or not.

As the music softened, Elisa's attention shifted to the entrance of the hall. Her heart fluttered in her chest as she watched Jackie descend the stairs with Urchin by her side. Tonight, Jackie wore a shimmering yellow dress that glowed in the candlelight. A memory crystal adorned her neck, its mysterious message kept secret from all. Her face was partially concealed by a black velvet mask, similar to Elisa's, but adorned with a golden rose.

Elisa couldn't see Jackie's eyes, and she was grateful that Jackie couldn't see the tears welling in her own.

"You two make such a beautiful couple," Theo remarked as they approached them.

"Thank you," Jackie replied with a smile.

Elisa embraced her friend, taking in the scent of raspberries that always lingered in Jackie's hair. It was ironic that even at a masquerade, they had to conceal their true feelings.

"I've missed you so much," Jackie whispered.

"Me too," Elisa responded.

Theo turned to Jackie. "Feeling nervous?"

"A little."

Urchin grinned at her. "I think we're all a bit nervous here. Let's try to pretend to be happy."

"That's something I excel at," Jackie replied.

A waitress approached them, offering Jackie a glass of red wine. She took a sip before Urchin gently took the glass from her hands. "Please, don't. You have an important role to play."

"Don't worry – I can handle it."

"I don't doubt that, but we need to be cautious," Urchin said, his expression serious.

Jackie tugged at his elbow. "Let's go dance then."

Elisa took the glass from his hands and flashed a reassuring smile. "I've got this. Go enjoy the dance, and we'll be close by, watching you."

As the music swelled, they glided gracefully in a waltz. Howard proved to be a skilled partner, his movements fluid and precise. The other dancing couples surrounded them, casting envious glances in their direction.

Jackie couldn't resist stealing glances at Elisa, who stood with Theo at the appetizer table, engaged in conversation. Her red lipstick left a mark on the rim of her glass that her lips had recently touched. Each sip Elisa took caused Jackie's heart to beat heavily.

"Jackie, stop staring," Howard chided gently.

She turned to him. "Sorry. I'm just relieved that she's okay."

"Elisa? Yes, she's more than okay. She's full of enthusiasm."

"What do you mean exactly?"

Howard allowed Jackie to turn in the dance, holding her hand before pulling her closer as they glided across the dance floor. "Ask her. She's your best friend, from what I recall."

Jackie glanced down at her memory crystal, which softly glowed, still safeguarding Elisa's heartfelt confession from their unforgettable night. Sometimes, she would listen to the recording from the crystal, her heart melting each time she heard Elisa's whispered words, *'I love you.'* Perhaps Jackie was expected to erase this message, but doing so would sever their connection entirely. No, even if Elisa rejected her and shattered her heart into a million pieces, Jackie couldn't bear to part with the memory of that night.

It was all she had left of Elisa. "Believe it or not, I maintain a distance between us for her well-being."

"Are you prepared to meet my family over winter break?" Howard asked, catching her off guard.

She opened and closed her mouth, unable to formulate a response.

He leaned in closer. "You would adore them. My mom is a chef at a restaurant, and my father, as you know, used to be a guardian captain, so you could learn a lot from him. They would be thrilled to meet you."

"You seem to be the only one here with normal parents," Jackie remarked.

Howard chuckled. "I know. Sometimes it feels strange. Like I'm the odd one out."

She laughed. "Sometimes I feel like I'm surrounded by broken people trying to pretend to be normal. It's reassuring to know that normalcy exists."

"We all have the power to create our own version of normal."

As the music faded, Jackie gave him a warm smile. "I'll consider spending the winter holidays with your family, okay?"

Howard kissed her hand. "Of course."

The music ceased, and they returned to their table. Walter approached them, dressed in a burgundy costume and a mask, though Jackie recognized him by his distinctive hairstyle. The men exchanged handshakes, and Jackie greeted him with a cool smile. While they may have moved past their previous conflict, the memory of his prank still left a sour taste in her mouth.

"Great to see all of you," Walter greeted them.

"Thank you for inviting us," Jackie replied.

"No problem. That was the easy part," Walter responded.

Howard lowered his voice. "What about the difficult part?"

Walter glanced around. "The boss will be out soon, so just stay close by."

"Can you tell me what made you agree to help us?" Jackie inquired, crossing her arms over her chest.

A smile spread across Walter's lips. "I always had a feeling that something was amiss with that misunderstanding. I initially suspected you of betraying me and jeopardizing my reputation, but when I realized it might have been him... it became a matter of honor to investigate it."

Howard offered her an encouraging look. "You've got this, Jackie. We're all counting on you."

She sighed as Theo and Elisa took to the dance floor, her gaze fixed on them while the men conversed. Her temples throbbed with the rush of blood, and she found herself tuning out their conversation.

Walter placed a hand on her shoulder, prompting her to turn towards him.

"Do you truly trust your friends?" he inquired.

"Yes," Jackie affirmed.

He scowled. "I just can't comprehend one thing. If Elisa was involved with the drug dealers, why didn't you just read her to get more details?"

Howard and Jackie exchanged glances. Jackie concentrated, attempting to formulate a suitable response, but she found herself at a loss for words. She couldn't read Elisa, and it was a result of the Gift blockage. She was too in love to be able to use her Mind-reading power on her. Walter may not have been the most trustworthy man she knew, but he was a skilled detective who could easily pinpoint vulnerabilities.

Thankfully, Howard stepped in. "The sellers Elisa talked to are merely small players in this game. Reading her wouldn't provide us with much."

Jackie squeezed his elbow in agreement. "Exactly."

Walter hesitated. "Well, perhaps. But –"

"Look," she interjected, pointing towards the ceiling.

The lights above the tables dimmed at that moment. The music ceased, and the dancing couples vacated the floor. A young guardian in an orange suit introduced the chief, and Trevor Harland made his entrance onto the dance floor. He waved to the crowd, eliciting applause and cheers from the attendees.

"I hope you all enjoy this evening," Trevor addressed the crowd, his lips curling into a smile beneath his mustache. His eyes were concealed behind a black mask. Jackie was grateful she wore her mask, too, because he could easily discern her intentions if their gazes met.

"Ladies and gentlemen, dear guardians," he continued, "I want to take a moment to express my gratitude for all your hard work. I understand that some cases are more challenging than others, but together, we will maintain order in this city!"

Howard chuckled in agreement. "Damn right."

Trevor's gaze lingered on Jackie, causing her feet to feel unsteady. The air felt stifling, making it difficult for her to breathe. She had a sudden urge to leave the room immediately.

At that moment, the lights flickered back on, and the music resumed playing.

Walter's hand gently nudged her forward. "Now or never."

Summoning all her courage, Jackie took two steps towards Trevor before coming to a halt. Her heart raced, threatening to burst from her chest.

"Jackie," Trevor greeted her with a soft voice.

"Trevor."

"It's been a while," he remarked, extending his hand for her to take.

As the other couples around them began dancing, Jackie and Trevor joined in. Jackie attempted to steady her breath in order to read him, a challenging task given their movements. The sound of his voice helped her focus.

"How are your classes going?" Trevor inquired.

She smiled. "I'm really enjoying them. It can be tough at times, but I'm giving it my all."

"You see, I told you. Just when you think life is over, it's actually just beginning..."

"Of another stage of your life," she finished the thought. These were the exact words he had spoken to her when she had been lying in a hospital bed, broken and thinking of suicide. As they danced together in the grand hall of the Guardian House, Jackie knew that the most challenging task lay ahead – to probe Trevor's mind. It was her duty, despite the difficulty of the task.

All her friends watched them closely, prepared to intervene if anything went awry. Elisa, Howard, Theo, and even Walter, though Jackie wasn't entirely certain about him. However, with Walter involved, she had no choice but to place her trust in him.

With a deep breath, Jackie prepared to take the next step – to delve into the depths of Trevor's consciousness. As they twirled around the dance floor, she placed her palm on his, feeling the connection between them. Closing her eyes, she focused on her Gift, ready to uncover any hidden truths that lay within Trevor's mind.

The darkness surrounded Jackie, a temporary shield that the guardians could create to prevent others from reading their minds. However, as Jackie had discovered, there was always a way to find a crack in that shield. She navigated along the barrier of Trevor's memories, searching for a sliver of light that would lead her to the truth. Finally, she found a faint beam of light seeping through a crack, and she leaned in to peer inside.

In the chief's office, she saw the mysterious man in the gray hat standing before Trevor. He was receiving instructions. Their voices were muffled, but she could make out some of their conversation.

"Keep an eye on a mind reader girl in case she appears at the fighting club," Trevor instructed.

"What if she reads me?" the man in the hat inquired.

"You'll eliminate her before she can leave. It will deter everyone from sending mind readers on such missions."

The man nodded in understanding. "Got it."

Trevor then produced a purse and placed it on the table. The sound of metal clinking against the surface indicated that it contained money. Jackie could sense Trevor's greed and adrenaline, a potent mix that hinted at the significance of the sum inside the purse.

Jackie opened her eyes as Trevor ceased dancing. The music continued to play, and the other guests moved around them. However, the two of them stood still, facing each other. Despite his eyes being concealed by the mask, Jackie could feel his intense gaze upon her.

"Did you just attempt to read me?" Trevor inquired.

Jackie placed her palm over her chest. Trevor possessed an exceptional Gift that allowed him to detect lies, making it futile to deceive him. "You have strong mental protection."

"Do I?"

Attempting to stall for time, Jackie nodded. "It's quite challenging to breach."

"But you managed to."

She remained silent.

Trevor placed his clammy hands heavily on her shoulders, his voice growing louder. "You have the potential to be an exceptional guardian, Jackie."

"And I will," she asserted.

"No, you won't."

Her voice trembled. "You can't fire me. You are not my boss."

Trevor's laughter echoed in her ears. "I may not be your direct superior, but I am the boss in this city. With a snap of my fingers, I can send you back to your small town, where you can drown yourself."

Jackie swallowed hard. Apparently, the chief was aware of what she had attempted last winter when Walter had rescued her from the lake. "I won't give up so easily," she said. "Not this time."

"I know. Fortunately, my associates are quite skilled at making things look like suicides," Trevor threatened.

A tear rolled down her cheek. Regret flooded her mind. *Why didn't I stay away and avoid this mess?* Now, there was no turning back, no escape. And she had no evidence against him beyond this fragment of his memory. Even if she went to court, no one would believe her.

"Now, tell me who instructed you to read me," Trevor demanded flatly.

Jackie shook her head. "No one."

"Come on, be a good girl and give me the names. Perhaps then I'll consider letting you stay in my team and assist me."

Tears welled up, making it difficult for her to speak even if she wanted to provide him with the names.

"Let's continue this conversation in my office, where we can both calm down," Trevor suggested.

Jackie took a step back.

"No?" Trevor's grin was menacing. "You know what, I'll find out one way or another."

"You won't," Jackie said.

"You're confident in your team, huh?" Trevor's voice was taunting. "Are you sure you can trust all of them?"

A fear washed over her. Jackie knew she could rely on everyone who took part in today's operation except for Walter. He was a dark horse. She had never been able to read him and was unsure of where his loyalties truly lay. It meant he might have destroyed their lives.

Trevor moved closer, his voice a whisper in her ear. "If you want to protect your friends, then run. That's your only option – keep running. Get out of this city and never look back."

Jackie nodded in understanding, and without hesitation, she followed his advice. She turned away and bolted through the crowd, using her elbows to push through the throng of people towards the exit. She didn't want to be seen or followed by anyone. If Trevor had caught her interacting with anyone, it would have spelled doom not just for her but for her friends as well.

Jackie tore off her mask and flung it onto the pavement. The cool breeze soothed her flushed face. Wiping away the tears that streaked her cheeks, she gazed up at the cold, dark autumn sky, the stars twinkling faintly above. It was the final day of October, a time when nature seemed to wither and fade.

"Excuse me, miss," a carriage driver said as he approached her. "Do you need a ride?"

Suppressing a sob, Jackie nodded. "Yes, please. And make it quick."

"Of course," the driver replied before walking away to prepare the carriage.

Sitting on the roadside, hidden in the shadows where she thought no one could see her, Jackie was startled when Howard materialized in front of her.

His voice was filled with concern. "What happened back there?"

Taking a deep breath, Jackie hesitated before responding. "It's all over, Howard. Please, just go."

"Over? I saw you speaking with the chief. Did you find out anything?" Howard pressed.

Jackie gritted her teeth. For Howard's own safety, he must never learn the truth about Chief Trevor. If he did, he would blindly involve himself and risk drowning alongside her.

"Jackie," Howard called out. "Please, talk to me. Whatever it is, we can work through it together."

"I didn't uncover anything, and the drug case isn't linked to the chief. I checked – he's clean," Jackie lied.

"Okay, but why did you run away then?"

Standing up, Jackie reiterated, "I said it's over."

"This investigation isn't over—" Howard began.

"Not an investigation. *Us.*"

His eyes widened in disbelief. "You're... breaking up with me?!"

She nodded, fighting back tears.

Howard gasped, then stormed over to the nearest bush, kicking it in frustration before returning to her. Jackie gazed down the dark street, waiting for the carriage, but it remained deserted.

"I knew it," Howard muttered.

Confused, Jackie turned to him. "Knew what?"

Tears welled in his eyes. "Theo. It was always him, wasn't it?"

"What are you talking about?" Jackie asked, bewildered.

Howard loosened his tie, his gaze piercing as he confronted her. "I'm not blind, Jackie. It all began a long time ago. I noticed the competition between you and Theo in class, and the shifts in your moods. Then you chose him for that first mission, the one you failed. I knew you harbored feelings for him, unreciprocated. I saw it all, Jackie. And I had hoped that you would eventually choose me, but all this time, you loved him. Tell me if I'm wrong."

Jackie cast her eyes downward, the weight of his words heavy on her heart. She never wanted to hurt him like this, but the truth had to be revealed. "I'm so sorry," she whispered.

Howard's eyes dimmed, the light within him fading. When Jackie reached out to touch his shoulder, he recoiled. "When were you planning to tell me about the two of you?"

"Howard, please listen. I'm not in love with Theo, and I never was."

"Why are you lying now?"

"It's the truth," she affirmed. "Consider this – my Gift has its limitations. If I felt anything for Theo, would we be able to perform our recent ritual together?"

"I don't know. Perhaps your connection rekindled after your heartfelt conversation by the fireplace, where you both shared your troubled past."

Shaking her head, Jackie explained, "My Gift prevents me from reading people whom I love or have loved in the past."

Howard stood still, deep in thought. "But I saw you tonight. The way you kept looking at them, damn it. Am I losing my mind?"

Her heart sank heavily. "Howard, please. Let's just say our goodbyes."

"Wait," he interjected, gesturing with his arm. "You're in love with someone, and you're not denying it. And if you weren't looking at him tonight, then..."

His eyes widened, a spark of realization dawning in them. Jackie always admired Howard's detective-like thinking, and she could see that he was piecing together the puzzle in his mind. Sometimes, the seemingly impossible explanation turned out to be the correct one, as Howard often said. In that moment, he explored this theory, fitting the missing pieces together until they aligned perfectly.

At last, the carriage emerged from the corner and pulled up to the entrance door.

Jackie's gaze bore into Howard with regret. Her career was in ruins, but she was determined to protect Elisa from suffering the same fate. "Yes, I looked at *her*," she admitted.

Howard remained speechless, his eyes fixed on her. The shock typically lasted for several minutes, a time they couldn't afford.

"I tried to move on from her. I truly did. Because she'll never be mine. It's agonizing to love someone who can never return your feelings."

He narrowed his eyes at her. "Yeah... tell me about it."

Seizing the moment of his silence, Jackie embraced him and planted a kiss on his cheek. "Goodbye, Howard. I'm sorry for everything."

He regarded her with disappointment as she made her way to the waiting carriage. Feeling his gaze on her, she glanced back only to find him gone. It was just her and the carriage on the desolate street. And the life she was about to leave behind.

As she settled into the carriage, the driver eyed her curiously. "Heading back to the Academy?"

"No. Do you know about the new club that opened this summer?" Jackie inquired.

"At the Eastern outskirts?"

"Yes."

"It will cost more," the driver warned.

"That's fine."

The carriage glided through the deserted streets, passing by buildings and quiet alleys lined with bare trees. Everything seemed to drift past Jackie's eyes in a slow, dreamlike manner. If this was to be her final night in the city, she wanted to etch this peaceful scene into her memory.

Choosing to visit the club where she and Walter had conducted their last investigation was a decision made on impulse. Perhaps she sought solace in a place where she was unknown, where her face and name held no significance. But before she could move forward, she needed to leave everything behind. Trevor's words echoed in her mind – running away was her forte, and he was right. Despite her attempts to break free from this pattern, she had been deceiving herself.

Though she had taken on the role of a guardian fighting for truth, she had been living a lie. Unable to continue this facade any longer, Jackie reached out and touched the memory crystal glowing on her chest.

"Erase," she whispered softly.

The crystal blinked once, and then the light faded, extinguishing the memories it held within.

Story 8

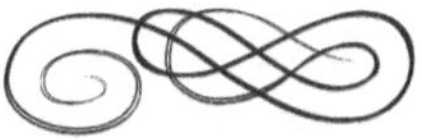

Reading Between the Lines

46

Two Shots

Thanks to the autumn ball, the nightclub wasn't very busy. The visitors were mostly people who came here for the afterparty. Among plenty of free seats, Jackie chose table number five. This was where the Moon Dust case got a new perspective. Well, here it was supposed to end.

The waitress, a woman in her thirties with sad black eyes, approached Jackie with a tray. As she was putting her order on the table, the scars on her wrists were revealed. Jackie's heart sank. She bet the waitress was one more victim of the man's cruelty, but tonight, she didn't want to think about it.

The woman gave her a polite smile. "Bon appétit."

"Merci." Jackie placed two bronze coins on the table. "Please, keep the change."

She put the coins in her apron. "You have a kind heart. May I bring you our special cocktail for free?"

"No, I have just enough."

She nodded. "Sure. Let me know if you need anything."

"Of course."

Her modest order was in front of her – a small plate of tree nuts and two shots of whiskey. The first shot of whiskey symbolized her personal life, and the second one was her career. Until this moment, she had only these two things she cared about, and she managed to screw up both. Jackie took one shot and raised it.

"For my broken heart." She drank it, and the hot liquid burned her stomach. She took several short breaths to cool down her tongue. The hunger that quietly slept before now awoke. She grabbed the nuts and ate them all, enjoying every bit of it. When Jackie emptied the plate, her head stopped spinning.

The second shot gleamed in the light of a single candle. Once Trevor told her that when life seemed to be over, it actually was about to begin. Only if she could tell him he was wrong! Jackie moved the shot closer, collecting her guts together to drink it. And then, the capricious Lady Luck finally decided to turn her face to her.

Two men sat at the next table, just behind her back, and the sound of their voices reached her ears. One of them was the owner of this club, and the second one... was Trevor.

"You're late," the owner said. "I hope everything is alright."

"It is," Trevor replied. "Just had to take care of the garbage."

Jackie scoffed. Well, it wasn't the worst thing she had heard about herself during her short experience as a cadet.

The waitress brought their order without asking questions. Using this moment, Jackie touched the memory crystal on her neck. She brought it closer to her lips and whispered, "Activate."

"So," the owner said as the waitress left. "What urgency made you come here personally?"

"Not much to worry about, Joe. Just decided to speed up our deal."

"Speed up?" Joe chuckled. "After you told us to slow down?! No, it doesn't work this way."

Trevor landed his glass on a table, its loud clunk causing Jackie to flinch.

"Listen carefully, Joe. I came here myself because I have some rats in my barn. They don't really have anything, but time plays against us. The sooner we close the deal, the better."

"Ok, ok. I've got it."

Trevor fidgeted on his sofa, and it squeaked under his weight. "The last fight will be tomorrow."

Joe breathed heavily. "Hold on. What about the guests? We need time to send invitations. Then we need to prepare everything and find a place. Plus, no one would come on Sunday."

"I'll provide a reliable place. No one would ever check there."

"Got it. But I need two days," Joe said.

Trevor paused. Jackie was motionless. In hanging silence, her heartbeat was so loud that she worried if Trevor could hear it too.

"Fine. Monday then," Trevor replied.

The men stood up. Jackie quickly switched the crystal off and held her breath. It was probably all the limit of her luck that night because the waitress approached her and started collecting the empty dishes.

"Hey, miss!" Trevor asked, and the waitress turned to him, exposing her.

Damn. Jackie literally had two seconds before he would notice her. Their talk with Laura awoke from the depth of her memory. It was the day when they held a Gift exchange ritual, trying to find a way to tame Elsa's Gift. As they figured, sometimes the best thing to do was to rely on instincts. Like now, when she had no time to waste.

Everything Jackie knew before and everything she learned now assembled in this particular moment when she was in this club. She took a short breath and let her instincts do the job. Her fingers detached the crystal from the chain, and she dropped it into the shot of whiskey. The brown liquid sparkled, keeping the terrifying truth that could cost her a life. Then, she did the most beautiful and the most disgusting thing she had never thought she was capable of doing. Jackie raised the shot and drank it.

She didn't choke. The whiskey made the crystal slide down to her stomach, and it comfortably settled. Then, a heavy hand touched her shoulder, and she turned to face Trevor.

"Jackie?!" His eyes flashed.

"Long time no see," she said, smiling nonchalantly.

His eyes kept piercing her. His ragged breath with a slight alcohol odor reached her face. "What the fuck are you doing here?"

Jackie stood up and landed the empty shot on a table. The glass cracked, but she didn't bother to check it. "I made up my mind," she said. "I want to work for you."

Trevor laughed. "Do you know what's the funniest thing? Even when people know about my Gift, they keep lying to my face."

He raised his hand and clicked his fingers. Jackie helplessly looked around, but the room was almost empty, and no one paid attention to them. Joe made a silver energy ball in his hand. *A Paralyzing spell.* Before Jackie could move, the ball reached her chest, and she stood motionless.

"You shouldn't have come here," Trevor said. He closed her eyelids with his fingers, and Jackie fell into the darkness.

47

Upside Down

Jackie didn't see any dreams. She just floated in the fog, lulled by the whisper of the waves coming from the lake. She kept her hand on her belly, and the crystal pulsed there, holding the dangerous truth. How many days did she have before it would leave her body? As she remembered from the anatomy course, she had a day, maybe two.

She chuckled. Her mother loved to repeat that the truth always finds its way out, and damn, she was right. At the end of this summer, Jackie wrote her a letter for the first time after she ran from home, just to let her know that she was alive and well. If only her poor mother knew where she was right now.

The fog around her dispersed, and her mother's face was revealed. Her eyes were full of tears. "Write a letter," she said. "Please."

Jackie nodded. The letter. If only she had a chance to write it to her – to lay the inks on a smooth paper and inhale its fragrant smell.

When Jackie opened her eyes, the sky above was gray. The whisper of the waves didn't disappear. Now, the fresh breeze touched her puffy face as she blinked and sat up. Her hands were bound with power-blocking cuffs. Usually, the guardians used such cuffs to prevent the criminals from harming them. Today, Jackie found herself on the other side of reality – a lawbreaker in the criminal world.

"Wake up and shine," Trevor said, standing two steps away from her. The waitress, a woman Jackie had met the night before, stood near him, her eyes conveying a sense of sadness.

"Shine yourself," Jackie replied.

Trevor chuckled. "You always had a good sense of humor."

"You too."

He approached and leaned over her. "Names, Jackie. I need the names of the people who are helping you."

She took a deep breath, allowing her detective thinking to kick in. Trevor still didn't know about her friends, indicating that Walter wasn't working for him. Trevor had lied to her the previous night, manipulating her fears – he had exploited her trust issues and made her doubt her team. And she had been foolish enough to let him play with her. It should never happen again.

"What if I don't tell you?" Jackie asked.

He raised his hand. "Isn't it obvious? I'll kill you."

Jackie looked around. The club building was nearby, and they were on a rocky lakeshore on the outskirts, the last place her friends would check when they realized she was gone. Of course, if someone was going to look for her, considering how she had said goodbye to Howard.

Trevor coughed into his fist, drawing her attention.

"If you were going to kill me, why am I still alive?" she asked.

He glanced at the waitress. "We decided to get the information first."

Her eyes sparkled with violet electricity, making Jackie's heart tremble. She possessed the same Gift as Elisa.

"You didn't deserve my tips," Jackie said.

"It's just business, nothing personal."

Jackie shifted her gaze to Trevor. "Do you really have time to torture me? What would you do at work – take a day off? Call in sick?"

"It's none of your business."

She persisted. "And the traces?! I left some traces, so the guardians will be here any moment."

"You lie," he said. "I see it. No one would come for you."

"I don't lie." She gasped. "I believe in my team."

He waved his hand, and the waitress approached. Her fingers touched Jackie's neck, and electric sparkles pierced her spine like a dozen hot needles. Jackie tried to shout, but her voice failed her, and she bit her tongue.

Jackie fell on the rocks, shaking, her mouth helplessly gasping for air.

Trevor approached her and shouted, "Names!"

She spat blood. "You need me, Trevor. I can work for you."

He clenched his fists. "Wasn't it enough?"

"When they discover my absence, they'll find me with the Searching spell. What would you say then?"

"No one will find you because I'll erase your traces."

Her hands stopped shaking, and Jackie sat up. "Why, Trevor? Use these traces. Use me. The worst enemy of a guardian is disinformation."

The waitress extended her hand to touch her neck again. Trevor raised his hand, and she stopped moving.

Jackie continued speaking. Unbelievably, her tongue, which had always been her enemy, now became her best friend. "Let's say they come to the club by noon and find a note from me. Then they follow the wrong trace, and you gain time to close your deal with Joe."

He nodded. "Suppose you do it. Then what?"

"You'll give me some money, and I'll get the hell out of this city. Win-win."

He sneered. "And you betray your friends so easily?"

She sighed. "Friends... Let me be honest, Trevor. There is no place for me in this Academy and among the guardians. The woman I love can never be with me, and yesterday, my ex-boyfriend figured it out. I'm done."

He looked at her with interest now. "So, you are gay."

Jackie nodded.

"Whatever." He gave her a wary look. "What about names?"

"It won't benefit you. At least four people besides me suspected you, including your team members. If I suddenly disappear, more people will start to worry."

He nodded. "I see."

Her belly rumbled, and Jackie placed her palm on it. She only hoped that the Lightning magic hadn't damaged the crystal and that her stomach wouldn't let her down. She had bought herself some time, but there was no guarantee that Trevor wouldn't kill her after she wrote the note to her friends.

A spasm pierced her guts, causing Jackie to bend at the waist and moan.

"What did you do to her?" Trevor asked the waitress. "Can she hold a pen?"

She leaned in and placed her palm on Jackie's, which was resting on her belly. "That shouldn't have happened. Unless something is interfering with my magic."

Jackie shut her eyes tightly, trying to block out their faces. The spasm eased, and she let out a sigh of relief.

Trevor approached. "What are you hiding, Jackie?"

Jackie gave him the saddest look she could muster. As she had learned from her practice, it does not matter *what* you say; it matters *how* you say it. She saw an opportunity to awaken his human feelings and jumped at it without a single doubt. "You want to know? All right, me and my fake boyfriend broke up, but I kept his present in my belly. And this is the only thing I care about now!" Her eyes welled up with tears. "And I... More than anything, I'm afraid to lose it. If I do, everything I went through was for nothing!" She dropped her face into her palms, sobbing generously.

The waitress patted her back. "Is that true, Trevor?" she asked. "Is she pregnant?"

Jackie cried louder, and now these tears were real. Trevor's Gift was to see the truth, and now her life was in his hands. But he was a human being, and humans make mistakes. His mistake could save her life.

"She is telling the truth," he said.

Jackie moaned with relief, her tears flowing without pause. She was freed. Protected. Saved. It was one small victory in this cruel game called life. *How many more challenges can I handle?*

The waitress hugged her shoulders, offering comfort. Unfortunately, Jackie couldn't use her Mind-reading Gift as her magic was blocked, but she didn't need to delve into the waitress's thoughts to understand that her problem likely involved her children. It was a good card to play later.

Trevor stood up. "Penny, stop it!"

She released Jackie from her embrace. Relieved, Jackie wiped her tears away. *Oh, if I were a criminal in this world, I would be a damn good one.*

Trevor gave her a stern look. "Bring a paper, Penny."

"And the ink," Jackie added, wiping her nose.

The sun was slowly rising above the horizon, and her pen glided smoothly across the paper. The scent of the ink brought back memories of her mother's request to write a letter. *Was it an actual warning from my mother? Had she performed a ritual to protect me?* Jackie didn't know, but she knew what to do now.

Trevor instructed her to write, and Jackie began to put the words on paper. After her first day of classes, she developed a habit of reading the first letters of the text to find a hidden message. It had never been useful before, but she hoped that someone would read her letter in this way. Perhaps it would be Theo, as he was the smartest person on their team and had cracked a message in a previous quest.

Writing the letter wasn't difficult. Trevor had first asked her to bid farewell, and Jackie included those words in the letter using her own style. It was a brief message, just half a page. Here is what she had written:

"Dear Howard,

Only if I could be with you... but
we live just once.
A new life is ahead, and
I have to say goodbye to you.
The truth is that I don't deserve you.
Maybe I wasn't a good girlfriend.

Or a guardian. Whatever.
Now, I only want you to know that
drug dealers will have something tonight
at five in the evening.
You will find them in this club.

P.S. I wish you the best in your career. And please, say "Goodbye" to Theo and Elisa. I'll never forget us and the quest we solved on the day we met.

- Jackie."

She handed the letter to Trevor, her heart beating in a frantic rhythm, ready to leap out of her chest. Don had once said that a felon must be an incredibly lucky person. A bad person needs to be lucky all the time to avoid being arrested, and a good person needs to be lucky just once to catch them.

Today, Jackie found herself on the other side, once again begging for luck. *Interesting, does Trevor's luck have limits?* She hoped so because if her plan worked, the guys would read the hidden message – *Do Wait Monday.*

Jackie only needed to find out where the fighting would be on Monday and let them know.

Trevor finished reading the letter and looked at her, satisfied. "You will remain in a special place for two days under the Hiding spell."

Jackie patted her belly. "Of course."

"Penny will take care of you," he said. "When the deal closes, I'll give you twenty gold coins, and you will leave immediately."

Jackie nodded.

Trevor started reading the letter again, frowning. *Shit, I need to distract him.*

She stood up. "Just twenty coins. How come?"

"Jackie." He folded the letter and put it in his pocket. "I could kill you right now. Do you understand how generous I am?"

She heaved a sigh of relief. "Sorry, Trevor, but I had to try."

He shook his head and turned to Penny. "Conspiracy first. Bring her to the place."

Penny stood up, removing her scarf. Jackie allowed her to cover her eyes.

"Just follow me," Penny said, taking her hand. "Everything will be alright."

Jackie smiled. "Sure, it will."

48

Lost in Words

"What do you mean she'll never come back?" Elisa sat at the table in front of Urchin, her eyes glaring at him. They had failed to find Jackie. After the ball at the Guardian House, she disappeared with Urchin, leading everyone to assume they had returned to the dorms to avoid suspicion.

However, the next morning, Theo discovered that Jackie had actually left in a different direction, prompting them to use a Searching spell to trace her energy to a nightclub. Now, back at the Academy, they sat around the kitchen table, arguing about their next move.

"That's what she wrote." Urchin crumpled a piece of paper with Jackie's farewell note and threw it on the floor. The paper ball rolled to the chair leg and stood there.

Theo pressed his palms together, deep in thought. "It can't be that simple. She never spoke to any of us before her sudden departure. Why would she do that?"

"I don't even know," Urchin replied, raising his dull eyes to Elisa. "Maybe because she broke up with me."

"She did what?" Theo gasped.

Elisa placed her palm on her chest, feeling her heart pounding. Urchin clearly knew something important about the true reasons for Jackie's decision, but he remained silent.

"I mean, I'm very sorry for your heartbreak," Theo eventually said. "But it's so illogical for Jackie. What about her career? Would she give up everything because of a relationship failure?"

"It was more than that," Urchin said, running his fingers through his hair. "To make a long story short, everything between us was built on lies. But I won't discuss it now. What we need to focus on is what she discovered – the dealers will be at the club at five tonight, so we need to be there to catch them."

Elisa and Theo exchanged glances. Urchin was right – their personal drama could wait until they completed their mission of catching the drug dealers.

"So, if I understand correctly, she told you the chief was clear," Elisa summarized. "And then, she goes to the club in the suburbs and leaves a note saying the criminals will be there."

Urchin nodded. "Exactly. I believe she saw someone at that club last night. That's why she hid the message under the bench – so only we could find it."

"It makes sense," Theo agreed.

Elisa glanced at the crumpled piece of paper on the floor by the chair leg. "Can I read it?"

"No!" Urchin stood up. "She wrote it for me."

"But you might miss something –"

He picked up the paper and tucked it into his chest pocket. "Can I have at least one thing that doesn't involve you?!"

Elisa narrowed her eyes. "What are you implying? Should I stay out of it because you're heartbroken?"

Theo moved his gaze around them. "Alright, let's calm down, both of you. We need to go see Don now and discuss the operation."

"Sounds good to me," Urchin said, giving Elisa a disappointed look before walking away.

Elisa stood up, her hand resting on the warm table surface. This was their special place, where they used to sit with Jackie during their first months of studying, sharing breakfast every morning and sometimes dinner. It was here that she had taken a potion on their very first day when Don had run his quest. It felt strange to think that they would never sit here again, chatting and laughing together.

"Don't let Urchin upset you," Theo said. "He's just going through a tough time. It will pass."

She turned to him. "Why was it him? Why didn't she say good-bye to me?"

"I think it was just too difficult for her," Theo replied with a shrug. "Does it really matter now?"

"I just realized that I might never see her again," Elisa's voice trembled. She raised her eyes to the ceiling, trying to hold back her tears.

Theo approached her. "Whatever happened, give it time. I'm sure she had her reasons, so you must trust her now. Can you do that?"

Elisa nodded. "I'll try."

At five in the evening, they found themselves in the club. Elisa sat at the bar with Laura, who had come to assist with the undercover

operation. They ordered two cocktails with bright paper straws and scanned the room for any suspicious individuals. So far, all the patrons seemed to be behaving normally.

Urchin was seated at a table with Theo, putting on a facade of a friendly meeting. Don was outside with a small group of guardians, poised to enter at a moment's notice.

"So, they broke up, huh?" Laura twisted her straw, stirring her drink in the glass. Her curious gaze met Elisa's.

"It appears so," Elisa replied. "But it doesn't change anything for us."

"Are you still planning to leave the city?" Laura inquired.

"I honestly don't know what to do," Elisa said, placing her empty glass on the table as the bartender approached to refill it.

Laura glanced at Elisa's drink with disapproval. "Drinking won't help solve anything."

She gave her an annoyed look. "We'll see."

Laura leaned in closer. "You know what would be fun? If I managed to nick her letter from Urchin."

Elisa glanced over at the guys, who were engrossed in their conversation and occasionally casting glances at the other patrons. Unlike her, they seemed completely focused. She turned back to Laura. "No way. It's in his chest pocket."

"Just watch," Laura said with a wink before standing up.

Adjusting her hair, Laura sauntered over to the table where the guys were seated. After a brief flirtation with Urchin, she asked him to dance. Theo remained at the table, nursing his beer with a sour expression. Elisa couldn't help but smile. It seemed he was feeling a twinge of jealousy, which she took as a good sign.

As the bartender approached a man nearby, Elisa shifted her attention to their conversation. She moved closer to eavesdrop on their discussion.

"Okay, someone will be at the backdoor in a minute," the bartender said.

The man in the black leather jacket had a star tattoo on his neck that shifted as he scanned the crowd, his gaze eventually settling on Elisa.

She flashed him an innocent smile and requested another drink from the bartender. As the suspicious man departed, she casually made her way through the crowd towards the front doors. There, a guardian was waiting for her, and she signaled to him with a wave of her hand. He nodded in acknowledgment and headed out to the street.

With their plan set in motion, everything was now in their hands.

49

✒

Choosing the Paths

That day, Jackie couldn't find peace. She was in the basement of a building, in a room without any windows. She paced the room again and again, like a wild tiger trapped in a cage. She didn't know if Howard had received the letter or if any of the guys had cracked it. She didn't even know what time of day it was. All she had was this gloomy room with shabby walls lit up by the torchlight from the corridor.

Jackie approached the narrow doorway, her hands squeezing the metal rods. She shook it hard, but she couldn't move them aside to get out. Then, a quiet clank of metal sounded at the end of the corridor. Jackie closed her eyes, listening. Someone was at the stairs – two women's voices argued.

"I've told you to use the cloth carefully. You just ruined the material for two jackets!" one of them said. Her voice sounded familiar.

"Sorry, Marta," the other woman replied. "I'll be careful next time."

"You know that I report to the chief, and he counts every coin!"

Silence.

Marta's voice rang out, "This is the guardian uniform! Please, be careful! I won't be able to keep you here if you don't do your job properly." Her voice muffled, then disappeared into silence.

The uniform. Only one factory in the city provided the guardians and cadets with the uniform. Jackie had visited this factory last year with Elisa, shortly after their first semester had started.

As it turned out, making the uniform with golden dragon embroidery was quite expensive. The young guardians never thought about the hard labor that went into creating it when they wore it in their free time, often neglecting to take care of it. In response, Don started organizing tours for the cadets to educate them and teach them to treat the uniform with respect. Hardly effective, but Jackie still remembered the woman who was the main seamstress. She had a stern voice and maintained strict discipline. This woman had a beautiful name that didn't quite fit her stark nature – Marta.

Jackie took a step back and inspected the walls around her. They were made of gray brick, the same as the sewing factory she had once visited, indicating that she was in the basement of this building.

She slid down onto the cold floor. Amazingly, her detective talent helped her establish her location, but this discovery did little to help her escape. Jackie shook her cuffed wrists. The metal hurt her skin, and the scratches tingled. She was still wearing her yellow ball dress, which sparkled in the torchlight. When Howard had seen her in this dress, he had remarked that she looked too beautiful for the dull hall room. If only he could see her now!

The sound of quiet steps made her turn towards the corridor. This time, it was Penny, the waitress who worked for Trevor. She carried a tray with sandwiches and a teacup, which was a good sign. At least they planned to keep her alive. Jackie stood up as

Penny opened the gate and walked inside, placing the tray on a bench.

"How is it going?" Jackie asked, trying to look nonchalant.

"The guardians came to our club today but found nothing. The distracting maneuver worked perfectly."

Jackie mustered a smile. "Good."

"I brought your dinner. I added more veggies so you can get some vitamins. You should eat well, Jackie."

She almost asked, "Why?" but bit her tongue. Obediently, she sat on the bench and started eating.

Penny gave her a pitying look. "You drank alcohol last night. Why?"

Jackie stopped chewing. "Just two shots won't hurt."

"Listen, I know it's hard for you, and your boyfriend dumped you –"

"I don't want to think about him anymore," Jackie said, switching her full attention to her food. "Please." Damn, she was really hungry. She hadn't had a crumb since last night.

Penny leaned against the wall, her hands clutching the folds of her snow-white apron. "Once, I had a similar situation, Jackie. And back then, I was totally alone."

"Yes. Alone in the whole world." Jackie took the mug and inhaled the aroma of the tea. Penny really cooked well.

Penny sat next to her. "But you are not alone anymore. You will have *him*, and he will always love you."

"I wish I could have *her*," Jackie said.

Penny shook her head. "It doesn't matter, boy or girl."

Jackie fell silent. No, she couldn't be a criminal. It took too much stamina to keep playing this game of words. And Penny... Something terrible had happened to her, and Jackie was afraid to ask, but she needed to establish a connection to get out of her prison. "Penny, I see something happened to you, and let's be honest – it's not easy for me to ask. But why did you start helping Trevor?"

She turned her palms up, showing the cuts on her wrists. "Jackie, you won't understand. He saved my life and gave me a purpose."

Her eyes widened. "He did what?!"

"Once, I was just like you, Jackie. I loved a woman, and this love wasn't possible because... you know why. I tried to forget her, and I got married to a respectful man that my parents chose for me. Then we moved to this big city with my husband, but I could never forget her. As a reminder of her, I kept a love letter from her under the floor of a guest bedroom, so my husband would never know. When he started renovating that room, we were expecting a child, and..." Penny took a deep breath, her eyes filling with tears.

"He found the letter," Jackie guessed.

She nodded. "He beat me severely, and I lost the child. Then I left him. He told my father about me to ensure I didn't have any support. I was on the street, starving... I lost everything."

Jackie hugged Penny tightly. "I know, Penny, I know," she whispered, caressing her hair. Her own eyes became wet, triggered by her own memories. That night when her ex-fiancée poisoned her, and then the doctor's words... it would always stay in the depths of her mind.

They sat together, shedding tears, and somehow it brought a sense of relief. The sorrow that each of them had endured was terrible, but at the same time, Jackie knew that she wasn't alone in it, and it gave her the strength to fight for them. For all women. To be the person who could stop this mess, or at least try.

Jackie wiped her face. "I chose to be a guardian to prevent this, but sometimes it seems like the whole world has gone insane. Like it will never stop."

Penny stood up. "That's why you shouldn't think about them. Think about yourself now."

Jackie turned to the corridor, where the flames danced, oblivious to their numb grief. "You know what my friend told me once? We can choose what to do – to ignore what's happening in this world or do what we can to make it a better place to live. I chose the second way."

"And how did it work?" Penny asked.

Jackie shrugged. "I couldn't become a guardian, but you know what, my life isn't over. When I get out of here, I'll do something using my Gift. Oh, I can do so much good!"

"Like what?"

She stood up and swung her arms. "I can be whoever I want! I can help women in difficult situations and support them."

"Don't you need money for that? Or special education?"

She thought for a moment, then replied. "You know what, I'll use the money from Trevor to continue my studies and become a lawyer. Of course, in another city."

"It sounds like a childish dream," Penny said, giving her a sad smile. "You are so naive."

"Let's do it together then! You can use your Gift, too." Jackie took her hands in hers. "Actually, how did you manage to keep your dangerous Gift and not get sent to Mercy House?"

Her cheeks blushed. "My mother knew the witch, and I learned how to hide my powers from others. I lied that I had another Gift."

"Seriously? And what's your cover Gift?"

She smiled. "I 'can' see dreams about the future."

Jackie laughed. "People must think you are terrible at it."

"Whatever. As long as I was alive and safe, it suited me. We hid it from my father, and when my mom passed, no one knew about my secret Gift, not even my husband."

"So, you can teach teenage girls how to control this kind of power."

"Like a witch?!"

"No, like a teacher. You can work in a school and educate girls with destructive Gifts. I've heard that such teachers are in high demand right now."

Penny lowered her eyes. "I would love to. But... what about Trevor?"

"Who cares?! We'll disappear from the city after the fighting. We will be free."

"No! He will never let me go. I know too much."

"Don't worry about that. Soon, he will be too busy with other things."

"Why?"

Jackie bit her lip. No, she couldn't tell Penny about her secret plan, not yet. Penny was too scared and too loyal to the wrong person. Jackie had to finish what she planned first. "Penny, listen. When it's over, I'll find a way to persuade him. You should trust me now."

"What do you want from me?" Penny narrowed her eyes.

"Tell me where the fighting will be."

Penny stared at the wall behind Jackie's back, thinking. Jackie counted the seconds as the blood pulsed in her temples. Penny could just say 'No,' and it would be over.

"Why do you need to know that?" Penny asked.

Jackie gave her a pleading look. "I'm just thinking about it all day, and it's driving me nuts. It's not good for me to be so stressed, considering my condition."

"I won't tell you, I can't," Penny shook her head. "He'll kill me then."

Jackie paused, thinking. It wasn't fair to ask Penny about it and put her life in danger. But she wasn't going to give up. "I'm not asking you to give me the address. Just tell me if it's close to here or not."

"It's right in this building. Just on the upper floor."

Jackie widened her eyes, unable to believe her incredible luck. Now, just one move was left. "Penny, I want to disappear after it's over. And I feel so bad to leave without saying goodbye to the woman I love."

Penny sat on the bench. "Do you love her that much?"

"More than anything. All that time, we couldn't be together, and we never will. Because now we are on different sides."

"Why don't you write her a letter?" Penny suggested.

"And how would I send it? Go to the post office tomorrow after the fighting? The guardians would find me right away!"

Penny nodded. "That's true – it's too risky. But how do you plan to get lost after you receive Trevor's money?"

Jackie gave it a thought. Fortunately, she was familiar with a classy kidnapping scheme, which would serve as a perfect explanation. "I want to hire a carriage and put a Hiding spell under the roof. Then, I'll get out of the city."

"Sounds smart."

"Thanks." She revealed a gentle smile. "Ah, Peggy... I'd appreciate it if you could help me by sending a letter. Maybe tomorrow morning, so she will receive it the same day and stop looking for me."

Penny stood up. "Say no more. I'll bring you the ink."

"And paper."

"Of course." Penny smiled. "If we hurry up, I can send it today before the post office closes."

"That would be awesome."

As Penny left, Jackie lay on the bench and hugged her shoulders. *Elisa,* she thought, *I hope you will understand everything I'm about to tell you.*

50

Bloody Truth

Elisa walked out of Don's office, panting. If she learned something from her failures, it was that the sense of despair never became easier. As it appeared, there were no drug dealers in the club, just a guy with a tattoo who brought a couple of boxes of liquor. Apparently, the whole operation was a waste of time, but the worst thing was that a slender thread that could have led her to Jackie was lost.

Laura was waiting for her in the corridor. Her silhouette was black in the bloody-red rays of the dying sun. Elisa came closer and just stood near, without having anything to say.

"What did Don say?" Laura asked.

She shrugged. "He doubts her common sense. And mine, too."

"Why yours? You did what you could."

Elisa scoffed. "Because if one man makes a mistake, no one in his sober mind would ever think to blame another man. But for women, it's different. If one of us screws up, the others are considered a huge failure."

Laura gave her a sly look. "But if you solve this case, they will respect us more."

"Maybe." Elisa turned to the darkening skies. "Only if I knew how to solve it."

"Let's try, then." Laura took an envelope from her pocket and gave it to Elisa. "I received it an hour ago. It's for you."

Elisa opened the envelope, and her heart leaped as she read the lines written in Jackie's hand.

*"**My** dear Elisa,*

Asking you to come with me would be
rather silly than romantic.
Then let's just say goodbye
and keep the fire of our love in our
souls. I loved you, and I always will.
Everything we shared together
with you, all the talks, hugs, tears.
I will think of you every day, and I'll
never forget the taste of your kisses.
Goodbye, Elisa.

P.S. Love you. Jackie."

"What's there?" Laura peeked over her shoulder.

Elisa wiped her eyes. "She is saying goodbye."

"Hmm..." Laura paced the corridor and walked back to her. This time, she held a wrinkled sheet of paper. "In her letter to Howard, she asks him to say "Hi!" to you and Theo. Why would she do that?"

Elisa stared at her. "Where did you get it?"

"When we danced in a club, I took it."

"You mean you stole it."

Laura gave her a teasing smile. "I can return it to him anytime."

"No fucking way!" Elisa took the letter from her and placed the two papers together. It was hard to read the lines written for Urchin, so her eyes slid through the lines, trying to make any sense of them.

"What do you think, detective?" Laura rushed her.

"There must be something in it." Elisa placed the letters on the window glass, trying to see the hidden words or symbols on the paper, but there was nothing like that. "It's like another quest from Don designed to torture innocent cadets."

"He does it to train you."

Elisa turned to her. "True. Our very first quest had a purpose of uniting us and making us work as one team."

They looked at each other in silence, Elisa's memory slowly awakening the complaints from Urchin, who blamed Don for making such a tough task that only Theo could resolve. And as she remembered, Jackie was absolutely in love with the idea of writing between the lines, as she called it. In her letter to Urchin, she even mentioned that she would never forget the day they all met. This must be the key. Elisa placed two pieces of paper on a windowsill with her trembling hands, and her index finger slid along the first lines.

"Marta. Sewing," Elisa read. The next message was meant for Urchin, and it said, "Wait for Monday."

"Something will happen on Monday, tomorrow," Laura said. "Today's operation was just an attempt to distract us."

"And it explains everything," Elisa agreed. "Someone made her write it, but she found a way to send us the warning."

"See? They underestimated her." Laura smiled widely. "But what about Marta? Do you know who she is?"

Elisa rubbed her forehead, thinking. "I remember this name from the sewing factory we once visited. They make uniforms for guardians and cadets."

"A sewing factory?!" Laura blinked. "The one in the suburbs?"

"I think so, yes."

"Then we must go there. This time, we'll catch them red-handed."

The doors to Don's office opened, and the rest of their team walked to the corridor. Elisa grabbed the papers and gave her a cheerful look. "Come on, let's cheer up these dull faces."

When Jackie awoke, she remained lying on the stiff bench. Her lower back hurt. She had no clue if it was morning or evening. She just didn't need sleep, so she kept staring at the ceiling. She put her hands on her belly, soothing the disturbing pulsing there. As she remembered, her moon cycle was about to begin.

"Please, hold on for a day," she whispered. Hearing approaching steps, Jackie sat up and looked at the corridor. Penny was walking toward her, and this time, she brought her food and clean clothes. Jackie stood up. Her ball dress was too tight, and she couldn't wait to change it to something simple.

Penny put the tray on a bench and gave her a cotton dress.

"Are you going to watch me?" Jackie asked, climbing out of the ball dress.

Penny turned to the wall. "I've sent your letter to Elisa. The post office was closed, so I walked to the Academy and dropped it right in their mailbox."

A sense of relief washed over her. Jackie stood as she was, completely naked, her hands squeezing the dress she had been given. "Oh, thank you so much! It means the world to me."

Penny turned to her, and her eyes opened widely.

"What? Never seen a naked woman?" She laughed, pressing the clothes to her chest.

She came closer. "How do you feel?"

"Fine."

Penny narrowed her eyes. "You are bleeding."

Jackie slowly looked down at a red smear on her hip. Well, her moon cycle was stable, but not her luck. "Crap."

Penny put her palm up and formed a silver Paralyzing spell in her hand. A ball of mist twisted in her hands. "You are not pregnant. You lied."

Jackie mustered a silly smile. "What a pity! Maybe I'll be more lucky next time –"

"It won't be next time!" The lightning flashed in her eyes. Then she threw her spell at Jackie.

She tried to dodge it, but it hit her in her chest, and she fell to the stiff floor.

Penny stood over her, her voice trembling. "And how could I believe you?"

51

The Last Fight

Jackie's head felt heavy, and her right shoulder throbbed with pain. It was likely due to the fall she took on the stone floor when Penny hit her with the spell. Slowly, she opened her eyes. Bound to the chair, she still wore the power cuffs on her wrists.

Taking in her surroundings, Jackie found herself in a spacious room filled with several chairs and cloth racks. A small window near the ceiling allowed the evening light to filter in, signaling that the impending fight was drawing near. Jackie's eyes landed on the familiar sight of shining bikinis and matching tiny shorts hanging on the racks. She remembered seeing these clothes on the day they failed the mission with Theo. The Incapable women had worn them during the ring fight. It didn't bode well. Attempting to move, Jackie found herself securely held by the ropes.

Just then, the door creaked open, and Trevor entered the room. He was dressed in a guardian uniform, the dragon emblem on his shoulder gleaming in the dim light.

"Look at this busy man," Jackie remarked. "Straight from work to a gig. Do you ever rest?"

He chuckled. "I've heard women are getting moody these days, but you seem to be in good spirits."

Jackie exhaled through her nostrils and remained silent.

He loomed over her with his hands in his pockets. "You're such a stubborn kid, Jackie. After the masquerade, I thought you would give up and flee the city that night. Yet, you managed to track me down and outwit us. You've changed a lot."

She shot him a sharp look. "People change."

Disappointed, he shook his head. "I had high hopes for you. After you made it through your first undercover mission, I decided to give you a chance. I thought you would be my loyal friend who would have my back. But you've dashed those expectations."

"Your idea of friendship is asinine. True friends respect each other."

He laughed and affectionately patted her head. "You're a naive, hopeless romantic. The world doesn't work that way."

"And how does it work?"

Trevor retrieved a cigar from his pocket and lit it. He blew a cloud of blue smoke in her direction, causing Jackie to cough.

Grinning, he continued, "Let me explain. People are inherently greedy and selfish. Concepts like love and friendship are mere illusions because everyone cares only about their own interests. If you believe your friends are reliable, think again."

She exhaled a sigh. "I pity you."

"And what about you? Why aren't you with the one you love?" Trevor probed.

Speechless, Jackie reflected on Elisa and Howard. Both were held back by their fears, which hindered their relationships. Elisa once said, *"If there is love, anything is possible,"* but she proved to be a hypocrite, preventing them from being together due to the fear of judgment and jeopardizing her career. As for Howard, his constant jealousy indicated a lack of trust in her.

Trevor smiled knowingly. "There you have it."

Jackie let out a sigh. "Perhaps I can't be with the woman I love, but that doesn't define me. I know who I am."

"And who are you, Jackie?"

"A dreamer. A fighter –"

"Exactly!" He raised his hand, and the smoke from his cigar formed a circle in the air. "That's why I haven't eliminated you yet. You have the potential to be a formidable fighter."

Jackie's gaze shifted to the cloth rack, where the bikinis shimmered in the fading light of the sunset. A chill ran down her spine. "What do you mean?"

"I believe you understand perfectly well what I mean. Are you prepared to fight for your freedom?"

"Will you truly release me if I win this fight?" Jackie questioned.

"Why not? Consider it my parting gift. It has been intriguing to witness your transformation."

"And what about you?"

"I'll continue to rule this city. Even though you and your Fire-Gifted friend caused a lot of damage, the earnings from tonight will compensate for it. Can you envision it? The entire underground will gather tonight to witness the showdown between the Incapable and a guardian woman," he declared, extinguishing his cigar underfoot.

Her hands clenched the ropes in frustration. "Son of a bitch! You'll pay for this –"

Before she could finish her threat, his hand covered her mouth, prompting Jackie to bite down. Despite his rough grip, her teeth managed to break the skin, leaving a metallic taste of blood on her tongue.

He yelped in pain and withdrew his hand, which was now stained with blood. Jackie met his gaze, panting heavily.

"I see you are ready for the fight," he remarked, wrapping his injured hand with a handkerchief.

In defiance, Jackie spat at him, the mixture of saliva and blood landing on his jacket. She wished it could reach his smirking face. Trevor turned on his heel and exited the room, leaving Jackie seething with anger.

As the room descended into darkness, illuminated only by the faint moonlight filtering through the window, Jackie's heart ached in her chest. Trapped with no means of escape, she pondered the fate of her letters. *Would I ever be discovered? What if both Elisa and Howard read my letters but kept them hidden from each other? Why would they disclose something as personal as a love letter?* The subject of the letters was a delicate matter for both Elisa and Howard, and they might have chosen to tuck them away in a drawer or simply destroy them. A solitary tear trickled down Jackie's cheek.

This was not how Jackie envisioned her life coming to an end. Trevor's harsh words had shattered her dreams, leaving her feeling abandoned and desperate. The faint glimmer of hope that had sustained her through the previous day had now disintegrated into a million shards of glass, causing her soul to bleed. A life devoid of faith held no value, and she found herself consumed by darkness.

Sadly, Jackie was nothing more than a pawn in the eyes of the wealthy spectators who had come to witness the fight. While they appeared to possess opulence and influence, the emptiness resided within them. Perhaps that's why they sought solace in extravagant jewelry, carriages, and mansions, desperately seeking new thrills through drugs and violent entertainment to fill the void within their souls. Perhaps they believed that the show would offer them a fleeting escape from their inner darkness.

Jackie remained seated on the chair, tears streaming down her face. She lost track of time as she wept. Eventually, she found herself devoid of tears, enveloped in a heavy silence.

The door creaked open softly, revealing Penny entering the room with a cup of tea. Jackie declined the offer.

Penny regarded her with a sorrowful expression. "I'm deeply disappointed in you."

"Sure, just eliminate anyone who disappoints you. That'll solve all your problems," Jackie retorted.

Placing the teacup on the floor, Penny took a seat. "You deceived me."

Jackie scoffed. "Apologies. I had a life to save."

"Why do you have to be so sarcastic?"

Instead of responding, Jackie glanced towards the door. "It's not too late, Penny. Let's escape. You and me."

Penny's lips curled into a grin. "Yes, let's rent a cozy apartment and live happily ever after."

"Why not?"

"You've already tricked me once."

Jackie met her gaze with a somber expression. "Believe it or not, I want you to have a better life. Truly. You possess the freedom to choose, and you must exercise it."

"It's too late," Penny said, eyeing the tea. "But I'm not a heartless person. I brewed a potion for you. It will numb any pain if you drink it."

In defiance, Jackie kicked the cup, causing it to roll against the wall and spill its contents, filling the room with the scent of herbs.

Penny raised her hands in confusion. "Why?"

"Because I'm not afraid of pain. It reminds me that I'm alive," Jackie declared.

"Then you will be hurting."

A man clad in a red shirt entered the room, instantly recognizable to Jackie. She had encountered him the previous year, as he was the one who entertained the audience in the boxing ring.

He glanced at Penny and commanded, "Prepare her! The final fight is about to start."

With that, he exited the room.

Penny began untying the ropes binding Jackie, who squirmed in her chair to make the task more challenging. As Penny reached for her neck, where her pulse throbbed, a faint spark of electricity coursed through Jackie's body, causing her to go numb.

After changing Jackie's clothes, Penny guided her to the door. As the doors swung open, Jackie had to shield her eyes from the blinding light. Though she could walk, her legs felt weak, causing her to stumble along the way.

In the hall, the crowd erupted in cheers, welcoming the female fighters. Elisa's gaze remained fixed on the ring, her heart heavy as she witnessed Jackie being drawn into the brutal and inhumane spectacle. Despite the overwhelming urge to intervene and rescue her, Elisa knew that such a rash move could ruin this operation, as Don had cautioned her. So, she stood by helplessly, an invisible shield separating her from the unfolding events.

Urchin grasped her hand, diverting her attention to him. "Please, try to calm down. Your anxiety weakens the shield."

"How can I possibly remain calm?" Elisa's voice quivered, betraying her inner turmoil. Thankfully, Urchin couldn't see her at that moment, or he would have insisted on her leaving immediately.

"Take a deep breath. It will help ease your distress," Urchin advised in a gentle tone.

Elisa followed his guidance, attempting to avert her gaze from the ring.

"Now it's better," Urchin said. "Let's wait a few more minutes before taking any action."

Elisa nodded in agreement, even though Urchin couldn't see her. Their newfound cooperation had blossomed since she had solved the puzzle, instilling hope in their mission to rescue Jackie. Urchin had readily set aside any past grievances to focus on their shared goal.

Surveying her surroundings for a potential escape route, Elisa noted only two guards amidst the night plants that illuminated the walls and tables. Their attention was fixated on the ongoing show.

The man in the red shirt paced back and forth in the ring, engaging with the crowd. Elisa paid little heed to his words, her focus solely on Jackie, who sat on the floor with her hands folded in her lap. Her complexion was pallid, and she appeared on the verge of fainting.

"Please, hold on, dear," Elisa whispered softly.

As the man in the red shirt gestured, the Incapable woman in a blue bikini entered the ring, eliciting cheers and applause from the spectators.

Jackie struggled to her feet, her weakened legs causing her to limp as she made her way to the edge of the ring. Despite her unsteady gait, she reached out and raised her hand, capturing the attention of the audience.

"You!" She pointed directly at the man with a gray mustache seated in the front row. He met her gaze with a smile.

Urchin leaned in close to Elisa's ear. "Damn, that's the mystery man we've been searching for."

"Are you certain?" Elisa inquired. "You've never seen him before."

"I've heard enough from her descriptions. Regardless, keep an eye on him once we're outside," Urchin advised.

"Understood."

The mystery man scanned the crowd, drawing curious glances from those around him. "Me?"

Jackie nodded firmly. "You deceive these people, all of them!" She then turned to the Incapable woman. "Do you truly believe you are fighting for your freedom?"

The Incapable woman nodded in agreement with Jackie's sentiments.

"Bullshit!" Jackie addressed the crowd, gesturing around. "And all of you are miserable! Your lives are so hollow and devoid of meaning that you derive pleasure from watching desperate women fight. Yes, I may be backed into a corner, but at least I have the freedom to choose. And I choose not to be a part of your perverted games!"

The man in the red shirt clapped his hands. "Silence!"

The crowd erupted in a cacophony of noise.

"You won't get what you desire!" Jackie retorted before defiantly sitting on the floor, her arms crossed over her chest.

Disappointed whistles emanated from the audience.

"Great speech," Elisa remarked with a smile. She pondered how much money Trevor would lose if his star fighter refused to participate.

The Incapable woman forcibly lifted Jackie and hurled her towards the edge of the ring. Jackie collided with the ropes before tumbling onto the canvas.

"Fight me!" the woman bellowed.

Jackie shook her head in refusal.

The crowd chanted, "Fight! Fight! Fight!"

Jackie covered her ears with her hands, lying prone on the ground. The woman loomed over her, delivering a brutal kick to her abdomen.

"No!" Elisa cried out in anguish. Ignoring the precautions, she broke free from Urchin's grasp and dashed forward. Now visible, she had barely taken two steps when he caught her once more.

Turning to face him, she pleaded, "Let me go."

"They shouldn't see any of us, remember?" Urchin's gaze bore into hers. "Or both you and Jackie will be in grave danger."

"I don't care! I would rather die than witness this."

"We are running out of time!" Urchin gripped her shoulders firmly. "Trust me, I'll ensure Jackie's safety when the moment comes."

"Will you?"

"Go outside. Now," he urged, releasing her. "You will be re-united with her soon. I promise."

Elisa nodded and hurried towards the exit.

Jackie curled into a ball on the ring, enduring the cruel taunts and kicks from the Incapable woman. A searing pain shot through her spine, causing her vision to blur as she struggled to focus on the frenzied crowd. In a moment of delirium, Jackie thought she saw Howard and Elisa in the audience, holding hands. She blinked, and they vanished, leaving her to face the harsh reality of her torment.

The Incapable woman returned, continuing her assault on Jackie. Each blow intensified the agony, leaving Jackie gasping for air. The memory crystal, still lodged in her stomach, seemed to be causing further damage with its sharp edges.

As Jackie braced herself for the inevitable outcome, she envisioned the guardians discovering her lifeless body at the end of the evening. With the crystal as evidence, Trevor would be apprehended and sent to Death Island, where his powers would be stripped away, and justice would be served.

Jackie's laughter echoed through the chaos of the ring, a defiant response to the pain and suffering inflicted upon her. In that moment, laughter became her cure, shielding her from the physical torment. As she continued to laugh, a sense of relief washed over her, fueled by the flicker of hope that had been reignited within her.

Despite her grim circumstances, lying battered and bloodied on the ring, Jackie found solace in the knowledge that she had lived a life filled with more meaning and purpose than those who sought to exploit her. She clung to her belief in justice, a beacon of light in the darkness that surrounded her.

Suddenly, a deafening explosion rocked the room, shattering windows and igniting a blaze that consumed the tattered curtains. Thick smoke billowed into the space, prompting the crowd to flee in panic. Jackie's gaze fell downward, but she no longer saw her own broken body. As if guided by an unseen force, she was lifted and carried out of the burning building.

Floating through corridors and stairwells, Jackie was gently guided to the backyard. Upon reaching a grassy hill, she came to a peaceful halt.

Jackie observed the factory building engulfed in flames, with the guardians and those who had managed to escape gathered in the yard. Walter and others with telekinetic abilities used their powers to hold up the collapsing structure, ensuring the safety of those exiting the building. Amidst the chaos, a surreal sight unfolded as a blue dragon soared above the inferno, unleashing flames.

Perched atop the dragon was a familiar figure with fiery red hair – Theo. Elisa embraced him from behind. As the dragon landed, Elisa sprang into action, racing towards the entrance doors. Penny emerged, wielding two crackling spheres of electricity in her hands. With a piercing scream, Penny unleashed her magic, but to no avail. Jackie breathed a sigh of relief. Luckily, similar Gifts were ineffective against each other.

Elisa swiftly cast a Paralyzing spell, immobilizing Penny before securing her with handcuffs. Jackie watched with a heavy heart, feeling a pang of regret for Penny's fate. She wished she could plead for Penny's forgiveness and a second chance, but Elisa was too far away to hear her quiet plea.

A comforting warmth enveloped Jackie from behind, and she found herself visible once more, draped in a black guardian jacket. Looking up, she felt a wave of dizziness that caused her to fall backward. Howard knelt beside her, his expression filled with concern.

"You came for me," Jackie whispered, her voice barely above a murmur.

Howard sat beside her, gently stroking her hair. His eyes glistened with unshed tears. "I couldn't bear to lose you."

"I knew you guys would decipher the message," Jackie remarked with a faint smile.

Howard returned the smile. "It was Elisa, actually. She mentioned your knack for reading between the lines and uncovering hidden messages. Who would have thought it would come in handy?!"

"I'm relieved you're not angry with me," Jackie said, the taste of blood lingering in her mouth as she swallowed.

Howard let out a sigh. "All I want is for you to be alive and happy."

Jackie chuckled softly, grateful to see the familiar warmth in Howard's eyes. However, the pain returned, causing her to clutch her stomach. "Howard, I don't think I'll make it."

"Don't say that."

"I don't know how much time I have left, so please listen carefully," Jackie implored, guiding his hand to her belly. "When Trevor mentioned the fight, I recorded it using your memory crystal. You need to retrieve it."

His eyes widened in surprise. "Where did you hide it?"

"Right here," she replied, squeezing his hand. "I swallowed it."

Howard's mouth opened in shock before closing again, processing her words.

Spitting out the blood, Jackie continued, "It's inside me, and it caused damage during the fight. Retrieve it when... when it's time. You'll have the evidence to bring that bastard to justice."

"You're not going to die, Jackie," Howard insisted, his voice filled with despair.

As the sky darkened above her, Jackie's vision began to blur. The rare clouds in the sky reflected the glow of the burning factory below. Two dragons soared through the clouds, heading south. One was Rei, the blue-scaled reptile, and the other one was red. Regrettably, Jackie never learned the name of the red dragon.

Howard brushed a stray hair from her forehead. "The other dragon is a female. They named her Rose."

A faint smile touched Jackie's lips. Over a year ago, Elisa had shared stories about the dragon farm, leading to the daring act of stealing dragon eggs.

Struggling to speak, Jackie whispered, "Tell Elisa that I love her."

"You'll tell her yourself," Howard assured her, his voice sounding distant.

With a final exhale, Jackie closed her eyes and saw no more.

52

A Heart of a Dragon

The darkness enveloped Jackie as she sat in a prison of her consciousness. She was in a cold, dimly lit room, trapped within its walls. No voice or light could penetrate the darkness that surrounded her. Hugging her shoulders, she waited, unsure of what she was waiting for. Suddenly, a flash of pink energy materialized before her eyes, swirling into a ball of Light. Jackie stood up, reaching out with numb fingers, but the ball darted away from her grasp.

She chased after it, the ball moving swiftly ahead of her. As she ran, Jackie realized that she was not in a room but a tunnel, the light at the end growing brighter with each step. Shielding her eyes from the blinding glare, she slowed her pace, allowing the warmth to envelop her. With each breath, her heart raced in anticipation. Finally, summoning her courage, Jackie opened her eyes.

Jackie found herself in her room, the daylight streaming in through the window. As she sat up, she noticed a lady in a white veil sitting on her bed. The veil obscured her eyes, but her smiling lips were visible as she donned her white gloves. The lady appeared young, perhaps around Jackie's age.

"Who are you?" Jackie's voice rang out, surprisingly strong.

"I believe you already know who I am."

Jackie's eyes widened in surprise. "It can't be... Are you a Healer?"

The lady nodded, placing a finger to her lips in a gesture of silence.

Jackie's heart raced with excitement. To have a person with such a unique Gift before her was beyond belief. Jackie couldn't resist asking, "Did Elisa summon you?"

The Healer nodded. "My husband and I were called here by Elisa, and we arrived just in time for the rescue operation. You were teetering on the edge, Jackie, but now you'll be alright."

Jackie lifted her nightgown, revealing a small pink scar that crossed her belly. It mirrored Elisa's scar, symbolizing a newfound connection on a deeper level between them.

The Healer lady gestured towards the scar. "You underwent a minor surgery to remove the memory crystal before I could perform my healing. The scar remains as a reminder of the remnants of my Gift that lingered after the wound healed."

Jackie shrugged. "A small price to pay for survival."

The Healer's expression turned somber. "It's more than just a scar. My Gift carries unforeseen consequences. Once you receive a new lease on life, you forfeit the ability to give life."

Jackie reflected for a moment. "That ship sailed long ago. No regrets."

"You possess great strength and fortune, Jackie," the Healer remarked. "Not everyone is granted a second chance, and there won't be a third, even with my Gift. From now on, live the life you've always desired."

Jackie regarded her with a tinge of sadness. "I wish I could follow your advice."

"You'll need time to process what happened. But I hope you find the answers you seek soon."

"Me too. How is Elisa, by the way?" Jackie inquired.

"Why don't you ask her yourself?" The Healer stood up and made her way to the door.

Elisa appeared at the threshold, observing the exchange. After the Healer departed, Jackie and Elisa embraced, and Elisa took a seat on the edge of the bed.

"Thank you," Jackie said. "You saved my life. Again."

Elisa chuckled. "Oh, dear... Do you realize the impact you had on the chief's arrest?"

Jackie glanced down at her scar, concealed beneath her cotton nightgown. "What do you mean? Will they allow me to remain here and continue my studies?"

"Absolutely. They've already arranged for both of us to reside at the local Guardian House," Elisa revealed.

Jackie placed a hand over her heart in astonishment. "That's incredible. They accepted you as well?"

"Of course. We're a team, remember? After all, Theo and I brought the healer and the dragons. No one has ever done such a thing before."

"Right, I recall seeing Rei and Rose. They've grown so much!"

Elisa chuckled. "They do grow quickly. The reactions in that building were priceless. No one even attempted to flee! That's how we apprehended the mystery man and Chief Trevor. Despite his denial the next morning, we had your crystal with the incriminating voice recording, leaving him no chance to evade justice."

Jackie's eyes widened in admiration. "You've done an incredible job, Elisa."

"It wasn't just me, it was all of us. Urchin ensured your safe evacuation. Walter orchestrated the operation discreetly, catching Trevor off guard," Elisa explained.

A sense of pride washed over Jackie. "Walter successfully brought the investigation to a close, then. Look at us – we've truly become guardians. Isn't this what you've always desired?"

Elisa grasped both of Jackie's hands in hers. "I was mistaken. I believed that my sole purpose was to be a guardian and save lives, neglecting the most crucial aspect. It was my greatest error."

"We're only human, and mistakes are inevitable."

"But we must learn from them. Upon arriving here, I thought I was prepared for anything. However, meeting you unearthed all my fears."

"Am I truly that scary?" Jackie teased.

Elisa chuckled. "No, you're adorable. But love can be daunting. I feared losing my career, yet more than anything, I dreaded you losing yours."

Jackie's heart raced. "And you rejected me."

"I know." Elisa's eyes glistened with tears. "I tried to remain strong, but I eventually turned to drugs to numb the pain of missing you, and it nearly cost me everything. I contemplated leaving the city, but when you departed without a farewell, I felt as though a part of me would die if I never saw you again." She wiped a tear from her cheek. "Then, seeing you in the ring last night, I realized one thing – we are the guardians, so our lives are constantly at risk. All we can do is live our lives, cherishing our time together, even if it goes against their rigid code."

"Are you afraid now?"

"I'm only afraid that you'll never forgive me."

Jackie gently lifted Elisa's chin, locking her eyes with her shimmering gaze. Like two vast oceans, her eyes held depth and mystery. "I don't think I'll ever stop loving you."

"Really?" Elisa's face lit up with a smile.

"Yes. But please, don't let your fears ruin what we have," Jackie implored.

"I love you deeply, Jackie. If you grant me a second chance, I promise I'll never disappoint you."

Jackie leaned in, and they shared a tender kiss. Elisa's touches were gentle and precise, causing Jackie to tremble in her embrace. Jackie yearned to hold her close, but Elisa pulled back, giving her a mischievous look.

"Hold on. We have something prepared for you."

"We?" Jackie glanced around. "You mean with Howard and Theo?"

"I mean everyone," Elisa clarified, rising and extending her hand. "Let's go!"

Elisa led Jackie down the corridor, and they hurried to the glass doors leading to the veranda. It was where they had spent evenings together the previous year, gazing at the city lights and anticipating the Light signal. It felt like a distant era.

As they stepped onto the veranda and approached the stone railings, they were met with a bustling crowd. Cadets, teachers, and members of the guardian team had gathered, with Walter among them. He waved at Jackie, who returned the gesture.

The crowd erupted in cheers and shouts of her name. Jackie's gaze fell upon the dragons as they descended lower, circling above them. The lady in the white veil rode the red dragon, while the man in black attire rode Rei. They waved at the crowd before soaring off into the distance.

"You see," Elisa remarked, "the dragon farm is no joke."

Jackie smiled at her. "I can't believe this is really happening."

"I told you. When there is love, anything is possible."

"I love you so much," Jackie expressed, embracing her.

The guardians raised their hands, releasing their Lights. The energy spheres shot into the sky, exploding into a dazzling display of multicolored sparkles. Everyone watched in awe as the lights ascended, eventually dissolving and revealing a cloudless blue sky.

All Jackie had ever dreamed of seemed to be within reach – a life shared with Elisa, their loyal friends and colleagues, and a career they could continue to build together. It was the second chance the healer had spoken of, a chance they both deserved. And there was one more goal Jackie wanted to pursue.

Giving Elisa a mischievous look, Jackie asked, "What do you think about me becoming the first female lawyer?"

"I think you would be a fantastic one," Elisa replied with a smile.

~ The End ~

Encyclopedia

Welcome to Crystal World!

You can find all the information about Gifts, Spells, and more here. Since this book has a print limit, I collected only the glossary for the specific words I used for this particular story.

To access a full encyclopedia, feel free to visit this link: www.magical2worlds.com/encyclopedia

Flora

Crystal World's nature is abundant and whimsical. All the herbs and flowers have valuable elements, so mages and witches use them to prepare various mixtures and potions. For instance, **chamomile** and **mint** have strong sedative effects, which makes them perfect foundations for relaxing teas.

Many flowers have unique energy, so their buds open at dusk and glow, illuminating the space around them. Mages learned to select such plants and use them to decorate their rooms and add more colors to their interiors.

Trees also vary depending on the climate zone. In the areas where seasons change, such as Lake Kingdom, the trees are covered with moss, making the barks shine. The color of the tree trunks changes depending on the season:

Spring – from light blue to mint-green
Summer – bright green
Fall – from orange to red and dull purple
Winter – the moss fades away, and the naked barks shine with a sapphire blue color.

In warmer regions, the barks might have brighter colors, such as indigo or magenta.

Fauna and Dragons

The animal world includes multiple species of fish, birds, and mammals. Many mages have cats, dogs, bunnies, and other small pets. Because horse-drawn transport is the most popular, people keep many kinds of horses at their stables.

Dragons are among the most unusual creatures. They prefer to live in wild areas and roam free, triggering the curiosity of scientists and adventurists who periodically visit their habitats to observe them. Eventually, the mages find a way to tame these reptiles and raise them as domesticated animals.

In later stories, dragons become essential companions for the guardians involved in defense forces.

Dragons' classification
(the breeds mentioned in this book):

Ogosis

Size - 10-12 m. (32-39 ft.)

Appearance - Red scales. Paws and tail can be maroon to black.

Strengths and weaknesses - When the dragon is about to release the fire, its scales shine. This breed is the biggest one, so Ogosis doesn't have natural enemies.

Ehdianoptus

Size - 6-9 m. (19-30 ft.)

Appearance - Dark yellow scales. Head and tail are darker than their body.

Strengths and weaknesses - This breed is hard to tame because of its stark nature.

Nozimos

Size - 5-7 m. (16.5-23 ft.)

Appearance - Blue with a dark violet tail and paws.

Strengths and weaknesses - Good for local flights and friendly. Nozimos is popular among guardians who live in smaller towns.

Time Crystals

Time is merciless, as mages say, so we must use it wisely. In Crystal World, all mages measure daytime using special time crystals.

Until people discovered time crystals in a cave on Death Island, they used sunlight to count hours and days. Now, they can simply look at their pocket crystal, which gradually changes color. When the day starts, it is red at midnight, then orange, yellow, and so on, until it goes through the whole spectrum and becomes red again at noon.

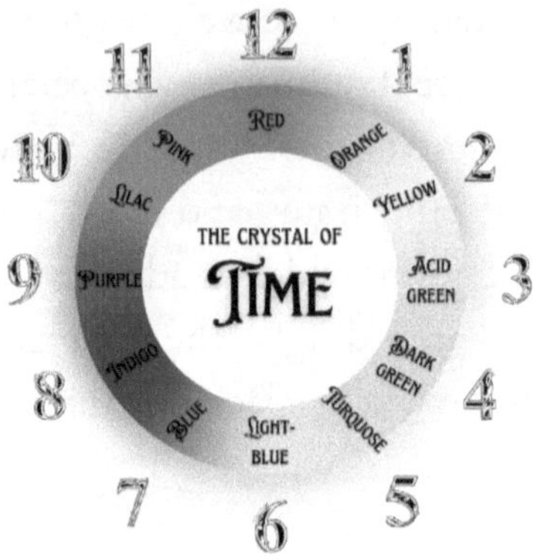

Mages like decorating public places with these crystals because this is how everyone in their town or city can keep track of time. Plus, it looks beautiful. In the stories, you will find many such places - a fountain on the central plaza in Santos, the courtyard in Middle Lake, and the bridge of wishes in Triville.

Guardians

The guardians are equal to police forces. They are responsible for catching lawbreakers and minimizing criminal activity. The word 'Guardian' originated in ancient times, when the primary job of defense forces was limited to guarding a king and law. Nowadays, this term applies to all members of security and defense. Each guardian has a military rank, such as sergeant, captain, lieutenant, general, etc.

How to become a guardian?

Everything starts at Guardian Academy. After completing two years of study, cadets receive multiple career opportunities. They can choose to become detectives, criminal experts, engineers, lawyers, or continue their training in the military.

Each town and city has its own **Guardian House,** which provides safety on the streets, investigates accidents when someone uses forbidden spells, and does its best to prevent crimes. The guardians also check the areas near the town for any illegal activity of local witches. A guardian team usually consists of different talented mages, as a unique combination of Gifts lets them work more effectively.

A shift in traditions

Historically, only men were allowed to become guardians, as people believed they made the best warriors. In the era of Mercy Houses, every Guardian House had an assigned Gift Hunter whose identity was kept secret. His task was to spot and report teenage boys with destructive Gifts once they manifested. If an adolescent girl happened to have destructive power, she was captured by Gift Hunters and sent to the nearest Mercy House, where her powers were taken away.

With time, women were allowed to perform guardian duties. The trilogy *Two Worlds: Beginning* is about the women who made this shift possible.

Incapables

Mages inhabit Crystal World, but some people don't have powers. They are called Incapables. Who are they, and where did they come from?

Historically, people who committed serious crimes were sentenced to imprisonment on Death Island. There, they eventually lost their magic because of the strong magnetic anomaly. When these prisoners retired or deserved their freedom through excellent behavior, they were allowed to return to the continent. Without magic and despised by society, they couldn't find a place in this world. So, they had no choice but to live the rest of their lives in special closed reservations, usually in the small villages hidden in the forests.

With time, communities of Incapables grew bigger, and not only because of the number of returning prisoners. There were also natural reasons, such as the births of Incapable kids. Incapables were always considered 'cursed' creatures because they spread their curse to their prosperity – ex-prisoners' kids became Incapables, too, even if their chosen women had magic.

The authorities attempted to control the population of Incapables by limiting their access to the civilized world. Thus, all Incapables who wished to work in the cities were obliged to pass a special exam and get a permit. There were many limitations in their lives. For example, they were prohibited from marrying mages and growing their families outside their reservations.

With time, Incapables became a source of cheap labor. They often worked on farms, cleaned houses, and did other low-paid jobs, letting the mages focus on education and building prestigious careers. This inequality has existed for centuries. Incapables kept being obedient mainly because they considered mages to be a superior race who had more rights and privileges. However, this system started cracking with time. One day, Incapables will find their voice and start fighting for their freedom...

Soul Light and Spells

Everyone in Crystal World (excluding Incapables) has magic. People can evoke their visible energy and use it as a foundation for different spells. This visible life energy is called 'Light' or 'The Light of the Soul.' It has a unique color and structure because everyone's energy is different.

Thus, mages use their Light to create unique lockers on their doors or sign important documents such as wills, bank loans, or business contracts. In terms of structure and color, Light can be solid or contain sparkles, spots, or stripes of other shades and hues. It might also be sparkling or matte.

Magic channels are located at the fingertips. Mages can release their energy through these channels (for instance, they can cast an energy ball in their palms). That's why when the criminal gets caught, the guardians use blocking cuffs to prevent the usage of destructive spells against them.

All mages are able to release their Light from childhood, and they are introduced to applied magic in middle school. So, what is applied magic?

Applied Magic (Spells)

Life energy or Light is a foundation for different spells, such as Fireballs, Paralyzing, Life Support, and all other temporary spells from the table below.

The Spells mentioned in this book:

Erasing

Permitted usage - to erase the energy traces.

Structure/color - when this spell touches the energy traces, it soaks them and cleans the area.

Notes - People leave their traces when they touch something, and it can be identified within 12 hours with the help of the Revealing spell. Sometimes, educated criminals use Erasing spells to destroy their energy traces.

Fireball

Permitted usage - to make a fire.

Structure/color - a ball of flame.

Notes - forbidden against living creatures (as a weapon) for everyone but guardians. They might use this spell against criminals only if there is no other way.

Hiding

Permitted usage - to hide the person from Searching spells.

Structure/color - invisible but takes purple when the object is under the influence of the spell.

Notes - when people don't want to be found by the Searching spell, they use the Hiding spell as a temporary shield that preserves their privacy. Sometimes, criminals use this spell for kidnapping.

Hypnosis

Permitted usage - to persuade people.

Structure/color - can be transferred to the object by touching or with the ball of Light. This spell is invisible.

Notes - guardians often use hypnotic charm during interrogations to make the criminals tell the truth. Sometimes, they make victims calm down if they are in shock. It's illegal to use the spell against regular people if the goal is to get a benefit from manipulation.

The effect of Hypnosis is hard to hide because as soon as the effect evaporates, the object realizes that the spell was used on him/her.

Life support

Permitted usage - to improve physical condition due to severe injury.

Structure/color - the Light becomes brighter and sinks an injured person's body.

Notes - this spell is used to help people who experience pain or fatigue or are about to die. This spell is a temporary measure before the patient gets proper medical help.

Locking

Permitted usage - to create a magic lock.

Structure/color - a thin metal plate needs to be charmed and placed on the door. It can be opened only with the Light of a particular person.

Notes - this spell is widely used to protect households from thieves. Usually, the plate is placed on the entrance door.

In some places, like banks or secret archives, the doors are also locked with such locks.

Magic Traps

Permitted usage - to catch a person/living being.

Structure/color - invisible but takes a bright green color when the object is caught.

Notes - this spell can be used only with a foundation (a roof or a net if it's outside). It must be placed over the head of the object. The spell is invisible, but when someone steps into the area below the spell, they can't leave this circle, trapped in invisible walls. Hunters use this spell to catch the prey.

Muting

Permitted usage - to protect a space from eavesdropping.

Structure/color - an invisible shield. If it is used outside, the air becomes fuzzy around the protected area.

Notes - this spell is often used during private conversations to prevent any information leak.

Paralyzing

Permitted usage - self-defense.

Structure/color - grey color. The spell looks like a ball of mist.

Notes - the magic channels of the one who shoots with this spell get blocked temporarily (blockage time depends on the spell's strength).

Revealing

Permitted usage - to make energy traces and hidden spells visible.

Structure/color - looks Like a Light ball but becomes brighter when activated.

Notes - guardians use this spell to find energy traces and check the objects for hidden traps. This spell is also widely used by doctors to make correct diagnoses.

Protective

Permitted usage - to prevent the other spell from interfering.

Structure/color - the spell looks like a mist when in progress and becomes invisible when it is completed.

Notes - it is used to protect sensitive spells or secret information.

Searching

Permitted usage - to find a missing person.

Structure/color - the Light foundation takes a blue color when the spell starts working.

Notes - this spell should be used on a personal belonging. It twists around the belonging, then this belonging becomes active and flies in the direction of the missing person. It might not work if the spell is miscast or if the person is dead. Guardians often use this spell. Ordinary mages can use it if it doesn't violate the rights and freedoms of the person they are looking for.

People who develop their skills and boost their stamina can become professional magicians, wizards (mages of a high rank), or witches (mages who perform illegal activities).

Most people have basic knowledge and master their skills only if it's required for their work. For instance, guardians shoot criminals with Paralyzing spells to deactivate them; detectives use Searching spells to find the missing person; and doctors can check the patients with Revealing spells to figure out a diagnosis.

All these spells are temporary, meaning every person can create an easy or advanced spell relying on their skills.

Most easy spells are allowed for broad usage, and some are forbidden to use against people because they can be fatal (such as fireballs). People who use forbidden spells against other living things might be punished or imprisoned.

Applied magic is not tricky, but Gifts are another pair of shoes.

Gifts

Gift is a unique magic capacity that manifests in adolescence. Each time, it happens under certain circumstances, often due to intense emotional turmoil.

There are many Gifts in Crystal World; some are common, and some are very rare (such as time magic). Each Gift has its limitations. Many people can't use their Gifts against blood relatives and people they love (it is called genetic blockage or emotional blockage). The only common limitation between all Gifts is the inability to avert death.

Gifts mentioned in this book:

Fire

Appearance - flames coming from the fingertips.

How it works - the mage with Gift of Fire can cast flames and is resistant to high temperatures and destructive magic.

Limitations - this power is limited by a person's life energy (too long exposure to magic can dehydrate a Gift carrier).

Future teller

Appearance - invisible (mind force).

How it works - the mage sees the dreams about events that will happen in the near future.

Limitations - the Gift doesn't work on close blood relatives and/or people the Future Teller loves.

Healing

Appearance - pink energy.

How it works - the energy sinks in the chest of a sick person and heals them.

Limitations - doesn't work in case of death for more than 5 minutes, blood relativity, and romantic attraction.

Invisibility

Appearance - invisible shield.

How it works - the mage can become invisible by slowing their breath. Mages can also make the other objects temporarily invisible.

Limitations - this power is limited by a person's life energy (too much magic exhausts a Gift carrier).

Lightning

Appearance - electricity lightning of violet and white colors.

How it works - the lightning comes out of palms (might be rolled into a ball or shot directly into the object).

Limitations - this power is limited by a person's life energy (too much magic exhausts a Gift carrier).

Mind reading

Appearance - invisible (mind force).

How it works - the mage needs to touch the person physically to read his mind. They catch memories in the way the person saw it and identify a time when these events happened. Mages with such Gifts also can see the fears and desires of others.

Limitations - the Gift doesn't work with people the Gift carrier loves or once loved and with close blood relatives.

Poisoning

Appearance - dark green energy.

How it works - the mage can make the organic subjects toxic by touching them.

Limitations - gift carrier can't poison himself or people with the same power.

Speed

Appearance - invisible (muscle force).

How it works - the mage can move at high speed and quickly travel long distances.

Limitations - this power is limited by a person's life energy (too much magic exhausts a Gift carrier).

Telekinesis

Appearance - invisible (mind force).

How it works - the objects move without physical touch as per Gift carrier will.

Limitations - this power is limited by a person's life energy (too much magic exhausts a Gift carrier).

From early childhood, all the mages are told to use their Gift for good purposes. Using magic powers against living creatures is forbidden if it causes harm.

Thank you, dear reader!

Thank you so much for reading _The Academy_! This is one of my favorite stories because it shows the times when the era of dragons has started in this fantasy world.

I hope you enjoyed this fictional journey about four friends. And if you want to know what happened to Elisa, Jackie, Urchin, and Theo, you can keep reading their story in the next book of the _Magic Squad_ series!

The events of the next story unfold three years after this book ends. This time, all four must unite to solve two supernatural mysteries...

P.S. If you enjoyed this read, please don't hesitate to check the store where you bought it or the _Goodreads_ website and give this book a good rating.
Your support means a lot because it lets the story find its new readers!

Sincerely yours,
-Lubov Leonova

Lubov Leonova

I always loved reading. I guess all the books I've ever read impacted me greatly - they let me expand my worldview and inspired me to pursue my dreams despite the obstacles.

Born in Russia, I immigrated to Canada in 2014, where I faced multiple challenges, including building my own life from scratch and figuring out what career path would let me use my full potential. My searches led me to feministic studies in college and volunteering in female support groups.

My experience slowly formed into ideas for my fantasy series *TwoWorlds*, where females shape the sphere of justice using their natural talents.

Today, I live on the East Coast of Canada with my husband, Alex, and our three pets: a cat, Grayson, and two sneaky bunnies – Boris and Flora.

Let's connect!

Do you want to win Giveaways for my books and receive daily inspirational content? Yes? Then follow me on any of these platforms on your preference:

Instagram - author's official page
https://www.instagram.com/authorleonova/

Instagram - 2 Worlds Series
https://www.instagram.com/magical2worlds/

Facebook
https://www.facebook.com/magical2worlds

Twitter
https://twitter.com/LeonovaLubov

Also, I have a **Goodreads** account where you can always get the newest updates on my stories release:
https://www.goodreads.com/author/show/21216748.Lubov_Leonova

What will happen next?

It's been three years since the events of The Academy. Four friends have matured, and each of them works on their chosen path: Jackie is a lawyer helping victims of domestic violence; Elisa and Urchin serve as the guardians in Middle Lake; and Theo lives in Triville with his dragon Rei and solves the crimes happening in the suburbs of Lake Kingdom.

All of them do their best to catch the criminals; however, this time, they face a dangerous religious cult called Daughters of Divine. Its leader sacrifices a young woman when the full moon rises.

Will the four friends find a way to get together again to stop this cult?

Forbidden Manuscript

CHAPTER 1. AN ANNIVERSARY

The chilly morning wind brushed against the curtains, causing them to flutter against the window. Elisa sat up in bed, rubbing her eyes as she took in the sight of her empty bedroom. The only reminder of the previous night with Jackie was the wrinkled sheets. *Had Jackie already left for work?* Elisa let out a sigh. Regretfully, their busy schedules often kept them apart. Jackie had left without even saying good morning.

Her bare feet touched the cold wooden floor as Elisa made her way to the window to close it. Outside, a new day had dawned, with gentle sun rays illuminating the rooftops and half-naked trees. The deserted street below was coming to life, with shopkeepers in a gray coats opening their doors. It was Wednesday, a typical workday for most, but not for the guardians like Elisa. For her, it was one of the quieter days, as the lawbreakers tended to take a break before the busy weekends.

Middle Lake was renowned as a criminal capital, with its history of gangs and illegal activities. It had been three years since the leader of the drug gang was apprehended, but new criminals had since risen to take their place. This turnover in criminal leadership had made Elisa and Jackie's jobs even busier, often causing their days off to not align for weeks at a time. Elisa missed Jackie deeply on days like today, but she never voiced her complaints aloud. After all, she had willingly chosen her duty despite the challenges it presented.

The sound of the entrance door squeaking open caught Elisa's attention, and her heart leaped with joy as she saw Jackie entering the room. Jackie was dressed in a black coat over her work clothes, her hair now dyed a captivating charcoal-black shade that cascaded over her shoulders.

"Where have you been?" Elisa asked, surprised by Jackie's sudden appearance.

"Guess," Jackie replied, placing a paper bag on the floor and beginning to remove her boots. "You're the detective here, after all."

Elisa gave her a puzzled look. "Well, you'll have to give me another hint then."

"Do you know what day it is today?" Jackie asked, her eyes flicking to the calendar on the wall. Elisa's heart quickened as she read the date: *November 2nd.* How could she have forgotten their anniversary? Elisa hadn't even bought a present for Jackie, which was completely unacceptable. But she still had time to come up with something.

"Happy anniversary, my dear," Elisa said, smiling. "I bet you thought I'd forgotten."

Jackie shook her head. "I don't believe you remembered. You look surprised."

Elisa had a ready excuse. "I'm just excited to see your face tonight when I reveal my present."

"Okay, okay," Jackie relented with a laugh. "I know you've been working six days in a row. I'll buy it."

Elisa crossed her arms. "You should trust me more."

Jackie lifted the paper bag, and the scent of warm baking with strawberries wafted through the room. Elisa's stomach rumbled, craving a mouth-watering breakfast.

They sat in their cozy kitchen at a table adorned with a white cloth featuring a forget-me-not pattern. Elisa's aunt had gifted her this cloth as a graduation present when she and Jackie had started living together. Elisa sighed, wishing her aunt knew the true nature of her relationship with Jackie, beyond just being neighbors and best friends. However, she had already caused her aunt enough trouble, and revealing the full extent of their bond might shatter her heart.

Jackie set her coffee cup down on the table. "Ah, Lissy. I've been planning something special for us all this time."

Elisa finished the last bite of pastry and smiled. "This romantic breakfast is the perfect way to start the day. We can continue celebrating in the bedroom."

Jackie's eyes sparkled with mischief. "I can't afford to be late for work. Again."

Elisa reached out and gently wiped the remaining crumbs of pastry from Jackie's chin. "Are you sure?"

"Patience," Jackie replied, brushing her hand away. "Actually, I have a real present for you."

"Darling, you don't need to buy me anything. Your thoughtfulness is more than enough."

She stood up. "Wait here."

Elisa raised her coffee cup. "Alright."

Jackie hurried to the bedroom and rummaged through a drawer, her voice softly humming a tune. Elisa gazed out the window, noticing that the shops were now open. She contemplated buying something beautiful for Jackie, who had a fondness for shiny things. The trade street boasted numerous jewelry stores, and Elisa even had some savings she could dip into for the occasion.

Returning to the kitchen, Jackie held a leather notebook, her cheeks flushed with excitement. "Guess what it is?"

Elisa gave her a puzzled look. "Are you suggesting I start a diary?"

"Nope."

Setting her empty coffee cup down, Elisa remarked, "Good, because I believe diaries only bring trouble."

Jackie sat down and placed the notebook in front of Elisa. She ran her fingers over the cover, which bore the inscription *Our Memoir*.

Looking up at Elisa, Jackie held her breath.

"Is this your story? Have you finished it?" Elisa asked.

She nodded. "*Our* story. I've had so many experiences over the years that didn't quite fit into my diary. So, I started writing about us, about everything that happened since the Academy. And voila, now I have a novel!"

Elisa flipped the first pages, skimming the lines. "I see you've included some personal moments."

"Personal moments, as you call them, make it more interesting," Jackie replied, her eyes sparkling mischievously.

"Who said that?"

"Beth. My literary agent."

Elisa paused before responding. "When did you get an agent?"

"Did you know that Theo spent a significant part of his childhood under the roof of the bookstore? He made some connections in that world."

"Theo is in Triville now, caught up with Rei and investigations. I doubt he had time to assist you with your manuscript."

Jackie waved her hand in explanation. "In case you forgot, we live in a modern world, and we have mail! Theo simply sent the letter to the bookstore owner, who then introduced me to the agent. She's actually a nice woman."

Elisa shook her head in disapproval and closed the book with a thud. "So, you've decided to share our story with the whole world. Why didn't you consult me first?"

Her eyes dimmed. "I thought you would appreciate it. I put in so much effort."

Elisa stood and wrapped her arms around Jackie's shoulders. "I'm sorry. I didn't mean to upset you, especially not today. But you know how challenging it is for us to be who we are, and I just want to protect you."

"Can you at least give it a chance and read it?" Jackie's emerald eyes pleaded. "I can edit out anything you find too revealing."

"Of course," Elisa replied, gently brushing an eyelash off Jackie's cheek. "Please don't take it personally, my love. You know I can be too blunt at times."

Jackie chuckled. "Oh, I know."

"Then go to work, and I'll prepare something special for you tonight. Deal?"

"Deal." Jackie sealed the agreement with a strawberry-scent kiss.

To find out what happened next, read the next book in series:

Amazon Book Store:
http://author.to/lubovleonova

Check all my books on my official website:
https://www.magical2worlds.com/books